Hades, & Persephone

USA TODAY BESTSELLING AUTHOR
AMELIA WILDE

KING

of

SHADOWS

ONE

Persephone

THE MOST VALUABLE FLOWERS IN THE WORLD ARE A DEEP red.

Vibrant. Sharp. The color of fresh blood. Anyone who got close enough to my mother's fields to see them would gasp at the contrast. Shocking against early summer green. Nothing competes. Not the dandelions turning into white, floating seeds. Not the thistle. Not the ground ivy. The weeds compete for space only as much as my mother allows.

Nothing ever threatens the poppies. Aside from my mother and me, no one is allowed to get close.

No one is allowed to touch them, which is a little sad. We're the only two people in the world who get to feel the delicate softness of the petals. I've held and tended hundreds of flowers in my life. Thousands.

These are the softest, and the most beautiful.

I run a fingertip over one of the petals. The color of fresh

blood, yes, but there's fire, too. Tiny filaments of white and orange and gold.

They're the most valuable flowers in the world because they don't exist anywhere else. They're my mother's creation. They exist at her mercy.

I have that in common with the poppies.

It's a pretty dramatic thought, but it's true.

The outside world is dangerous, and filled with dangerous men. That world is the reason we don't have a computer. It's the reason her phone stays in a locked drawer next to her bed.

It's the reason I'm here, with the most valuable flowers in the world. Protected and safe.

Stifled, a voice whispers. *Suffocated.*

If I said that to my mother, she'd laugh. Who could claim to be suffocated in wide-open fields filled with flowers?

The sun's gentle on the back of my neck as I trace the petals, one by one, over and over. Warmth gathers in the middle of my chest. A sweet, gold warmth. It whispers through my veins. Down to my fingertips. Into the petals and through, following those filaments to the stems and to the roots, down in the dark.

The poppy grows.

Its growth is like a sigh. A stretch. So subtle I can hardly see the extension in the petals. The echo of gold heat in my chest is just as soft. I'm not really trying. Just tending. Just thinking. It's a bit early in the summer for poppies, especially these. They thrive in full sun.

This one craves a little more light. A little more heat.

I can give it while I'm sitting here, thinking. Relaxing.

Waiting, really. Waiting with my legs tucked under me in the fresh green grass. It's something to pass the time and my most important work. The most valuable flowers get the most individual care. We lose fewer of them that way. My mother doesn't like to lose any at all. That was one of my earliest lessons as a girl. Expensive blooms go to the city for weddings and parties.

Other flowers go into one of her greenhouses to become something else.

I've seen the mortars and pestles she uses there. Separate sets for separate projects. One set reserved for the poppies. She's taught me plenty of things in the greenhouse. Remedies that grow from the earth. How to boil and extract and grind. How to render plants helpful.

How to render them harmful.

Death is part of life, Persephone. I can hear her say it. I was ten when we moved beyond identifying dangerous plants to using them for emergency purposes. It gave new meaning to the phrase *deadly serious.*

I feel the footsteps before I see him. Before I can hear him. I feel the soles of his shoes through the plants on the ground. The weight of his body crushes the stems. Flattens the petals. Snaps some of those little lives in two.

Decker's not paying attention. He doesn't feel the flowers breaking as he strides over them, daisies and dandelions breaking with every footfall. He doesn't care. I can't hold it against him. How could I, when he doesn't know what he's doing? Grass and clover don't mind the occasional flattening. Flowers are different.

I've never tried to explain it to him. Secrets are meant to be kept, not shared.

His pace slows as he crests the top of the nearest rise in the earth. Decker's long and lanky in his work clothes. Reinforced linen worn soft at the knees. A sand-colored shirt pushed up to his elbows. He picks his way toward me, keeping his eyes on the poppies. It's impossible to miss those.

I take my fingers away from the petals and look out over the fields. Nobody's in view. My basket remains gently nestled in a small patch of field grass.

"I'm not supposed to be here," he jokes as he gets closer. "Swear you won't tell?"

I laugh as he lowers himself to the grass. "Secret's safe with me."

His green eyes take in the flowers. The sky. My white dress. "You know how many flowers I saw on the way here?"

"At least a thousand. Probably more."

"And none of them were as pretty as you."

I roll my eyes. "You have to stop telling that joke."

"Who said it was a joke?"

"*You're* the joke."

Decker sighs, propping himself up on his elbows. "I risk my life for you, and you think I'm funny."

"I think you shouldn't risk your life just to come bother me."

His eyes roam over the clouds. "I had nothing better to do."

I check again to make sure nobody's watching. My mother has a soft spot for Decker. He's brave enough to approach her in the fields, or in the greenhouses. He's been that way since he started working for her five years ago. Or is it six? He charmed her into letting me talk to him in the yard behind the farmhouse, where she could supervise.

Being alone in the fields is still a risk.

"Something on your mind, Sepphie?"

How many more seasons can I survive here before I wither away?

The truth is that the fields have seemed smaller with every year that passes. The fence more confining. The books my mother buys me get worn through in a matter of weeks.

I'm twenty years old. How bad could it be in the outside world?

I'm beginning to doubt it's any worse than in here. My mother talks about danger like it's a wild animal lurking in the night, ready to pounce. Something that only exists outside the doors of the farmhouse.

I know better than that.

"Tell me about the city."

Decker plucks a dandelion from the ground and twirls it in his fingers. "It's a big collection of tall buildings made from metal and concrete. None of it's as pretty as you."

I purse my lips, trying my best not to encourage him. I don't feel that way about Decker. He's not afraid of my mother, and he's always been kind to me. As a friend. Nothing else. Decker's a part of this world—the fields and the sky and the growing season.

And I want out.

"I know there's more," I needle. "What about the library?"

This is the place I imagine when I think about freedom. My mother thinks about danger. I think about the library. I saw a picture of it when I was six or seven. It couldn't be more different than the farmhouse, and the fields.

"Well." He gives an indulgent sigh. "The main branch of the New York Public Library looks like something out of history. It's made from these big, white stones. It's got tall arches in front. And inside, there are books."

"How many?"

I already know what he'll say. I want to hear it anyway.

"Hundreds." Decker lies back on the grass, settling himself carefully, avoiding the poppies. He skims his fingers lightly over one of them. Touching it, not taking it. If he did, I'd have to tell my mother. "Thousands. More than you could ever read."

"I don't know about that."

I love to read. If I push my mother hard enough, if I seem sad enough, I can get new ones. An entire building filled with books would be a dream come true. I'd spend the rest of my life working my way through the shelves.

"And…" Decker sits up and leans in, lowering his voice. "It's guarded by lions. Two of them outside the front doors. Huge stone statues."

"Patience and Fortitude."

"People say that if you watch them in the moonlight for long enough, you can see them move."

My chest squeezes. It sounds like something out of a story. Not the magical lions. The city itself. If I could stand on the street and look at lion statues in the moonlight, that would be magic. If I could do it without looking over my shoulder to see if my mother was watching, that would be freedom.

"I want to go," I admit to Decker, not for the first time.

"We'll go together," he offers.

My mood darkens like a summer thunderstorm. Like a flower being lashed in the rain. Decker says it like it's simple. Like heading to the city is just a matter of hopping on the train. In another life, maybe. In this one?

Not a chance in hell.

My mother lets me have this land, and this life. Tending the most valuable flowers on earth. It's a privilege to do it, and I wish, I *wish*, I could stop. Just… walk away without her noticing. Get on the train without anyone noticing. Disappear.

That's the dream.

What would happen afterward is less dreamlike. I don't have any money. I'd have to get a job to support myself. From what Decker says, I could try to find a place at a flower shop, but that's the first place my mother would look.

I'm not sure she'd stop looking even if I went beyond New York City.

Guilt clouds over all those thoughts. My mom, searching for me, having to leave her fields? It wouldn't be good for her.

I let out a breath and tip my face toward the sun.

"I'm sorry." I can feel Decker watching me. "I just meant we could go, if you wanted to try."

"It's okay." When I open my eyes, he's pinching the stem of the dandelion, eyes rueful. "Someday I'll figure it out."

"Why is your mom so intense?"

Intense is a nice way to say it. My mother is not just intense. When she's angry, she's terrifying. It's not just her knowledge of plants, either. Not just the fact that she can make poisons in her greenhouse. It's what she can do to people. She speaks, and they listen. She smiles, and they'll do anything to please her. Decker's the first person I've met who's willing to go this far.

"She doesn't want me to get hurt." My eyes go to the mountain on instinct. It looms in the sky, a masculine black against pale blue. That mountain has watched over the fields all my life.

"Because of him?" Decker's eyes follow my gaze.

"Yes."

The man who lives in the mountain is as mythical as the lions in front of the library. I've never seen him. I only know that he's the devil. I only know that my mother is most intense when she talks about him.

Hades.

Decker narrows his eyes at the mountain. "Is he looking for you?"

"She thinks he's dangerous. She says he'd hurt me if I ever stepped foot off the farm." I keep my eyes on Decker's face. The corners of his mouth turn down. He looks like he expects for Hades to stroll out of the mountain right now and take enormous, godlike footsteps all the way to the farm. "She says people go into that mountain and they don't come out again."

"She might be right," Decker says, finally.

"About him?"

"Yeah." His eyes come back to mine, and my heart jolts with something cool and electric. It's curiosity. This is new information.

"Have you ever seen him?" My curiosity speeds through my veins like a new flower reaching for the sky. Decker glances away, and I can tell he's planning to lie to me. "You *have* seen him. You've met him."

If Decker's met Hades, seen him in person, then it's proof.

Proof that my mother is *wrong*.

She acts like he's the most dangerous man in the world. The biggest threat. She lowers her voice when she warns me about him, as if he might overhear all the way from the mountain.

"I knew it."

Decker sits up straight. "Knew what?"

"I knew she was exaggerating. Trying to scare me. Acting the way she did so I'd think—" A laugh bubbles up like a new green shoot. "So I'd think I couldn't leave."

"No." Decker puts his hand on my arm. His touch startles me, but not as much as the expression on his face. He's not flirting now. Not joking. "I don't know what she told you about him, but I wouldn't brush it off."

"What are you saying?"

"I'm saying—" This time, his glance at the mountain seems almost out of his control. "I'm saying that it's different out there. People could be dangerous to you. People could hurt you."

I feel her, a heartbeat before she crests a hill at the opposite side of the field. My mother chooses each footstep carefully. I shake his arm off and grab my basket as I stand, heart pounding. And then, like I haven't done anything wrong, I wave at my mother.

She's beautiful, out here in her white dress, with her hair tumbling down her back and her basket tucked delicately over her arm. She could be a flower herself. Her hand lifts in a little wave.

Decker waves too. He lopes away across the field.

My mother watches him go.

All around me, the fields are in motion. Breezes rustle the grass. The poppies bow their heads this way and that. The hem of my dress plays at my shins. My curls lift from the back of my neck, then settle in.

But I'm like one of those statues in front of the New York Public Library. I wouldn't be called Patience, or Fortitude. I'd be called Caught. Trapped. Frozen.

The wind shifts. It's coming down off the mountain now. My mother turns her head toward it. When she turns back, her expression is unreadable.

"The poppies, Persephone," she calls from the top of the hill.

"I'll be done soon."

I replace my basket. Sit down next to it. Focus all my attention on the poppies. The hairs on the back of my neck pull up with the sensation of being watched, but when I lift my head again, my mother's gone.

TWO

Persephone

I CAN'T AVOID MY MOTHER FOREVER. HER FIELDS GO ON and on, stretching away from the train tracks. There are stands of trees and a burbling creek. She'd find me eventually, or one of the fieldhands would.

I'm too old to hide, anyway. Twenty is old enough for escape.

For at least… planning to escape. Planning for a life that doesn't end at the fence.

In the south fields, I tend the more delicate blooms. The ones that need extra help to be perfect enough to sell in the city. I make lists of jobs in my mind. I could clean houses, or tidy up a store. I could look for work in a library. The planning keeps my worry from rising.

It's not like my mother not to comment on something that makes her angry. Me, alone with Decker—that made her angry. The fear I can't bury entirely chafes like nettles. Too old to hide. Too old to spend the morning fretting about my

mother's mood. Better to make the flowers grow instead, and plan. Lay them carefully in my basket, and plan.

I pick wildflowers. Weave them into my hair.

Plan.

I'll need help. Decker might do it. I'll need money. He could figure out a way to get some. I'll need time, once I've escaped.

I'll need to figure out what to do about my mother.

I don't want to hurt her. Any plan I make will have to involve some kind of explanation. She wouldn't be okay if I just disappeared.

Maybe I shouldn't care about that at all. Maybe I should just care about myself. But I don't.

It all seems simple, in my head. It's a matter of asking for help and then going. Trying, at the very least. I won't know exactly what to do until I'm away from here.

The first step is a conversation with Decker. That'll be harder if my mother reacts badly to seeing us by the poppies.

When the sun gets high in the sky, I head for the farmhouse. It shines, neat and whitewashed, on top of a gentle hill. My heart beats faster as I get close. There's no point in trying to guess what she'll be like when I open the door. I imagine rage. I imagine betrayal. Tears, even.

One more breath of the fresh air, and I push the door open, bracing myself for the scene that's sure to come.

My mother stands at the kitchen counter with a knife in her hand. She's cutting up carrots, fresh from the smaller plots of vegetables she grows. A faint smile crosses her face in the moment before she glances at me.

"Persephone. Did you finish with the poppies?"

Her voice is so mild it sends a chill down my spine. I smile at her in spite of it, stepping closer to put my basket on a shelf by the door. "They're all right here, along with some of the new varieties from the south fields."

"Is that where you're working after lunch?"

"No, I'm done with those. The east fields after lunch." I step up to the sink and run the water. Lather my hands with a bar of soap made with my mother's flowers. Buttery sunlight streams through the double windows over the sink. Light splashes over the countertop and the heavy wooden table that takes up most of the kitchen. Everything outside blooms lush and green.

Dread tastes like half-dead dandelions. Bitter and rotten. My mother's sleeve brushes mine as I dry my hands on the dishcloth hanging by the sink. It's embroidered with flowers. They're pretty and delicate, like the blooms in the fields and the soap and everything else.

Even the knife's edge looks delicate as it chops through the carrots. It bites through them with a *snick* and a *thud*.

The wait is unbearable. I open my mouth to offer some excuse, some explanation, but my mother speaks first.

"What were you doing with that boy?" My mother's silver eyes meet mine. They look different when she's not out in the sun. Darker.

"We were talking. That's all." It's the truth.

"About?"

I don't have to tell you, I want to say. It's none of your business. Why can't you see that?

Her knife pauses over the carrots. My mother shouldn't have been able to hear us, but lying seems risky.

"About the city. Decker's been there."

The knife comes down and bisects another carrot slice. "Stop thinking about New York City. It's too dangerous. You know that. And we have planting to do."

"I know. He was just telling me about the buildings."

An enormous, sprawling field of buildings. Other girls—other *women*—get to live in the city. Other girls get shopping malls and restaurants. Other girls get to leave home.

My mother huffs a laugh, her disappointment curling through the center of me like a parasitic root. She chops harder at the carrots. "You think I can't tell? I see you looking out the window all the time. Looking at the mountain. Imagining the buildings that are beyond it. And now I discover you've been meeting with that boy."

A split-second decision—argue about Decker, or risk her anger for the city?

"Would it hurt to go for a visit? I'd come back."

"Would you?" Her eyes snap back to mine.

"I would come back to you. I swear."

"You'd come back to me." The inexplicable smile brightens her face and disappears. "And what would I find when you did? That you'd been beaten? Kidnapped? Murdered? I've told you what happens to young women who go to the city. What would happen to me if you were killed? How do you think I'd feel if you never came back?"

I'm a tangle of guilt and frustration and longing. Guilt because no one else cares about me. Frustration because I'm suffocating. And longing for more. A selfish longing that grows like a weed.

I'm withering here. Disintegrating as surely as I would if I were buried six feet beneath the ground.

I feel her panic and her anger like a cold frost. The knife in her hand glints. Sun reflects off the blade, daring me to look at it. I want to be the kind of person who stands up to her own mother. But now that another chance has come to do just that, I'm afraid.

The thought of me leaving, or being taken, makes her desperate.

And desperate people do desperate things.

"You're right," I say, my voice shaky with adrenaline. Her eyes. The knife. The way I felt when she caught us in the field. "It's too dangerous."

My mother takes a deep breath and faces the window. I'm not the only one who watches the fields, and the mountain. Her hair is bronze, a shade or two darker than mine, curls springy and full. It's gathered at the nape of her neck with a pink ribbon.

The sun kisses her face. She tips her head back, closing her eyes.

Beautiful. She's beautiful.

She's also selfish and cruel.

She's the only mother I have. How could I think about leaving her? How can I stay when it feels like death here, day after day, year after year?

My mother opens her eyes. They've lightened up. So has her grip on the knife. "What does the city have for you, Persephone? What is it you're so anxious to visit? It's a grave-yard made from glass and concrete. Men who'll rape you as soon as they'd look at you."

Her voice wobbles a little on the last word. She flicks her eyes down to the carrots. To the knife in her hand.

"I can't let that happen to you. You're the only thing I have."

She's told me this so many times. "I'm sorry, Mama. I know."

"I have to keep you safe."

"I—" I step closer, though it feels like getting closer to a hornet. "I'm twenty years old. I'm not a child anymore."

"You're far too innocent for the city." Her tone changes again. Light, like the afternoon sun. She pats my hand, rubbing at my knuckles. "You're far too innocent to be meeting with farmhands in the fields. Don't lie to me. You were just talking? He didn't touch you?"

"He didn't. Please don't be angry. Decker was only being polite."

She laughs. "I'm not angry."

I don't know what to say to that. She can laugh all she wants. It doesn't change the glint in her eyes or the way she snaps between suspicion and cool detachment. But my heart has been racing all morning. I want to believe her.

Just this once.

"Really? I'm sorry for meeting with him. I won't do it again."

I say all these things in place of the questions I don't dare ask. If all men are ruthless killers, why does she hire them to work for her? My heart aches for the fear that holds my mother here. It holds me here, too.

My mother lays the knife next to her cutting board and puts her hand to my cheek. "It's better if you don't. Believe me, Persephone."

There's a pressure in the air. Or maybe it's in my chest. *Agree with her*, it says. *She's right. Can't you feel how right she is?*

My gaze drops to the ground. "I trust you."

My mother catches my hand in hers and squeezes. "You said the east fields after lunch?"

"That's where I'll be."

"There's my good girl."

Is it over? I wonder all through lunch. While I collect my basket. While I wave at my mother through the dining room window and head east. While she paces with her phone pressed to her ear. Am I forgiven? Is Decker?

Does it matter?

My mother only wants to protect me. That's why she has these rules. That's why there's a fifteen-foot high fence at the border of her land. I know she only wants what's best for me… but I'm not a flower bed she can water and weed.

I need to leave in order to bloom.

THREE

Hades

THE FARM BOY COMES TO FIND ME IN A CORRIDOR LEADING up from the mines.

I've hired many spies over the years, and Decker is among the more desperate. It shows in his voice every time he opens his mouth. I'm not concerned with the specifics of his desperation. It made him easy to buy and easier to keep.

My dog Conor pads alongside me in the corridor, tucked within reach. One of my workers drags his feet on my opposite side. My hand in his collar is all that's keeping him upright. He mumbles something that ends in *can't see*.

"Enough," I snap. He has taxed my patience for long enough tonight. "Stop whining and open your eyes."

"They're. Open."

"Have you broken your legs in the last ten minutes?"

He can hardly breathe to answer me. "No."

"Then concentrate on walking."

It's the least he could do after the unrest he's caused this

evening. The lights in my diamond mines are calibrated to each shift and can be keyed to smaller groups or individuals, if necessary. A glitch in one of the sections caused a brief period of total darkness. The other workers were unaffected. This one had a near-complete breakdown even after the lights were restored. It can be contagious in underground spaces.

It was a mess when I arrived. Oliver, my head of security, contained most of the scene. I handled the rest. I understand it to be unusual for a man in my position to deal directly with workers. Situations like these require personal involvement, which costs less than replacing an entire team and has the benefit of keeping my mining operations running.

Footsteps approach from up ahead in the corridor. I could adjust the lights, but I don't. This is all I need to see by. Everyone else will have to cope.

Decker's shadow appears out of the dark.

"You're late."

He startles, as if he couldn't see me at all. Perhaps it's darker than I thought. What little light remains catches dimly in his eyes. Open wide. Trying to see.

"I missed the first train. I had a run-in with Demeter." He's shifty. Unsettled, no doubt, by the presence of the man I've brought with me. "What are you doing with him?"

"Delivering him to his next assignment. You can keep standing in my way, but I wouldn't recommend it."

The farm boy lets out a breath that sounds like indecision and more wasted time. My patience runs thin. After all the hysterics tonight, it was already threadbare. A pressure at the base of my skull is headed toward a sharp, throbbing pain.

I drag the worker another step forward and Decker abandons his noble ideas. His shoes scrape on the corridor floor.

The farm boy loses all sense of his body in space when he thinks I might snap a man's neck while he watches.

Attempts to watch.

Decker stays just ahead of me. It gets lighter in gradual increments as we go up. As we reach the split in the corridor, a set of lights in one of the halls dims. I enter a code into the keypad by the door. It pops open.

At the sound, the worker dangling from his own shirt collar jumps. "I'll go back down. It's fine. I'll go back down. I will. I will."

I change my grip and drag him closer, so we're face to face. His toes barely reach the ground. "You are *useless* to me in this state. That's a breach of contract. Do you want to discuss the penalties for breaking it?"

He shakes his head. Once. Twice. A third time, harder.

"Then get out of my sight." I push him through the doors, where there are two people waiting to catch him. A third in scrubs with a clipboard. "I don't want to see him again until he can fulfill the terms of his employment."

Their murmurs of agreement are cut off by the door clicking shut.

Decker snaps his eyes back to mine at the sound.

"I don't pay you to have run-ins with Demeter. I pay you to watch her and report to me. What the fuck are you doing to provoke her?"

He puts a hand to his hair. "I met with the daughter. I've been talking to her. Trying to get close, so I could get better information. She wants to go to the city."

I step away from the door. Decker moves backward on instinct until he's up against the wall. The pressure has become pain. It will only get worse the more I stand here, listening to this fool tell me absolutely fucking nothing.

"I don't give a fuck what Demeter's daughter wants."

He fumbles in one of his pockets and comes up with a package, which he presses into my hands.

I know as soon as I feel its weight that it won't be enough.

"That's all you brought?"

"She's been doing smaller plantings. I couldn't take more without her noticing." He gives a nervous laugh. "I thought that's why she came to see me. Thought she figured out I'd taken them. But it was about the daughter. Wanted to know what we were talking about. I said it was only a couple minutes, but—"

His voice fades into a rush of pure, hot anger. It combines with the pressure in my head. Expands. Demeter's been playing games for too long. I'm reaching the end of my patience. I'm reaching the end of my supply.

The scale tips.

The risk becomes intolerable.

I meant for this smuggling operation to be a temporary solution to my need for Demeter's flowers. A specific breed of poppy in particular. One that was made for me.

The headache rises fast, like my skull is fracturing. I can only manage it for so long. The floor shudders beneath our feet. It's barely a vibration. Decker sucks in a breath like it's an earthquake.

"What was that? Is the mountain coming down?"

The worst pain is to need. It feels like a diamond cutting through flesh, slicing the headache. Multiplying it. I can feel the shape in my palm, though I'm not making a fist. I tuck the package with the flowers into the crook of my arm.

"Which fields?"

"What?"

He's tensed, like a quick sprint would save him if the

mountain collapsed. "Which fields is she using for the planting?"

"South. But I can't get more. Demeter keeps track."

She won't have to worry about it when I'm finished. Demeter broke the terms of our agreement. Unfortunately for her, I have no more mercy to spare. It was beaten out of me years ago at the hands of my foster father.

I reach into my pocket and pull out folded bills and hold them out to Decker. He grabs for it quickly, like I might take it out of his reach. He doesn't flinch the way he did at the beginning. Conor nudges my leg. He would like for me to exit the hallway and go back to my rooms. Lay the fuck down in the dark.

That's the inevitable end to Demeter's bullshit games. The world has been closing in for two years now. Getting smaller. There's no such thing as a sunrise in the mines. Soon I'll have to shut it out completely in the rest of the mountain.

When I've done that, I might as well let all the rock collapse and crush me.

I take out another bill and hold it in front of his face. The farm boy's eyes lock on the money like it's edible.

"You're going to do absolutely nothing tonight."

Wide eyes meet mine, then go back to the money. "Nothing?"

"Don't draw attention to yourself. Don't go hunting for the daughter. Don't talk to anyone."

He does not understand. "Why?"

"Because you want to stay alive."

Decker manages not to look at the dark corridor leading down to the mines, but he's tense. He's been afraid since the first time he stepped foot on the mountain. He's a superstitious fool. He believes that if he stays where it's light, I won't kill him for fucking up.

"What are you going to do?"

A bold question.

Take matters into my own hands. That's what I'm going to do. There is no fixing the weakness that stays at my heels like my own loyal dog. It refuses to be excised from my brain. It can only be managed. And if Demeter has gone back on her word, then I'm going back on mine.

"I'm buying your silence." I push the money into his hand. "If you want more money, you'll stay out of sight."

"But—"

Another whisper through the floor. A shake. Earth settling. I feel it for what it is. A match to my headache, which has escalated from a dull thud to an icepick through the tempers.

"Get the fuck out of here. You'll miss the train."

Decker barely makes it out of sight before he runs.

I wait for his footsteps to fade, then follow after him.

No more games. No more bullshit. No more rationing.

No more smuggled flowers.

I'm taking what Demeter has tonight. She'll be lucky if I let her live.

FOUR

Persephone

THE STONE LION'S AMUSED WITH ME. IT SHAKES ITS HEAD in the moonlight, fur rippling down the rest of its body. The lion's sweet. It bows its head for me to pet, rumbling low in its throat.

"I didn't know," I tell it. "I thought it was a myth."

Something clamps down around my arm and yanks me away from the statue. The lion's eyes narrow. It bares its teeth. But then I'm awake. Not in the city at all. In my bedroom.

My mother's fingers dig into my arm. The silver of her eyes burns in the moonlight. Her hair's wild, expression wilder, and I gasp as she pulls me out of the bed.

"You're hurting me. Mama."

"You weren't listening." She drags me the few steps to my bedroom window and shoves it open.

"I was. I heard—"

My mother stabs one finger at the open window. "He is coming for you."

I blink, clearing the sleep from my eyes, scanning the yard for the figure of a man. There's no one out there.

Of course, it's not the yard she's pointing at. It's the mountain.

Black rock cuts across the stars. The moon hangs over sharp angles. Light glows behind it. Light from the stars, yes, but also light from the city. It's a dream in the distance. All those buildings are so bright that the light reaches the mountain.

And then it disappears into the outcrops. It can't get to me. I send out a prayer to the leaves and the sky. *Not again. Not again.*

"Nobody's out there." It's the middle of the night. The clock by my bed says it's two in the morning. "Nothing's happening."

"Do you think he won't find you? Do you think he won't kill you?" My mother's whisper is broken up by fear and rage. It hurts to hear it. Hurts, because her grip gets tighter. Hurts, because I'm afraid, too. For her. For me. "If Hades comes down from the mountain, you won't survive."

"There's no—there's no reason for him to do that."

"You don't remember the last time he came here. You don't understand."

"I do," I insist. I want her to let go.

A vine curls gently in through the window, almost as if it was blown there by the breeze. It wasn't. The dark-green leaves are different. They're bleeding into rose petals.

"Look." She shakes my arm, pushing me closer to the frame. I follow her eyes back to the mountain. It's calm in the night. Still. Silent under the stars. "Can't you feel it? He's angry."

Energy trembles through her body. A defensive, snarling anger. I don't know how to tell her that the mountain doesn't scare me. I don't feel its darkness, or its anger. It's just watching.

The way it always has. There's no way to know if the man inside is angry. He's probably just sleeping. It's the middle of the night.

A new shoot of frustration pushes through the soil. "Why is he angry, Mama? I haven't done anything to him."

She purses her lips, and I feel a flash of recognition. A cold understanding.

"Did you do something to him?"

It's the first time I've ever considered that she could have.

I know my mother is capable of hurting other people. My arm throbs in her grip even now. She rules over her farm like a queen. But in all the times she's spoken about Hades, she's never hesitated like this.

In the stories she's allowed me to read, the hero is pursued by a villain who has been corrupted by the outside world. Who is made evil by that corruption. Not because he has a good reason.

My mother narrows her eyes at the mountain.

"Of course I didn't."

Her tone is all wrong. She's lying to me. "What did you do?"

I've pushed her too far. She pins my wrist to the window frame, her silver eyes pale in the moonlight. She's worked in the fields for longer than I have. She's stronger than she looks. The white dresses, her long hair—they're a distraction from how dangerous she is. My wrist is going to break.

The vine from the window curls next to her hand.

I don't feel the thorns until it's too late.

"Let go. Mom. Let go."

The vine contracts and I gasp at the pain. The thorns bite into my skin. My mother's doing it. She made something hellish out of the vine and the rose bush that grows nearby.

She's lost control.

I push my hand toward her, trying to get the vine to release. It doesn't. Every move I make shoves the thorns in deeper.

"Listen to me," she demands. Blood wells up around the thorns. It stings, and aches, and I'm terrified—terrified that it will cut down to the bone and I won't be able to get away.

"I'm listening. You have to stop. It's cutting me."

The vine stills, but it doesn't recede from my arm. My fingers are starting to go numb from how tightly she's holding on. I hold my breath. Try not to move. If I don't move, maybe she'll calm down. Silver glints in her eyes. Little pieces of bone-white color.

"You were sleeping when he tried to take the fields."

"Take them?"

"Destroy them. Take them for himself." It doesn't sound real. Another story. Why would a man like Hades want anything with flowers? Murderers don't need plants to keep them company. "Do you think he'd stop at hurting you? If he found you, he'd kill you."

"Mama, please. I don't think—" Her fear is real. Her anger, too. But these stories. This obsession. It's so much larger than life. "I don't think anything's going to happen tonight. I'm right here, with you. I've been careful."

"You haven't been careful. I saw you in the fields with that boy."

"You like him." The thorns dig in a little further. "It was just Decker. One of your own people. I would never talk to anyone else."

"I know what you're planning." Her eyes darken. Deaden. "I know you're planning some kind of escape. I know you're going to run for the city. I can't let that happen. I can't let him get to you."

"I won't talk to him again," I promise. The thorns have

looped around my arm another time. My legs ache to run. How far will the vine wrap around my body? Up to my neck? Up to my eyes. "He didn't mean any harm."

"He knows better than to talk to you now."

My stomach drops. "Did you hurt him?"

"I reminded him of the rules. I reminded him that you're not to be disturbed. That you're my daughter, not some whore from the city." Her voice rises. "You're not here for them. You're not here for anyone. You have to be careful, Persephone, and you haven't been careful."

"I will be." Another row of cuts, these ones smaller. I can't have these going all the way up my arm. "Mama, please. Let go."

"Promise me you won't leave." Her eyes go wide and scared, and I don't know what's going on in her mind. I don't know how her thoughts leap from one thing to another like this. I don't know why the sunset upsets her so much.

"Promise me."

"Mama—"

"Promise," she orders, and bruising pain spreads through my wrist. The thorns sink in. "Promise. Persephone."

"Let *go*." I wrench my wrist away from her. Claw off the vine. It retreats to the window, the life going out of it. I've never seen her this angry. I've never seen her this… disconnected from reality. I hide my wounded wrist behind my back. The last thing I want is for her to change again. For her to try to fix it. "I'm not going to leave you. Please. You're just—you're tired. It's late. Let's just go to sleep and talk about it in the morning."

"That's right." Her hands fall to her sides. Something in her face changes. "That's right. You're not leaving."

"No. Of course not."

She crosses the room to me, and I hold my breath. A

droplet of blood falls from my knuckles to the floor. My mother puts both hands on my face and looks into my eyes.

"It's not safe out there," she says softly. "Stay where it's safe. What would I do if anything happened to you?"

"I'm okay. Nothing happened."

My mother blinks. She could take me back to the window. She could do worse.

Instead, she releases my face. "It's too late for all this," she decides, like I'm the one who woke her up. "We can talk tomorrow. Go back to bed."

"Okay," I whisper.

She leaves my bedroom, closing the door tightly behind her.

And then—

Another sound.

A softer one.

The lock on the outside of my bedroom door sliding into place.

She meant it when she said I wouldn't be leaving. I listen hard for her footsteps going down the hall to her room. As soon as her door shuts, I suck in a breath. Another one. My body shakes with adrenaline, and with certainty.

There's a locked door and an open window.

I have to leave.

Not in the morning. Not tomorrow night. Right now. She'll remember the window eventually. She'll have one of the workers come to nail it shut. She won't take any more chances.

I steady my breathing enough to listen for her. There's no movement from her bedroom. The wood floors are silent under my feet as I creep to the fabric. Everything in here is white. I pick a lightweight dress with sleeves and pull it over my head. In the back corner of the closet, there's a gap between the trim and the wall. If I wedge my fingernail into it, I can pull out the money.

It's not much.

In all my plans, I thought I had time.

I know, down to my core, that I don't. That this is worse than she's ever been. That it won't get better from here.

I force myself to listen.

Crickets chirp in the yard outside. A wind chime tinkles on the front porch. The high, mournful whistle of the night train howls through the trees.

My pulse pumps hard. That train is the only way out. She'll catch me if I go on foot.

At the windowsill, I brush the vine back into its place and hoist myself up onto the frame. There's no time, really, for a graceful exit. My arms burn as I lower myself down as far as I can and let go.

I hit the ground harder than I thought, stifling a yelp with my hand.

And then I turn around and run.

FIVE

Hades

AN ANGEL APPEARS IN THE FIELDS.

No one shimmers out of darkness like that—like a light source is beneath her skin and woven with the fabric of her dress. The breeze plays with her hem. The motion hooks me in the center of my chest.

One glance, and the flowers are forgotten.

Look at *her*.

She's hurtling across the grass, her eyes on the ground. Protecting the flowers, for God's sake. Her body moves lightly, gracefully, something clutched in her fist. Her dress is a soft, virginal white, made thinner by the moonlight.

I'm jealous of that light touching her skin. I didn't know I could feel things this strongly anymore. I had no idea how fresh the air could taste. No idea my heart could beat like this, as if it had been squeezed back to life.

What the fuck.

Conor makes a questioning sound. Almost a whine.

"Stay."

He stays. He always does. He's always been a good dog. A loyal one. It hardly took any training to make him into a guard dog and a companion. Animals are oftentimes better at understanding than humans.

Curls spill over her shoulders, held in check by a braid at the crown of her head. This is the girl the farm boy was smitten with. This is Demeter's daughter.

I want her.

Consequences be damned. And there would be consequences. Fatal ones, perhaps.

There will be consequences regardless.

I had a long-standing deal with Demeter. I killed a man for her. She supplies me with the flowers I need to keep the pain in my head under control. She became more sporadic in her deliveries some time ago, making it increasingly difficult to live.

I want Persephone more than I want the poppies.

So much more.

It's not an intellectual want. It's animal. In the wordless, feral part of me, sensations crash together in a hail of lust. My blood thundering through my veins. The tease of the night breeze on my skin. A senseless pulse at my cock. I want to know what's underneath the light, summery fabric of her dress. Little to nothing, judging by the hard little peaks of her nipples.

Fuck the flowers.

I take a single step, putting myself directly in her path. It looks very much like Persephone is running for the train platform. I'm not fifteen feet inside the fence.

I spare a glance back toward the open stretch of the fields. She thinks she's all alone.

Persephone grabs for the hem of her dress, bunching it into her hand along with whatever else she's hiding. Head down, she

31

puts on a burst of speed. Thirty feet away. Twenty. Fifteen. She's barefoot. She's innocent. She thinks she has a prayer of success.

Conor shakes, stretching out.

Her eyes come up from the ground, and there's a moment when she doesn't understand what she's looking at.

By the time she does, it's too late to stop.

Persephone gasps. Her steps falter.

And then she cuts right, sprinting for the trees. It's the bravest, most foolish thing I've ever seen anyone do.

I consider letting her try, but…

No.

It only takes a few steps to catch her. The feel of her body in my arms is so familiar my heart stops. She thrashes, fighting.

"Screaming would be a better use of your energy."

"Don't do this. Please," she begs.

I turn back from the fields and go toward the train.

"You're running out of time," I tell her. "Once we're in the train car, no one will be able to hear you."

It's a coup, kidnapping Demeter's daughter. I can hardly focus on the triumph for how much I want to strip her naked and see how brave she is then.

"Just let me go. I'm just trying to leave."

"You did a miserable job. Didn't your mother warn you about the dangers of going out alone?"

"Yes." She's crying now. Silent tears. That—I want more of that. The edge of fear, the end of the word slipping into a whimper. "She did. I know who you are. Please don't do this."

A short laugh. "You know who I am."

She throws her body one way, then the other. It doesn't make a difference. "Hades."

"And how do you know that?"

"Because—" Another attempt to wriggle free. "Because

I've never seen you here before. Because my mother said you were dangerous. Because she said that if you found me, you would—"

"Take you?"

"Kill me."

I laugh at her. Demeter, telling stories about monsters in the night as if she's not a monster herself. "You're worth more to me alive."

"I'm worth nothing to you now. You can just put me down. Pretend you never saw me."

Impossible. There's no such thing as forgetting what she looked like, running across that field. No matter how I use her, I'll remember. How her hair shines in the moonlight. How her heart pounds underneath her skin. How she smells like spring flowers and sunshine. The kind of light that doesn't hurt.

Her voice sounds true, and clear. It's a shift in the universe, a boulder rolling away from the open mouth of a cave, dawn splitting the sky above.

But what she's saying is false. I can't let her go. I can't put her down. She is not worthless.

Persephone struggles harder the closer we get to the train. She puts her back into it. Her fists. I've been hit enough times that her blows are soft touches.

"No." I'm not sure she's talking to me or herself. "I was almost there." Three steps from the train. Two. "Stop. *Stop*. Please."

I put her on her feet on the step leading into the train car. She's trembling, head to toe, but her face is determined. I hold her in place with both hands just above her elbows. Her chest heaves.

Her eyes, huge and silver, stay on my face.

I know what she's seeing.

"Did you have a request?"

"Please." She takes in a ragged breath. "Please don't kill me in there. Take me back out to the flowers first."

Those words in her voice defy description. They carry the pressure of one of my episodes without the pain. They have the weight of a memory. More than one. I know the shape of them on my tongue.

There are consequences for this, my foster father's voice whispers. *She'll see you for what you are.*

"As I said before, you're worth more to me alive."

Persephone swallows. "Why?"

Because I want to fuck her. Because I want to *have* her. Because I saw her running in the field, hopeful and sweet, begging to be defiled. I came here needing something. She got to me first.

"Because I've never fucked anyone as sweet as you."

I give a sharp whistle and shadows detach from the trees. The train echoes the sound. Persephone's eyes widen. One hand goes out to brace herself on the train car door.

I slip one hand around her throat. Fuck, she's delicate, her pulse fluttering underneath the skin. Persephone goes still and stays that way. She pants as I run the pad of my thumb over her chin. It quivers, along with the rest of her body.

"Do you promise you're not going to kill me?"

"You keep mentioning death. Is that because you want me to give it to you?"

A flicker of fear is chased off her face by a nameless expression, determination flaring in her eyes. She glances down at Conor, who waits patiently at my side.

"No," she says. "I want to live."

I lean in close. Her heart races under my fingertips. That sunshine smell. The fresh softness of her. Fuck, the things I'm going to do to her. The urge to throw her down into the dirt is so strong.

No. It's time to move on. Things are going to be different now that I have Demeter's daughter for my very own.

The poor thing.

SIX

Persephone

I SHOULD KEEP FIGHTING OR DIE TRYING.

That's what I should do.

My mother warned me about this. I dismissed her, because I thought she was exaggerating.

She wasn't.

I've never seen a man this powerful. He's so tall he blocks out the moonlight. The dream of seeing the New York Public Library—gone up in flames. Cicadas scream on my behalf.

Why wasn't I looking? How did I not sense that he was here? How did I not feel those footsteps on the flowers?

It's too late to think about that now. He straightens up, keeping his hand on my throat. I will never accept that I don't entirely hate it. That there's something almost comforting about a person this confident.

No. No. That's not right. I'm just trying to survive this, moment by moment. Shouts come from farther down the train. I

jump. None of them sound like my mother. It's not that kind of commotion.

Hades stops me from turning my head. He makes me look at him instead.

I know, instinctively, that it's over if I get on the train. That these are the last moments I have to make an argument.

"Isn't there anyone else? Anyone else for you to f-fuck?"

The corner of his mouth curves in a deadly line. "No one else I want."

My mother told me he wanted me dead.

It only occurs to me now, belatedly, that being alive for what's next might be worse.

"What are you going to do to me?"

"Whatever I please."

A frustrated sob escapes me.

"Don't hold back." His hand tightens on my throat. "I'm very much enjoying the sound of your tears. It's such a…" He cocks his head to the side, leaving a bare inch of space for the night to rush into. "It's such a pure sadness. Lovely."

"I hate you."

Hades laughs. My knees wobble. I hope, I pray, that he didn't feel it. He lets go of me and steps back, considering me from a few feet away. Silhouetted there in the moonlight, the night drawing him in bold strokes…

Something is different about him. Something's wrong. Shadows play over his face in a way that's not right. Like he's pulling the moonlight into his dark heart and bleeding it dry of its brightness. The moon loves him, the night loves him, and he takes all that love for himself, all that moon-glow and darkness.

There's none left for me.

My own breath is harsh over the hum of the train and the whoosh of the wind in the leaves.

"I haven't hurt you, have I? Not yet." A grin flashes across his face, teeth white in the strange shadows. He radiates a mean confidence. It comes off him in waves. My mother said the city has violence, but Hades is violence. His dog whines. "I've left the flowers in your hair."

"If you were being kind, you would have killed me already, rather than playing with me like this." He's torturing me now without touching me. A better man wouldn't put me through this crushing terror, but he loves it.

An unspeakable fear closes my throat. The wondering tone about the flowers shakes me to the core.

"Playing with you?" He slips his hands into his pockets, standing tall. "If I recall correctly, you were running for the train. Now you're on it."

"Whatever you're going to do, just... do it now."

Hades tips his head back and laughs. Even in the summer warmth, it's the coldest sound I've ever heard.

And yet.

Something about it strikes me as beautiful.

It fits him, even while it gets under my skin, down to the bones. I'm not going to cower. Even if he picks me up in his arms again and takes me to the farmhouse.

"Is that what you want, Persephone? You want a rough fuck in the dirt? You'd like for the workers to hear you scream and beg?"

"I want to be free."

"That's not an option for you." He shrugs. "I don't have to do it here. Perhaps you'd prefer to go back to your mother's house. Fucking on the floor wouldn't be so different from the dirt."

Hades steps toward me, reaching for my wrist, and I

scramble backward. Never mind that there's nowhere to go but onto the train.

"No. Not there."

"Astonishing." He's so close I can feel the heat of his body. "Of course, there's another explanation for begging to stay with me."

All I said was *no*. I didn't beg to stay. I just don't want him to take me back to my mother's house.

He lets the statement hang in the air until I'm ready to burst. The train whistle sounds again—this is the third time—but Hades doesn't so much as blink.

He's watching me.

More than watching. This is no casual gaze. He's pinning me here with his eyes. Making me wait. Stripping me down. Heat sears my cheeks.

I force the words out. "There's no other explanation."

"It's this." He puts his hand back at my throat. "You want this, and it's hard to admit it." I shake my head, horrified. No, no, no. "Not on the surface. Deep down, where you feel the most filthy and dirty and shameful. You like a hand on your throat. You like my hand on your throat."

My lips have gone numb, but even worse, the heat has fled my cheeks and settled between my legs. Fresh shame presses my thighs together.

"No. I was only trying to escape. I hate everything about you."

"I like the way you cry." Hades takes his hand away again, and I wish he would put it back. It's a horrible wish. One I should never have. Instead he draws two fingertips down my cheek, burning a path along the tracks of my tears. "I like the way it makes your body shake. A man could get drunk off that feeling."

AMELIA WILDE

I press my lips together, trying not to let any more tears leak out. It's futile. I couldn't stop them if I tried.

"That's what you want from me? Tears?"

"I don't want anything from you. I want everything." Hades presses one thick finger to my lips, keeping me silent. My breath superheats in my lungs. I have a chestful of mortification. He's right, that little voice taunts. He's right, and you know it. "No. I misspoke. It's not about wanting. It's about taking. I'm going to take everything. Turn around."

The air rushes out of my lungs. "What?"

Hades leans in. "Turn around."

A montage of awful things stampedes through my mind. Now? Here? On the steps of a train car? It's too much, too soon, and at the same time, I'm seized with a desire so powerful the hairs on my arms stand up. The anticipation is always the worst part. I've learned that enough times, living with my mother. If he'd start, if he'd do what he's going to do, I could exhale.

But I can't, because I'm frozen here on the steps, his eyes concealed by the thickening night, and if there's one thing I know, it's this—you don't turn your back on the monster in the room. His dog watches me silently. It reminds me of Hades. They're too similar. Too big and terrifying.

Hades drops his hand.

"You're slow to obey, I see. That won't be a problem for very long."

"I…" There's nothing I can say to that. He looks like he could stand at the bottom of the stairs forever and never get tired. There's no choice but to do what he says. It's this, or he takes me back to my mother.

A full-body shudder moves through me. I have to do this, and I have to do it now. Something like excitement sparks

40

through my veins. It's the wrong kind of desire. I should never feel it for this man. I should never hope for him to destroy me.

"Turn around and do what?"

Another slow smile, the hint of a laugh. I hold my breath, the air around me pressing in on my head and on my heart and on the sick desire knotting in my belly.

"It's not obvious?" Hades puts his fingers beneath my chin and moves my head back and forth, watching, watching. Conor whines again. "Hush," he says to the dog, but then his focus returns to me. "I liked it when you lied before, even while you pressed those thighs together and pretended you didn't feel it. But don't lie to me now. I'll know, and then you'll have to pay the price."

"It's not obvious," I blurt, I beg. "What do you want me to do?"

"Turn around," he says again. "And get on the fucking train."

SEVEN

Persephone

THE OUTSIDE OF THE TRAIN CAR GAVE NOTHING AWAY, ITS shell the same black, sleek exterior as the other cars. I edge into the train car sideways, breath shallow.

I don't want to turn all the way around.

If I take my eyes off him, God knows what he'll become.

It's not his looks that make my knees weak, though he's the most stunning man I've seen. It's the fact that he's taking me. Kidnapping me. Like my mother's nightmares made him real.

Or maybe it *is* his looks. I don't know anymore. My brain is nothing. My brain is the breeze in the leaves—leaves I might never see again.

Hades steps into the car behind me, his frame filling the door. For an instant, I think he might not make it through. Then he angles his shoulders, the movement graceful and controlled, and I have to scoot out of the way so he can rise to his full height behind me.

I don't mean to stare, but in the warm, golden light of the train car, I have no other choice.

Hades is exactly as tall as he was outside, only more so now that we're in an enclosed space. My mind can't put all the pieces of him together at once. I wasn't wrong about the way the light reacts to him. He wears a rich suit as dark as a black hole. There's not a hint of shine to it, like the suit jacket I found at the back of my mother's closet once upon a time.

And the body underneath the suit...

Flawless. My thighs press together again at the sight of him. Hades looks like he was born to wear expensive suits as much as he was born to steal me away in the dark. Everything about him is symmetrical. Lean. Perfect. The suit slides over hard biceps, and I bet if I pulled his shirt out of his pants and looked underneath...

I bet...

Oh, God, I can't even think of it. I swallow hard. All the books I've read are fantasies. In real life, men as evil as Hades don't have to have an outward mark to tell you they're the devil. Hades certainly doesn't. This isn't a man. This is a god. I try to bat the thought away, but it's foundational and true.

I never once felt lighthearted about Decker. I never pressed my thighs together. I never wanted him to touch me.

A jagged tear appears in my mind. Everything about Hades's clothes and his train car is supposed to be about refinement, but all I can feel is the violence coiled underneath all that fine fabric.

He took me out of the fields.

He didn't let me run.

His clothes don't hide his cruelty, or his strength. They enhance it. He could kill wearing the most expensive piece of clothing I've ever seen.

Hades snaps his fingers in front of my eyes.

I blink up at him, breath stopping again at the sight of his face. His body is one thing, but his face—I've never seen any man so cruelly beautiful.

Even with his eyes.

Black. They're black. Too black, for a man with white-blond hair that catches the golden light in its short glossy strands. Wait. Not black. A thin line of blue, pale blue, like chips out of the springtime sky. Not enough to push back the darkness at the center. Who has eyes like this?

Hades tracks the movements of my eyes over his sharp cheekbones and cut jaw.

"Ah. So you *do* like what you see." His lips curve upward in something between a sneer and a smile. "I didn't tell you to stare."

"No. I hate you." Yes. I do like what I see. I can't help it. He's beautiful, and his clothes are beautiful, and this train car is a dream. I expected to stow away with the crates of flowers. "It's just hard to look away."

Behind him, the door slides shut. He slaps a palm to the wall beside him. It glows, then fades away, and the train starts moving. My balance is off on my unsteady knees, and I fall sideways, unceremonious, one palm thrown out to stop my fall.

I never hit the floor. Hades catches me. The place where he's touching me hums with heat.

"Pay attention." A cool command. "If you hit your head on the furniture, you won't be of any use to me."

He wraps his other huge hand around my waist and pushes me backward.

This time, the landing is a soft one—plush and overstuffed. It does nothing to calm me. His dog is between us, looking back and forth. A growl rumbles in his throat. He's more like a wolf—too big and powerful to be a pet. For a second I think he's guarding Hades. That he's growling at me. Then I realize he's trying to protect me. He's my unlikely ally.

"Conor," Hades warns.

He ducks his head in reluctant obedience. Conor is the color of midnight and strong, not an ounce of softness on him. He crosses the train car, nails clicking on the floor, and curls up in front of the fireplace. A low fire burns in a grate by the train's outer wall.

I have the distinct sensation of the sun going behind a cloud.

Hades is not the sun, and he's not the moon. He is total darkness, a place no light can touch.

Hades moves through the train car. He stops to pat Conor's head, which gives me time to catch my breath. At the edge of a desk, he removes one of his cufflinks. The desk has clearly been made to fit him—sturdy polished wood, gleaming in the firelight, a deep, dark color with a hint of red.

The other cufflink is next. He drops them both on the surface of the desk with a muffled metallic *click*. The desk must be bolted to the floor. Everything in here must be bolted to the floor, because it all sways with the movement of the train. It would have been a different ride in the dusty interior of one of the cargo cars, sitting on the hard floor.

This car must've been built to his specifications, so Hades travels in complete comfort. Every detail could have sprung from his bones fully formed. The rich paneling on the walls. Deep green-gray furniture, the hue of the summer grass at night. He turns from his desk and undoes the buttons of his jacket. Slips it from his shoulders. My heart stops. Stutters to a start.

Behind the desk is a door. Past the door is the corner of a bed, done up in sheets the color of his suit. My stomach clenches, and I dig one hand into the armrest on this—what is it? A small sofa.

Hades takes out his phone. The glow lights up his face. Most people look washed-out by the electronic light, but he only appears sharper. More beautiful. How? His black eyes snap to mine over the phone.

"Still paying attention?"

"Yes." I sit up straight. It's wrong—how hard I've been trying to do what he says. How hard I've been paying attention to this man and his dog, both of whom could be the end of me right now. It doesn't matter that the dog wanted to protect me. He takes orders from Hades. All it would take is one decision from him. A snap of his fingers.

I should wish I was dead right now. From the shame, and the danger. I should wish this was over already and I was safe in the ground, all of my pain over. But I don't wish I was dead.

It's foolish, all the thoughts humming in my mind like a swarm of bees. I don't want Hades to be the man my mother said he was.

Do I?

I don't, I don't. Some small part of me knows that even if I obey him flawlessly, it will never, ever change him.

It's not up to me to change him. It's up to me to survive until I can get free.

"I'm paying attention," I confirm.

"Good. Then we'll begin."

I lick at dry lips, folding my hands into my lap. Oh, God. I thought I talked myself down from the panic before but it comes on again, thick and suffocating. A thousand questions wither on the tip of my tongue.

Hades sits on the wider sofa across the train car, feet planted on the ground. He surveys me, eyes cold. I'm afraid of those eyes. A shiver crawls down my spine. My heart races, thrashing around inside my rib cage, screaming to get out. Just start already, please, please, please. I open my mouth to let the plea slip out into the air, but Hades speaks first.

"Come here."

Already, the sofa has come to represent the safest place in the room. Ridiculous. I'm not safe because of the sofa. A firework explodes, sending shards of shame through every part of me, and I get to my feet. My knees start up again, going loose and useless, and I have to lock them to stay upright. Don't faint. I unlock them, rocking them forward an inch.

Just move.

I take the first step, and Hades holds up a hand.

"Not like that, Persephone."

I don't know what he means. There's no other way to get across the floor except by walking.

Unless—

I don't know what he means, and then suddenly, awfully, I do.

"I-I'm wearing a dress."

A glint in his eyes, and I want to clap a hand over my mouth. I'm here because of my reckless words, and now I'm going to end up without any clothes at all. He'll see everything. The linen tank I have a hundred of. Had a hundred of. The… the white panties.

Oh, God, no.

And on top of this, I have to crawl past the dog. As if I'm a dog, too.

"So you do understand." He laughs, that same sound that burns my cheeks. "Come here."

I drop to my knees onto the plush carpeting, which still carries the scent of a lightly perfumed cleaner, something like fresh laundry. Before I can stop myself I dig my hands into it, eyes burning.

"Don't hide your tears." I look up into Hades's face, and his intense gaze is changed, brightened. He's enjoying this. "I want to see them all. Keep that pretty chin up while you crawl to me."

My hands are cement blocks, my knees totally ineffectual, but I put one palm after the other, one knee after the other, while hot tears slip down to clean carpet. At the last moment, he points between his legs.

I'll never make it. I'll never be able to make myself do this, not with humiliation sloshing over every last inch of me.

And the most humiliating thing of all?

It's not every last inch.

Between my legs, desire builds with every sway of my hips and every press of my palms into the carpet.

I stop between his legs and look up at him, trying to keep my breathing even. Hades reaches down and puts a hand under my chin, jerking my head up another inch, peering down at me. That filthy, hidden part of me sighs with relief even as the rest of me recoils.

I have to let him do this if I'm going to live. But I cannot feel anything but hatred about it. I can't.

Hades smiles, and I can't tell which parts of me have gone cold and which parts have gone hot. All I know is I want him to let go, to let me go. Yes. That's what I want. That's what I need, and I don't need anything else.

"You took too long, but you get extra points for crying. I fucking love that." His teeth scrape at his bottom lip.

Then his eyes go to the flowers in my hair. His gaze settles there. It changes.

"Don't move."

I don't. I wait to see how cruel he'll be. Whether he'll tear them out along with strands of hair.

He does not.

Hades takes them out of my braid one by one. He puts

them on a table nearby. Not one of them is damaged by his hands. I don't understand it. I don't understand how he can be so careful, and so terrible.

"Can I go back to the sofa now?" I ask when he's done. More tears work free, my heart throbbing. This is enough for now. It has to be enough for now.

"Do you really think I'm done with you? Tell the truth." The simple words have the same weight as curses. He leans down, the scent of him surrounding me. He smells so good. Like the first hint of cold in winter. Like ice and mint. Like a wide-open sky. "Tell me now."

"No," I choke out. "I didn't think… I only thought, since—"

"Shut your pretty mouth."

I snap my lips closed.

"I'm not done with you yet. I won't be done with you for quite some time."

My life is in his hands.

Hades lifts me up by the chin, quickly enough that I have to scramble to my feet. He holds me off-balance, leaning close, and I want to collapse into him and sob against his shirt.

It's sick. It's wrong. I want it.

The train carries me away from my mother's house, away from everything I've ever known, at a breakneck pace. My mind floats back to those fields.

I hated the fences.

Now I want them back.

Hades snaps his fingers in front of my eyes again and I startle.

"Now." It's all I can do to stay upright, even with his hand gripping my chin. "Let's find out what else you'll do."

EIGHT

Persephone

I TREMBLE IN HIS HANDS, AND HADES WATCHES THIS AS dispassionately as you'd watch a flower grow. Unlike my mother, he wouldn't think twice about crushing blooms under his heel or in his hands. He'd just as soon tear out the petals and spit on them.

"The crawling was fine." A cold assessment. The way you'd talk about a thing. "The tears are delicious, but you'll have to do better than that."

He rises to his feet, towering over me. I can't move. I can't anticipate what he'll do or what he'll say, so I stand there, rooted to the spot, staring at the buttons on his dark dress shirt. I've never seen a shirt like that. It must be expensive. It looks nicer than any linen dress I've ever owned.

"I have to say, Persephone, the sight of you scared…" He makes a low noise in the back of his throat. "You were such a courageous little thing out there, trying to run away from me."

I want to sink down to the floor and hide my face. More

than that, I want to hook my fingers in the space between the buttons of his shirt and hold on for dear life.

"I'm not afraid of you. I've known you were dangerous all my life. That doesn't make me afraid." I have never been so terrified. It's become the air I breathe and the rise and fall of my lungs. "It makes me hate you for doing this."

"It's strange you weren't looking for me, then. After all those warnings." His eyes rake across my face. My lips. My neck.

"I would have been, but I had other things on my mind."

"Like what? Were you fucking one of your mother's farm boys?"

I turn my face away.

His bristling silence tells me I've stepped in the direction of defiance. The air crackles.

"How many of them were you fucking?"

"None. And I don't know why you care."

He turns my face to his with a firm grip and searches my eyes as I force myself to look back.

"Prove it to me."

"Prove what?"

"Prove you're innocent." He clicks his tongue. "It would be disappointing if you weren't. I have such plans for you."

I close my lips, pinch them tight. Terror mixes with confusion, all of it wrapped in the overpowering need to survive and a burning embarrassment that I like the way he looks. I like the scent of his skin. I like the sound of his voice.

Oh, I hate him.

"How do you want me to prove it?"

He turns me to face the desk.

"Bend over." Hades's hand curls around the back of my neck. "Here. I'll make it easy."

I can't breathe. I can't think. I can only obey. I thought

crawling was the worst of it. I thought the nightmarish images that came to mind about what men do to women were the worst of it.

I was wrong.

The desk meets my hips, a hard, unforgiving line. I'm painfully aware of the curve of my back and my ass and then the press of my breasts against the unyielding surface.

"What are you going to do?" I try to ask it in as normal a voice as possible. "Just tell me."

He gives my neck a shake, and my cheek makes contact with the desk.

"I don't share my plans with property." Another shake, harder. "In fact, I've already held up my end of the deal." Hades rubs a thumb absently up and down the side of my neck, underneath my hair. "I didn't take you back to your mother's house and fuck you there. I didn't kill you, though I could." My body fights between tensing up and giving in to the slow slide of his thumb. Why would I ever want to let myself relax? It's not me wanting it. It's my traitor of a body. I pin my legs together as tightly as the muscles will allow. "You're so small. It would be nothing."

The heat of my cheek has already warmed up the desk beneath it.

"I thought you wanted me alive." I keep my eyes firmly focused on the shuttered window on the opposite side of the train. The thought of him seeing me like this, bent like this—

It can't get any worse.

It gets worse.

"I'll get far more value out of a live woman than a dead one." The hand lifts from the back of my neck, but I stay pressed flat against the desk. He hasn't said to get up. Hades makes a satisfied sound. "Look at you, trying to anticipate my wishes. Can you guess what will happen to you next?"

My breath stops, and there it is, my chin going again. A million scenarios run through my mind. A million horrible, filthy scenarios, snapshots of things depraved people would do. I know that not all sex is bad, but most of it must be. My mother kept all of it from me for a reason. The things I read about in books were nothing like this. They involved gentleman and marriage proposals, not bending over a desk, ass lifted up toward a man who'd just as soon kill me as—

"No," I breathe. "I don't know."

"You're lying." He kicks my legs apart. "You might wear a white dress and live on your mother's farm, but she'll have told you things. She must have taught you about the birds and the bees."

"No." My desperation rises in another round of tears. They drip onto the polished surface below my face. "She's never told me anything about this. About any of that."

His hand slips down my spine, counting each ridge, until he stops just above the swell of my ass.

"You bleed every month without knowing why?"

"I know why." I'm incandescent with shame. How can he say all this into the open? And so casually? "I know about getting pregnant."

The warm air from the train car glides underneath the hem of my dress and strokes me between my legs, where all that separates me from Hades is a thin layer of cotton. Every movement in the air, every movement of his hand—all of them are magnified, intensified. The hem of my dress lifts.

I feel every inch of my legs as he exposes them, little by little, torturing me. The dress reaches up above my white underwear, and a sob rips from my lungs. I've had my thoughts, late at night, about someday lying down with a man, somebody normal and gentle, probably fumbling. It never seemed like such a big deal, like something that would swamp me so completely with feeling. With humiliation and desire and the tug of linen up to the small of my back. The desk vibrates beneath me, the train vibrates beneath me, and I shake along with it, my body out of control.

Hades curses behind me, voice laden with something dark, edging on needy.

"You're a liar. These clothes are all for show, aren't they? You want people to believe you're as innocent as these panties say you are."

"I didn't think anyone would ever see them." I don't know what could possibly be a performance about what I'm doing now. If I had anything else to wear, I'd have worn that.

"Except one of your favorite farm boys." He puts one finger under the elastic and traces a fiery path underneath, and then it's gone. "Did you have a favorite, Persephone? Did he like to play games with you?" I've never heard a tone so deadly in my life. "Push you against a tree somewhere and let his hands creep up beneath your dress?" One big hand caresses the back of my knee and slips upward, upward, another inch upward. "Did you let other things beneath your dress?"

My legs betray me. I'm frozen, hardly able to breathe, but at the touch of Hades's hand, I move one thigh out another inch.

He laughs. I squeeze my eyes closed, which does nothing to keep the tears in.

"I told you. I wasn't with anyone like that." Hades's fingertips play at the edge of my panties. He slips one underneath again, tugging the elastic out, letting it snap back against my skin. He's getting closer and closer to the softness between my legs… and the dampness, and if he touches it, if he finds out, if he can see, I won't survive. There's no way I can live with it. I'll be disgraced.

The moment comes anyway.

Hades cups a hand over my panties, fitting it between my widespread legs, and it forces a cry out of me.

He goes still, but doesn't move his hand.

He waits.

Each horrible moment bleeds into the next.

"That's right," he murmurs. "Push back into my hand." My body obeys him, even if the rest of me wants to collapse to the floor. He fits his thumb into the cleft of my ass, and his fingertips brush a place only I have ever touched, and only secretly, only furtively. "You're wet," he comments, a gravelly edge to his voice.

There's no arguing with him. I can feel it too. And I can feel the tendrils of electric desire moving outward from that pressure. I grit my teeth. I will not move my hips to get him to make contact with my clit. I will not. I will *not*. But my hips betray me too. It's hardly any movement, but it's there. I hate myself. I hate him.

"Who taught you to play this game?" He's searching for something. Some piece of information. I don't know what.

No one's ever touched me like this.

But you want Hades to touch you, says that viper's voice.

I don't.

"How many of the farm boys did you fuck? Speak, Persephone."

As Hades asks, he works his fingers into the waistband of my panties, and the entire world grinds to a halt on its axis. There's only the vibration of the train beneath me, my hands somehow gripping the other side of the desk, and my bare toes trembling on the floor.

He's going to take the panties off, and then he'll be able to see everything.

He'll be able to do everything.

Hades's fingers curl at the waistband of my panties, and the spiky edges of anticipation tear through me like a clawed beast. The words follow on a gasp, on a cry.

"I didn't fuck anyone." Tears, rain, there's no difference. "I'm a virgin."

Hades pulls the elastic away from my skin, hard enough that it digs in. The hard snap when he lets go brings me to my senses and restarts my lungs. I'm still wet between my legs. There's nothing I can do about that. But at least I have my panties.

This momentary relief doesn't last. My stomach turns over. Hades walks to the opposite side of the desk. I don't dare move until he reaches down and lifts my face from the wood, holding my chin in his hand.

"Don't lie to me."

"I didn't—"

Something in his cold eyes chases the shakes from my muscles. I'm not fast enough for him. He plucks me off the floor and positions me in front of him in a heap of linen. My legs burn from standing on tiptoe. They sigh with relief.

It doesn't last.

Hades pulls me to my knees on the hard surface of the desk. Wraps a hand around the back of my neck. Holds. He's inches away, smelling like cold and cedar and something else, something I've only ever smelled on him, looking into my eyes like he's seeing all my thoughts skittering away. He's waiting, menace embodied, and every breath makes my breasts rise, aching for something. His touch? Not likely.

"I told you not to lie to me." A voice like a blade. "Be a good girl and tell the truth."

Hades twines his fingers through my hair, tugging my head back an inch. Resisting him feels impossible for the moment.

"I'm telling the truth." I swallow, and his eyes drop to the front of my throat and come back up to meet mine. I sound hoarse, pained. "I'm a virgin. Nobody's ever done that to me."

Hades smiles, displaying a row of teeth sharp enough to tear my skin. "But you've been waiting for it. Longing for it."

"No. I don't want it." I want it more than I can say. I want it enough to run away from home. I want it enough to leave my mother and everything I've ever known. But it's not just sex that I want. It's everything that comes along with it. Everything I thought came along with it. "I especially don't want it from you."

"Liar. You threw yourself at me. I've never seen a woman more desperate to be fucked."

"What if I trade that, then? Sex in exchange for letting me go?"

His smile turns taunting. There's a certain softness to it that I'm certainly imagining. "No. I don't accept."

Something breaks inside me, crumbling under the tension and exhaustion from the night.

"I wasn't throwing myself at you. I was trying to get away. I wanted to get away."

"And you got what you wanted." I hate that he's right.

"Why were you even there? What do you *want*?"

"I want you to cry. I want to watch your face go red with shame. I want to make you beg. I can promise you will."

A painful sob changes into a laugh in my mouth, and I fall, tipping forward. I can't hold myself up anymore. I'm so tired.

He catches me in his arms, saying nothing. I'm laughing too hard to do anything about it, swallowing the sound, putting my knuckles to my lips to keep it in. Better to let him think I'm crying. At least he likes that.

I like how it feels to be carried by him. Everything else is in terrible motion, but he's steady.

A door opens on a draft of air, and a spike of panic drives deep into my mind. The bedroom. I land on the bed—a firm mattress, I've always wished for a firm mattress—and curl up on the pillow. I need a minute to collect myself, that's all. My vision swims. There's no way I'll fall asleep here. No way I can rest with him in the room.

The world is already fading away.

Hades lifts my hand from the pillow next to my cheek. I'm miles away. Lying in a grassy field that belongs to me and no one else. I'm escaping, if only in my mind. I wish I had a book. Any book. But I couldn't stay awake to read it.

He pushes my sleeve up a few inches. A few more. My eyelids feel heavier by the second. His voice brushes by me. Once, then again.

"Persephone." A fingertip skims the cuts from the thorns. "What's all this?"

I try to open my eyes and discover I can't. I'm done for the night. That run across the fields took everything I had. "My mother got angry. She didn't mean to do it."

Hades puts my hand back on the pillow, and then I really am dreaming.

Because in the dark, I feel him leave, and I feel him return. Careful hands fold my sleeve back. A stone lion murmurs curses under its breath. Something cool sinks into each mark left by the thorns, and they don't hurt anymore.

A dream, because monsters don't tend wounds. Kidnappers don't worry about infections. And Hades doesn't care.

NINE

Hades

GIVING IN TO URGES COMES WITH A CERTAIN AMOUNT of pleasure, but nothing compares to denial. Denial of the body. Denial of the soul. Persephone could destroy what's left of my soul.

I thought there was nothing left, nowhere more depraved and wasted to go.

Yet here we are.

The train hurtles through the night. Persephone makes no move from the bed after I've finished with her cuts.

I recognized them easily enough. Thorns, wrapped around her wrist. In all of Decker's reports, he's never mentioned behavior like this from Demeter. I had assumed she didn't care about breaking the terms of our agreement. It was clearly an incorrect assumption.

Persephone's breathing turns soft and even. A few shapeless words escape her lips, sounding like a question.

She's dreaming.

Unbelievable. That she's managed to fall asleep and stay asleep while I was watching, while I was touching her…

It does something to me. Brings the world closer in. I like the daylight to be kept at arm's length, along with the complicated emotions of the people in it, but Persephone is the sun bursting into my sanctuary and turning me into a fool.

She must know how defenseless she is, falling asleep here. She must also know it doesn't matter. Persephone could have all the defenses in the world, and I'd still get to her.

Everything is different now. She's changed all my plans. Changed the calculus of my life.

Captivating—that's what she is. I've never been captivated before.

I hold out a hand to shake her awake and hesitate. She is a tumble of curls and linen. Pink-cheeked from what I did to her. Soft and warm.

There's no need to rush this, other than the insistent throb between my legs.

I made it clear I could kill her. She knows it down to her bones.

I won't kill her. I can't.

Her heartbeat matters to me now. It has nothing to do with Demeter, or those goddamn poppies. It's that seeing her in her white dress, her face pale with fear, was like being shocked awake. I've sunk into darkness enough times to be familiar with a slowing heart. With death, held close. Mine beats again. Throbs with the ache in my head.

I wanted a clear mind to visit Demeter's fields, and the painkillers are already wearing off. The pressure increasing. If anyone cared to look, they'd find the evidence dotted along the train tracks under a thin layer of earth.

If only the headaches were as simple as migraines.

I could break Persephone. Reduce her to a little puddle of a woman. I have the skills to do it.

I won't do that, either.

She'd be alive, but not really living.

Denying myself her body is like wrapping my cock in barbed wire. I'm not into that, but I can't resist waiting. She wants me to get on with it so badly. I could, but I'd lose all those delicious tears, and the begging, and the way she fights so hard not to cry.

If I break her now, all those tears will dry up. It would be such a pity.

I run my hands over my mouth and listen to her breathe. The shadows in here are far more tolerable than the lamp I left on outside. It almost seems plausible to lie down next to her and drift away.

Almost, but not quite.

I am more practiced in denial than most people I know, including and especially my brother Zeus.

Zeus, who owns the city's most upscale and notorious brothel. He's taken our father's place at the helm—or, as Zeus prefers, at the center of its largest room, where he can hold court like a fucked-up king. He loves to toy with people. All the factions in the city jostle for his attention. I know why they bother. He knows everyone's business. He keeps their secrets. Takes their money. Sells them women.

He keeps his parties running smoothly through the sheer force of his will. An illusory mood, dropped over people's minds like thin, gold cloth. Being near him sets my teeth on edge.

I go back out into the main section of the train car, turning that over in my mind. Both of my brothers—Zeus and Poseidon—know about Demeter's daughter. Neither of them have tried to use her for their own ends. Poseidon is continually at sea, and hates Demeter more than anyone. Zeus must need Demeter and her supplies more than I thought.

My lips curl into a snarl. There's nothing I loathe more than needing something from someone else. I've devoted my life to exorcizing every possible weakness, save the one I can't cut out.

I wave a hand over the light and it turns off, plunging the train car into darkness.

Better.

I let myself sit heavily on the couch and press at my chest, trying to get that odd, painful sensation to go away.

It's not a heart attack. Deeper than that. Maybe an overabundance of lust. Or perhaps it's extra adrenaline, held back from the moment I swept her into my arms. If I'm honest in the privacy of my own mind, I'm glad I didn't kill Demeter tonight. I'm glad I took her daughter instead. I hate the humanity of that gladness. It exists nonetheless.

Should I turn the train around? I consider the question instead of assessing adrenaline-soaked emotions. I taste the sweetness of giving in to what I want and imagine every detail of what it would be like. The way the train would slow, the tracks rearranging themselves in front of us. Most people know there are provisions to change direction. It can be done in an emergency. It would be well within my rights. I own it from start to finish. A tenuous agreement with Zeus keeps it running smoothly through the city. It would throw off his timetables, which would be delightful.

No. It's too simple a taste, that sweetness. I won't turn the train around. I'll let myself want Persephone while we travel through the dark. Let that want scratch at my skin. Let my cock pulse against my pants.

I'll let myself suffer while she sleeps.

The communications unit pings on my desk. It's built to blend in with the surface and can generate secure lines, if I need them. Its most convenient feature is its connection with my head of security, even when the train loses access to wi-fi.

"Answer," I tell it. Conor comes over and puts his head on my knee. I absently rub behind his ears. He whines a little, tensing. "I'm fine. Settle down."

My dog believes me for the moment. Conor has been with me for ten years. For a decade, I've kept him safe and well—not that I place a high priority on saving anyone or anything. It's almost always a pointless expenditure of valuable resources. My brother Zeus has a fetish for pointless expenditures. I hold a special well of hatred for him in my heart. The fucker wouldn't know what to do with a good dog if it bit him, which a good dog would.

I've tried not to become attached to Conor. He's only a dog, but he's good at what he does. He keeps me from wasting energy when it matters. And he has the virtue of being mine.

He huffs, letting his head rest against me.

The call connects.

"Callahan here."

I hired Oliver Callahan almost directly off the streets, where he'd been living until the moment he decided to hitch a ride on the train and come raid the mountain. Never mind the audacity of attempting to perform petty theft in a fortress guarded by private security and by me—the motherfucker watched as the tracks split to send the train car into my seldom-used private entrance, let himself get three electric shocks, and balanced on one of the connectors until he could get inside. I wasn't the one who gave him the long scar down his face. He survived that *and* the shocks. Anyone with that kind of willpower is best kept loyal to me.

"Do you have an update?" I ask.

"No. All's quiet here."

Conor lifts his head up and returns to the fireplace. Curls up. Falls asleep.

"If you don't have an update, why are you calling me?" I lean my head back against the sofa and close my eyes. With a family like mine, there's a certain need for vigilance. The best part about the train is that it's exceedingly difficult to attack when it's going at full speed, and I know my men cleared the cars before we started moving. This is one of the only places I can even pretend to relax. "If you had to kill someone again, there's no reason to give me all the details. Bury the body and move on."

He chuckles. "The train left earlier than usual. I wondered if you planned to reschedule."

"Circumstances changed."

I didn't go into the field to get the flowers. I took Persephone instead.

That needy, obnoxious ache in the center of my chest starts up again, and I sit up straight, rubbing at my eyes. The fucking moonlight. This problem, this weakness, is why I need the flowers in the first place. It should have been simple to get me.

Demeter was smart to hate me. Her paranoia keeps her safer than she would be otherwise, and to my great disgust and irritation, I do need her to be safe.

I need a great deal more from her.

Persephone is one way to get those poppies. I knew that, on some instinctual level, the moment I saw her. I won't go that route. I didn't take her as a hostage. I took her because I want to taste her. Fuck her. Break her.

"If I wanted to turn back, I'd have given you the order already."

"Of course."

"Don't bother me again."

The call disconnects with a two-toned beep, and I'm left alone in the train car. Wind whistles along the outside, a pleasant white noise. The very moment the call ends, Persephone is back at the front of my mind, struggling in my arms, telling me not to take her back to that house. My cock reminds me of every angle—her delectable body bent over my desk, the way she had to spread her legs so wide to fit my hand, the way she loved it.

I stifle a groan at how much she wants it, how much her body wants all the filthy things I'm going to do to her. And that admission she's a virgin—fuck. I knew she wasn't lying the first time she said it, but who doesn't like to push a little here and there? Make her spill a few more tears? Make her think it's her very last breath she's sucking in?

It's painful how much I need to use her. I get up from the sofa in the dark and go over to the desk. Brace against it. Undo my pants with a swift jerk. Let her see me now. I'd love to see a brand-new wave of tears spill out of her eyes. How she'd hate it if I made her come on my fingers. She'd hate it down to her bones, down to the center of her soul. Persephone has a soul— that much is obvious—and I want it to be my mission in life to dirty it up until she can't see any way to live without me.

Think. I need to think.

I can't. I want her too much. I played with her, humiliated her, to illustrate my power over her, and in the process I've fucked myself over.

I wait as long as I can, precum gathering on the tip of my cock, and then I take it in my fist and pump it hard, hips angled toward the wastebasket, straining for the sound of her breath. I've *taken* her.

Getting the poppies from Demeter will be more complicated now in any number of ways.

But none of those complications do a thing to relieve the unfiltered lust rocketing through my bloodstream.

The release is an anticlimax, empty and base, and as soon as it ends, the cycle begins again. Sunrise, sunset. I lean against the desk and catch my breath. Taking her, that was easy. Making her cry, easier still. But keeping her at arm's length?

Curses fill my mind, and I fall back onto the sofa. Persephone believes I'll destroy her, and I will—in every possible way that will still let me enjoy her. Only here, in my train car, my cock already getting hard again, can I sit in the knowledge that this could be the end of me too.

TEN

Persephone

MY EYES OPEN TO A DARKNESS SO COMPLETE A SCREAM lurches up in my throat. I clap my hands over my mouth, holding it back while I get my bearings.

Where am I?

I can't see anything, and this makes the memories from last night even worse.

Hades, appearing out of the night, a massive dog at his side. His threats to *trade me back*. His hands between my legs.

A pillow. A bed. *His* bed.

My heart beats hard and sharp like I've been running. In a way, I have been running. I sprinted toward freedom—and I failed.

I belong to Hades now.

Temporarily.

Until I can find a way out of here, too.

I press my knuckles against my eyes, wiping away dried tears. My skin is puffy, and my face is probably still red. The

main improvement is in the marks on my wrists. They're a lot better than they were last night. I can barely feel them. My hair—I don't have any way to fix the mess it's in. I smooth my hands over the curls and feel Hades's hand there too, the ghost of his touch from last night.

Last night, or another night. How long has it been? How long did he let me sleep? A man like him wouldn't care about me getting an adequate amount of rest. I fumble my hands together and whisper a half-remembered prayer I read in a book once. I can't remember all the words, and I seriously doubt anyone will hear me. If last night taught me anything, it's that there is probably no God.

There is only Hades.

The door opens, sending me scrambling back on the bed, eyes stinging. The vibration of the train slows. Stops. I blink at the enormous figure in the doorway. Light streams in around him. I'm a mess, and he looks like he just stepped out of a walk-in closet.

His jacket is back on. "Get up."

"Where are we?"

"Did I invite you to ask me questions? No. I told you to get up."

I tip myself off the side of the bed. I ran away without shoes, so I have to move toward him without them, in my rumpled dress. Hades's eyes are hidden in the shadows, but I can still feel where his gaze meets my skin. A strange heat. What happened before I slept taunts me. My cheeks must be the color of my mother's garnet-hued orchids. Or deeper.

I open my mouth. *Don't say anything.* Shut it again. *Don't.*

"But where are we?"

I have a small, wild hope that maybe we're in the city and Hades has decided to set me free. He could let me off the train

68

right now and I could proceed with my plan. Find somewhere to stay. Keep running. It's the tiniest thing, like a newly hatched bird, and I know I'm being ridiculous by indulging it.

The slightest inhale of breath, which I recognize as a laugh.

"Where do you think we are?" He folds his arms over his chest, blocking more of the light. "Do you think I've brought you back to that godforsaken farm? Come here."

This time, I don't hesitate. Hesitation only ends with me crawling across the floor, and I don't want to cry again this soon after waking up. I stand one step away from him. With a rough grip, he forces my face upward, fingers tight around my chin, so tight I gasp.

He was playing with me last night. He was being gentle.

"You're. Never. Going. Home." Hades doesn't bother to raise his voice. He lets the words cut me like the small knives they are. They hurt, but part of me is relieved to hear it. "Not ever. I've decided to use you until you take your very last breath."

"Or until you take it from me." I shouldn't say it. I know I shouldn't say it, but it slips out on a wave of homesickness and regret.

A moment's pause, and then—

"That's right." His grip doesn't loosen, but there was a note of tenderness in his voice. A note that said *I won't take it from you*. Either that or I'm still half-asleep. "Let's go."

He walks away without looking back, and I want to throw myself into the darkest corner of the room and stay there until he forgets about me. Conor pauses in the middle of the train car and looks back at me. It feels dangerous to be near Hades, but the dog's tail wags a little. That means it'll be okay, doesn't it? It doesn't matter. Hades won't forget. He won't leave me behind.

And.

As much as I hate Hades—and I do hate him, for the fact that he's exactly as evil as my mother always said he was—I want to see what happens next.

I can't sit down and shut up now that I finally have a chance to do something other than roam my mother's fields. We're headed toward a logical conclusion. A terrifying logical conclusion. My heart thrums in my throat. The waiting will be awful. But if he throws me down outside this train car and has his way with me, I'll be wishing I could go back in time to when it was all shrouded in mist, part of the future.

So I follow him.

I catch up as Hades steps down off the car. Conor's footfalls are close behind me. The dog's nose brushes the back of my dress, and my legs tense, ready to run. But running is the last thing you should do in front of a wild animal.

Conor isn't a wild animal, not really, but the back of my neck bristles like he is. Instead of biting me, instead of rending flesh from my bone, he licks me. It's a small comfort, but a real one.

The platform outside is not just a platform. I get an impression of high ceilings and dark marble, a cavernous, echoing space. And then I get an impression of something else, something that needs a second look. Hades holds his hand out. The movement doesn't make any sense. What is he doing? What does he want me to do?

Oh.

He's offering me his hand. I ignore it and climb out the door, wobbly and uncertain.

Hades glares.

"Is it that you want to fall onto the tracks? I can promise you it wouldn't be a pleasant escape." His voice is so light and so cutting all at once.

"No, I don't." I put my hand in his.

The touch is electric, bordering on a firestorm. He touched me last night, but the only thing I had under my palms were Hades's clothes. His hand is so big, and mine so small. It feels like putting my hand into an alligator's cage. Utterly reckless and dangerous if the alligator is in a bad mood. Hades is far more dangerous than any of the animals I've read about or seen outside the fence, except for his own dog. Is that what this is? A warning? Or my own body tricking me into thinking a monster might not be so bad after all?

He tugs, and I step down. He doesn't seem to care that I'm not wearing shoes.

We're very far from alone. I've only ever seen pictures of one of the train stations in the city, which was an antique design built before all the skyscrapers went up. At least that's what one of the placards on the wall said. This station doesn't have any placards.

It's busy. Nobody spares a second glance for Hades's dog, which must mean they're used to it. I don't know how they could get used to a dog that size—one with so many teeth. Even if he is being nice to me.

What did I expect when Hades caught me? An empty room at the center of the mountain? This isn't it. Far overhead, the ceiling moves smoothly over us in a high arc. The rock is a matte black with streaks of gold painted onto it.

No. Not painted.

In an instant, it clicks into place. Hades didn't hire artists to come hang from the rock, carefully imitating seams of precious metals. They *are* seams of precious metals. He's carved his train station out of his own riches.

I'm in his world now, and it could not be more different than the one I came from.

"Close those lips or I'll be forced to put something there."
Everything he says is a casual promise.

"I…" What's the use in apologizing? There is none. I
think—and I could be wrong—he likes it when I'm a little in-
solent. Probably because that'll give him an excuse to punish
me later. A full-body shiver rocks me from head to toe. Who
has thoughts like this? Not me. I can't let myself sink into that
kind of depravity no matter what happens to me here. If I do,
I'll never be the same. And if I'm going to hold out any hope
of escape, I have to keep myself intact. As much as I can manage. "This is huge."

People pour out onto the platform from doorways gashed
into the walls. They don't look afraid. They look like they're
going home from work.

Are they really leaving?

As if he's read my mind, Hades speaks. "They're not leaving, so wipe that precious expression off your face. They stay
on the mountain, just like you will."

The trap of his hand closes over mine.

"You keep people here?"

Hades looks at me like he's never seen a person quite as
dense. "Who do you think works for me? Commuters?"

"They all made a deal with you?"

His eyes narrow. "Yes. That's the nature of employment.
There's work to be done in the mines and in my home. I set
the terms. Workers agree."

"Mines?"

"She didn't tell you anything, did she?" He flicks his eyes
to the ceiling. "You'll do your part to keep my business running, just like everyone else."

"Me?"

"Did you think you were special?"

Maybe I did. Maybe the way he tended my wounds last night gave me the idea his cruelty is hiding something else.

I must have dreamed it.

The way he's looking at me now, eyes harder than diamonds—no. I'm like everyone else in this station. I'm his property too. My heart aches for them and for me. I was desperate enough to throw myself on his mercy. They must've been too. It's a cold comfort.

"You're nobody," Hades says simply. I already know it. I've been bracing myself to hear it all along, but tears prick the corners of my eyes. "You're nobody now, and when I'm done with you, you'll still be nobody."

Then he lifts my hand to his lips and brushes them across my knuckles.

He drops it before I have a chance to react.

"Keep up with me. I don't have all day."

ELEVEN

Persephone

THE MOUNTAIN IS MUCH FARTHER FROM MY MOTHER'S fields than I thought.

Nothing drives the point home more than walking up the wide stone steps to a set of massive double doors that look like they've been carved from the same rock as the rest of the train station. Those doors swing open as Hades and I approach, Conor right behind him, and it's only after a few seconds that I see the men holding them ajar. They both keep their eyes on the ground as we pass through and enter what can only be described as a capital city.

That's what it looks like, with Roman architecture and a soaring rotunda up at the top. A series of hallways branches out from the room's round center. The halls are so long I can't see the ends from here.

Now it makes more sense why my mother would have been so paranoid. A man who could own a place like this could own anything else he wanted, including the hands of

an assassin. There are no rules for him. His house makes that crystal clear.

Something is not right about the space. The places like this that I've seen in books—the few of them that I've seen—are carved from white rock. The black rock shot through with gold isn't what's wrong about it, however. It's something else. The shadows shift on Hades's face. I try to blink away the difference in case it's my eyes. Nothing changes.

People come and go here too, but fewer of them, and they're dressed in dark suits and maids' uniforms. All of them glance up as we pass, waiting for him to give them an order. There's a certain eagerness in their eyes, as if they're hoping to be useful, but only one man dares to approach. He matches pace with Hades and hands over a leather folio. Hades opens it, not breaking his stride. The man puts a pen in his hand. He signs. Hands the folio back. They don't exchange a word, and then the man is part of the crowd again.

I can't help staring as Hades moves through the giant space. He's not hurrying, not exactly, but there's not much time to look and so much to see. Carvings up in the dome of the rotunda, and windows. White, fluffy clouds roll against a blue sky through the windows, but the tint is off. Tinted windows in a rotunda? Who would want that? It's doing something to the natural light. Making it wrong. It's not until this moment that I miss my mother's fields with a vengeance.

I miss the sun on my face.

Hades strides across the rotunda, footsteps echoing, to a bank of elevators. Conor keeps up, completely focused on following Hades. He doesn't pause to sniff the floor or get a pat from anyone else. He stays right by Hades's feet like it's his job.

Maybe it is.

There's one button inset into a panel outside the elevator,

and Hades presses it. The doors slide open soundlessly. Every set of doors reminds me of how far I am from home and safety.

I don't want to go in.

My pulse beats faster. The elevator door feels like the steps on the train car. It feels like a last chance.

I bolt. No plan. Just feet flying over the marble for one step, two, I could get to the train, I could ask someone for help—

Or I could get caught on someone's arm. It wraps around my waist and yanks me back without any effort at all.

Hades carries me into the elevator like a stack of books and deposits me on the floor. I break away and press myself against its back wall, panting. My reflection pants back at me.

Conor pads into the elevator. Hades follows. The doors close behind them. They're taking up most of the space.

"What are you doing?" Hades asks.

I'm gripping the handrail so tightly my knuckles have lost all their color. I'm surprised there is a handrail in a place like this, where everyone is nobody. The elevator is far smaller than the train car, far more closed in, filled to the very top with my own fear.

"I'm—" Dying, maybe. "I'm afraid of you."

"Is that the reason for your little escape attempt?"

"Yes."

"You're not concerned about being punished?"

Maybe he wants me to let go, to stand closer, but I can't move. "I had to try. You wouldn't punish me for that."

"My, my. I didn't think we'd come quite so far yet. Let's go back out so I can give you what you really want, you filthy thing."

"No, please." I hold on to the railing for dear life. "Don't do that. Not now. Not on the first day."

Hades saunters over. "I don't think you understand the

terms. I'll do whatever it is I want with you, and you'll do whatever I say."

"Why should I?"

"Because you'll want to avoid the consequences."

My mouth goes dry, my face hot. "What are those going to be?"

Hades's eyes have gone deeper than the center of me. They've gone all the way through. He can see everything.

"I can't fucking believe it." He sounds wondering. "Demeter's daughter is a virgin who wants a man to punish her."

His hand is around my throat faster than lightning, too fast for me to raise my arms. He's not squeezing hard. Not yet. Just enough to let me know he has absolute control. And my body responds. My nipples tighten, and I press my ass against the wall of the elevator. Hades stares into my eyes, watching my shame, and then he curses under his breath.

I have never, never thought those words, even late at night when I know my mother is so soundly asleep that she'd never catch me thinking about it. But the truth—the worst possible truth—is that I'm a liar.

I'm a liar, and I have thought about a scenario like that, with a man's big hand and a woman bent over his knee, ass raised to accept it. There were some books that slipped by my mother. Some books I burned to keep her from finding them.

"No." It's a weak denial. There's no fight behind it, and Hades notices. A cruel smile curves his lips.

"You do." He dismisses me outright, and I want to slide down the wall of the elevator to the floor. "And to answer your question, though I don't believe you deserve an answer—I don't believe you deserve anything—you'll do anything I demand of you. You'll take it because you have no choice."

At some point, the panting breaths have turned from panic

to desire, which is terrible. It's the most terrible outcome I can imagine, aside from Hades dragging me back out into the center of the rotunda and punishing me there. I don't even know what that would entail, other than…

I can't even think about it. My body, however, has thought about it, and I can't deny the new slickness between my legs or the way my nipples brush against my tank top, sending electric shocks down to the center of my belly.

Hades studies me.

He studies me like I'm a foreign language to learn, and the only way to learn it is to absorb me into his skin until the humiliation eats me alive. Blessedly, that should happen soon. There's no way I can survive my embarrassment much longer.

"Keep your hands on the railing."

I try to say *okay*, but no sound comes out. Nothing comes out. I concentrate all my effort on the railing.

Hades kneels down in front of me, and even kneeling, he is absolutely in control.

"Punishment," he says, and as if I've been a naughty schoolgirl, as if I've been intentionally obtuse, "can take many forms." He wraps two fingers around my ankle and lifts my foot off the ground, exposing the tender arch. "I could punish you here." He draws a finger down the center, the spot so sensitive I throw my head back against the wall and squeeze my eyes closed. Then the quick swipe of a fingertip on the tops of my feet. "Or here." What kind of horrible things does this man have up his sleeve? Is there no limit? *No*, whispers that voice. *There is no limit.* He drops my foot and runs two hands hard up the backs of my legs then squeezes the backs of my thighs. "Here, until they're crisscrossed with stripes from my belt." His *belt*. I might not survive this, not even one single day. His hands go upward, and he's testing the curve of my ass. "And here. This is what you were thinking of. I'm sure of it. A spanking. But you know, Persephone, there are far more interesting punishments."

I'm speechless, lips parted, struggling to take a breath. Heat, heat, heat between my legs, running up between my breasts. Hades thrusts his hands up beneath my dress but over my tank to my chest, taking one breast in his hand. He studies it like he watched my face before, with complete concentration.

"Tits are an excellent thing to punish too. The sounds..." He makes a noise of satisfaction. "You'll see. But more than that..."

There can't be more. There can't be more, because I'll die. I'll turn to dust in his hand and float away on the non-existent breeze in the elevator. He would love that, wouldn't he? Or would he hate it? I can't tell anymore, and the only thing that matters now in all the earth is the way he's touching me, roughly, squeezing, pinching. Why does it feel good? Why do I want to lift my hands from the railing, not to push him away but to pull him closer? What the hell is wrong with me? It's all so, so wrong.

Then he slips his hand down, over my panties—the same panties he palmed last night—and brushes his knuckles over a part of me that throbs in a desperate, aching way. He doesn't stay there. He reaches back behind me, takes two handfuls of my ass, and spreads. He's not truly touching me. A thin layer of fabric is keeping him from touching me. It's keeping his hands off my skin, and it's not enough at the same time. It would be better if he took them off. But it would be so mortifying. I would never be able to stand it. I would never live through that.

One of his fingers goes to a place so private I whimper, knocking my head back against the wall. Anything to release the pressure. He pushes his finger in harder.

"Here."

I'm babbling something, God knows what, the words meaningless. Hades pays no attention to them. He slots his hand between my legs, exactly where it was last night. He doesn't have to force my thighs open. He's already arranged me how he wants me, and I didn't notice. He scrambles my brain. He does something to me that's worse, somehow, than killing me would have been. My mother was wrong. She was wrong.

"And here."

All the sound and breath in the elevator goes still. Letting go of the railing hasn't been on the table since he told me to keep my hands there. Hades holds me up with his hand between my legs. It's awful, it's wonderful, and it's going to tear me to pieces. Seconds tick by in the silence. He's waiting for something. I pick my head up from the wall and look down at him, my face burning.

"You wouldn't. You wouldn't do that."

He has the most beautiful, serious expression. Hades is a judge handing down a sentence, paternal in a way and vaguely concerned. *I've taken you through this as simply as possible*, his black eyes say. *Are you still not following?*

"I would. Know it in your heart, Persephone. I would."

Hades stands up, brushing his hands together like he's done dirty work. The moment snaps apart. I bend forward, bare feet hot and then cold on the elevator floor. He turns and presses one palm to a panel on the wall that glows. The elevator drops, my stomach rises, and we ascend into what has to be Hades's private space.

TWELVE

Persephone

THE ELEVATOR COMES TO A SMOOTH STOP AND THE DOORS slide open. I swallow back a surge of fear. The way time passes is distorted by standing so close to Hades, so I have no idea how long we've been going up. We could be on the top of the mountain, for all I know.

Outside the doors, the hallway drops into shadow. Anything could be waiting in those shadows. Is he going to lock me up in a cage for trying to run? He could. He could shut me behind a solid rock door with nothing but my clothes and keep me there, the weight of the mountain crushing me bit by bit until there's nothing left.

Or.

He could do the things he talked about in the elevator.

He steps out into the hall. Conor moves first, going directly to his side. Hades looks back. His face in profile, even wearing an expression of impatience, is so beautiful it takes my breath away.

"Let go of the fucking railing. Don't be tedious about this. It wastes my time."

I hate him for saying it. And I hate my grudging instinct to follow his orders. He caught me so easily that I know it's pointless to run again.

So if I'm going to escape, it's not going to be by sprinting through his house. I'll have to plan. And in order to do that, I'll have to be good.

Good enough to survive.

Good enough for him to be pleased.

What does that make me, if I want him to be pleased?

I follow him out and try to keep myself calm by going over the details.

There's no jail here. No cells. It's not a prison, like the ones I've read about in my books. Prisons don't have walls carved like this, with the same gold streaks I saw before. This floor—this wing?—has no echoing rotunda. The ceilings are high enough that Hades looks at home. This place was made for him, as custom as his suits. I steal a glance behind us. The hall disappears into darkness in either direction.

He sighs.

I snap my head around, expecting to see him glaring at me, but he's standing with his eyes closed, hands in his pockets. Conor nudges him below the knees, almost like he's coaxing him to go somewhere. Hades opens his eyes, frowns at me, and moves down the hall, Conor at his feet. I'm not even as good as his dog.

"Keep up."

What was that I saw? Relief at coming home, maybe. Hades is a man who should be as comfortable here as he is anywhere else. Nothing can touch him, out there in the world or here at home. Maybe he likes being at home. Needs it, like regular people. I don't know. It doesn't seem possible.

And yet.

We pass four doorways, and the gloom lifts at the end of the hall, where a double door is set into the end. We're almost there when I can't force my feet to go another step. Hades stops and scowls at me.

"I told you to keep up."

"Just tell me what's going to happen."

He rolls his eyes. "When I said I'd make you beg, I didn't mean over every obnoxious thought that goes through your mind. I thought that was understood."

Anticipation and anxiety twist together at the center of my chest, filling up all the space where air is supposed to be.

"I can't stand it," I say breathlessly. "I want to know what's coming. I need it."

Hades makes his way back over to me, a half-smile on his face. Oh, he understands. My heart cracks open with relief. I know he's a bad man. I know he doesn't care about me and never will. That doesn't mean he's incapable of all empathy. He must see in my face how much I need this. My thoughts become more tangled, more knotted with every step he takes.

He puts a hand on the top of my head, and I let my eyes flutter closed. A comforting touch. I thought I'd never feel a comforting touch again. Tears come free of my eyelids.

His thumb rubs over my temple, smoothing back my hair. I need this so much. I clench my teeth to keep my chin from quivering, because I don't want him to stop. I don't want—

Hades digs his hand into my hair, twists his fingers, and tilts my face up to his. It pulls a gasp from my mouth. I've never seen a harder, more narrowed set to his eyes.

"We're not going to do this." Nothing about him is loud,

which makes his voice sound far deadlier. This is a man who doesn't have to shout to keep people in line. "I'm not going to pet you and indulge you at every doorway. You need to know what happens? You already know what's going to happen, Persephone. You'll do anything I say, and I'll use you for my own purposes. But let's get to the truth at the very heart of this, the one you keep flirting with. You belong to me now."

I stare, open-mouthed, caught halfway between abject terror and disbelief at how beautiful he can look when he's being so mean.

Hades gives my hair a shake, and I cry out at the pain.

"Do you understand me?"

"Yes." My voice is high, pained, and he doesn't care. Conor barks at his side.

"That's not good enough, precious. Tell me what it is you understand."

"That I—" I suck in a deep breath, hoping it'll give me enough momentum to get the words out. "—I belong to you now."

"Again." He pulls my hair harder, yanking my head back. Hades leans his head down until his lips are an inch away from my pulse. He could bite me now, break the skin, and let me bleed out on the floor. All I feel is his breath as he exhales, and then he stands tall. "I said *again*. How many times do we need to go over this? Or are you truly begging for punishment? I promise you, I can make it so you'll never, ever forget what I've told you."

"I belong to you now." This time, my voice is low and frantic.

"I can't hear you."

"I belong to you now!" He changes the angle of his hand, and it doesn't hurt anymore, not really. It's pressure. He's tugging. Controlling. I hate it. I want it. I keep repeating it, over and over. My cries are broken up by Conor barking, more and more, like an argument. "I belong to you now, please. I belong to you now. Please. Don't make this feel good."

It's not good. It isn't.

Hades's grip gentles.

He lets me down slowly to the floor, and I hate him, I hate him. I can't catch my breath. I liked how rough he was, and I hate him. I liked how he didn't treat me like glass, and I hate him.

A hand cups my chin and pulls me up to my feet. His hand. I can't catch my breath. He steadies me. Something else does too—Conor, pushing against me. Almost like he's pushing me up. The dog makes a low noise, and for the life of me, I can't tell if he's comforting me or trying to get me back on my feet to do Hades's bidding. I think he might be growling... at Hades.

"Oh, stop," Hades says. "She'll live."

Conor presses his nose against the crook of my arm, the rest of him warm and solid. Everything is upside down. I should not feel any safer here with Conor at my side. But I do.

Hades's eyes trace my face, following my tears down to my chin.

"Excellent," he murmurs. "You have no idea how much I loved that."

"You're sick." I shouldn't say it, not if I want to keep breathing, but the lingering pain overrides what's left of my good judgment. "Disgusting. Vile—"

"That's it," he prompts.

"You're a terrible man!" I shout.

"Well, yes."

"You're the worst person I've ever met." The last tears fall and dry on my cheeks. The air here is not still or stuffy, despite the lack of windows. It's always moving, always whispering against my skin. "I hate you."

"Good." Hades pats my head again, a light in his eyes, a smile playing at his lips. "I intend to strip you down to the core, Persephone, and make you mine in every possible way. But this bullshit of yours, these little fits of terror over things like doors? Save them."

"Save them?" I cross my arms over my chest to hide the shake in my hands. "Save them for what? This is all very, very bad." My throat tightens with the urge to cry, so I clear it roughly.

"Save your pretty fear for when I have you naked over my knee or tied spread-eagle on my bed." He swipes his thumb across the remnants of my tears, the salt tracks that seem to be a constant fixture on my face now. "That's when I want it. Don't spend it on things like entering a room. You'll exhaust yourself, and that will limit the amount I can enjoy you."

"Enjoy me? You take pleasure in this?"

His expression darkens. It looks like honesty. "So much pleasure. Say it one more time, so I know you understand."

His words echo in my brain—*naked over my knee, spread-eagle on my bed*—and I imagine burying them deep beneath the earth. It's the only way I can make myself say it. Because I don't belong to him. I'll never belong to him, not in my heart.

"I belong to you now," I repeat, voice level.

"That's right." He whistles. "Conor, go in."

The door swings open at his touch like it was waiting for him, and Hades sweeps one hand around my back and pushes me into the room. Conor shoots past us and disappears down one hallway. One of my bare toes catches on the smooth floor, and I stumble, but this time there's nobody to catch me. He's behind me, and there's no way for anyone to—

A hand flies out just as I catch my balance, and I take it like it's the last life preserver on a sinking ship.

"Thank you. Thank you so much." The gratitude dies on my lips as I straighten up, the new information falling into place.

Someone reached out to catch me.

Someone has been inside this room the whole time, hearing what happened, hearing me scream.

I lift my chin and look, only because I can't stand the wait any longer.

Five women in black uniforms, their hair combed back in sleek buns, wait in a semicircle in the entryway to the most enormous room—no, it must actually be a set of rooms, because this is no bedroom, or a living room. To call it a living room seems like a ridiculous understatement. Thick pillars separate an enormous sunken sitting area from the rest of the space. It looks ancient and modern at the same time, like you could curl up at the base of it and stare into a screen or sit around the edges and attend a performance. My heart zigzags frantically at the thought of what kind of performance that would be. Knowing what I know of Hades, it could be...

The blood drains out of my cheeks, and I take a step back toward Hades. He nudges me forward with a sharp exhale. I've annoyed him again.

One of the women—the one who put out her hand to break my fall—looks to be in her forties, with silver hair and red lipstick that makes me feel utterly naked in its perfection. I'm wearing a linen dress, handmade for me by an old lady my mother pays by the season, and I want it off. If I could have anything else to wear, I'd wear it.

"Fix her," says Hades. "Don't disturb me until it's done."

He moves past me as the women close in, the nearest lady reaching for my hand again. Hades doesn't look back. He heads to a wide hallway leading God knows where.

"You're leaving?" I call after him.

"What does it look like?"

"I thought you would stay." I try and fail to keep the quiver out of my voice.

"If you wanted me to stay, you shouldn't have run." Hades doesn't turn back, doesn't bother to see if I'm all right. He doesn't care. Of course, he doesn't care. "Obey their orders as if they've come from me."

"I'm Dana," says the lady with the silver hair. Her eyes hold a flicker of concern, but then her face settles into seriousness. "Come this way. We can't keep him waiting."

THIRTEEN

Hades

PERSEPHONE WOULD LOSE HER MIND IF SHE KNEW ABOUT the two-way mirror.

It's made with slightly different technology than the rest of my windows, which means the wall doesn't appear to have a window in it. There are many reasons for me to have a room in my private quarters that allows for observation, but of all of them, this is by far the most enjoyable.

The bright lights are *not* enjoyable. They're killing me. All the bulbs in my space were designed for me, but that doesn't matter if I don't have painkillers. When I'm running out, when I have to ration them like this, all light hurts.

I sit on a sofa designed to my exact specifications, to fit someone of exactly my height and stature, and watch through the window as Dana and her team do their work.

I had the team brought here while we were on the train. A helicopter flight from the city. Very discreet staff to help with a very discreet guest.

This is for me, of course. But it's also for Persephone. She won't see it that way yet.

Make a decision, pay the consequences. It's simple.

Persephone stands up to me, which takes true bravery. Especially since Demeter was obviously a terror of a mother. She hasn't changed since she was a child. It explains everything, from the farm-girl dress to the way Persephone blanches at the sight of an unfamiliar door. She's been kept under lock and key all her life.

It makes her perfect for me. I've acquired a blank slate. She's a raw diamond, waiting to be shaped.

Waiting to be used for my purposes.

This experience will have an effect, no doubt. Dana strips off Persephone's dress, her movements efficient, leaving her shivering and clutching her arms to her chest.

"Oh, please," I murmur. "It's not cold."

She can't hear me. I focus instead on her pink cheeks and the nipples poking out underneath her tank top. What the hell is that thing? Demeter obviously wanted to keep her defenseless and virginal. To dress her in nightgowns for the rest of her life. She thought it would keep her safer.

A miscalculation.

Dana demands the tank top next, and Persephone reddens, shaking her head. I could turn the sound up and hear the audio from the next room crystal-clear, but this silent-film situation is better. It forces me to pay closer attention to her body when I'm not distracted by the sound of her voice.

The team is performing quite well. Dana only lets Persephone argue with her for a short time before she calls the other women. I assume she's threatened to hold her down and cut the clothes off, because Persephone strips in a hurry.

She stares down at her feet, hands clutched in front of that sweet little pussy of hers, her cheeks blazing red. But I felt how wet she got yesterday on the train, and again on the elevator. I saw how much she wanted me to fuck her.

Perhaps she gets off on the humiliation. She wouldn't be the first.

The difficulty now is that I don't want anyone else to touch her. At least this denial is familiar. I want my hands on her, but Dana's are on her instead. I'm depriving myself of something I want.

My phone rings, interrupting my view of the first bucket of lukewarm water hitting Persephone's naked skin. I catch a glimpse of her gasp and the way she raises her hands to her eyes to wipe the droplets away.

The phone rings again and I pull the damn thing out of my pocket.

It's my brother.

"What do you want?"

"Manners, Hades." Zeus sounds mildly disapproving. Like he has any right to have the slightest opinion on how I answer the phone. "I'd think you'd have a more pleasant greeting for your favorite brother."

"I'm busy."

"So that's a no."

"It's a no to you, asshole. If you're calling me to be irritating, hang up the phone now and spare us both the breath."

The women have coordinated forces to scrub Persephone clean, standing there in the middle of the room. I can't see the drain from here, but I know they've arranged her over it. They lift one of her arms above her head, which has the effect of lifting her tits along with it. Then the other arm. Hands on every part of her, none of them mine.

I grit my teeth.

Dana points to Persephone's feet. Points again. With an expression of agony, Persephone parts her legs so they can wash her there too. I would do this myself—fuck, I want to—but I don't want to give her the impression this early on that I care for her in any way.

Even if I do. A strange thought.

"—very rude," Zeus is saying. "It's obvious you're not listening."

"It's obvious you didn't have a reason to call." I shift positions on the sofa. "Here's some politeness for you. Goodbye."

"Don't hang up."

"And why not? Does it ever occur to you that I might be busy? I don't sit around waiting by the phone like one of your conquests." I almost called them *whores*, but the women who are attracted to Zeus aren't anything of the sort. If I cared, I might call them victims. But I don't care. I gave up caring a long time ago.

"Of course you're busy." He sighs. "You're always busy. Too busy to participate in the family."

"Where did you get the idea that I wanted to participate in any family you're in?" I don't want to see Zeus. I don't want to see Poseidon. I do not, for fuck's sake, want to see Demeter. They've seen too much as it is. I hate Zeus for seeing me that way and insisting that I continue to live through it. I didn't want him to witness me then. I don't want to bond with him now.

Although… if I'd died, I wouldn't have Persephone.

"You wound me."

"You make me ill."

It's difficult to keep up my end of the conversation. I've been rough with Persephone, but it's different when it's someone else. The urge to keep her safe is growing. Something happened when I brought her onto the train. Something I don't want to admit out loud, and perhaps I never will.

I'm a danger to her. To her heart. To her soul.

And she's a danger to me.

"I'll wait if you need to be sick."

"Fuck off."

"Tell me the truth, Hades." His voice has dropped. "Did you take her?"

My heart slows to a stop. Persephone is doused with another bucketful of water. One of the women is filling them again and again. They turn her so I can see her wet curls falling down her back. I want her bent over my desk again. Need it.

"Damn it, Hades, answer me."

"Yes."

There's a rare moment of dead silence from Zeus.

"Is there something else you wanted to know?"

"You took Persephone." He sounds astonished, frankly.

"It's tiresome when you can't keep up."

"What the fuck." It's sinking in, then. What I've done. "What the fuck were you thinking?"

"It was an impromptu decision."

I leave out the fact that I was only going to take the flowers. I leave out the fact that when I saw Persephone, I forgot the flowers. I leave out the fact that I wanted her. That I still do.

"Is this about the shipments?" he asks.

"Those are none of your concern. And no."

The shipments from Demeter have nothing to do with Zeus. Whatever painkillers I have or don't have will never be any of his business. The mountain can function as his money laundry whether I can get out of bed or not. Whether I'm conscious or not. Whether it hurts like this or not.

My pulse presses out against my veins, the blood too thick

for the space it occupies. It's a distraction from the things I'm trying to focus on. Like Dana leading Persephone over to a waxing table, and Persephone's eyes getting wider and wider as Dana explains what she's going to do. I get to my feet and pace over to the window, swallowing hard. Half of me wants to run in there and throw all their hands away from Persephone. *Mine*, I would growl, loud enough to scare the shit out of them. The other half is relishing her embarrassment and fear. I discover I'm on my feet, standing close to the window.

"This isn't the way to resolve this." I'll be damned. A note of stress is creeping into Zeus's voice. "Kidnapping the girl?"

"She's not a girl. She's twenty. Fair game. And I'm not sure you have any moral high ground."

"My women are here of their own free will."

"Tell me again. Maybe this time I'll believe you."

"Hades—"

"What do you want?" My patience frays. I'm going to die of a heart attack, watching this scene, denying myself entry. "You're entirely free to leave me the fuck alone."

"You know I can't do that."

"You can't stay at your whorehouse and fuck with your women? You can't pretend we've never met?"

"You *kidnapped* her. Demeter says—"

"Demeter wasn't there."

More silence. "She said you took Persephone from the house."

"I didn't."

I do not offer him more explanation. If he wants to believe Demeter, there's nothing I can do about it. And I don't care about convincing him in this moment.

Dana is a professional, but Persephone shakes so badly the other women have to hold her down. To spread her open so Dana has the access she needs. Dana must guess there's a window, because I catch the flicker of her glance in my direction. She must know I'll be watching to ensure the job is done correctly.

To ensure it takes perhaps longer than necessary.

Persephone's chest rises and falls, quickly, quickly, tears leaking down her cheeks. Dana applies the wax, the strip, and waits.

A heartbeat. Another heartbeat. She says something to Persephone and rips it away.

Persephone arches on the table, biting down on her lip. It takes all of them to keep her in place. She lifts her head, and I can tell by the wide-eyed look in her eyes that she's begging.

But Dana is my employee. She knows better than to cross me. *We have to keep going*, her lips say.

Persephone squeezes her eyes closed.

More wax. Another strip.

I am desperate to go into the room right now and shove my fingers inside her. She'd be soaked, no question. Those red cheeks, those nipples—everything about her gives her most private thoughts away, as if she said them out loud.

The third strip.

She turns her head into the palm of one of the women holding her down and weeps.

But she doesn't close her legs.

Fuck.

The scene draws all the blood down from my brain and into my cock, splitting my concentration in a very unpleasant way. I have to turn away from the window to finish the conversation. Conor stirs on the low bed in the corner and lets out the beginning of a whine. He thinks something's going on, that I have to get out of here. I do, but not for the reason Conor thinks. I signal him back to his rest. I'm still fine. Mostly.

"I'm far too busy to stand here listening to you breathe in my ear, Zeus."

"She's very upset," he says, voice sounding far away. It works to my advantage for Demeter to be upset. The more upset she is, the more willing she'll be to bargain. "She's hysterical. No doubt Persephone is the same."

Persephone is not, in fact, hysterical. Persephone did not, in fact, want to be returned to the farmhouse.

You're not going to return her, teases the voice in my mind.

It's a mystery to me why Zeus has allowed himself to care about Demeter's feelings. About Persephone's. Zeus doesn't care about anyone, or what they want. That's the core of his personality. That's why he probably has bastard children all over the city. People flock to that man because they confuse beauty with trustworthiness. A smile with a kind heart. They can feel his energy like an invitation. He slips those disguises on and off like a comfortable jacket, whenever and wherever it suits him. They can call me what they want—a killer, a monster, a sadist—but no one can ever say I hid it from them.

"It's not my concern if she's upset because Persephone ran away."

"Because you took her."

"Yes. As she was running away from home, trying to hide on the train. If you want proof, I'll send paperwork."

What would she have done if she succeeded? She'd have gone into the city, which is rife with men like Zeus. I have no illusions that I'm not what Perspehone dreamed of, but being chained in a whorehouse wouldn't be better. Other men would touch her.

Demeter can't possibly have expected to keep her locked away in her home forever. She can't be unraveling already.

Anyway, it's too late now. I have her here. Unfortunately, turning away from the window has only made it harder to think. Imagining what's going on a few feet behind me makes my heart pound. I steal a glance. Dana has Persephone in the most humiliating position on the waxing table, and her face is such a gorgeous red color that I wish I could capture it in a painting. Her lips form one word over and over. *Please, please, please.*

"What was that noise?" Zeus scolds. "Are you fucking her already?"

"You're the only one rude enough to take phone calls when you're using a woman," I shoot back. But something else is happening behind my breastbone, something very unexpected. I want to be fucking her already. The thought of her in Zeus's whorehouse makes my head split. I lean hard on the sill of the two-way mirror. I can't take my eyes off her. A screeching alarm sounds in the heavy silence of my thoughts. A weakness, it cries. *She is your weakness. She's the one who can kill you.*

Fuck.

He sighs. "You could bring her here. Broker some kind of deal."

"I'm not interested in a deal."

"Hades." A weighted pause, signaling a change in topic. "There are better ways to motivate her if she's not sending as much as you're demanding."

He thinks I'm throwing a tantrum.

My body bristles while I try to manage the emotion. The pain at my temples deepens. "If you want to gossip, call in one of your whores."

He's still trying to talk to me when I stab my thumb down

onto the button to cut off our connection. It falls to the floor with a loud clatter. I crush it under the heel of my shoe again and again and again until the plastic casing splinters and the wires inside come apart. What have I done, and what am I doing? In the end, I sweep the shattered phone into one corner with the toe of my shoe, rage hardly spent.

Yes. Fine. I've created a small problem, a dangling thread that will irritate me until I cut it off at the neck.

My uses for Persephone do not include leveraging her for the poppies. Regardless, I have to have them. I won't return her, but keeping her here puts the mountain at risk. It puts *me* at risk of developing a weakness I can't afford.

I can't live without the poppies.

I don't want to live without Persephone. Without at least the chance to fuck her.

It's an absurd thing to admit, even to myself. It doesn't suit me to feel this way about anyone or anything, even in some dim, vague way that disappears as soon as I look at it head-on.

On the other side of the window, Persephone sits up on the table, breasts heaving with every breath. She turns toward Dana, my name on her lips.

FOURTEEN

Persephone

DANA SLIPS A DRESS THAT'S MORE OF A NIGHTGOWN OVER my head, eyes sharp and lips pursed. She tugs the hem into place. It barely covers my ass. It was made to barely cover my ass. I don't bother asking if there's a bra and panties to go with the set. Clearly, there's not, and clearly, her orders came from Hades himself.

"Good." She gives the rest of her team a crisp nod. "I'll be back in a few minutes to assist with cleanup." Dana flips over her wrist and glances at her watch. Her eyes widen at the time. "If you'll come this way…"

I follow her without a word, because what's the point? I'm officially nothing. My own embarrassment has burned me so many times it's surprising to discover, at every new moment, that I'm not just a pile of ashes. Sweep me up with a broom and set me free on the wind. Again and again, every heartbeat reminds me that I'm still here. In this body that's been waxed and stripped and buffed until I'm not sure I have any original

skin left. They put lotion on my stinging flesh, every inch of it, and worked out all the tangles from my hair. I've never been so sensitive and so numb at the same time.

"This way," Dana says, tone urgent.

I pick up the pace. I've been staring at the floor, the polished marble beneath my feet. "Where are we going?"

The question comes more out of resignation than anything else.

I don't expect her to answer. I think of Hades's fingers in my hair and how Dana probably heard me begging and didn't do anything about it. Nobody will ever do anything about it again.

And how maybe, maybe…

No. I can't let myself think that way, otherwise all my sacrifice will have been for nothing. It's not a sacrifice if some twisted part of your soul enjoys it. And I don't. I can't. Hades is evil. I'm in shock. That's all. It's been a shocking turn of events.

It's not my fault that the makeover session made me think of him.

It made me want comfort from him. Comfort I'll never get.

"To meet with Hades." Dana's voice breaks into my memory.

"Meet with him?"

"I was to prepare you for a meeting," she says, sounding as if she's reciting direct orders.

I laugh, the sound surprisingly real. Dana raises her eyebrows and picks up the pace.

"Is that what he calls it? He's a very proper man."

"He likes things to be a certain way." Her silver hair bobs behind her in its bun.

The hallways of Hades's house are proof of this. Every one of them gleams with a kind of blank perfection that makes the weird quality of the light seem less unsettling. That can't possibly be for other people, so there is a man underneath the cruel façade who has feelings one way or the other. There must be.

Dana takes me this way and that until I've lost all sense of where the prep room was, and then, abruptly, she makes a sharp right turn off the hallway, almost colliding with a woman in a black dress and white apron, one of the maids.

"I'm on my way in," says Dana in a low voice. "Anything I can take for you?"

The maid nods, lips pressed into a serious line. "This." She hands Dana a small silver tray with a phone, shiny and sleek, in the center. "Thank you."

Dana waits until the maid has scurried off down the hall to push open the door with one elbow.

It's an office.

Hades's office.

Dana goes directly to his desk and puts the tray down.

Hades sits behind an enormous desk, head bent over a stack of papers. Conor curls on the floor by the fire. The office is too normal for him, all dark wood paneling and low lights. I feel like I'm seeing him stripped down to nothing in a room like this. The rotunda in the entryway of this fortress is meant to impress people, but this looks like a truly private room.

"Mr. Hades." Dana glances around for me and gestures me forward into the pool of light surrounding the desk.

Hades looks up from his papers. His eyes land on me like ice water, cold and assessing.

An answering heat sears through my lungs, down to my belly. My body doesn't know how to react to him. My stomach twists. I'm glad to see him. Which doesn't make sense.

His eyes travel slowly from the top of my head down to my still-bare toes, and when they meet mine again, the frigid stare has slipped away. It's darker now. Hotter.

The hairs on my arms stand on end.

"Go now."

Dana leaves, shutting the door behind her with a soft click that seems to echo.

I'm alone with him. Heart hammering. Legs trembling. He makes me shake and shiver. The skimpy dress isn't helping. All the things he could do rush through my mind. The dress might not survive those things.

I might not survive those things.

No matter how many times I tell myself it doesn't matter, it still does.

Hades seems to take up every spare inch of the room. There isn't a single breath that's not suffused with him. And he smells clean. Like a lungful of cold air. I resist the urge to fold my hands over my chest. It won't hide anything from him. It'll only make him notice me more, and now that Dana's done with me, there's more to notice.

A blush creeps across my cheeks.

"Sit down."

There's more than one chair in his office, and that familiar panic crawls up the back of my spine and shakes the base of my neck. Hades must mean the chair in front of his desk. Easy enough. *Breathe.*

While I pad forward and take a seat, he lifts the phone from the tray and flicks it on.

Puts it down on the edge of the desk closest to him.

Hades watches me for far longer than is necessary. The wide desk separates us and nothing else. I bite my lip. It's strange that he's not bending me over that desk, fisting his hand in my hair. Isn't it? Or are things different in his fortress?

Hades curses low under his breath. "I can smell you from here."

My stomach sinks, and I curve forward, wanting to disappear

underneath the desk, underneath the floor, and underneath the earth itself. "I didn't know. I didn't—"

He leans forward. "It's making it difficult to proceed with our task. Don't hunch over like that, Persephone. It doesn't suit you. If I want you humiliated, I'd do more than this. I promise."

I stare at him, shocked.

A shake of his head like he's clearing his thoughts. "With a pussy like that, you'd think someone would have laid claim to you already. Not that I care about other people's claims." This last bit is soft, almost like he's talking to himself. "It does explain why your mother kept you behind bars."

"She wanted to protect me." We cannot be talking about this. My face will superheat, and I'll never recover. The question hovers at the tip of my tongue, but I don't dare ask what the task is. "She thought men might want to hurt me. That *you* might want to hurt me."

"I won't hurt you." A fleeting smile. "Very badly, at any rate."

He will. He already has. But it could get worse. "You don't mean that."

"I won't hurt you enough to mark you. Or kill you." Hades gazes at me from across the expanse of wood. "How much time are you planning to spend arguing with me?"

He sounds different. Like something happened when he handed me off to Dana.

A mask. It reminds me of slipping on a mask.

"What's our task?"

He pushes the stack of papers across to me, and I try to get control of my breath and my mind. "It's time to formalize the terms of our agreement."

"What agreement?"

"The one we have together. It requires a written contract."

None of this makes any sense. He took me. He's already

made me over to his specifications. He's made it so clear that I'll never leave. What difference could it make for me to sign a paper? "But why?"

The corner of his mouth rises, and he shakes his head. "Because I want your fall to be explicit."

"What am I promising?"

"You'll stay here with me. For as long as I want. And in return... I don't take your mother's farm."

My stomach drops. "What?"

"She's already reneged on the terms of our agreement."

I pretend to be in a business meeting, though I've never sat in a business meeting in my life. "How?"

"By not selling me the flowers."

"She doesn't have to sell them to you."

A growl. "I paid for that whole goddamn farm, flower by flower. They're mine."

I glance around the hard, minimalist room. There's not a flower pot or floral arrangement in sight. "You don't seem like you need fields of flowers."

"It's a certain strain of poppy. I'm sure you know the one."

The ones that had to be protected at all costs.

You were sleeping when he tried to take the fields. That's what my mother said. Hades has tried to get those flowers at least once.

"That's why you were on the train that night. To steal from the farm. To sabotage it. I don't know, but it wasn't anything good."

"Instead I found you, wandering outside like an innocent little lamb."

My stomach flips. "Why do you need those poppies?"

"That's irrelevant to you." He taps the papers with his fingertips. "You wanted to know what was going to happen. Here it is. I'll use you for my entertainment. And I'll leave your mother's farm alone."

It's the hardest thing I've ever done, scanning the words on the papers.

They all blur together, the letters switching places and taunting me. My mother's name. My name. The offer he's making me. In the contract, Hades has written *submission without limits*.

I bite my lip and read it again. And again. It doesn't sound like something I should want, on any level.

A part of me wants it anyway.

If I sign this paper, I would never have to question what my life would be. There would be no more making plans to get away. No more wondering if I could make it on my own. No more worrying about running into dangerous men on the street. The most dangerous man would be here, right where I could see him at all times.

I crave it, that relief. My hands tremble around the paper. I'm not supposed to be this way. I wanted to be free.

Now I don't know what I want, with my skin still humming from all the contact and every part of me leaning closer to get another breath of him. It doesn't make sense. I want to scream.

I swallow that scream and try again to order my thoughts.

Instead I found you, wandering outside like an innocent little lamb.

"What happens if I don't sign?"

Hades looks at me. The answer is in his eyes.

My heart stops. Starts again. "You would hurt her."

"If she got in the way."

She would die before letting Hades take her farm. "So I have no choice."

His mouth tightens. "There's always a choice, sweetheart."

I read the papers again. "You don't want to trade me? For the flowers?"

"If I did that, I wouldn't be able to use you, would I?" Hades taps his fingers on the desk. "I'm done answering questions,

Persephone. If you're going to take advantage of my offer, do it now."

I feel small. Unworthy of understanding this contract in my hand. It has clauses guaranteeing I'll be fed and clothed. It says he can discipline me at will. The more I read, the more I want to cry. Only I don't know if I'm crying because there's no way out of this or because I don't want a way out of this. It doesn't bother me as much as it should, his control over my body. It bothers me more knowing I'm giving up on my dream. I'm giving up on freedom. There will be no trip to the New York Public Library. I won't check out a thousand books on every subject under the sun. I won't do anything but exactly what he commands.

Hades holds out a pen, thick and black and shiny. "Make your choice."

Why is he doing this? It was easier when he didn't give me one. The cruelest, most beautiful man I've ever seen sits across his desk from me, watching with ice in his eyes. I squeeze my eyes closed and force myself to picture my mother's devastation at losing her farm.

All my plans would be for nothing.

"I don't want to belong to you. I hate you."

He smiles. "I'd expect nothing less."

"Give me the pen." As I reach for it, I glance up into Hades's face one more time and catch an expression I never thought I'd see—relief. He narrows his eyes, and it disappears.

I don't ask any questions. I know better than that. I just take the pen and sign my name.

It's done.

FIFTEEN

Persephone

THE MOMENT I LIFT THE PEN FROM THE PAPERS, everything changes.

Hades stands and leans over to put his own signature on the contract. It's a manly scrawl that runs over mine in places. He doesn't care where mine ends and his begins.

Then he tears a sheet from a notepad at the corner of the desk.

Fuck off, he writes on it.

"They're ready," he calls. The man must've been standing outside the door all along, because it takes him no time at all to collect the papers from Hades's hands. "File them with the rest. Send a copy to Zeus along with my note."

It takes me a moment too long to rise from my seat, which earns me a scowl that makes goose bumps rise up and down my back. What now? I allow myself to think it. I don't allow myself to say it.

Whatever happens, I'm not going to stop hating him.

Not for anything.

I don't know how to plan around this. He took me from my mother's fields. He could get to her, too. And I never wanted my freedom to mean her death, no matter how unstable she could be.

There's not enough air in the room. Now is when it happens, isn't it? Now is when he takes what he wants from me. Whatever's left. I steel myself for a hand around my throat and close my eyes. Soon, his hand will be a collar there, and he'll be in charge.

But the only thing that brushes against my exposed throat is a shift in the air as he moves past me, Conor at his heels. They wait at the door.

"Come here now."

I stub my toe on the chair leg in my hurry to get to him. My heart beats so hard and fast it's like a horse given its head for the first time, racing across an open field. The dress—nightgown, whatever it is—rides up. It's hard to keep it in place and follow him at the same time. We take one hallway down to the big living room area at the center of his private rooms and make another turn. Down another hallway, rooms branching off. At the end of the hall is a set of double doors. Hades stops before we reach them at the last door on the right.

Hades opens it with the air of a man who has run out of time and patience.

"Go in."

This time, I don't hesitate. I'm a little proud of that.

"Your personal maid will be here soon." He turns to leave.

"Wait." I'm still turning when I catch Hades by the sleeve, and he pauses, staring down at my hand like I've shocked him. My heart has gone off-rhythm. I drop my hand and draw myself up to my full height, though I still feel unsteady. It was one thing to tell him I didn't want to go back to my mother's house. It's another to have our names scrawled together on what looks like a very official document. I don't know what he plans to do with it, but dread pools at the base of my belly. "Where are you going?"

Hades looks at me, questioning. "I have business. Did you think I'd be spending every waking moment with you?"

His fingers in my hair, his laughter in my ears. *Did you think you were special?*

Yes.

No.

I want to be special.

He comes back across the threshold.

"Are you admitting you need supervision in order to hold up your end of the agreement?"

My end of the agreement is to be here. Submission without limits. What else could I do?

"That's not—no." *I only thought you would keep me with you.* I should be crying tears of joy right now, or tears of relief, if he's willing to leave me alone. After the morning I've had, the last thing I should crave is a rough man's touch. "I wondered. That's all."

"You didn't wonder anything of the kind. That much is clear." He's taken up all the space between us, compressing the air down to nothing. "If you'd thought at all, you wouldn't be wasting my time."

"What was this morning for, then?" My voice rises, getting away from me. "You left me in that room with those people—"

"With Dana and her team." It sounds like scolding, and it pisses me off. "You needed their services."

"They took my dress, my clothes. Now I only have this, and you're leaving?"

Hades puts his hands in his pockets, a heated expression playing slowly across his face, making its way to his eyes.

"Are you angry because they made you into something tolerable or because I didn't bother to inspect their work?"

"You don't need to inspect—"

That's all I get out before his hand comes down over my mouth, huge and immovable. He turns me as easily as a doll, walking me into the room and over to a four-poster bed. It's the biggest bed I've ever seen. Compared to the twin mattresses we had at home, it's huge. But Hades doesn't use the space there. He marches me over to one of the posts and snatches both wrists in one of his hands.

"Up here. That's it. Keep them up if you'd rather avoid a punishment." He laughs, the sound wicked and dark. "Though if you insist on it, I can always rearrange my schedule."

I gasp against his hand, and then his palm is gone, leaving my lips open to the air. Words bubble up, a hundred questions, a jagged pulse of anxiety, but before I can speak, a length of cloth covers my mouth and slips between my teeth. A gag. Hades tugs it tight behind my head, making a satisfied sound at his handiwork. When it's tied off he gives it a cruel twist, and I cry out against the cloth.

"That's better." He strokes down the back of my neck, lifting the extra fabric away from my skin so he can blow a breath against my spine. "Now that you can't get yourself into trouble with that mouth of yours, you'll finally be able to relax."

I let out a wild laugh. Relax? Like this? Holding onto the post of the bed like it could possibly save me? I won't relax. I would never be able to.

"Now. You were upset I didn't pause to appreciate Dana's work." He reaches down and jerks up the hem of the nightgown.

It's thin, and having it raised lets the slowly circulating air caress the naked skin underneath.

I have nothing left to protect me. Nothing to keep me from him. He can see everything.

Hades twists it into itself, so it stays lodged at my shoulders. This is so much worse than being naked. I'd rather be naked. No—I wouldn't. I wouldn't. At least he's letting me keep this.

He slaps the back of my thighs.

"You know better than that."

At first, I don't know what he's talking about, and then I realize I've clamped my thighs together so hard the muscles are already trembling. I manage to inch my feet apart, caught between wanting to avoid the punishment he'd be so happy to give me and wanting to cling to the very last shreds of my modesty. There are practically none left. I don't know why it matters, only that it does.

Hades has no patience for this. He pushes one foot between my legs and shoves them apart. Wide. Conor growls, disapproving, and appears at my side. Hades turns my face so the dog can see.

"I'm not hurting her. She's fine," he snaps. Is this what fine is? "Go lay down." Conor grudgingly pulls away. He finds a fireplace. My heart slows a little bit.

"Keep your legs here. Do you understand?"

I nod, trying to keep my composure, feeling the tears leak one by one out from under my eyes. Only I'm not crying out of fear. I'm not even sure why it's happening. I could be wrong. It could be fear. Maybe I've stopped feeling it. Maybe this last day has done that to me. Maybe he's done that to me. Hades works a hand down over my ass and squeezes.

"Good." His hand is slightly rough and calloused. Every

ridge imprints on my skin as he tests my other asscheek and unceremoniously spreads them apart. I lean my forehead against the post of the bed and try to keep breathing. My stomach sinks down to my toes, knees weakening. It's hard to keep my legs spread like this. My thighs ache from the position. He's looking at me. He's looking at me there. I thought it was bad before, in the elevator, when he touched me. That was nothing.

The moment goes on and on, stretching out into eternity.

Hades is being awful.

The longer it goes on, the weaker my knees get. A strange warmth arcs across my chest, winding itself up with an ache that feels like wanting. The drop of shame melds with a fluttering anticipation until it's hard to tell one sickness from another. This can't be happening.

He strokes one finger over my most sensitive, secret place. My head falls back and a sound escapes me, a sound so sultry I don't recognize my own voice.

Hades rewards this by letting go and grabbing one of my hips with another light slap.

"You are a fucking liar," he murmurs in my ear, the heat of his body covering my back. "You're such a wide-eyed, innocent little liar." One of his hands comes up to grip my jaw, pulling the gag even tighter. "I'd say I would train it out of you, but that would be such a waste."

His lips brush my cheek, which is wet with my tears. He braces my head against his chest, or somewhere near his shoulder. I don't know. All I know is I'm still upright, and it's a miracle.

Then his other hand traces a path to the front of me, circling each nipple with the sharp edge of his nail. I can't stop the sounds any more than I could let go of the post. *This is wrong, this is wrong, this is wrong.* The chant goes around in circles in my mind until it's a meaningless song.

His hand moves downward.

Inch by inch by inch.

He circles my belly button.

He goes lower.

I can't breathe.

I'm doing nothing but sucking in air through the fabric between my teeth. The sound is harsh compared to Hades's even breathing.

His hand stops moving.

He's inches away from my clit. It throbs just from the proximity, painful and wanting and bad. It's bad. It's so bad. The prickling sense of being in trouble runs over my skin like a cascade of hot water, dropped from above by a woman in a dark uniform. I wish he would touch me. Please, please touch me. Bring an end to this torturous anticipation. The waiting is the worst thing by far. My knuckles tighten on the bedpost.

He doesn't move his hand.

He's so close, the buttons of his jacket brushing against my spine, but he keeps his fingers splayed low on my belly.

Why?

He waits.

Hades is the king of waiting. That's what he is. He pretends he has no patience, but it's not true. His silence. His patience. What does he want? What do I have to do to get him to touch me, to finish this? My body is already bent for him. But I push my hips out another inch.

"It's terrible, what I'm going to do." That voice in my ear is enough to make my knees give out, but I don't let it. "Do you remember, Persephone? I promised I'd make you beg."

But I can't beg. I can't say anything, not with this gag in

my mouth. The whimpering sound I make next embarrasses me more than everything that's come before it.

"Please. Of course you can beg. You've done it just now. Only that's not enough for me to give you what you want. It's not enough for me to give you anything you want." His lips brush against the side of my neck—the shadow of a kiss. "I could decide to give you something you want. It wouldn't go against our agreement."

Another sound. I can't stop it. And the heat and want have grown so powerful that my mind clouds, hiding the sharp mortification of this moment behind something dirty and hot. No, I can't do this. I can't give in to him. It's very, very bad, and it's very wrong.

It's not up to me now. It's not my rational mind that moves my hips again, rolling them. I can't move far. I can't move much. But it's enough. I do it again and again. It's obscene. I'm fucking the air, with his hand on me and his gag in my mouth and my name on his papers. It's the worst thing I've ever done.

He slips two fingers down between my legs, down into the wetness that's already waiting for him, and pulls them back up to circle my clit. I'm nothing now, an animal, a bundle of nerves that don't know what to do with themselves. The noise that comes out of me is barely human, and if anyone ever heard it, it would be the end of me. But Hades hears it, and his hand goes still.

"No," I cry into the gag, but it's muffled and distorted. "Please don't stop."

"If you want more, you'll have to get it yourself." He sounds completely detached. "You'll have to admit that you want it. You'll have to prove that you want it."

God help me, I do.

I work my hips up into his hand, legs spread wide, arousal

dripping down my thighs. Sweat beads on my forehead. I can't let go of the post. I can't let him let go of me.

I'm almost there, on the brink of something obliterating…

He takes his hand away and steps back.

I howl into the gag, sagging against the bedpost.

Hades leans down over me.

"Almost, but not quite." He reaches forward and wipes his hand against my back. His next touch is a ghost of a kiss against my shoulder. "I almost believed you, liar. Conor, come." His footsteps retreat toward the door.

Don't leave.

"Oh," he says lightly. Every cell in my being bends to him, calling him to come back across the room. "Dana could have done better. But you were a difficult case."

SIXTEEN

Persephone

HADES LEAVES THE ROOM.

His footsteps retreat in the hall, each one softer than the last, and I hold tighter to the bedpost.

I.

Hate him.

I can't believe he left me like this. I'm nearly at death's door, only it was the most pleasant death I could have imagined. Even thinking about his touch sends new sensations zinging between my legs. I'm so focused on it that time goes by without me marking it. I couldn't keep track if I tried, but I'm not trying. I'm busy imagining his fingers where they were and trying to get there on force of fantasy alone.

And hating him for stopping.

Who am I?

When the footsteps come down the hall, I'm too far gone to notice I should be doing something other than clinging to a bedpost with my dress hiked up to my shoulders, rolled around

itself, and a gag in my mouth. Something like rearranging my clothes. Anything. But I'm not. I'm still frustrated and over-heated and lost to myself.

Where is he? Why would he do this to me? What do I have to do, run naked through the hallways to get his attention? Why do I even want his attention? I'm used to dreaming of empty fields, without a single person looking at me, and now—him?

I wish, desperately, for flowers.

For the comfort of them. The familiar silkiness of the pet-als. The warmth when I make them grow. The quiet exchange between us. I want to bury my face in those poppies and hide. I want to forget the cold, diamond smell of him and the heat of his hands.

I would settle for dandelions and daisies. Anything to set-tle my mind.

The footsteps get closer.

They're too light and too soft to be his.

But why would he leave in the middle of making me come? He's a terrible man, even more terrible than I thought.

The footsteps can't be his, because they're so light and measured.

The footsteps can't be his.

The footsteps arrive at the doorway at the same time all the disarrayed puzzle pieces of my thoughts fit themselves to-gether. I let go of the bedpost with a shriek and leap to the left. There's nothing there to hide me. The door opens, and the air moves over my skin. Dress first. Oh my God, I can't get it down.

"Miss?"

It's definitely not him, this woman with a soft, even voice, and I burst into flames and crumble into a burnt-up husk. When the flame recedes, I'm unfortunately left in my own body. My dress won't come untwisted. This can't get any worse. Maybe she hasn't seen me. Maybe she'll just leave.

"I can help you with that. I'd be glad to."

I blink at the bed, too frozen to turn around. Her footsteps come across the plush carpet behind me. Every step is amplified in my newly perished state. Then a pair of gentle hands untwists the dress and tugs it back into place. She, whoever she is, smooths it down at the hem with a touch that's somehow professional in its intimacy. Next comes the gag. He tied a tight knot, no doubt to leave me in this exact situation. Frustrated tears wend their way down my cheeks. When is this going to stop? I was never a crier before. It was useless in the face of my mother.

It's not useless to Hades. He likes it.

Which makes him far worse than my mother.

Once, I read a book where the heroine finally felt safe enough to cry. That can't be happening with Hades.

Can it?

The gag comes loose, and I turn around before I lose my scrap of nerve. The woman who helped me wears a long black skirt and a black vest over a white dress shirt—one of the maid uniforms I saw on the way in. She has eyes the color of cocoa and hair a few shades lighter. The maid folds the fabric that made up the gag delicately, as if it's precious. Now that it's in her hands, I see what it is.

It's one of Hades's ties. Black, like the rest of his clothes. He must have taken it off to put it in my mouth.

She presses it into one of her pockets—out of sight, out of mind—and looks at me with a smile that reveals nothing. A knot at the center of my collarbone releases. Her expression is far softer than Dana's. There's no fear in it.

"Good morning." She extends a hand to me and we shake,

like I'm not standing here in a dress that could be lingerie and she didn't just help me hide my naked ass. "My name is Lillian. I'll be your personal assistant." She wrinkles her nose. "I think that has a nicer ring to it than maid. Though some of the people around here don't think so."

I drop my hands in front of me. "You already know my name, I think."

She nods slowly. "I do. But I don't know anything else about you. Not much information was provided when I was reassigned. Come this way and tell me what you like to drink with your breakfast. Tea? Coffee?" Lillian drops her voice. "I'm sure I could sneak you a mimosa once every so often."

A mimosa?

Is she joking?

And reassigned from where? How many other household staff does Hades have, and where do they work? Does he have other women here? The questions explode like fireworks at the front of my mind across a dark backdrop of jealousy. I let them fizzle out.

"Anything but herbal tea." If I have to keep drinking herbal tea, I'd rather close my eyes and depart from the world. My mother didn't believe in caffeine. Rising at dawn, yes. Caffeine, no. Decker told me about coffee shops in the city. Drinks that made you feel awake. Fresh morning air—that's the thing I'll miss. The dew beneath my feet. The soft calls of birds. My flowers. All my flowers. "I've always wanted to try coffee. If you have any."

She wears a small, sly grin, like the two of us are close friends and she doesn't work for the man who owns me. "I'm sure we can make that happen."

Lillian leads me across the room toward an inner hallway.

The lights adjust for us as we reach the threshold and go down the hall.

She puts her hand flat against the first door on the right. "This is your closet. I'll take care of it for you. If there's anything you ever need, all you have to do is tell me, and I'll have it repaired or replaced depending on your preference." Another door, on the left. "The bathroom."

"This is a suite." I don't remember anything about a suite in the contract. Every breath I take erases more of the words on the page from my mind. Fear is a slippery thing. It puts itself between you and everything you think you should know, and it pops up again and again, like a weed that can't be killed. "I thought…"

"You thought you might be kept in some empty cell?"

I whip my head around to look at Lillian, blood fleeing from my lips, leaving them numb and buzzing. "Does he do that? Are there people in a dungeon here?"

A shake of her head. "Not a dungeon, but a place of this size has to have somewhere for people to be kept, if necessary." Lillian reaches down, takes my hand, and gives it a brief squeeze. "If it's any consolation, I don't think that's where you're headed. Hades isn't in that kind of business."

"What kind of business is he in, then? He mentioned mines. He didn't say anything else."

She presses her lips together. "How much do you know about him?"

"I know he's ruthless." One word slips out, and another, until they become a stream I can't stop. "I know he's mean." My eyes fill with tears. "My mother always told me that if he ever found me, he'd kill me. I never knew why. I still don't know why. I just know he's the kind of man who could take someone's life without even thinking about it. Without even a second of regret." He could take my mother's life. He could take it in retaliation for this conversation, even. Pain presses in on my lungs until it's hard to take a full breath. "I shouldn't be telling you this at all." I turn my face away and swipe away my tears. "You work for him." Another surge of horror. "You might go and repeat everything I've said, and then—"

Lillian takes both my hands and squeezes hard. Hard enough that I let out a yelp. Her dark eyes look like thunderstorms in miniature. The pain clears my head, makes it easier to breathe. She drops my hands.

"I do work for Hades," she says softly. "But I'm assigned to you. I'm your personal assistant. I can do your hair. Get you something to eat. Whatever you need." Lillian laughs lightly. "Basically, my job is to keep you happy." She gives a sigh. "I won't tell your secrets. My job is to help you, not spy on you."

I don't trust it.

I want to, but I don't.

What I want is a minute alone. What I want is several *days* alone. What I want is to cry out the disappointment swelling in my chest. The confusion. The hatred.

"Do you have orders to stay with me?"

Her brows draw together. "No, miss. Just to be available."

"Then I think it would be best if you left. I'd like to be alone." It sounds too curt coming out of my mouth. "It was nice to meet you. I'm sorry. I just—"

"I understand." Lillian's face stays warm. "I'll have a tray sent up."

She goes back out through the bedroom, closing the door softly behind her.

In the bedroom, there's a chair by the window. A bedside table. I drop into the chair, staring up at miles of blue sky.

With no flowers, with no plants, all my feelings are a

shaken mess. Nothing is how I expected it to be. I *knew* Hades would kill me if he found me. Now he wants to use me to get something from my mother. He's dangling her over my head, using both of us against each other. I thought he'd keep me jailed. This is the nicest bedroom I've ever seen.

I don't want to accept a maid from him. I don't want to eat his food, or sleep in this bed.

And...

I *do* want all those things.

I cry for as long as I have the tears, ignoring the knock at my door. Me, giving orders to a maid. What's the use in pretending I'm worthy of a maid?

Noon rolls by. The early afternoon. The sky changes hue. I hate him.

The next person to come in doesn't knock. The door opens with quite a bit of force.

"You dismissed your maid?" The ice and cedar scent of Hades hits me at the same time as his words.

"I don't want a maid."

He stalks around the side of the bed, to my chair. "Going on a hunger strike won't release you from our agreement."

"I'm not hungry."

Hades narrows his eyes. They're so black. It sends a shiver down my spine. "You'll eat, Persephone."

"Fine." I stand up and face him, anger blooming. "I'll eat. I'll follow the terms of our agreement. But I'm not going to be happy about it. You can't impress me with a fancy bedroom."

"Impressing you is the least of my concerns."

"Then why not just put me in a cell, then? Why not just put me where I can't see outside?"

"Do you want to be isolated in the dark?"

"No." Fresh tears close my throat. "I wanted to have my

own life. This is just—this is a joke. A cruel joke. Pretending that this is a life."

"You were clear about your wishes, not that they matter. And I wouldn't call what your mother gave you a *life*."

"I didn't want to go back to the farmhouse. That doesn't mean I like it here."

He scoffs. "What do you think the world has that I don't?"

"I don't *know*. That's the point. I never got a chance to see. You could give me a minute to be upset about it. You could give me a minute to get used to it."

"You've had the better part of the day, and now I find that you've decided to become an ungrateful brat. And all because you didn't get to come."

My face flushes so deeply it's painful. "I don't care about that."

"Liar."

"I care about… more than that.

His smile is cutting. Dangerous.

"You think you've been deprived in some way?" Hades hooks his hand through mine and pulls me through the bedroom, then throws open the closet doors. "These are all your clothes. Decent ones, not like those linen bags you were wearing. There is food you requested gone cold outside the door."

"Those are things. Those aren't living. At least you got to do that before you came here to be rich and awful."

The muscles around Hades's mouth quirk. "You have a fascinating imagination."

"You probably wouldn't understand what that's like. You probably got to go to school." Hot tears prick my eyes, and I snap my mouth closed. He doesn't care. He'll never care. But I always wanted to go to school. I thought the New York Public Library could make up for some of what I'm missing.

For a flash, Hades's eyes go dark. More shadowed than they already are. As if the idea that he'd gone to school is hurtful, somehow. As if something in his past hurts.

"Well," he says, voice etched with irritation. "If it's books you're throwing this little tantrum over, then here you are."

He tugs me to another doorway and shoves it open with the flat of his hand.

It's a library.

My bedroom has a library.

One wall is completely covered in shelves, and those shelves are full of books. There's an overstuffed chair by the window. A round table. A throw blanket.

"Go ahead," he prompts. "Storm off and tell me how you'd rather be working your mother's fields."

I step past him, drawn to the books. They're not flowers, but they smell so good. I could read them for hours.

My fingers are inches away from the spines when I force myself to stop and turn back to him.

Hades stands in the doorway, expression shuttered.

"Can I read them?"

His eyes narrow. "What the fuck could you possibly mean?"

"Are there any I can't read? Any I'm not allowed to touch?"

I expect him to tease me. To punish me for my outburst. To make me work for it.

Hades straightens up. "No. They're all yours."

I whip around, facing the shelves. There are so many books here. So many new books that I've never read. All kinds. My mother isn't here to take them out of my hands.

"Thank you," I say.

Hades doesn't answer. He's gone.

SEVENTEEN

Hades

THE DIAMOND MINES ARE THE FARTHEST I CAN GET FROM Persephone. They're the closest source of people who require correction in any number of ways. But mainly, they're the safest place for me to be when the pain in my head is intense, the way it is now.

Well. The safest place for everyone else. A potentially mortifying place for me.

I'm pushing the limits, and I know it. That's the nature of running out of the painkillers that make it stop. I have to save the last few for real emergencies.

Of course, I could be the cause of an emergency, if it gets out of control. Best to be in a place that can accept the appearance of additional diamonds.

Unfortunately, stalking through the mines doesn't help the burning in my blood. It does nothing to tame this emotion stampeding through my veins. An intolerable emotion. One that grows with every second that passes.

Fucking Demeter. Seeing Persephone's face when she saw that silly little library was like discovering those thorn marks on her skin. The bruises. Demeter cut her off from the world completely.

The night bleeds by.

The next morning.

An afternoon.

Another night.

Another day.

No word from Demeter. No poppies.

I leave Persephone be. Deny myself.

There's a limit for me, and the people on the mountain know that. When I'm finished in the mines I go to my office for meetings and signatures and to survey the stream of money entering my accounts. I stay until Conor insists. He shoves me away from the office lights, toward the hallway, toward the elevator.

The pain is awful.

And it will be getting worse. My business will be vulnerable soon. I don't want to pull the whole enterprise down on my head. What a waste it would be. All this pain. All those diamonds. All those deals, for nothing.

The easy solution is to make my demands to Demeter.

I can't bring myself to do it.

The news of my mood has spread through the staff. All of them scurry out of my path on the way back to my private wing. Not one is in sight by the time I get inside.

I slam the door to my office and pace behind my desk. Back out toward the door. Back to the desk. If I had less self-control, I'd pull everything off the shelves and crush it in my hands. I need destruction like I need air and water.

What happened in Persephone's room could be my undoing, as much as it is hers.

I've touched Persephone before. It should have been meaningless. But it wasn't. And I don't know whether it was the press of her head against my chest or the sounds she made with my fingers on her naked flesh. I don't know if it was the way she looked completely clothed as part of my household, not a stitch on her from anywhere else. She tried so hard to please me, and not only because she was afraid.

I *saw* her.

How queenlike she could be. How perfect.

Fuck.

Persephone is right to be afraid. I'm a dangerous man. I'm not dangerous to her, at least not in the way that makes her tremble and fret. I won't hurt her any more than she can take.

I sit down behind the desk and run my hands over my face.

Sending Persephone back to that place would be the act of a soulless bastard.

I slap my hand down on the switch that controls the lights in the room. Today is a bad day. The worst yet. In the dark, I let my eyes settle. Conor pushes his nose against my knee and rests his head on top of my thigh. I don't have to see to lean back in my chair and continue controlling myself moment by moment. And I don't have to see to answer my cell phone when it rings.

"What?"

"Let's settle this. Tell me what you want from Demeter, and I'll mediate the deal." Zeus is walking somewhere, and quickly.

"I love when you call me to make demands. Especially when you know it's pointless."

It is, though I don't tell him that. I don't have enough painkillers to stay in the city long enough for that kind of bullshit.

"There was no need to resort to kidnapping if all you want is an increase in deliveries."

"Is it your contracts with her you're worried about? There are other suppliers, Zeus. No need to keep it all in the family."

"No need?" Now he's incredulous, and I can almost see his face contorted into disbelief. "You have the biggest stake in this by far."

"I have other priorities." The desk was built to withstand me. It doesn't budge when I brace my hand against it and push until the wood threatens to cut into my palm. "If Demeter is that important to you, come here in person and see what happens."

Zeus has never set foot here. He calls it the Underworld, and the nickname became so pervasive that eventually I had to take control of it myself. The worthless fucker. Always with his hands and his dick where they don't belong, causing chaos wherever he goes.

"I might have to, if you're going to be so unhelpful."

"Unhelpful? Your little empire in the city would be nothing without me. Are you sure you want to upset our special relationship just because Demeter's daughter stepped out?"

This will have gotten him where it hurts. He hates to admit that our businesses have a mutual dependence, though on my end it's more out of convenience than anything else. But he needs me. So do many of the players in the city, even if they'll never admit it out loud.

"Bring Persephone here. We can deal in person. Come to a resolution."

Zeus wants to play the good cop. My lip curls, disgust welling up from an endless supply. If he weren't hiding such an evil personality, I might find something in him to admire. If he hadn't forced this life on me for the fun of it, I might tolerate him. But I don't want him here. I have no plans to ever let him into my private quarters, but there's no telling what he might try with my staff. If he came here, there's a chance, however small…

"I'm not interested in a resolution."

"Demeter might be. She's come a little unhinged."

A chill creeps along the base of my spine, and Conor growls. Persephone hasn't been here long. And Zeus is telling the truth. I can hear that in his voice.

"Again, this is entirely useless information." It's the most important information I've ever received. My hackles are up, the hairs on the back of my neck standing straight. The stakes are higher now. Zeus. Demeter. Me, with Persephone here, with her books. A tangled web indeed.

"Come to the city. Bring Persephone. I don't believe your contract wasn't coerced. We can still solve this."

We. Coerced. The nerve of him. Acid burns the back of my throat. No. Fuck no. I don't want anything to do with Zeus or the brothel he keeps so people can fawn over him like a charming prince. But what is the alternative? He can't come here. I'd have to kill him before I let him this close to Persephone. General upheaval would follow. It would be the kind of distraction that's impossible to ignore.

"You could consult with some people." He sounds so fucking sincere. "I have a new doctor on call. She's very good. She might be able to find you some alternatives."

I want to squeeze this phone until it shatters, but that would be two in one week. So I deny myself the pleasure.

"I don't want to consult with anyone. Least of all someone you've chosen."

"If you don't—"

"What the fuck does it matter?"

"You could die," he says flatly.

"Wouldn't that be a shame. And after all your hard work."
I end the call.

The phone vibrates a second later. I open my eyes—fuck,
it hurts—and read the text on the screen.

**Zeus: I forgive you for what you said when you had a
headache.**

**Hades: Next time the train arrives, you're free to stand
in the tracks.**

Zeus: She's going to fuck you over.

I ignore it and close my eyes again.

The silence of the office without Zeus's voice is welcome
after the clashes and clangs of the mines and the chatter of
the office.

Welcome for a moment, anyway.

One moment flows into the next, and for a while, it's relatively peaceful. Then my mind catches on image after image.
Tears spilling from Persephone's eyes. Her trembling body
under my hands. The sway of her hips while she crawled across
the floor. No amount of denying myself can keep them away.
I want her. I want her too much to sit here, but I keep my feet
firmly planted on the floor and my hands against the edge of
the desk.

The mountain moves around me, alive with people whose
movements feel like ants in an anthill. All of them running to do
my bidding. Only one of them matters. Down in the mines, the
evening crew comes on, pickaxes ready to carve out gemstones
from the rock. There are new diamonds there, moment to moment. Small vibrations in the rock. I can feel the earth shifting.

And Persephone waits.

I don't know how long it's been when I finally stand up. The hall on the way to my most private rooms is still and empty, the way it should be. There's a certain pleasure in the late hours, when it could be any time at all. The night is liquid on the way to my sanctuary within a sanctuary. Even if Zeus came here, I would never let him into my private apartment. A fortress within a home within a fortress. Some people might label this paranoia. But I live every day with the knowledge that anything brave and strong enough to kill me is an earnest threat.

The silence grows as I get closer to my bedroom and send Conor in ahead of me. The night attendant will have put his food out. It's a deep enough silence for a thought to occur to me. Maybe she escaped. There is only one way to escape from here. I did, after all, leave her in a room with considerable furnishings. Something like fear grips my throat. It's such a foreign sensation that I try to rub it away.

The door to her suite opens beneath my hand as easily as it ever has, the turn of the handle as soundless as the room within. For a few moments, I can't hear anything.

Then...

Even breathing.

Persephone sleeps in a circle of light from the bedside lamp, almost hidden from view by the hangings at the head of the bed. Her small frame blends with the pillows and the blankets.

She's surrounded by books.

Neat stacks of two or three, perhaps fifteen in total, are fanned out around her. She holds one under her arm, like she fell asleep reading it. My heart tugs at the sight of it, and I rear back, turning away.

What the hell?

She looks so defenseless, so vulnerable, so young. And

the feeling that sloshes through me, messy and uncontained, is one of tenderness.

Fuck me.

I can't feel tenderness toward her. Or anyone. Ever.

My own dark needs come thundering in a moment late for this party. The surge of violent energy is a relief. I don't want to caress her. I want to spank her. Or maybe it's both. I don't want to let her sleep. I want to haul her out of the bed, shove her dress up to her waist, and cover her mouth while she cries underneath me. I don't want to deny myself any longer. I want to take her now, with thrusts that will make her feel so alive it hurts, and then hurts again, until there's nothing left but me inside her.

It's absurd, and I loathe it—more than I loathe Zeus, more than I loathe my deal with Demeter, and more than I loathe the endless dance of keeping people in their places. She's so close. I turn back around and look at her again. She does not sense me here. If she did, those eyes would open wide, and she'd know to be afraid.

It's another man who isn't me, or who isn't all me, who stands up tall.

Who walks around to the other side of the bed and reaches over her to shift the book from under her arm.

Who considers the title, stifling a laugh. I had them set up the smaller library for a woman while we were on the train. This is the kind of thing she'd like—of course it is. It's the kind of thing Demeter would never let her read. I put it on the bedside table.

It's another man who pulls the blanket up around her shoulders and turns out the light.

And it's another man who closes the door tightly behind him and goes to his own room without touching her at all.

EIGHTEEN

Persephone

THE DOOR TO MY ROOM—MY SUITE—OPENS WITH A breath of air, and Lillian comes in with her silver tray, dark eyes alight. The way she has every morning for the last two mornings. She's forgiven me for sending her away, I think.

Hades isn't with her, but something else is.

A small pot with a flower arrangement inside. Live flowers. Growing flowers, not cut.

She gives me a warm smile, eyes flicking over me. I'm already awake, just under the covers with a book. Waiting for him. "You brought flowers?"

"Good morning, Persephone. I thought you might like them." Lillian makes her way to the side of the bed and positions the tray over my lap like we've stepped right into one of the historical books from Hades's library and I'm the lady of the house. A lady with a suite attached to the library by a private door. "Did you sleep well?"

"Yes, of course." No. I woke up several times, thinking I

heard him in the room. I lay the book next to me, touching my thigh so I can be sure of its continued existence. I push my fingertip into the soil in the pot. Oh, only a few of them have sprouted yet. Lillian's brought me a project. The root filaments reach down into the dirt, freshly watered.

Lillian goes over to the curtains by the window and draws them open one by one, letting a bit of light in. Like everywhere else in Hades's home, it's a strange light. It makes me miss the sun. He must hate the daylight so much that he only allows it through his windows in diluted form.

"These are lovely." I keep my voice casual. "Is there anything scheduled for today I should know about?"

The set of Lillian's shoulders—relaxed and easy—tells me before she speaks that no, there's nothing on any sort of schedule. The only schedule that matters is the one Hades sets for me. He would tell his plans to Lillian for the express purpose of making my face turn red and hot.

"Not that I know of." She's constantly on the move, gently transforming the room around me. Straightening the hangings on the bed. Moving a stray book from the chair by the window to the table by my elbow. I don't keep much in the suite. I don't have much to keep. But somehow, when she's made her rounds back to the door, it looks fresh and new. "Are you reading this morning?"

I smile back at her, but it's only to cover the frustration twisting and turning like a creature wending its way through my ribs and settling between my thighs. Where is he? Where did he go? The questions are steam in a tea kettle, waiting for the chance to scream. Maybe he went to get those flowers. Maybe he went to take the seeds. Maybe he went back on his word.

"Until something happens." I drum my fingertips on the cover of the book.

Lillian leaves with a swish of her black skirt and the whisper of the door closing behind her. I manage the coffee, which is a revelation. Sugar and cream changes the color to a delicate tan.

The food is fine.

Half a piece of toast later, I've abandoned my breakfast to the tray and the tray to the bed. I've brought the flowers to a spot on the windowsill. The book fails to hold my attention. I take a shower and dress. I wear blue, because I can.

I pick up my book and start again. How much would I have given to have unfettered access to this many books in my mother's house? I'd have given a lot. Maybe a change of scenery would help. But even the library can't compete with my insatiable need to know. The answers aren't in this book, or any of the others. It's more frustration—frustration I shouldn't be feeling.

I. Should. Not. Miss. Hades.

And I don't. I don't miss him. That's not it, not exactly. What it is, exactly…

Unfinished business.

An unfinished orgasm, for one thing. That's at the top of my list. I get out of bed and go to the window, hardly seeing the harsh drop down the side of the mountain. Why is he staying away? Is it supposed to be a kindness or a punishment? The odds of Hades doing anything to be kind are slim, so it must be the other option. He must be trying to torture me. He must know, somehow, that I've been lying under my sheets for the past few nights with flushed cheeks and a clenched jaw and all my efforts have come to nothing but lost sleep.

Now I do focus on the mountainside, the wall jutting out of it and the drop into misty nothingness. The wide sill is the perfect place to brace my hands so I can press my forehead to the cool glass. I stare until my vision blurs, but it still doesn't erase the tightly wound feeling at the apex of my legs, pulsing and begging. It's relentless.

Instead, after the window chills the heat in my face, I put a fingertip to one of the buds in the flowerpot.

I think of sunshine, and life, and spring. Gold in my chest. Trickling down to my fingertip and into the bud.

It stretches. Grows. Lifts toward the sun. It tries, anyway, but the sun is different here. It reaches toward me instead. It feels so good to do it.

The petals spread open. The flower blooms.

"What did you just do?"

His voice hits first, and then a chill in the room, like he's come in out of the cold and it's sticking to his skin. Then the heat. Heat in my face, heat between my legs, heat streaking down, all of it gold. I jerk my hand away from the flower and whirl to face him.

This is the biggest secret I have. It's the one I'm never supposed to tell. More than that, I know better than to trust him.

"I didn't do anything. I was just looking out the window."

Hades strides through the bedroom. Conor follows him closely, like he always does, but sits near the edge of the bed.

"I saw it. You made that flower grow." He peers down into the pot, then pushes it toward me. "Do it again."

"I don't know what you're talking about."

He winds his fingers in my hair, pulls my head back, and stares into my face like he owns every part of me. Like it's just a matter of convincing me. But… I have to hold this back from him. I can't give in.

"Do it again," he orders, and uses my hair to angle me over the pot. Hades takes my hand in his and holds it near one of the other flowers. "There's no use pretending, Persephone."

I want to.

That light, gold feeling builds in my chest. I hold my breath. Hold it in.

Hades drops my hand and puts his palm between my breasts. Slides it down and down and down until he reaches my hips.

"Make it grow."

I want him to touch me so badly it hurts. I want him to finish what he started. And I can't do this in front of him. I've spent my life hiding it from people.

"I won't."

"Refusing me isn't part of our agreement."

"But we have an agreement. Arrangement. Whatever you want to call it." My head throbs. My throat tightens. I could combust. "You've been gone for days, with no word. I don't even know if you've kept up your end of the bargain." I'm grasping at straws, trying desperately to keep a secret I've already let slip. "Is my mother still alive?"

"Yes. And you are being cared for. Make the flower grow."

"I told you. I won't."

He pulls me upright, so I have to face him. His eyes look bright. Almost happy. But there's no smile at his lips. It's another expression entirely.

Almost like he wants to kiss me.

Hades takes my wrist in his hand and hovers my hand over the pot. He leans in close.

That winter-wind scent takes my breath away. He just smells so *clean*. So good. I want to push my face into the side of his neck and breathe. I feel myself leaning in. My mind resists. I can't lean in for a kiss. Can't.

He lets me get an inch away before he stops me, giving my wrist a little squeeze.

"Keep refusing," he says. "You won't get anything you want."

"I don't want anything from you."

He comes in close, again, and my whole body leans into it, rising up on tiptoe. I'm ashamed, head to toe. On fire, head to toe. I wouldn't be surprised to find out that my skin is lighting up from the gold around my heart, buzzing in my fingertips.

Hades pulls back.

"I hate you," I whisper.

"You're my favorite sight. I missed you. Now make the damn thing grow."

"Never."

"We'll see about that."

He locks his hand around the back of my neck, sweeps up the flower pot with the other, and moves. What else am I supposed to do, other than stumble forward? Nothing. My feet go numb, clumsy with the thrill of his words. *I missed you.*

Hades's legs are so much longer than mine. He is so much more powerful. And I am so, so scared. The only way to avoid being dragged is to keep up, and I try. I try my best. All the way out of my bedroom. Down through the halls, and out.

I haven't been outside his apartments for days, and the hall outside is huge in comparison. He's built himself a palace fortress, with layers inside layers, all of them as impenetrable as he is.

We take the elevator down. It's not quiet when the doors open. Conor's nails on the floor are the backdrop to a chorus of other sounds. The big rotunda is alive with people. I feel them seeing me as acutely as I feel his fist in my hair and the cooler air of the hall slipping under my dress to the delicate lace underthings I found in the closet. I blink away tears. Some of them escape and evaporate off my skin.

I screwed up. I didn't hear him coming.

Hades takes me through the center of the rotunda, his footsteps echoing louder than any of the others. A path opens up for us wherever we go. A wide space. An empty space. No one dares touch him or touch me. He barks an order at someone, but I can't hear it through the haze of pain.

A set of doors opens, and we cross over the threshold. A large room. Flashes of leather and steel. A wide glass desk. And the most massive windows I've ever seen. Hades releases his grip, only so I can straighten up and see where we are.

His office. His real office. And his office overlooks...

An enormous factory floor. His hand goes around the back of my neck, and I lurch forward again, following him through a set of glass doors. Conor stays where he is. He must know this play already.

The sound is like nothing I've ever heard. It's an enormous, never-ending sound, an echo off the impossibly high ceilings and a storm made up of all the work that goes on below us. Rows of worktables line a room bigger than some of my mother's fields. It's not a space that should fit indoors, and yet it does. Hades has made the impossible absolutely real.

At the far end of the room is a yawning chasm, a rip in the rock. From here, I can make out a line of people in a constant stream. I blink in the face of the noise. The steady beat of machines. A foreman's voice, rising above the fray. Tools on metal. And a deeper hum. Mining. They're mining something over in that tear.

He pushes me to the railing. This is more than a balcony. It's a viewing platform with an opaque, waist-high wall. There's a ledge running along the inside. We're high above the people below. But not that high. High enough that a drop wouldn't kill me. High enough that if they looked, they could see us.

Hades puts the pot on the ledge. Pulls me close to him.

I suck in one ragged breath after another. "What—what—"

"Isn't it gorgeous?" Hades's voice sounds like a murmur against all the noise in the room. This is the sound of him pulling his wealth from the earth. So much money. So much power. "Everyone down there is working for me. Everything they do is for me. You're one of them, too. Only your work isn't with jewelry and metal and all the other things people want to buy."

Jewelry. Metal. Something new I've just learned. I'm nervous enough to ask another question. "What's in the mines?"

"Diamonds," he says, his voice low.

Diamonds.

So much money, buried in the rock.

Hades traces a path around to the front of my collarbone, then clamps his hand around the front of my neck. I can't take my eyes off the people below us. They're noticing, one by one, pale faces glancing up and then back down again.

"We'll start again. Make the flower grow."

"Here?"

"I gave you plenty of opportunities to do it in private. Now you'll do it here."

Confusion is hot and horrible. It feels good to have him handle me like this. I'd fall if Hades didn't have his hand around my throat, pinning me against his body. Every inch of him is as hard as the rocks making up his palace walls. My body struggles for a moment, unthinking, and he only holds me closer.

I pin my hands to my sides.

Hades steps back, putting space between us. I feel like I'm dangling in midair. With a sharp tug, he tears my dress in two. It flutters to the floor. He pauses, running his fingertips along the lace of my panties and bra. "Do you want to keep these?"

"Yes," I gasp. This is a room full of people. They won't ignore me forever.

"Then show me what you did."

When I hesitate, Hades takes my wrist and holds my hand over the pot again. "If I don't?"

"I'll punish you here. I have time, Persephone. We'll stay as long as it takes. Keep your hand where it is."

The heat in my face must give me away. My entire body feels scarlet. I'm practically naked. There are so many people.

Hades changes his grip. He wraps his left hand lovingly around my throat, putting just enough pressure to keep me in my place. And with his other hand...

He touches me.

The hollow of my collarbone. My cleavage. When he slides a hand under the bralette, a strangled cry floats above the noise. Both nipples, already peaked, feel exquisitely sensitive as he pinches one then the other. He goes lower. I can't breathe.

"They're watching you. Make the flower grow, and I'll take you where nobody can see."

"I'm not—supposed—to do this in front of other people. I won't do it for you."

Hades shoves my panties down to the center of my thighs and strokes his fingers between my legs. Casually. Possessively. Like he's owned me forever.

It's good. It feels good. And I'm so guilty. I'm awful for wanting this. It's not right. "Please. This is—this is—"

His hand stops moving, and my breath catches. I can't tell if it's Hades's heart or mine that's beating so hard.

"It's something you want. And you can't have it until you make the flower grow."

"Yes," I admit, sounding wretched. "I do."

"Concentrate on the flower." Another stroke, and I sag

141

against him, a wicked desire spreading outward from his fingers through every inch of me. It hurts, and it's so good. "Touch it."

He does it again.

My fingertips meet the flower bud. It's a few inches tall. Ready to bloom. It wouldn't take much.

"Good girl."

"No," I whisper.

"Yes," he hisses back. "Make it grow. And stay on your feet."

He reinforces this with a squeeze against my throat. Then he uses one leg to knock mine apart, the panties stretching to the limit. He buries his hand between my legs, stroking and pinching and oh no, oh God, circles against my swollen clit. He rubs it with his knuckles, with the pad of his thumb, with the palm of his hand.

I can't stand. I can hardly see. Everything narrows down to where his hand meets my skin. My traitorous, wanting skin.

Hades makes a noise that's half frustration, half satisfaction. Another sensation breaks through the cloud that my mind has become—him. He's hard too. Is he going to fuck me in front of all these people?

The moment I have the thought is the same moment I switch to wanting him to start. It's an endless echo. If he's going to do it, do it now. If he's going to do it, let it happen right now. Right now, right now.

Instead, he touches me while the factory watches.

How can they not be watching? Each set of eyes is another set of pinpricks. He works two thick fingers into me. My slickness helps him on his way, but they feel huge, so huge. There's no way anything more than this can ever fit. Too much, too much. I try to squirm off of them and fail. All I earn is his laughter, rumbling against me.

A sob rips itself from my throat, but to my total shock, it's not because of the stinging push and spread of his fingers. Or everyone watching him do this to me. It's because I'm so desperate to come that it's tearing me in two.

Too much becomes *not enough* in a sickening instant, and I find myself—I discover myself, like I'm coming upon myself in a deep wood—rocking against his hand. Begging out loud. Are they even words? I don't know, and I don't care. I'm touching him now, my hands against his hand, against my throat. Pressing harder. I want more. I want it now.

"You're only hurting yourself. I won't let you come until you do this for me." His hand works harder, pushing deeper, flicking my clit with his thumb. "Now, Persephone."

"I can't." My wail has to be loud enough for everyone to hear.

"I won't let them see," he promises.

I need something else. I need… I need… I need—

Hades lowers his head to the curve where my neck meets my shoulder and bites.

His hand stills, and it breaks me. I suck in a breath and let the gold swim through my veins and through my fingertips and through the petals. The flower blooms under my fingertips and keeps blooming. More petals than should be possible. They fall to the dirt.

"There," I pant. "There. I did it. Please."

Hades pins me to him hard, both arms trapped, his fingers inside me. One small movement of his thumb, and I'm coming on those fingers. The gold turns gossamer under the ice of him. My body shatters. Pleasure is warm, and so overwhelming. All I want is to fall, but he keeps me standing, keeps me upright while I shudder and shake and cry.

When the wave subsides, he's still there. He builds it again, agonizing in its slowness, in its precision.

Hades makes me come again in front of his factory. In front of the flower. I did a bad thing, showing him, a terrible one, but it makes it feel good.

It hurts more the second time.

And it also feels better.

The intensity is too much for my mind to handle, too big for my body. And I can't get away. I'm half-naked, spread open in front of all the other people he owns. I am nothing but nerves and pain and pleasure. A flower, burst into bloom.

At the end, he scoops me up like the empty shell I am and carries me back to his rooms, back to the bed, and into a blessed dark rest.

NINETEEN

Persephone

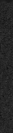HEAR HIM IN THE NIGHT.

Maybe what I'm hearing is only a dream, but it hauls me bodily out of my sleep and into the darkness of my room. My mind is blank for a few breaths, numb, but then the sound makes its way in.

His voice.

Hades is here. And close.

What night is it? How long have I been asleep?

I don't care.

The floor is warm under my feet, even though this place has been carved out of mountain rock. A heated floor. Even so, I pull a blanket from the chair by the window and wrap it around myself. I'm going to find him. In the sleep delirium, it seems like a good idea. But how asleep am I, really? I'm not. I'm awake, just tired. Just worn out from what happened.

Everyone saw that happen.

Most importantly, Hades saw what happened. He knows about me now.

I pad across the floor, open the door to my bedroom suite, and look out.

The voice wasn't a dream. But it's farther away than I thought. Much farther.

Why not go on an adventure?

I follow the sound of his voice down the hall. Through the living room, with its pillars and sunken floor. I cross another threshold.

That's when I see it.

Light, coming from the cracked door of his office. Not a normal yellow hue, like the lightbulbs in my mother's house. Not even candlelight. What is it? What kind of lamp makes light like that?

Why not find out now?

"Why not?" I pose the question to nobody while I go down the hall. I could be a spirit floating above the floor for all the sound my feet make. This is not a bad idea. It might even be a good idea. I watch myself from outside my body, moving down the hall, sleep-rumpled and wrapped in a blanket. I observe myself pushing open the door to Hades's private office. And then I'm slammed right back into my body, because that is the effect of looking at him. It brings me to myself.

He sits behind his desk, phone pressed to his ear.

"It's a developing problem." If it weren't for the tired soreness suffusing every muscle of my body, I might be more shocked to hear it. Hades having a problem? He raises one hand to his eyes and covers them like they hurt. I can't imagine him feeling pain. But it looks like he does. Maybe monsters *can* feel pain. "I need people in the field. I'm not in a position to leave the mountain for the amount of time that—" Hades sits up straighter. "No. I don't have enough of the source."

He must sense me, because he uncovers his eyes and turns his head, all of him on high alert. It's something to see. He hasn't changed the way he's sitting, and yet he's changed everything about the way he's holding himself. Muscles tensed. Sharp eyes narrowed. He ends the call without saying another word and lets the phone fall to the surface of his desk with a muted clatter.

"You're awake."

I'm here now. There's no going back, so I step farther into the office. "I heard you talking."

A smile curls the corner of his lip. "And you decided to come wandering out of your room in the middle of the night?"

Something about him seems slightly softer in this timeless place between midnight and dawn. At least, I'm assuming it's between midnight and dawn. No, not softer. Not exactly. He's still as sharp and as hard as he's ever been.

"Yes." It's as good an idea as any to drop into a chair across from him, so that's what I do. "I wanted to find you."

"You wanted another demonstration of how cruel and dishonorable I am?"

He's toying with me now, but I'm too drunk on his fingers inside me and the orgasms he stole from me, too worn from the days of wondering to care. A layer of him has been stripped away by the night. Conor snores by the fireplace, the orange light playing over his fur, and something else clicks into place.

"I wanted to know why you have a dog. I didn't think you would have a pet."

"I have my uses for him."

"But that's not all, is it? You don't just use him to scare

people. Or maybe even kill people." In the haze of the night, I have much less of a filter. "He helps you, doesn't he?"

"Nobody helps me."

"I think he does."

"What else do you think?" Hades's expression is hard, but when he glances over to where Conor sleeps, a hint of softness appears at the very edges. "Do you want to keep pushing me until you get the punishment you want? Or do you want to close those pretty lips of yours before you get into trouble?"

I don't want to say anything. I want to *do*.

"No. I wanted to say that you kept your promise." Guilt tumbles over me, like soil spilling from a bucket. "You didn't let anyone see the flower."

And you finally let me come.

"If I'm not the worst man you've ever met, I'll be shocked." Hades's eyes catch the light. Huge black pupils with a thin ring of blue. Less of him is in shadow now. "I can't imagine Demeter paraded you around the city. Or even let you off the grounds." He laughs, the sound low and rich. "And now look at you."

I don't want to look at myself. I want him to look at me. And he is. He's watching now. My wish came true already. The memory of his fingers pushes into me, again and again. I'm swimming up from a great depth.

"I've had problems too. Complicated ones."

He narrows his eyes and steeples his fingers in front of his chin. "Eavesdropping is a bad habit. I should train that out of you."

I pull the blanket tighter, but lean toward him all the same. "How would you do that?"

"It's very simple." The light plays in his eyes, highlighting the blue. Why are they like that? "A system of rewards and punishments."

"Like an animal?" Someone else has taken over my body and is now having this conversation like I can't still feel him touching me, even now. "Like how you'd train a dog or a horse?"

"Are you a dog or a horse, Persephone?"

"No." The room takes on a bizarre hue, and I blink it away. "Why is the light so weird in here? You've never explained that." I shouldn't say anything else. "Does it have to do with your dog? I think it might. I think it all has to do with each other. But it doesn't make sense."

Hades makes a sarcastic gesture. *Go on, little fool.*

"Why did you care so much about the poppies? And why won't my mother give them to you, or… sell them to you, I guess? She normally likes money. She likes being safe, too. So I don't understand why she's withholding them from you."

I don't understand why she'd take that risk.

He stays silent for a long moment, then leans forward in his chair, black shirt moving with him. I can't stop looking at his arms in that fabric. His biceps. His strong hands. His fingers.

I try to summon up my hate for him like a shield, and I can't quite do it. Maybe it's too late at night. Maybe I'm too curious.

"She's doing it to get back at me," Hades says.

"For what?"

"For interfering in her business practices."

I don't care very much about my mother's business practices right now. Her fields seem very far away. The missing piece is the flowers. They're what Hades came to my mother's fields for. They're what he wants to use me to get. They're everything to him.

"How is it getting back at you if she's the one losing money?"

For a split second, almost too fast for my mind to process,

worry flashes through Hades's eyes. His brow furrows just slightly. He looks vulnerable.

I imagined it. I must have. Because his face returns immediately to that cold, impassive expression.

"Because I'm in pain without them. The poppies can be processed into painkillers that were designed for me."

"Designed?"

"By your mother. Grown. They have certain attributes that make the painkillers safer. There are no side effects. They don't get less effective over time. They're not addictive."

Of course. I can make the flowers grow, but my mother has a different gift. She can make new strains of flowers. Hybrids. Like a vine of ivy with rose petals and thorns. Like blood-red poppies with golden filaments.

"What kind of pain?"

"Headaches."

"Do you mean..." I swallow. Focus harder. "Like migraines?"

"Worse than migraines."

Decker told me about his mother getting migraines when he was younger. They left her unable to get out of bed. For something to be even worse...

"Does it hurt all the time?"

"When I don't have access to the poppies, the pain is constant."

"Even right now?"

"Especially right now." Hades seems to search for the right words. "The last few days have been difficult. I've spent as much time as possible in the dark, but it's not enough."

My stomach sinks. I don't feel anything like hatred now.

"She knows about it," I say. "She's hurting you on purpose?"

Hades nods.

I'm horrified on his behalf. I've had bad headaches before from staying out in the sun too long. I can't imagine if they were worse. And lasting for hours. Days. Maybe longer. The horror sinks in. Turns to a clenching ache in my heart. He made me feel good today. I felt pleasure, even if it was shameful. And he felt nothing but pain.

"I would grow them for you." My heart races with sorrow for him and anger at my mother and a strange helplessness. "I would. If I had the seeds. I could make them grow faster. But I can't make the poppies from nothing. They're hybrids. Only my mother can do that."

A smile ghosts across his face. "I thought you'd find it comforting."

"Well, I don't. I don't think anyone should suffer. Even you."

Hades studies me for a few moments. "You didn't come here to ask me about the poppies."

I did, in a way. I came here to ask him everything. Or I came here because it's the middle of the night and something about the late hour has torn down a barrier between us.

And it has. I'm electric, with pulses of energy seeking him with every heartbeat. I want to get closer.

"There's something else I want to know." I lick my lips, which have gone dry.

Hades's eyes fall to the movement, and when he looks back up at me, he's changed again. As if another veil has been stripped away. "There's nothing I need to tell you."

"There's something I *need* to know." The blanket is soft and insubstantial under my hands, but I gather it up anyway and move to the edge of my seat. Cool leather against my bare thighs. "I need to know when you're going to fuck me."

For the first time, I've caught him by surprise. Hades's

shock is momentary, there and gone again. He threads his hands behind his head and leans back.

"Why would you think I'd bother fucking you?"

"Don't say that." The numb, dreamlike feeling has spread across my entire face and over my shoulders. What's the worst that could happen—he kills me? Some twisted part of me would probably like that too. "I know you want to."

In this light, and with those words hanging in the air between us, his eyes are as black as they ever have. Black as midnight. Almost no day left. There's hardly any color. I shiver under the chill.

"Tell me," I demand. "Tell me why you haven't done it yet."

"Come here."

There's no point in hesitating. Once I'm on my feet, he motions for me to drop the blanket. The moment he does, I want to keep it wrapped around me, but I know the game he plays. He'll only take it off himself. So I let it fall to the floor and go stand next to his chair.

It's a massive thing, built for him like everything else in this place has been, with no arms. Hades has created space between him and the desk. Just enough space for me. We look at each other in the weird, impossible light.

"Bend over my lap."

I suck in a breath, loud in the quiet of the room. My nerves, numbed by what happened before, rear back to life with a thousand sparkling cuts. Needles all over my skin, tiny thorns, have me painfully awake.

Hades clicks his tongue. "Still so slow to obey."

He shoves me gracelessly over his lap, legs splayed open, gasping like I'm breaking an invisible surface. A flash of pain, lace raw on my skin—he's torn off my panties. Then his hand, searching between my legs. Stroking. I'm a little sore from earlier, and I flinch away without meaning to. He presses his other hand down at the small of my back, pinning me.

"Here's your answer. Is this what you wanted?"

"I—" I'm struggling for air, for anything. My hips rock uselessly against his legs. I can't stop. I can't stop, and it's so embarrassing, so awful, that another wave of tears comes. Yes, yes, yes. "No. I can't want this."

"But you do. You're wet." His tone lifts to a register that could be awe. "You're so fucking wet that if I…" He shoves his fingers inside me, roughly, without warning, without waiting. "You want this. In fact—" He leans even closer so that his breath brushes my ear. "—you need this. And I love watching you cry and squirm and beg for it."

"I'm not begging."

"You will."

"I thought…" It's difficult, thinking, with the slow thrust of his fingers in and out, in and out, so casual. Almost as if he doesn't know he's doing it. But he does know. "I thought you wanted to use me. And hurt me."

"Hurt you?" A note of surprise in his voice. He pushes his fingers in deeper. Too deep. Fresh tears. "Does this feel like pain?"

This is, without question, the realest thing he's ever said to me. The words shimmer in the air, behind my eyelids, through the tears. "It's more complicated than that."

"Because you want it so much." He's fucking me with his fingers, but his voice betrays none of it. "It's dangerous for me to give you what you want."

The sensation builds until it's too much. His fingers. His lap. His office, the furniture looming around me as much as he is. His other hand on the small of my back. He's so big. He's so strong. It's a breathless, needy, desperate hum at the core of me, and it's too much. It's too much. It makes me come again. This orgasm is raw, almost painful, a thousand sunburns all concentrated into a bomb.

From far away, I can hear him coaxing me, surprisingly gentle. "That's it. Yes. Let it happen, Persephone. It's beautiful."

And then—then—I feel myself twisting, my own body moving, like I'm a puppet on strings. Twisting in his lap. Pushing myself up. Throwing my arms around his neck and kissing him.

It's a deep, vicious kiss, his hand on the back of my neck and the other braced against my hip. I'm straddling him. I don't know how I got here. But the most tender parts of me, bruised from his fingers, brush against the fabric of his suit. The orgasm peaks and fades. He tastes like snow and mint and something I can't begin to name. My heart is ready to fly out of my chest. My heart's ready to explode.

Before it's done, before I've managed to re-inhabit my body, he pushes me off his lap. I catch the edge of the desk and force myself upright, trembling. By the time I'm on my feet, he's standing. Backing up. Eyes blazing. He was telling the truth. I'm dangerous to him. I make him dangerous. It takes my breath away, or it gives my breath back—I can't tell. He puts a fist to his mouth, breathing hard. I've done something to him. All this time, he's done things to me, and now I've done something to him.

"Get out."

I open my mouth to argue, but Hades raises a hand and points behind me.

"Get. Out."

There's no arguing now.

I turn and go, feeling his eyes on me every step of the way.

TWENTY

Persephone

NO DOOR WAKES ME UP IN THE MORNING, NO SWISH OF Lillian's skirts, no footsteps in the hall, nothing. I swim in a deep and dreamless sleep for a long time and wake up slowly, muscles aching, almost naked. It takes quite a bit of stretching before I feel like climbing out of the bed.

A silver tray balances neatly on the table next to what I've come to think of as my reading chair. And that's not all—a new robe, pure white, hangs over the back of the chair. I shrug it over my shoulders and slip into the seat. I've been sleeping forever, and I'm starving. What happened yesterday laps at my mind like an endless series of waves on sand.

The flower. The poppies. The pain.

I have to stop thinking of it like that—as what happened, as the thing that happened, as what Hades did. Because what he did was make me come. Many times. A sick, twisted, intense pleasure. Words that shouldn't belong in the same sentence, but there they are.

It's dangerous for me to give you what you want.

He made me come, and he told me a secret.

My mother shouldn't be doing this to him.

Hades gives me pleasure anyway.

I rub both hands over my face and look over my breakfast.

Three plates. One with a slim slice of chocolate cake. One with a fan of strawberries soaked in sugar. One with a cloudlike pastry drizzled with chocolate. Two small pitchers of cream. A mug of coffee, black. A jewelry box. A note.

These are not the normal trappings of breakfast.

A jewelry box?

Note first.

I recognize his handwriting instantly—flawless, masculine, taking up every inch of the small slip of paper.

I've instructed Lillian not to wake you this morning in light of our activities yesterday. You haven't been eating enough, so I had the kitchen replace your meal for the morning. Do better, Persephone. I won't have my property self-destruct. You'd be useless to me then. —H

He's left a postscript underneath.

The box is for you.

The note falls from my fingers.

A gift.

I can't make myself wait. The velvet box feels new in my hands. Too light for what it means. It's wide and flat, and when I lift the lid, the box ceases to matter at all. Because inside is the most beautiful necklace.

A diamond pendant. A delicate chain. The diamond is large. Glittering. The shape is… I don't know how to describe it.

It's black, like his clothes. Black, like his eyes.

I've never owned a diamond. I've never owned anything like it. I've woven countless daisy chains, but this makes my heart race. It makes tears come to my eyes.

When I lift the backing from the box to take it out, another note flutters to the floor at my feet.

A reminder of where you belong.

Here, with him.

Of course I do. I signed a contract. But this means something else. It has to.

I put it on, and the diamond dangles between my breasts while I eat a miniature assortment of some of my favorite foods.

While I shower, working the shampoo through my hair inch by inch and slicking conditioner through every curl.

While I tilt my head beneath the most expensive, quietest hair dryer I have ever used.

While I hunt through the closet for a new dress to wear.

There's a rainbow of dresses in here. Dresses and tops and leggings. The dresses mainly hit above the knee, and the fabric is soft and gorgeous. There's no hiding what I'm wearing—or not wearing—underneath.

I choose a black one to match the diamond.

It's perfect.

It's light, for summer. A strong breeze could take it away. But the fit against my body makes me feel new.

"Persephone?"

"I'm in here."

Lillian comes to the doorway of the walk-in closet and looks at me in the mirror. "Is everything all right?"

Maybe. Maybe not. He was angry that I kissed him, and now jewelry appears on the bed.

"Is Hades up here or is he down at work?"

Lillian blinks. "He's downstairs."

157

"In his office or in the factory? Or the mines?"

She bites her lip, hesitating. I'm not allowed to go down there alone. "Let me find out."

While she's gone, I come back into the bedroom and straighten up my books. Finish the last of my coffee. Brush my teeth. I'm not going to wait all day to find out what the necklace means.

A minute later, Lillian returns. "He's almost done dealing with a situation in the mines."

"What kind of situation?"

"Sometimes, in the dark, people… get overwhelmed. And they need someone to take them out."

"So *Hades* does that?" He's the richest man on the mountain. He's the person who owns everyone else. Surely there's a person on his staff who could handle this for him. "Do you mean that he kills them?"

Lillian startles. "No, he doesn't. He takes them to a place where they won't interfere with the mining. It's not safe down there for a person who's not in his right mind."

I should wait.

I should follow his instructions.

"Take me to him. Please."

She shakes her head, eyes wide. "I don't think that's a good idea."

"Take me to him. And if he's still busy, we won't interrupt. You can bring me back here and he'll never know."

His note wasn't an apology for how angry he seemed after I kissed him. I'm not sure he's the kind of man who apologizes. But I want to talk to him about this necklace. I want to understand whether this gift is a symbol of change or whether it's misdirection to make me feel more comfortable here.

I want him.

Lillian taps her fingers against her thigh. "We'll have to be quick. I can't be seen taking you out of his rooms."

"Of course." I hurry back to the closet and slip on a soft pair of shoes. Goose bumps run across my shoulder blades. If I really lived here, and not just as a bargaining chip, I might do this same thing. Find shoes. Go down to meet Hades wherever he was, wearing the color he likes best. Back in the bedroom, I push those thoughts out of my head and square my shoulders. "Okay. Let's go."

We move quickly through Hades's rooms. I expect for Lillian to take me to the elevator, but she stops halfway down the outer hall and steps into an alcove I hadn't noticed. At the back of the alcove is a door. When she opens it, lights click on.

"This way."

I follow her through narrow hallways and down staircases.

"Staff access," she explains. "And maintenance. And for emergencies."

There are no windows to give me a sense of direction. Luckily, there's only one way to go, and Lillian's leading.

We go through another series of doors. A hum travels through the walls. "What is that?"

"The generators. Most of them are under the mountain, near the mines."

They're loud. They have to be, I suppose, because they're creating enough electricity for an entire mountain.

A door with a window in the top panel comes up on our right. Lillian doesn't pause, but I glance over. Do a double-take.

"What is that?"

It looks like buildings. At least two stories. And this door is looking *up* at them.

"Where we live." Lillian puts her hand above my elbow and tugs me along. "It's like a village. Or a town. There's an exit at the base of the mountain for the people who like to go outside."

"But where is it? Compared to everything else?"

"You can get there through the factory floor. An entrance near the mine shaft."

The hallway widens. Gets darker. It's louder here, too. Random *thud*s through the walls.

"They're breaking off pieces of rock," Lillian says. "Then there's a process to get the diamonds out. Okay." She stops at a door that's covered in red and yellow warning signs. "This is where he'll be, if he's still down here."

The noise level decreases a little, and Lillian bites her lip.

"What does that mean?"

"They shut down mining in this section. Just… stand out of sight."

I back up, and Lillian opens the door a few inches.

It was blocking more sound than I realized.

Someone is shouting, their voice ragged, almost incoherent with rage. That's what it sounds like at first. Except it's not rage. It's fear, and an almost inhuman sadness. I step forward to help, and Lillian puts her arm out in front of me.

I can see the man who's yelling. Sobbing. Dust from the mines streaks his face. He's muscular and strong, but he's holding onto the rocky wall for dear life. I can't understand a word of what he's saying.

"That's not what you saw." Hades's voice slices through the sobs and the distant noise of what must be other sections in the mines. He steps forward, into my line of sight. "Your eyes deceived you."

Another stream of words. He's shouting directly into Hades's face.

"She is up above." Hades is absolutely calm. He uses a level, no-bullshit tone. My heart pounds anyway. He's supposed to be a killer. A terror. "Working in the café, just like she was when you came on shift. No—*no*. I won't allow you to go up like this."

"They hurt her."

"Your team members didn't touch her. They've been down here with you."

The man takes a choked breath. "Then it was you. You killed her. It was *you*."

He launches himself at Hades, and I clap both hands over my mouth. My chest fills with ice. Because Hades won't let him live after this. He'll kill this man, this worker, and I'll never be able to forget.

It doesn't happen.

The man doesn't even make contact. Hades catches him, stopping his tackle mid-jump. Hades ends up with one hand locked onto the collar of the man's protective vest and the other across his chest, holding him still.

I see why he's the one down here now. Nobody else would be strong enough.

The moment he's held in place, the man breaks down completely. He's crying harder than I've ever seen anyone cry. My hands shake at the sight. I thought I might watch him die for this. Now I don't know what I'm seeing.

I think it's Hades. The real him. The one he hides from everyone.

"That's enough." Hades is still calm. He whistles, and Conor comes padding to his side. "No more of this."

"Did I hurt anybody?"

"Do you think it felt good to be hit in the shoulder with a chisel? Of course it hurt. Lucky for you, it was the blunt end. Come on. Walk."

Lillian lets go of the door handle, her face pale. "We have to go," she whispers. "Now."

TWENTY-ONE

Hades

DEMETER IS OUT OF CONTROL.

Messages from Zeus have been coming in all day. Demeter stormed into the city to demand he intervene. I was in the mines when he attempted to arrange the meeting. By lunch, she'd gone back to her fields.

And now the farm boy has come with a report.

He stands across the desk, next to Oliver, shifting his weight from foot to foot.

"She's burning the fields," he says. "One by one."

Of course, Demeter and I have always hated one another. She has always had an interest in killing me. She's always been evil, down to her bones. It's the same at her farm, with her little concubine field workers and the bodies she buries.

Two years ago, she started using some of her workers as test subjects and killing the ones who didn't respond to her experiments. She was not pleased when I paid her a visit. Even

less pleased when I told her that if the killing continued, I'd come for the poppies myself and have her arrested.

Demeter started by adjusting the painkillers themselves. They lasted for shorter and shorter periods of time, so I took over the processing with an in-house team. But then she started sending fewer flowers.

She wanted me to feel it coming.

I rub my hands over my face. It's awful today. I'm nearing a blackout. The pain has radiated down my spine. Down my back.

"Is it true?" I ask Oliver.

Oliver nods. "Went to confirm myself."

"I need to know which fields she started with." This, to Decker. It's the information that means the most to me now. I have to know. Lives depend on it, mine included. "As quickly as possible."

"The train—"

"Oliver will go with you. You'll deliver a message."

Deliver the poppies, and I'll give her back. Destroy them, and I'll kill her.

I will do no such thing. I won't just send her back. I won't ever kill Persephone.

Desperate times call for desperate lies.

They leave without another word. I follow soon after. Silence expands around me as I go. It's later than I'd normally leave, but fuck, the disastrous news has made me want to tear down all the glass just to hear it shatter.

I might die for this, but I don't think so. Not yet. My supply is almost at nothing, but it's not gone yet. And Demeter won't have burned the poppies. They're her bargaining chip.

As much as Demeter likes to pretend she's in the bridal business, that's only a front. It's always been a front. Her real business is far more lucrative and far more dangerous than bouquets wrapped in white ribbon.

But there's a chance, if she's become so unhinged that she's burning her business to the ground to force my hand…

I can see it now. Demeter with lighter fluid on a dry evening in early summer. Demeter lowering a match to the ground. Flames swallowing the fields whole. Red poppies going up in smoke.

The woman is going to kill me. She'll kill me, and then what will happen to Persephone? If I'm dead, this place slips from my control. Zeus's business is the next domino. We'll all end up under the ground, but it'll be me first.

And then who will protect Persephone?

No one.

My skin feels too tight, my mood too thunderous to be contained in this body. I have been containing it for years. I have been denying myself for years. I have kept everything so close to my chest that my biggest secret is a throbbing dagger through my heart. I can't take a step without feeling it there, lodged in deep. Not a single step. Conor shoves against my legs hard. He wants me the fuck out of here, away from the factory's bright lights. Not even the tinted windows of my office can mitigate them fully.

And it already hurts so much.

There's no way to ease the pain. Not when Demeter's fields burn and Oliver takes the train at top speed to see whether it's my life or someone else's that's rising into the sky like so much ash.

I don't know I've gone to find her until I'm pushing open the door to Persephone's suite. Conor stays in the hall to guard.

The lights are low, but they're on. No sign of her in the bed.

Her dinner tray, with a ruby red pomegranate in a silver dish, sits nearly untouched on a table by the window.

Where the fuck is she?

I don't call her name. She'll learn soon enough that hiding from me like this is not an option. She'll pay for this. I strip off my jacket and let it fall to the floor. If I have to search the entire mountain myself to find her, I will.

She'd better pray I don't have to.

Every sense is jacked up to its maximum sensitivity as I make my way down the narrow hall, shoving open doors as I go. She's not in the bathroom. The shower is dry. She's not in the closet, with her dresses and lingerie. I put many items in here to embarrass her. It's been worth it to see her face every time I scan her hemline.

For a heart-stopping moment, the library looks empty too. Rage squeezes at the muscle in the center of my chest until my blood flows backward. Then her foot, curled up at the edge of the overstuffed chair, catches my attention. She's here. My eyes burn, but not from tears. Never from tears. I don't bother to quiet my footsteps on my way to the side table.

Persephone doesn't stir. She doesn't seem to feel me looming over her, and I breathe in that innocence.

She doesn't know how much I need her. She doesn't know how this choice is eating me alive.

She doesn't know.

For this one final moment, she doesn't know. She's nothing but flowing fabric and bare ankles, a small heap in the chair with a book held tight to her chest. Asleep in the glow of the moon.

She has echoes of Demeter in her face.

I can see Persephone laughing as she burns down the

world. She is already burning down my heart. My want for her is turning me to ash.

I did this. I let this happen. I knew there would be consequences, and now I'm paying them. Something about her makes it impossible to choose. Let her go. Put her in danger. I can't do either one.

My pulse pounds in my ears.

But I make myself wait.

Even now, I make myself wait.

I unbutton the cuffs of my shirt and roll the sleeves up to my elbows. I loosen the top button. I watch her breathing, slow and even.

What does she dream about?

Not this.

"Get up."

Persephone's eyes snap open at the sound of my voice, wide and terrified. The energy in a tight ball at the base of my gut bursts apart, all static and lightning and anger. She doesn't know where she is, and now it's dark. I can see her in the kind of stark detail that makes her panting mouthwatering.

"Does *get up* mean *keep lying there* to you? Get up."

She scrambles to get up, but her arm is asleep or else I've scared her so badly she can't move. "I'm trying." Her cry reverberates off the glass statue on the top bookshelf. "I'm trying."

"Get. Up."

"Why?"

Her gasp blows apart the very last shred of my restraint. It's been weakened by the drumbeat of my own heart in my ears, by the flames in the fields, and having to touch her sweet body and not fuck her for what seems like an eternity.

I haul her up from the seat by her clothes, the seams

ripping in my hands. Into the air. Up until she's level with my face, her lips opening and closing.

"Because I need you," I growl into her mouth, and then I kiss her.

Because I want to.

Because I've waited.

Because last night, when she turned over in my arms and flung herself into me and kissed me like that, it almost killed me.

And I'd rather die this way than any other.

She tastes sweet and clean and soft, and the panicked little noises at the back of her throat drive me wild, wilder, until there's not much man left at all. Do I haul her into my arms, or does she climb up, her legs wrapped around my waist? Does she cry before I yank her head back by the hair and lick up the length of her neck, or is it after? I bite down on her bottom lip until the moment she starts to scream, and then I pull back.

"You didn't eat your dinner."

Persephone is the picture of confusion. "I wasn't hungry."

"Liar." It's nothing to carry her back out to the bedroom, put her on her feet, and bend her over the tray. "You're starving. You just don't know it."

"I was reading." Her voice shakes. "I meant to come finish it."

"When I tell you to finish something, you do it first or you'll suffer the consequences."

A shiver rocks her under my hand, electric, and she murmurs something into the pomegranate.

"I can't hear you."

"Please."

Her voice is a bolt through the room, and that's all it takes. I thought I was undone before. That was nothing compared to now. I force her down onto her knees and reduce her clothing to shreds. Indiscriminate. I want her skin exposed to me now. Her perfect pink nipples are already peaked, her thighs spread—she wants this. Fuck me. She wants it as much as she hates it.

The pomegranate next.

I rip it in two, the halves glistening in my palms, and drop most of it back to the table. Persephone's chest heaves with every breath. She has perfect little tits, a lovely shape, and they'll be even lovelier covered in the juice from the pomegranate.

She doesn't struggle when I take her chin in my hand and tip her head back. She looks up at me with her huge, depthless gaze, lips slightly parted. I work a thumb between her teeth and force them open farther.

"Eat."

It's awkward for her, because I make it awkward. I make it mortifying. I make it awful, and it drives me to the very edge of my own control. One by one, I lift each piece of the fruit to her lips and make her scrape the seeds out with her teeth. After the second section, she tries to lift her hands to wipe the juice away from her chest.

"Put your hands behind your back. Move them again, and I'll put you over my knee and spank you until you can't sit down."

I can see the tremor in her muscles. It's a dead giveaway. She considers disobeying me, but I shove her mouth full of the fruit. Again, and again, and again. Until her mouth is full. Then I make her chew. Swallow.

Again and again.

"You're not leaving," I tell her, and her eyes get wider. "Ever."

I have to get down on one knee to kiss her, to lick some of the juice out of her mouth. A surge of life hits my blood like the world's best painkiller. The ever-present agony in my eyes and my head subsides, at least for the moment.

This time, I can't stop.

I'm exhausted, and I'm wide awake, and reality shears away from what's happening with Persephone. This reality, with her mouth on mine, is the only one that matters.

The floor, the chair, the bed. I can't say how we get to either place, only that it must be me. I'm holding her hands pinned behind her back. I'm kissing her. Scraping my teeth over her nipples. Biting the sensitive skin at the curve of her neck.

I can't stop.

I have to stop.

If I cross that bright line, everything else that matters is going to burn.

Maybe it already has.

But on the off chance it hasn't, I shove her away, onto the pillows. Persephone falls hard, not bothering to put her hands out to catch herself. I'm halfway to the door when she gets herself up.

"Don't go." Her voice is wobbly but clear. "Please, don't go."

"Why not?"

"Because I want you."

TWENTY-TWO

Persephone

HE STOPS. TURNS. LOOKS.

I'm nothing but a throbbing bundle of nerves on the verge of an even more drastic destruction. If he leaves me here now, with every sense on edge, on fire, I'll scream and never stop screaming. I hate him. I want him. I don't want him to hurt.

I need so many dark and twisted things that I can't even fathom how depraved I've become. The necklace he gave me has twisted around and hangs down my back. I can feel it between my shoulder blades.

I am destroyed, and I'm looking at a man coming close to his own destruction.

I felt it in the way he kissed me. I've never met a man like Hades, but I felt it. I've only met a few men in my life, and I've always been ushered quickly away by my mother. There was never time. There was never a chance.

His black eyes catch an available bit of light, making him

look otherworldly, like something out of a dream or a nightmare. He's so beautiful it hurts. He is so flawless it cuts me in some place I didn't know existed. The wanting could turn me inside out all on its own. If I couldn't see him breathing, I would think he wasn't a man at all. Something more. Something darker. Something that could consume me.

Something that already has.

"You don't know what you want."

His words land, one stone after another, connecting with all my softest places. I get up onto my knees on the bed. I'm already naked. There's nothing else he can take from me, except this.

Is it really taking if I give it to him?

Power surges through me like I've taken all the sun's light and pushed it through my fingertips. I never thought I'd have this feeling, not ever in my life. Power. I thought it belonged to my mother, and to Hades. I thought, I thought, I thought. All those things are meaningless now.

"Yes, I do. I want you."

Hades hasn't moved. He's half-turned, the long lines of him illuminated by the lamp on my bedside table. His expression has never been so open to me before, so readable. Hades, the most powerful man I have ever known, is not hiding his pain.

I wait for the door to slam shut between us. For him to turn on his heel and walk away, leaving me here to writhe under the covers all night and into the morning. For the wall he builds every day to close over my knowledge of him like a prison gate, hiding him from me.

"You have no idea." A rough edge to his voice. "You don't know what you're saying. You don't know who I am. You don't know *what* I am."

"Who are you, then? Tell me. Please."

Please. Because I saw you in the mines. I saw you.

Hades turns toward me, and once again I'm struck by how tall he is. How he is cloaked by strength and power. I'm tempting death itself by arguing with him.

Death in a black dress shirt. Death in pants that hug the muscles of his legs like the fabric was grown perfectly formed around his body. Death in his eyes—a warning, a promise. Danger, all wrapped up in expensive cloth.

Danger and pain. One more than the other.

He comes to me. Each step makes my heart beat faster. I raise my chin for him to put his hand around my throat, but his fingertips go to the chain of the necklace instead. He tugs the pendant back to its place, then holds it in his palm.

"How was this made?"

"The necklace?"

"The diamond."

My face heats, but the question isn't particularly mocking. "Diamonds are made from… pressure. Extreme pressure."

A faint smile. "Correct. Pressure I feel in my bones. In my muscles. Pressure that feels like it's crushing my skull. Pressure that hurts so much it blinds me."

"Do you mean…" It's slow to sink in, because what he's telling me is awful. It's worse than migraines. Far worse. "Do you mean that you make the diamonds?"

"The same way you make the flowers grow. Except when you do it, it's graceful and soft. It's warm. There might as well be butterflies around. When I make diamonds, there's only pain. Only thousands of pounds of force." He exhales. "Extreme pressure."

"No," I breathe. Not because I think he's lying. But because I don't want it to be the truth. No one should have to experience that pain. *Pressure that hurts so much it blinds me.*

"The pain is a reaction to the light. If I stay in the light too long, it reaches unbearable levels."

"And then... diamonds?"

Hades meets my eyes. He looks so tired. "And then my body tries to protect itself by offloading the pressure into the ground, where it becomes diamonds. My brain tries to protect itself. The episodes are like seizures. They leave me unconscious. Defenseless. When I was a child, I couldn't control it. I couldn't... direct it."

"But you can now?"

"I can encourage the pressure to go elsewhere, but not indefinitely. Eventually, the pain overwhelms me. Without the painkillers, there's nothing I can do to stop the seizures."

I reach for him.

I can't help it.

This mountain, his home—it's on top of the mines. Filled with diamonds. It takes teams of people to carve them out of the rock.

They're from him. All of them were made by his pain. I can't bear it.

And so I put my hands on the sides of his face. I touch him as carefully as I would touch one of the poppies in my mother's fields.

Hades closes his eyes.

"Is there anything you can do?"

"Nothing stops the episodes. There's nothing to do but wait."

"Is it bad right now?"

He swallows. "Yes. I'm on the edge."

I run the pads of my thumbs over his cheeks, my heart aching. My soul aching. He's suffering, right in front of me, and I don't want it. I don't care whether I should want it, or whether

I shouldn't, or whether I should be glad that this cruel, beautiful man is being crushed from the inside out.

"Let me help you." My voice falls to a whisper. "Please. I need to help you."

His eyes snap open. "I don't want your pity."

"It's not pity."

"You just need to help me." His lip curls, but all that pain is still in his eyes. "What is it? Do you want me to fuck you like a whore?"

My heart absorbs the blow and rejects it, spitting it out like poison. "That's not what you really think." A tear slips out the corner of my eye, and I see how it affects him—see his eyes widen, his lips part. He loves my tears, yes. He needs them. And he feels them. "I know it's not."

"You should be terrified." This, delivered so lightly, his breath on my lips.

"Of what?"

"That it'll work, Persephone. That your sweet little cunt will take away some of the pain. Because if that's the case, I'll never let you go."

"What does it matter? You're keeping me here anyway." I sound desperate, and I am. I don't want him to feel this. If there's anything I can give to make it better, I'll give it. "Why shouldn't I stop you from being in pain, if that's the only solace you can get?"

His face is a firestorm. "You should hate me."

I can't sit with this knowledge about him and do nothing. I can't let him keep living like this. "Because you kidnapped me? Maybe I do hate you for that, but I care for you, too."

"Don't waste your energy. I'll touch you when I please. I'll bend you over when I please. I'll ruin you when I please."

"But you won't." I eke out the words on a breath. Another

crack in his armor, quickly disguised. "You can't get the flowers. That's why you're hurting. And it's my fault. My mother's fault, technically, but you can take your revenge out on me, can't you?"

He's silent for several painful heartbeats.

"It will be the end of you," he says simply. He means it. His face settles into a cautious expression. "It will be the end. No going back."

"We both know you don't care." The words are a knife slipped gently through soft flesh. It's what he's been saying to me all along. Hades glances down at his shirt like I've actually stabbed him. When he lifts his head again, his eyes don't just burn. They blaze.

I'm frozen.

End me, I want to say. *Do it now. Don't suffer another second.*

"You're right." A wicked, twisting smile crosses his face. He reaches for one of the arms of his shirt, shoved up near his elbows. I have never seen forearms like his. Not even from far away. Perversely, I want to lick them. Bite them, the way he's bitten me. "I don't care."

It's comforting, in a way, that he says it before he yanks his sleeves down one by one and strips off his shirt to reveal a pristine black undershirt. His clothes are always so clean.

"You do," I whisper. Too soft for him to hear. He hears it anyway. "You're just in pain."

Hades drops the pendant, takes my face roughly in his hand, and pulls me toward him. He licks the salt from the side of my face and leans in close to scrape his teeth across my bottom lip, stinging. His hand comes down on the table by the bed. A switch. The lights go off, plunging us into darkness. My eyes adjust while I gasp for air.

Moonlight.

It streams gently through the windows, bathing us in white light.

Hades leans down and kisses me again. He says something, silent, against my lips.

I do.

TWENTY-THREE

Persephone

I WANT HIM TO USE ME. HOWEVER HE NEEDS.

It still takes me by surprise when Hades drags me off the bed and stands my feet on the floor. He kicks them apart and shoves me down over the bed, bent over, exposed. My breath comes fast and hard and hot. He catches one wrist in his hand, then the other. A tie slips and slides over my skin. Hades tugs at the bindings he's made, the movement dispassionate.

"Rotate your wrists."

I can do it. Tenderness. Maybe this is because he doesn't want to cut off circulation in my hands, but even this small act of care is proof he feels something. Anything at all. Not that feeling is part of the deal. His emotions are not on the table. They have never been on the table.

But his pain is in the air between us tonight. I can taste it. Hard edges. Extreme pressure.

He stands up behind me and caresses my ass with one wide palm.

I've almost let myself relax into the sensation when he spanks me, once, hard. I lurch up from the bed, crying out, and he pushes me back down like I'm nothing.

Spanks me again.

"I could do this all night."

I believe him. I don't know what I'm being punished for, but it could be any number of things. Falling asleep. Knowing his secret. Wanting to ease his pain. But the more he spanks me, the more I want it.

A stinging heat spreads across my backside.

Ten or fifteen later—I've lost count in the haze—he shoves his fingers between my legs.

"Is it working?" I've been crying again, without knowing it. And I know I didn't do anything. I know this is punishment for the sake of punishment. I also know that my questions wind him up. Coil him tight. I keep my feet firmly planted on the floor even as my thighs tremble. "Does it hurt any less?"

"It's making it easier to fuck you." He adds a few more for good measure, and I gasp every time. "It's making you slick and swollen inside for my cock. Because you love it."

"Only for you. Only when you—"

"I've done things to you that made you so wet you could hardly stand up straight. But I'll give you this one, Persephone. You waited quite a while to beg me to fuck you. You're an angel. Now shut your mouth."

Angel sounds worse than *slut*. *Angel* sounds like a woman who wears only white and sleeps with her hands above the covers, never getting pleasure out of anything. *Angel* sounds like a punishment. You can't be an angel and be anything else. I want him to take my wings.

He spanks me to remind me until my ass burns. It must be red. He can't see how red it is, not in the moonlight, not bound over my bed, and that's one saving grace. Hades rubs at my sore flesh absently. Out of the corner of my eye, I can see him watching me.

"Those tears." He sucks in a breath. "Those, more than anything, make me want to keep you how you are."

He said to shut my mouth, but I can't help myself. "I'll stay this way for you."

Hades pushes thick fingers into me, as deep as he can, before he answers. "Don't make promises you don't intend to keep."

"I promise." One shuddering breath, followed by another. "I mean it."

He curls his fingers, and I am ended.

I don't know what he's touched or where, but he does it again and brings down all the lightning the world has ever seen in one massive bolt at the deep center of me. I can feel myself clenching on the fingers, tighter and tighter. Again. Again. Again. I lose count of how many times I jerk and come because of him. They blur together, one ending, another beginning, peaking constantly until the tears on my cheeks are from being completely overloaded by his hands. By his fingers.

"There's more than one way to punish a woman," he says. Or at least I think he says it. It could be my own brain finally losing its grip on reality. "More than this, Persephone."

I brace for another spanking, but instead I hear a sound I can't immediately place.

Clothes hitting the floor.

His clothes.

I'm bent over the edge of the bed, panting and quaking and only upright by the grace of Hades himself.

I've had too much to turn my head, though I want to see him.

I want to see him, but I don't need to see him. All I need to do is feel him. He touches me, making the first contact. The air around us ignites. He slides his palms down my back, traces a path down my spine. Then he braces them against my hips.

"I'm going to hold you still while I take you." Like he's commenting on the weather. "You weren't hoping for someone to kiss you and wipe away your tears, were you?"

I shake my head.

"Good."

Hades shifts behind me, and I can't for the life of me figure out what he's going to do. It doesn't feel like being fucked, which I'm assuming has something to do with a cock, not—

Not a tongue.

Not a tongue pressing possessively against me.

Licking. Long, broad strokes. My flesh is already swollen and wanting, and his tongue on it sets me on fire as much as his hands do, spreading me even wider. I didn't think it was possible.

It's possible.

He licks and nips in endless strokes that push wave after wave of pleasure over me. Pleasure so intense it aches and stings. A pleasure to meet the pain of his hand on my ass before. I hate him for it. I need him for it. Hate and need hold each other with a tight grip. They show no signs of letting go.

How can he be the one to do this to me? How can I want it so much? The questions loop around and around until they finally drown themselves in pleasure. In pleasure, there are no questions. There are only answers. And the answer is an earth-shattering orgasm that has me bucking against the tie around my wrist. I would be rocking into the side of the bed, but Hades's hands on my waist pin me in place. Just like he promised.

He pushes his tongue inside me, farther than I thought it could go, then pulls back. I howl against the bedding. It's awful. He's awful for stopping. I wanted more, and he could have given it to me.

But he was only preparing me for what's to come.

Which is the thickness of him pressing harshly against my opening. Which are his hands pressing tight against my hips, tight enough to bruise. Which is *say goodbye*. Say goodbye to who I was. I don't have the time to wish the old me farewell before he takes me with one single, powerful thrust.

It barrels through me, pain screaming between my legs— or maybe that's me screaming. He's torn something inside me, he's hurt me, and I know that's what's supposed to happen. I asked him to do this. But I didn't know it would feel like this. I didn't know he would feel so huge. There's not enough room. He can't fit, but he makes himself fit. He's stretching me too far. I'll never be able to take it all.

But I don't have a choice.

I don't want a choice.

He pulls out and drives back inside, inch by inch, and I feel everything. Every ridge, every iron millimeter. My body convulses around him in something like an orgasm, only wretched and tear-filled and bad. It's bad to have this happen to me.

And it's so, so good.

At first all I feel is the pain. Hades doesn't stop for an instant. He doesn't let up. He fucks me hard, like he has always owned me. Like this isn't special. It's just something he does.

It's not special. It's the end of the world.

Thank God, it's the end of the world.

Blood and pleasure mix around him, and slowly, gradually, it doesn't feel quite so sharp and cutting anymore. He might fit. He does fit. It's a near thing. He takes up all the room inside me. He fills me to the hilt, but I'm handling it. I'm managing it.

I'm more than managing it.

I discover that I'm murmuring pleas instead of crying, rocking back against his hands, since I can't move enough to get more of him into me. I'm moving with him. There is no other way to move. He sets the rhythm, he chooses the thrusts, and he is in control of everything.

It sets me free.

He's a vicious lover, never seeming to care what I need. Or maybe he did care, and I got what I was going to get at the beginning. Or maybe he knows me better than I know myself. Because the more he fucks me, the tighter the pleasure winds until finally he's driving into me so hard I can't catch my breath, holding me hard enough to bruise, and I come harder than I ever have.

It's blinding, heart-stopping, unearthly. Who's screaming? Me, or someone else? It doesn't matter. The spiral twists and releases again. I'm dimly aware of him working harder. Faster. And there's a deep, final thrust, a sound from somewhere in the back of his throat, and something hot spilling into me.

"Fuck," he murmurs, and his voice is graveled with relief. It worked.

I made him feel better, if only for a little while.

Opening my eyes seems out of the question.

After a long time, or maybe only a few minutes, Hades works himself out of me. I'm left knock-kneed and panting on the bed. I still don't open my eyes. I'm not going to open them. The tie slides off my wrists, and he moves onto the bed and rolls both wrists one after the other, making sure I can move them. Sometime later he picks me up. Carefully removes my necklace. Water runs in the bathroom, steam kissing my face. I notice for the first time that there's a ledge in the shower wide enough for a man to sit with a woman in his lap.

Soap on a washcloth. His hair, wet in the shower. Eyes carved from the sky and black mountains trace every path along my body, wiping away the sweat and the blood and all the evidence that nothing is the same now. His hands in my hair, working in the shampoo and working it back out again. The sweet scent of conditioner.

A towel so soft I could cry, rubbed in gentle circles over every aching inch of me. He wraps a softer towel around my hair, leaving it on long enough to draw out most of the moisture.

Hades gathers me into his lap.

Runs a wide comb through the tangles.

It's a process, with hair like mine, but he sees it through.

I keep my eyes closed.

If I open them, he'll disappear—I know it. Or I will discover that all of this has brought me back to where I started. I don't want to go back there. I never want to go back. There's nothing there for me. I have this now.

Hades carries me back to the bedroom. He peels back the blankets and deposits me between cool sheets. Tugs up the blankets.

A kiss whispers against my forehead. That's a bridge too far for Hades. It must be a hallucination.

Now I do try to open my eyes. I should ask him whether the kiss was real. Whether any of this was real. But I've kept them closed too long, and now I'm drifting, his body warm next to mine.

I try to get my lips to form words, but they won't cooperate. My only choice is to sink down into the pillow and let go.

Someone pounds at the bedroom door.

Hades curses.

I push myself up in the bed and hold the sheet to my chest. He swipes his clothes off the floor and pulls on pants. A shirt. He yanks the door open to reveal a man out in the hall.

The man has a scar running down his face.

"Make it quick," snaps Hades.

He's still trying to catch his breath. "There's a problem at the farm. With Demeter. She's dying."

TWENTY-FOUR

Persephone

I'M FROZEN IN SHOCK. MY HEART BEATS IN MY EARS. I'M going to be sick.

My mother, dying. I fought to be free of her hold. I know she hasn't been a good mother to me, that she's not entirely sane, but that doesn't mean I want her to die.

"It's a trick," Hades says, his voice grim.

The man with the scar shakes his head, wordless. "He's here. The boy."

Hades strides out of the door. I pull the sheet tight around me and rush to follow him. I half expect him to lock me in, but he doesn't notice. He doesn't notice because the sight in front of us is shocking.

Decker's in Hades's sitting room. Grinning, insouciant Decker who works on my mother's farm. He's been scorched. That's the only word for it. The scent of smoke permeates the air around him. There's soot in his hair and on his face.

The worst part, though, are his hands. They're burned.

They're red and blistering. I've seen that on a small scale, when I've touched my hand to the edge of a boiling pot. But these burns are covering his hands, as if he shoved them directly into a fire.

He's shivering, almost sightless as he stands there.

"Report," Hades snaps.

All this time, Decker's been working for him. All this time.

"She went insane," Decker says, his voice shaking. "She had already burned some of the smaller fields. But by the time we got back to find out which ones, she wanted to burn the entire farm. She went around with a torch, lighting field after field."

A gasp escapes me. I can picture the manic light in her eyes. "No."

Decker's gaze snaps to me before glazing over again. "It got out of control. The fire was faster than her. It caught at her skirt."

She always wore long flowing skirts. I push past Hades and confront Decker. I put my hands on his arms, careful not to touch his scorched hands. "Is she alive?"

"I don't know." Tremors run through him. "She was when I left. The burns… they're everywhere. It took three of us to drag her out of there. I'll never forget the screams."

"I have to see her." I turn to face Hades, to see the refusal stamped on his handsome features. "Please."

He's going to say no. No matter how much I beg or plead, he'll refuse. This will be the perfect revenge on a woman who's caused him pain. She could die tonight, alone, without even her own flower hybrids to dull the pain. She's burned the flowers away.

I would come back to you. I swear.

If I came back for anything, it would be this. The end of her life. Only a monster would stay away. If this is my last chance to see her...

He glares at me, eyes darker than I've ever seen. "Come with me."

I follow him back into the bedroom. Find a spot near the bed. "Please."

"Get dressed," he says.

I don't understand. I feel buried beneath layers of dirt. So much soil it's hard to breathe. My mother is dying. What am I supposed to do?

"I have to see her. I know what she's done to you. I know how she's wronged you, but she's my mother."

He leaves me standing there and goes into the closet. By the time I open my mouth to speak, Hades is already headed back, clothes in his hands. Underthings. A dress. A lightweight shawl to wrap around my arms. Shoes. He knocks the sheet out of my hand and starts pulling the clothes on for me.

"What's happening?"

Hades doesn't look at me. He just guides my legs into my panties and pulls them up with brisk efficiency.

"Hades."

"I'm sending you home."

The sentence feels like frozen earth. Like snow. "What about our contract?"

"You have something else to do right now."

"What about the flowers?"

"I don't know." Pain breaks through in his voice. "I don't fucking know, Persephone. She's burned the fields. There's nothing left. It's a question for another time."

"You're letting me go?"

My dress goes over my head. The shawl around my arms. He puts my shoes in front of me, and I step into them.

Hades wraps his hand around my chin and makes me look into his eyes. "I'm not releasing you from our agreement. You're coming back to me."

It sounds like an order, but underneath, it's a question.

"I'm coming back," I promise, though I shouldn't. I should take the chance to run. To finally find freedom. I ran away from the farm hoping for a new life. And somehow, I found one. It wasn't what I expected to find. It wasn't in New York City. It was here, on this mountain.

He drops his hand. "It's time to go."

I walk with him through the mountain in a daze, holding the shawl tight to my body. Conor follows on Hades's other side, Oliver and Decker behind us. A shell-shocked Decker steps onto the train. He holds his burned hand out to help me up, but Hades pushes it out of the way. There's not enough room for both of us on the steps, so Decker retreats into the train car.

Hades guides me to the top step, and I turn back.

His hands are on my face before I can blink. Before I can move. And then his mouth is on mine. He tastes like kindness and cruelty, he tastes like ice, and I hook my arms around his neck.

I can't get the breath to beg him to come with me.

Hades pulls back. Looks into my eyes. His gaze moves over my face, hard and determined.

The train whistle blows.

"Please," I say.

Hades unhooks my arms from around his neck. "Get on the train. And don't come back."

It starts to move, and I catch myself on the doorframe. "What?"

"Don't come back, Persephone." Pain falls over him like

darkness. "Say your goodbyes to your mother and go. Stay the fuck away from me. Stay free."

And then the train is picking up speed.

"Wait," I shout, but my voice is clouded with tears and confusion. It doesn't make a difference. Nobody hears.

I stumble into the train car and collapse into a seat next to Decker. He puts an arm around me and holds me close. I want to sob, but my lungs feel stiff. My face frozen.

"It's okay," Decker murmurs into my ear. "We'll get you there in time."

"Where is she? In the house? Or still in the fields?"

"She'll be happy to see you."

The train speeds through the night. I stare out the window, numb, looking for familiar landmarks. My eyes are burning by the time I spot my mother's fence.

We'll be stopping soon.

And then…

I'll help her. I'll help her through the burns. Through the pain. I'll help her survive. Do whatever it takes. Or if it's truly too late… at least I'll hold her hand for the end.

I brace myself against the seat. Wait for the hitch of the gears. The metal screech of the train slowing down.

It doesn't happen.

I lean closer to the window. Those are my mother's fields. I know the rises and falls in the earth. I know the fence.

The wooden train platform flashes by. Decker's arm tightens around my shoulders.

"Why didn't we stop?" When he doesn't answer, I turn to him. Cold dread snakes around my ankles like climbing ivy. "Decker. Why didn't we stop?"

Decker's eyes shine. His eyes are too bright. Too wide. He

grins but it looks lopsided and sad. His face is still tense with pain. He shakes his head. "You're not going home, Sepphie."

"What?" My stomach tumbles and falls, left behind on the tracks. "What about my mother?"

"She's fine." He holds up his hands. "I was the only one who got burned."

"Are you serious?"

He looks at me, green eyes colorless in the dark. "She had her men hold my hands to the fire. Literally."

Hope withers like a field of dead flowers. "Tell me where you're taking me. Right now."

"Don't worry, okay? I know she's crazy, but she just wants you to be safe. I have orders to take you where you'll be protected. Somewhere Hades will never find you."

SUMMER
QUEEN

ONE

Persephone

I T WAS A TRICK.

It was all a trick, just like Hades said.

The train moves through the night, and thoughts float in and out of my mind. My body is frozen in place. I can't jump off a moving train. I don't think Decker would let me go. Even with the burns on his hands, he's strong enough to stop me.

I cut a sideways glance at him. He's staring straight ahead, sweat beading at his temple. His hands have to be killing him. I wish there was something I could do. It doesn't make any sense to want it. I know that.

Maybe he's the one who's lying. Maybe my mother did catch fire in the fields.

What happened to him? What made him want to work as… as a double-agent? As some kind of spy? What made him so desperate that he'd work for someone like my mother? If there's one thing that rings true, it's the detail about her holding his hands in the fire.

She would do that.

Decker blinks hard and clears his throat. The burns look bad. He's going to need help.

I feel bad for him. Bewildered. Angry. There's nothing to do but sit here in the dark and feel.

It gets lighter the closer we get to the city. Skyscrapers grow toward the sky. Under the rush of the train, there are hints of other sounds. City sounds. Car horns and sirens and another train's whistle.

My heart beats hard.

I'm so close to freedom. This was supposed to be it, and instead…

I don't know where I'm going. Somewhere safe from Hades.

I don't want to be safe from him, not anymore.

But then… I didn't have a choice.

My body aches as the train rolls into the city and stops. I pull the shawl tighter around my body. The air's cool at night still, and my outfit was chosen in a hurry. It's not for a city like this. It's not for being taken to some safe house against my will.

Decker stands up and opens the door with a soft groan. "Come on, Sepphie. You'll be there soon."

"Where?"

"You'll see."

I want to flinch. To argue with him. To press myself against the wall of the train car and refuse to get out. But that will only delay the inevitable.

I walk out with my head held high and my heart in my throat.

The train platform is mostly dark.

Many places in the mountain were dark, or dim. Here, it's not right. There should be more lights. Decker steps out in front of me and whistles, the sound like one of the birds in the forest by my mother's house.

"Deck, this doesn't seem like a safe place. Maybe it would be better if I got back on the train."

He whips his head toward me. "You're not. Don't make me chase after you, Sepphie. My hands hurt."

I brace to run anyway, but the train's not going anywhere. It won't, I realize. Not until I've been taken from the platform. Fresh panic crawls across my gut like ivy. Decker says this is for my safety, but I don't feel safe right now.

Four men melt out of the shadows.

"I've got her," says Decker.

"Who are they?" Deck starts to step aside, but I catch his fire-scorched sleeve. "Decker, who are they?"

"It's okay," he answers.

The men surround us. They're wearing dark suits, all the same, like security guards.

"Why did you do this?" I whisper.

He blanches. It must be the burns. "I had to get paid."

It seems normal to cry. Appropriate, even. But that only happened on the train and with Hades. A switch has been flipped, and here, on this platform, not a single tear falls. Is it because I'm courageous, or is this shock? Warm air swirls up from the platform, laden with summer humidity.

For a moment, I can breathe. For a moment, there's space between me and the men. It shrinks and shrinks until finally one of them takes my arm.

They've been waiting for this, to see if I was going to fight back. The hand above my elbow makes me nauseated. But what am I going to do? Terror is bitter. Every breath is sharp.

Another man comes alongside me and takes my other arm. Then it's a hustle off the platform, into a building, and out the other side. Into shadow. Into darkness. Each heart-beat is a call to run, run, run. Get out of here. Get free. But my thoughts won't line up in a neat row. Or else they're too neat. It all makes too much sense.

Because Decker had to get paid. My mother had to get me back.

The men move me onto the sidewalk. It's a clear night, and even amid all the tall buildings, the air is alive in a way that it wasn't in the mountain. In the mountain, everything is tightly controlled, from the temperature to the mines. And me.

Even in the middle of the night, there are lights every-where. It would hurt Hades to be here.

If my mother steps out of the shadows, I'll be the one getting hurt.

I can't think about it too much. It'll make me fall apart. It'll make me collapse onto the concrete and sob. I shouldn't want to go back there, but I do. A canary shouldn't want to live in a mine.

Say your goodbyes to your mother and go. Stay the fuck away from me. Stay free.

Hades cared enough to say that. With time running out, he made sure to say it. I want to go back to that man. The very same one who put his hand around my throat and his fingers between my legs and made me come in front of his entire fac-tory floor. I want to go back into the dark, where he hurt me, where he ended me, where he let me live.

He made me give him my secret, and it feels so much lighter now that I'm not carrying it alone.

He gave me his, and it's so much heavier than I realized.

But I'm willing to bear the weight.

There was something in his kiss. There was something dark and wretched and hungry. I wanted it. And he wanted me. There was something pure about that desire. Something broken and lonely and pure.

A big black car comes down the street and pulls up at the curb. The men tighten their hands around my arms like I'm going to make a break for it. Where would I run? There are four of them, plus Decker. There's nowhere to go.

My pulse crawls, then sprints, my heart shaking the bars of its cage. How did it come to this? All I wanted was to be free. All I wanted was to visit those lions outside the library. I'm so close, and I'll never get there.

I only want one person now, and he's not here.

One of the men steps out of the circle and opens the door.

The other two shove me forward. No, no. I twist in their hands, struggling to get purchase on the sidewalk. I was going to cooperate, make it easier on myself, but I can't. I can't. One of them claps a hand over my lips and gives my face a violent shake.

"Not so hard." The voice from inside the car is surprisingly mild. "She's here to be protected, not terrified. And get the boy to the hospital."

The man grunts and lets go of my face. Then they're lifting me. My head goes under the doorframe. They're putting me in the car. This is it. This is the last moment I could have escaped. I squeeze my eyes shut in spite of myself. There's no point in seeing my new jailer.

Is there?

I open them again.

A man sits on the other bench seat in the back of the car, facing me. But he's not looking at me. He's looking down at something in his hand—a phone or a small tablet—and the light from the screen caresses his face.

He's gorgeous.

There's no other way to describe him. Languid and luxurious, in clothes that were undoubtedly made for him. Charcoal pants. A white dress shirt with the collar open. He's unbuttoned in a way that Hades never was, but it's purposeful, calculated. The tiny hairs on the back of my neck stand.

I've read books before, illicit books that describe characters as golden. This man is golden. From the way he fills out the seat, my guess is he's very tall. As tall as Hades. And burnished, like he's spent hours in the sun. His brown eyes have a golden sheen, and his hair looks gold, too. Not blond. A gold sheen, transparent over blond.

I find my voice. No more sitting here in silence. No more. "This isn't what I wanted."

He looks up from his tablet and smiles. Perfect teeth. Glittering eyes. It's the most charming thing I've ever seen, and the second most dangerous.

"You're conscious, then. That's good."

"Who are you?" I am not going to let my voice shake. I'm not a little girl anymore. I might have been when I stepped on that train with Hades, but enough has happened since then to make me a woman. "I don't know what you think you're doing, but I'm not property you can steal."

He considers me, using one finger to flick off the tablet. The light goes away, leaving his gold-dark eyes visible by the lamplight.

"But you *are* property, Persephone. You signed a contract in recent days. Did you not?"

"Anything I sign of my own free will is my business, not yours."

"Your mother would beg to differ."

My mother doesn't have anything to do with this. Or she has everything to do with this. If she'd let me have a life, I wouldn't have had to make plans to escape from her. Either way, I'm not going to discuss her with this stranger.

"You don't know anything about my mother." My palms are slick on my lap. "I'd appreciate it if you'd let me out. Right now."

The man tips his head back and laughs. "Into the city? By yourself? That would be a foolish thing to do, especially when you mean so much to your mother. No. That's not what we agreed on."

"I didn't agree to anything."

He studies me. "That's the crux of the issue, isn't it? You've been stolen once already. To hear your mother tell it, you were terrified. Screaming for help."

"That's not true."

"So you enjoyed yourself on the mountain, then?"

The car pulls away from the curb. My body tenses, getting ready to throw myself at the window, but of course I don't. I'm frozen here in my seat with a man Hades never warned me about. Why would he? He had no reason to think I'd ever be here. I had no reason to think I'd ever be here. We both thought I'd be trapped in the mountain.

He's frowning at me, that man. Studying me. It's the kind of expression that hides more than it shows. The kind of handsome I know instinctively not to trust. Something flickers across his expression, too fast to name. It reminds me of guilt. Or reluctance. It's a crack in his perfect shell, and it's gone in a heartbeat.

A sense of calm comes over me.

It doesn't match the situation at all, so I shake it off.

"What does it matter to you?"

It takes forever to look him in the eye, and another forever for him to smile again. Handsome. Relaxed. If I didn't know better, I'd think he could be kind. A low laugh, easy and warm. It's nothing like the bitter shards of Hades's laugh. If I met a man like this first, I don't know what would have happened. Terms like *better* or *worse* don't seem to apply.

"Caring for someone means they're kept intact. And I have a suspicion that if I examined you, I'd find one small part of you missing. Your hymen."

A lurch, a fall. The floor of the car isn't steady any longer. It's tipping in front of me, shuddering back and forth. Rocky ground. No part of me longs to go back to my mother's fields. Maybe I did when we were speeding past in the train, but now?

"Why did my mother send me to you? Why didn't she come for me herself?"

"Do you want her to be here?" His expression is open when he asks.

No. She's the real danger. She always has been.

Or is it me, for wanting to escape? A sudden ache at the back of my throat and the center of my heart makes me sit up tall, trying to relieve it. If only she had been able to love me, really love me, and not possess me the way she did, none of this would have happened.

"Don't take me back to her. I don't know who you are, but I know you can't be that evil."

He offers his hand with a flourish that makes my heart skip.

I take it, because what other choice do I have?

"How rude of me to neglect our introductions when you'll be staying with me." His other hand taps lightly against his chest. "Everyone calls me Zeus."

TWO

Persephone

ZEUS'S PROPERTY COULD NOT BE MORE DIFFERENT THAN Hades's mountain. Hades's home and his mines and all his other secrets are in a place blasted from black rock shot through with gold. It's night incarnate.

Though the sky is pitch-dark, this building shines. It glows. Enormous windows take up the first floor. Frosted glass allows light out but doesn't let me see in. My heart beats wildly. Zeus's smile hides secrets. I'm sure of that. His building must hide even more.

But he's proud of its façade. Miles and miles of white marble, soaring into the sky. If Hades lives in a fortress, Zeus lives in a castle. A castle transformed into a city block. I wouldn't be surprised if it took up the whole thing.

Zeus extends a hand into the car, a true gentleman. "Come, Persephone."

I look into his face. His expression is neutral. Almost

reassuring. He says terrible things, is amused by terrible things, but right now, when it counts, he's different.

"I don't want to go with you."

"Be that as it may, your mother's asked me to supervise you for the time being."

"I'm twenty. I don't need supervision."

"Agree to disagree."

He keeps holding out his hand for mine until I give in, then helps me out of the car.

My legs shake, weak, which forces me to lean on him. We walk together between two planters of flowers. The blooms remind me of Hades.

Two men wait in sharp uniforms in front of a pair of huge double doors. The doors are a solid white, like the rest of the building. The men step forward and open them for us in a smooth, choreographed motion.

And inside…

It's a party.

Music spills out from a ballroom into the massive lobby, the melody flawless, along with the low hum of people chatting. A woman laughs, the sound contagious, and my mouth twitches reflexively. Suits and gowns are briefly visible in an open doorway on the other side of the lobby, bathed in more warm light. Near the door into the ballroom, a man at the other end of the room leans over a woman on an antique sofa. He kisses the hollow of her neck. She tips her head back to give him better access, and I think of inching my thighs apart for Hades in the black of the bedroom he gave to me. How did this get so out of control? How did I never see all the ties between the people I knew? They were there all along, and I was oblivious.

Zeus repositions his arm and my hand, and now he's escorting me in. Hot shame trickles down my back. I look completely foolish. The women in here are in short gowns with plunging necklines, fabric that shines in the light, and I'm wearing a simple black dress and a shawl.

We go into the ballroom.

A four-piece band plays in the corner. A woman with a violin is the centerpiece, and the music threads itself through my heart. It's nothing like the folk songs my mother insisted were the only things worth listening to. Sensual. That's what it is. It's sensual and upbeat, and the violinist seems lost in it.

"Zeus, you're missing the party." A woman with bright red lipstick approaches and extends her hand. Zeus bends over it and kisses her knuckles. She leans in and whispers in his ear, and he nods, murmuring something back. What is he doing? Is this really a thing people do? Maybe if you're as gorgeous as this woman is, with her dark hair in a shining wave and her dress showing off every curve of her body. Her eyes turn on me, and I'm swept away in another flush of embarrassment. Her hand drops down to my face, and she traces underneath my chin. "Did you bring us a new plaything?"

Zeus laughs easily, but his arm tightens to his side, taking me along with it. "Not a plaything. My guest. Be nice to her, Reya."

"Can't we play with her while she's a guest?"

He gently removes her hand from my face. "No."

The conversation feels scripted. Like they already know all the words. Like this is for the benefit of everyone else in the ballroom, not Zeus and this woman—Reya.

"Why not?" Reya pouts, her cherry lipstick perfect. "They enjoy fresh meat. If I'm honest, so do I."

Zeus catches her wrist in his hand and brushes his lips against the fine bone there. "Shouldn't you be playing elsewhere? You have a lot of admirers here tonight."

"They tip better if they're jealous." She winks at Zeus and

turns away, hips swaying with every step. The back of her dress plunges so low it takes my breath away. One wrong move and she'd be completely exposed. Maybe that's the point of it. I follow her path through the couples leaning breathlessly into each other and waiters with trays balanced carefully on their hands, the single women in tight black dresses and bright jewel tones, men on the prowl.

"What is this place?"

Zeus glances down at me. "My business."

"Your business is throwing parties?"

A smile quirks the corner of his mouth. "You could think of it that way."

I don't want to think of it. I want to know. The evidence is right here in front of me, but my brain can't connect the dots. Frustration rises, hot and choking. Anything for the cool of Hades's mountain.

But Zeus leads me farther into the warmth of the room. I feel his attention shift away, though he keeps me close. He's scanning the space, his expression easy but his eyes calculating. Searching.

The mood in the room changes, ever so slightly. It settles. Calms a bit.

Another woman comes close, a drink in her hand, the alcohol amber in the light. She hands it to Zeus, and he leans down to accept it.

"—you okay?" If I weren't so close, I wouldn't believe he'd said the words. The question sounds genuine. I can't hear her answer. It's too quick. Too quiet. "Which client?"

Zeus looks over her head, in the direction she came from. He straightens up.

"Upstairs. Now." He gives the command loud enough for

the nearest people to hear. "I don't want to see you down here again."

She looks relieved as she slips past us and goes out.

Zeus continues through the room, and I steal enough sidelong glances at him to learn that his smile never drops. People see it and react to it like they're bathing in sunlight itself. Everyone does. Men and women both. They all smile back at him.

"This is only the beginning of the party," Zeus says. "It continues throughout the building. Into the back. Into the bedrooms."

The ballroom has low tables tucked into alcoves, each one with its own overstuffed booth. Light glitters at the edges of shadows. The couples here are eating, drinking, leaning close to talk. *Did you bring us a new plaything?* What did Reya mean? And what else was she telling him? The girl with the drink—

A new wave of fear tightens around my ribs and squeezes, making it hard to breathe. Zeus brings people here to become playthings. It must be common enough for that woman to make an assumption. He could drop me at any one of these tables, any one of these couches, and then what? Would the men without a woman circle around me?

What is Zeus's business?

"It's not really a party." I chance saying it, because impending doom is creeping in with every step we take. There is an end to this stroll we're on. There has to be.

"Of course it is. Don't you see all these people enjoying themselves?"

A couple cuts in front of us then, the man growling, the woman laughing. He has his hands tight around her waist, so tight that her dress is hiking up. It could be above her thighs soon. Nobody seems to notice or care that he's practically stripping her down.

Nobody seemed to care when Hades pinned me to him and finger-fucked me in front of all his workers.

"I'm not supposed to be watching this."

Zeus stops and takes my face gently in his hand, turning it up so that I have to look into his eyes. Gold, all through his eyes.

"No. You need to see this. I want you to understand where you are. You're here as a favor to your mother, but you're also here for you."

Tears spring up in the corners of my eyes. This is not a gift, no matter how convincing he sounds when he says it. I don't let the tears fall. I won't.

"There's nothing here for you."

He turns my face away. Zeus has a soft touch.

"Look." I close my eyes. "No. Look." His grip tightens, and there it is, that familial resemblance. My heart skips. A soft touch doesn't mean he's less dangerous. A soft touch could mean he's far worse. A man with gentle hands in public doesn't have to be the same behind closed doors.

I don't want to risk what might happen behind closed doors, so I look.

"There. See? Nothing so bad as all that." Zeus guides my head so my eyes have a moment to linger on every booth, every sofa, every chair. All of them are occupied by at least two people. A man with a woman. Two men together. Two women together. A man with two women. Their hands glide along each other's bodies. The women laugh, low and lovely. "You were right on one count."

Zeus smells good—fresh and clean, like someone you'd want to be close to. It's distracting in a number of horrible ways. I tamp down the instinct to ask him how I was right.

"It's not a party," Zeus admits. "It's supposed to be like one for the clients. I don't like an atmosphere of secrecy. My clients shouldn't get the impression that their pleasure is a dirty thing. The federal government says it is, but who listens to them?" He laughs, and the sound blends in with the music and the chatter. There are other sounds too—the background music for all the rest. A breath catching. A soft, needy moan, almost a whine. The word *please*.

Money is being made here. Even the sound is expensive.

All of it flows to Zeus. That's what it means to own something. But he can't be the only one providing services, because he has his hand on my jaw, and nobody would pay to see that. Nobody would pay *just* to see that. I'm certain of it. And it can't only be that the servers are making money, because a dinner club would be for dinner. It wouldn't involve so much whispering and stroking and…

Oh.

"Ah," Zeus says. "You understand now."

"The clients are the men?"

He moves my head a quarter-turn. "Not all of them."

In the last booth on the right, a woman in a flowing black jumpsuit, her hair pulled back away from her face in an indestructible chignon, leans into the lady with the cherry lipstick. The jumpsuited woman strokes a hand through the other's hair. The intensity in their faces doesn't feel like a purchase. But that's what it must be. Red lips purse and pout and then, with a turn of her head, she suggests going somewhere else. The two of them stand up and move quickly toward a hallway at the back of the room.

"You sell women to your clients?"

Zeus puts a finger on my lips. "No, Persephone. They sell themselves."

After a quick circuit of the party, Zeus takes me to the back of a hallway off the ballroom. There's an elevator here. He produces a card from his pocket and slips it into a slot on the wall. The silvery panel opens. A private elevator.

Why would I need to see a place where women are bought and sold? What could that teach me that I don't already know? I've already given myself away.

I don't want to do it again. Not for those men in the ballroom.

Only Hades. Which I know is wrong. Hades has rough hands, and the things he did to me were worse than anything happening in that lounge.

And I begged for them.

But no. I'm supposed to be safe here. Safer than I was on the mountain.

Zeus's elevator lets us out into a wide hallway with plush carpet, all of it bathed in bright lights. Hades would hate it. It would hurt him badly. Tables line the edges of the hall, each with a big bouquet of flowers. It must be meant to look like a hotel, a high-end place. But it's not. I remind myself again and again. That's not what this is. It's not what it seems to be.

He stops at the second-to-last door on the left and opens it.

"For you." Zeus gestures me in.

As far as prisons go, it's lovely. A big bed with plush white sheets. A lamp glowing on the bedside table. Through one open door, there's a bathroom with an oversized tub. A chair by the wide window. A view of the city.

A view of the mountain.

It's far off in the distance, but even from here, it seems to take up the whole horizon. The sight of it pierces my heart. Why? I'm finally in the city, but I can't make this latest development turn into a new plan. None of my old plans mean anything now.

"I have to go downstairs." Now Zeus is all business. "There are clothes for you in the closet. You'll be comfortable here, and safe. No one will disturb you."

He turns to go.

"Why would you do this to him? What did Hades do to you?"

He blinks. "I'm not concerned with his feelings on the subject. I'm concerned with you. He sent me a copy of your contract. Did you know?"

I refuse to be embarrassed. "No. But you should have taken that as proof. I signed it. I wanted to be there."

"It looked to me like you were coerced. What your mother described—"

"My mother lied to you. Hades didn't take me from the house. I didn't scream and cry. You're not doing this for me. You can tell yourself that, but you're not. I'll always hate you for it."

Zeus winks, becoming the charmer all over again. "We'll see."

"That's all you're going to say?"

"I have business. We'll talk tomorrow. It's late, Persephone. Get some rest."

He closes the door behind him, and I can't help myself. I run for it, keeping my feet light and silent on the carpet. My hand meets the cool metal of the handle, a flare of hope…

It's locked.

He's locked me in.

You'll be comfortable here.

I'm going out of my mind, out of my soul. I don't know why my mother thought this would be better than having Decker bring me home. I'd rather be on the mountain.

If I was there, I could ask Hades what he was thinking when he told me not to come back.

I have to believe it's because he cares about me. But another thought sprouts. Maybe he was done. Maybe he regretted telling me his secret. Maybe it doesn't matter, now that the poppies are burned.

I want him. I want the man who took me from the fields and the man who insisted I leave him behind. They're both parts of the same person, and he's hidden from me now. Kept forcibly away.

They *tricked* me.

The worst part? I can't help him from here. I can't get the seeds, or the flowers. There's no earth to make them grow even if I had the seeds and the plants.

Zeus must be like my mother. That's the only explanation for why he'd help her. I thought he might be different, because he *seems* different. It's an illusion like everything else in this place.

He talks about Hades like he knows him. He talks about my mother like he knows her, too. It stands to reason that he knows about the flowers.

My chest aches. Is that what this is about? Taking me away from the mountain to torture Hades?

I try the door again. Still locked.

It's late, but I can't bring myself to lie down in bed. Instead, I fill up the enormous bathtub and climb in while the water's still hot. The burn is a pleasant pain, and I let it touch every inch of me, every wanting inch of me. Because even locked up with Zeus's prostitutes, even without a hope in the world, one awful thing is still true.

I want Hades with me.

THREE

Persephone

I FALL ASLEEP LATE, WET HAIR SPLAYED ON THE PILLOW, TO the muted sounds of people fucking on either side of me. Thick walls, I think, but not thick enough to block the noise. Moans and cries sink into my dreams. My dreams become the soul-searing night that Hades ruined me.

I wake up the next morning with aching thighs from pressing them together in my sleep.

In the bright sunlight, I try the door and every window.

I run my fingers along the crown molding, as if a secret latch will appear.

One of the heavy chairs would probably break the window if I managed to throw it, but that would draw everyone's attention. It would also be a two-story drop down to the concrete. I want to escape, not die.

After an hour, I give up and slump on the bed again.

Nobody disturbed me last night. Only my dreams.

But someone will be coming soon. I'm already questioning

whether that person will be Hades. It was so terrible and intense and real with him, but it could have been a dream too.

This could all be a nightmare.

I put on the clothes I came here in. They're still clean, and Hades chose them for me.

I wish I had the necklace, too. He took it off before he washed my hair. I didn't own it for very long, but I miss it like it's part of him.

It is, I guess.

I'm working at my curls, thinking, when a knock sounds at the door.

Zeus stands in the hallway in a fresh suit, a tray in his hands. "Sleep well?"

"No."

He comes in and pushes the door shut with his foot. Then he goes across the room and puts the tray on a small table by the window. Gestures for me to sit down.

Very gentlemanly.

I take my seat, and he sits across from me. There's coffee, at last.

And even if he's awful, Zeus has some of the answers I need.

"You still haven't explained yourself," I say, tipping a packet of sugar into the coffee. "It would be great if you would tell me why you're keeping me prisoner."

"This is only a temporary arrangement."

Anger stirs like a poisoned flower. "Temporary or not, I'm locked inside this room."

"For your protection." Zeus looks sincere, his handsome expression concerned. I could almost imagine him as a regular man, some billionaire playboy—not the owner of a brothel. "I couldn't risk you wandering around without security. I go to great lengths to keep my clients in line, but I needed to be sure no harm would come to you. Not after everything you've been through."

"And how is this protecting me? You basically kidnapped me."

"I *saved* you."

"I didn't want to leave the mountain."

Zeus sighs. "Stockholm syndrome. A nasty business."

I glare at him. "It isn't Stockholm syndrome."

"Oh? So Hades didn't kidnap you and use you for sex?"

My cheeks turn warm. I can't quite hold his gaze.

"And you didn't learn to rely on him for food and shelter? That reliance didn't lead to intimacy and even affection? You didn't learn to care for your captor?"

"You're an asshole."

"And you're a victim. It's your mother's job to protect you, even from yourself."

"Does my mother pay you? Hades can pay you more."

"I don't need money," he says, gesturing meaningfully to the expansive room and exquisite furniture. "And I especially don't need it from Hades."

"You hate him," I say, watching the way his expression flickers.

"Hate? Yes. And other things. It's complicated. I suppose it's always complicated with brothers."

The meaning sinks in at the same moment hot coffee hits my lips. I inhale it and scramble for a napkin. Oh my God. Oh my *God*. "Your *brother*?"

Zeus's eyes go wide. "You didn't know," he marvels. "My sister didn't tell you?"

His *sister*. "My mother didn't say she had brothers. She never said she had a family."

I don't see how he and Hades could be brothers. I don't see how my mother could be his sister.

Zeus shakes his head in disbelief. "Hades said nothing?"

"He didn't discuss his relatives." An old instinct for honesty stabs me in the back. I tried for scorn and missed by a mile. My thoughts race, chasing each other, tangling up together until it's impossible to tell one from another. Hades's brother?

I can't imagine him having a brother, or parents. Maybe he would have told me about them if there had been time. There wasn't time. Or he didn't want me to know.

I hold it together through sheer force of will.

"What did you discuss, if not family ties?"

Punishments. The things I would moan and scream for. The way he would ruin me. The way he did. I discussed things with his mouth and his fingers. His cock. "That's none of your business."

Zeus *tsks*. "I'm sure your mother won't be pleased to hear you had… discussions with Hades. I suppose it was too much to expect restraint from him."

"Why are you doing this?" My mind can't work around the new information. "Why do you care what happens to me?"

"Because my sister asked me to care. She requested my involvement out of concern for your well-being. If I let you walk out this door, you'd go right back to the mountain. And even if you didn't, if you went back to the farm, Hades would find you. You're safe here."

"But *I* didn't ask for your help. I don't want it. Not from you, and not from my mother."

He furrows his brow. "I know my brother. I know what he's like."

"Which is what, exactly?"

"Fierce. Angry. Ungrateful. He never wanted me to save his life."

"Why would you need to save his life?"

"Our childhood wasn't... good. It was cold and violent and harsh. That's the soil that Hades grew out of, and you know about flowers, don't you? You know what happens to a seed in bad soil."

It doesn't grow. Or if it does, it becomes stunted. Twisted. "That means you're the same way."

"Of course. We aren't related by blood, obviously. We were foster children. All three of us. Me, Hades, and Poseidon. The man who took us into his home had one child. A daughter."

"My mother," I whisper, my stomach in knots, the air thin in my lungs.

"She only wants to protect you."

I stare at him. "We're on the second floor of a whorehouse."

"Well, yes. It's my family legacy. My foster father owned it before me."

"Didn't you ever think of doing anything else?"

"Of course not." An unnamable expression flashes through Zeus's eyes. "This is what I was born to do."

Through my shock, I feel a green shoot of sorrow for him. A whorehouse. His family legacy. In a sick way, it's my family legacy, too. His foster father would be my grandfather, though I never met him. My mother never mentioned her father. "How can you be happy here?"

Another megawatt smile. "It's a living. There's room for you, if you want. You could work the floor with the other girls. Put on a pretty dress and a pretty smile, and—"

"No," I snap. "I don't want to do that."

"Then you don't have to," he says gently, with an air of

satisfaction, as if he's proving a point. "It's an option available to you. All the women here choose to be here."

"I don't believe you."

"That doesn't make it any less true."

I put down the coffee with shaking hands. My skin goes hot, then cold. The situation is beyond anything I imagined. It's far beyond. "This is just as bad as Hades kidnapping me. It's the same thing."

"No, it isn't. Because I'm not going to have sex with you."

"You're awful."

"Then again, maybe you're sad about that. Maybe he won you over with orgasms. From what your mother says, you were a naïve virgin when he plucked you from the farm. A few climaxes, and you were ready to become his sex slave for life."

"I really don't understand where you get off acting morally superior."

He laughs. "It's called irony."

"It's called being a shitty brother. You're hurting him for the fun of it."

Zeus arches an eyebrow. "If Hades told you that I was responsible for—"

"He didn't say anything about you. But now I think that's because you hurt him. That's why he has pain that won't go away. That's why he needs the flowers."

His expression sobers. "I didn't hurt him. At least not the way he wanted. I made him stay alive, and I'm not sure he's ever forgiven me for that."

"But his eyes—"

Zeus glances out the window, then back at me. "Every doctor I've spoken with said the condition is hereditary. There's no cure. Though I don't think it would have mattered. Cronos preferred to leverage it for his own purposes."

The way he says *Cronos* sounds like a curse.

"What purposes?"

He leans his head on his hand and watches me. "Our father discovered the side effect of Hades's light sensitivity early on. He made a frequent habit of dragging him out into the sun to force an attack."

Horror climbs up my spine. "No."

"Then he could pluck diamonds right out of the ground, like flowers." Zeus's expression is still mild, but his eyes are dark. "By the time we were adults—well. You can guess by the size of the diamonds."

I blink back tears. "What about you?"

Zeus straightens up in his chair. "Unfortunately, my asshole father was less of an asshole to me. He brought me to work with him at the whorehouse. Taught me to run the family business."

That was *not* all. I can tell, just from looking at Zeus.

A man who would force a child to be in pain like that, who would force a child to have seizures...

He might not have been as awful to Zeus, but there's no way it was that simple.

It makes me wonder about my mother.

Did Cronos also hurt her? Is that why she was so obsessively protective of me? "So when you say you saved Hades, you were serious?"

"Someone had to keep him alive. Demeter was always in her greenhouse, fucking around with plants. Poseidon was in no position to intervene. You won't know anything about him, of course, because Hades kept us a secret. You're not likely to meet Poseidon. He spends all his time at sea."

"And you spend all your time here."

Zeus's smile snaps back into place. "Where else would I go?"

Nowhere, I think. But there's somewhere I could be. "Did you tell Hades I was here?"

"No, of course not. I wanted to talk to you first. Find out what he did to you."

"You've done that. Now you can let me go." I lift my chin. "This is obviously not about my safety. If it was, you'd listen to my wishes. I'm wondering if you aren't jealous of your brother. Maybe you didn't want him to have something you couldn't get for yourself."

Zeus bursts out laughing, and if he weren't my captor, it would be the most intoxicating sound in the world. He laughs like nothing has ever gone wrong in his life. He has a beautiful, melodic laugh. He throws his head back, and it's like he's been kissed by the sun. It can't be real.

Underneath that laugh is pure hurt. As different from Hades as their two houses.

"Jealous? Of his sad little life, all holed up in his mountain? No, I'm not jealous. Who could be?" He sounds almost empathetic. His laughter settles, tapering off. Zeus clears his throat. "You'll have to excuse me. That's the funniest thing I've ever heard. Our mutual business arrangement is all I want from him."

"Do you pay your women in diamonds, then?" I cross my arms over my chest. If Zeus does that, he's worse than I thought.

"Aren't you a clever one?" Zeus presses a fingertip to my nose, and my entire body recoils. "No, I pay my employees in cash. Diamonds would be cumbersome for them. Less so for me." He sighs. "Our government, in all its wisdom, frowns upon businesses like mine. I'm shocked that your mother didn't explain this to you. She uses Hades in much the same way."

"So things will be heated when he comes to get me."

"Are you certain he can?"

That, more than anything else Zeus has said, makes the

floor feel unsteady beneath my feet. I can't imagine my mother striking a deal with Hades, and I can't imagine Hades being dissuaded from anything. What if they've done something to him? What if he never gets the flowers? I hate to think of him in pain.

"It's clear you care about him," Zeus says, his voice gentle now. He holds something out to me. It's a phone, pulled up to a photograph. "But you can't see him clearly right now. He's using you."

I don't want to take whatever he's holding.

He brings it closer.

Morbid curiosity has me taking the phone. There's a handwritten note. *Deliver the poppies, and I'll give her back. Destroy them, and I'll kill her.*

I recognize the signature. *Hades.*

He threatened to kill me. Even when I signed his contract, when I obeyed his commands. When I climaxed around his cock. He still threatened to kill me.

"This could be forged," I say, my throat tight.

He looks at me with an expression of sympathy. "Persephone."

I want to scream. Maybe it was Stockholm syndrome. Or maybe I'm simply going insane. "Is there something else you came up here for?"

Zeus smiles. "Only to tell you that you'll be coming downstairs this evening."

To the party. To all those men, scenting all those women. A thin line of sweat breaks out underneath my hairline. "I'm not coming to your party."

"Oh, you are." Zeus goes down the hall with a long, graceful stride. He turns his head halfway down. "You're the guest of honor."

FOUR

Persephone

PANIC RAGES IN MY CHEST. IT'S A STORM I CAN'T CALM, one that touches every part of me. My lips go numb. My hands go cold. My chest tight.

Guest of honor? No, no, no. I can only imagine what that means. How is this nightmare coming true? Once, I read in a book that we spend all our time worrying about the things that never happen. The real problems are the ones that take us by surprise. I never worried I'd be a prisoner in a whorehouse.

If Zeus thinks this is a favor, it's not.

He's been gone for an hour and my heart hasn't slowed.

Another knock on the door sends me lurching for it without thinking. If it's Zeus again, I'll run.

It's not Zeus.

The woman who wore red lipstick—Reya—stands in the hallway, a metallic case in her hands. I look like a wild thing with half-brushed hair and a prostitute's dress. She looks as elegant as she did last night, with a more muted lipstick and a

comfortable outfit. I'd kill for those leggings. I want her flowing top. When she sees me, her face falls.

"Oh no. You look so sad. Are you all right?"

I shake my head, once, twice. I can't seem to stop. The conversation with Zeus bangs around in my head along with everything else. The note. The thread. How could he?

"Come here, honey. Sit down."

She guides me to a chair by the window and presses me into it. Brings me a glass of water. Makes me drink. Then she crouches down in front of me and looks me in the eye.

"I'm Aurelia, but everybody calls me Reya. You probably heard him say it." Her smile is as warm as Zeus's, but it strikes me as completely genuine. "I'm sorry if I upset you last night. I thought you were another girl joining the ranks." *Plaything.* That's what she called me. "The clients pay more for fresh blood."

"I'm not fresh blood," I say numbly. "I didn't want to come here."

She purses her lips in a gorgeous frown. "Life gets hard out there. I know. Trust me, we all do. Thank goodness we have Zeus. Anything I can do to help."

"Thank goodness?" She's joking. Has to be. Reya's making it sound like this place is a refuge. There's no way it can be. Women are sold here. It's just dressed up in silk and satin. "You think of him as—" I'm lost for words. "You're really grateful to him?"

"Of course." I think she means it. "He's not always nice, but there are many good things about him."

"I—"

"This is the only place in the city where a woman can refuse a client. Did you know that?"

"No. I barely know anything about him." I put my fingertips to my lips to stop more words from coming out. I'm not sure what Zeus has told her, but I'm not going to blurt out all these things I don't understand. I've already been foolish enough. "I don't want to know, anyway. I won't be here much longer."

"You'll be here tonight, though." She pats my hand and smiles. "Zeus thought you might want some help getting ready. I always like to do it early in case I make any mistakes."

"This early?" The thought of sitting around, dressed up and waiting for Zeus for the rest of the day, makes me vaguely nauseous. There's also a nagging memory of what getting ready meant when I first arrived at the mountain. "How long is this going to take?"

Reya cocks her head to the side and grins. "A few hours, when you account for a late lunch." A knock at the door punctuates her smile and makes it even brighter. "Speaking of, there it is."

I swear I'm not hungry, but as soon as she opens the door and pulls a tray inside, I discover I'm ravenous.

Reya and I linger over lunch. She is the first person in years to treat me like a normal person would. Except she's not a normal person, and this isn't a normal situation. It's not normal to sit in a castle whorehouse eating BLTs with a prostitute. Still. I put the food in my mouth and eat it, and it dampens the raw hunger and anxiety. Food has a way of doing that.

By the time we're finished with our second course—tea and cookies, for some unknown reason—the sun has wheeled overhead into the afternoon. Reya brushes the cookie crumbs from her hands and stands up from the edge of the bed. She retrieves her metal case and drums her fingernails on it, an impish light in her eyes.

"Prepare yourself. I'm going to make you look good."

Every swipe of makeup makes me more nervous until, at the very end, Reya has to unhook my nails from the arms of the chair. "All done, sweet pea." She steps back and surveys her work. "Zeus will be pleased."

She pulls another dress out of the wardrobe and helps me step into it, fastening the zipper behind my back. This one at least reaches the floor, but I can tell from the air shifting in the room that it's got a low back.

"Is that a good thing?" I swallow hard. "I don't know why I'm asking. It doesn't matter what he thinks. I don't even know why he wants me at this party."

She laughs. "To show you off. Or to show you a good time."

"I don't need a good time."

"You might have one anyway," Reya says with a wink, and then she leaves to get her dress.

The train comes back into focus in my mind. It runs from Hades's mountain to my mother's fields to the city. It's a lifeline. It's a knot, tied tight around the three of them. But knots can always be undone if you pull the right cord.

Zeus is trying to tighten it.

I have to get out of here.

The window isn't an option, and when I try the door, it doesn't open. Please, I think wildly. Someone come get me. Someone come save me.

My prayer is answered a moment later. The door opens from the outside, and Reya sweeps in, a goddess in deep blue. How can she just unlock the door like that? Is it freedom she had to earn by pleasing Zeus? The thought sends another quake through me, through the floor, through the world. I do not want to go down to Zeus's party.

It's a bad idea. A very, very bad idea.

Reya doesn't give me any choice. She hooks her arm through mine and pulls me along with her. We're headed down the long hall, and toward a set of stairs. We're headed for God knows what.

She pats at her hair and puts on a big smile. "Time to make our entrance."

FIVE

Hades

THE VISE AROUND MY TEMPLES IS MADE FROM BONE AND diamonds.

Everything I've ever done puts the force of itself around my eye sockets and the back of my head, drilling in deep. If I could be in the dark, I would.

But fuck if I'll abandon my business now.

The business is all I have left. I sent Persephone away, and I've heard nothing.

Not a fucking word.

It should be a welcome sign that things have returned to the status quo. They have not. Demeter hasn't sent any more poppies. She hasn't sent anything. Perhaps she's dead.

Or perhaps she's recovered and still waging war.

I've been standing at my desk for minutes or hours. An eternity. At some point I considered sitting. Fuck that. I am not a superstitious man. I don't have time in my life for mysticism

and wonder at the workings of the universe. Yet a gnawing at the pit of my gut warns me away from taking a seat.

It would feel like giving up. I'm already sick with worry. I won't admit to feeling fear out loud, but I feel it. All the way to the tips of my fingers.

Conor pads close and nudges my leg with his nose. He'd like me to leave the office. Find somewhere dark. I've tried. In Persephone's absence, I can't lie still.

I have no business knowing where she is. I'm the one who told her not to return.

There's no telling what the fuck I was thinking.

All those tears in her gray eyes did something to me. She wanted freedom so badly. And if I had to suffer through watching her leave, why not make it mean something? Why not make her happy?

This is what happens when something good throws herself into my life.

This is what always happens.

I wanted her, I needed her, and the world took her away.

I knew this would happen. I've known since my father killed the first dog I allowed myself to love. The first one I kept for myself. I knew Persephone would be taken from me.

Everything I want always is.

The thought filters down through the pain circling my skull. Not for the first time, I consider taking one of the remaining painkillers. I hate this unease. The unsettled thoughts, searching for an answer. I can't stop hoping for more poppies to appear.

I can't stop hoping for Persephone to appear.

It was supposed to be simple. Fuck her and fuck her and fuck her, until I had drained every ounce of desire out of her sweet body.

And if her presence helps pry the poppies from her mother's hands, so much the better.

That won't be happening now, of course. I can't even wage an attack on the farm, not when I'm worried Persephone would get hurt in the process.

More pain taps at the back of my mind. It's a steady beat, like a dripping faucet. There can be a certain pleasure in feeling it. An extravagant one, if Persephone is any indication.

Not for me.

The miners will have to work overtime to deal with it. I'll have more money. More and more and more until I'm nothing but an empty skull. My bank accounts will be filled to overflowing.

A cold comfort.

This is unlivable.

It hurts to bring my own reflection into focus in the windows of my office. It's an image of a haunted man.

My heart drives blood through my veins in a violent drumbeat. Deny it. Deny it. I let her go.

I have torn rooms apart. I have torn people apart. But I couldn't tear apart my own desire for Persephone without killing myself in the process.

Maybe I tore her apart, too.

Sick worry explodes in my gut, a landmine made of bile and rage. Where the fuck is she? If Demeter has her, she should send me what she owes. If Demeter has her, I'll go and take her back.

If she's lost to the city…

My fist hits my desk with shattering force.

The surface holds.

Oliver steps into the office, and I yank on a mask of composure.

He's followed by the farm boy. They both come to stand on the opposite side of my desk. Conor growls at the farm boy. He's never liked him. Neither have I, but good, honest men can't be bribed to give information.

I look the farm boy in the eyes. "Is Demeter dead?"

He glances down and away from me. I want to put my hand around his jaw and crush him. I want to force him to speak. He opens his mouth after another eternity. "No."

"And the fields?"

"I don't know."

"What the fuck do you mean, you don't know? If she's alive, is she replanting?"

"I don't know." His face is slightly pale, I see now. I didn't care before. "She's lost it. She's got the whole place on lockdown. Nobody's allowed to leave. There are guards at the summer houses. I had to sneak out with one of the shipments."

"Locked down because she has the girl?"

"Persephone's not there."

My mind compresses. The flesh. The skull. The pressure is so intense that my vision goes black. Electricity burns through the synapses. I feel the frantic biological struggle to get it out of my body. A corner of the desk crumples under my palm. It hits the floor with a much-reduced *clink*. No wood left. Only a diamond fragment.

I knew this was a possibility. I told her to be free. The reality is more painful than I anticipated. My desk is all fucked up now.

"Where is she?"

Decker hesitates.

I force my eyes open. Pain splinters through my head. Carves.

He's drawn his body back, putting more space between

us. He instinctively shields his burned, ruined hands, curling them under his arms, hiding the weakest part of him.

And I can see in his face that he knows.

"*Where*?"

"Demeter sent her to the city. She doesn't think the fields are safe enough. She wanted Persephone out of the way in case you retaliated."

"Decker." He flinches at the sound of his name. The farm boy's bravado has all but disappeared. "What about the fire?"

He's shaking now, unable to hide it. "She made me do it. Five of her men. It took five of them to hold my hands to the fire. I screamed. I passed out. And then she sent me here."

"Is she at Olympus?"

"No."

He's lying.

He is fucking *lying*.

I can hear it, but I'm in too much pain to determine why. "Get out."

Decker opens his mouth.

"Get *out*."

"Should I—"

"Come back at the usual time," I snap. "Oliver, pay him and get him the fuck out of here."

Decker says something to Oliver on the way out. I don't know what it is. I don't care. I'm only listening for the sound of my office door closing. The moment it does, I dig a small pill case from my pocket, take one out, and swallow it dry.

Persephone.

With *Zeus*.

At that goddamn whorehouse.

No.

I cover my face with my hands. It's not my proudest

moment in the office. Oliver will no doubt stand outside the door until I've managed to stave off this episode.

It's a near thing. A very near thing. I'm right on the edge.

A few minutes away from seizing at my desk.

I concentrate on the ground. Deep rock. Below the mine shafts.

I can't always force the pressure into specific areas. If I have a seizure, it will find the earth without my input. So far, it has always jumped the foundations of houses, including the base of the mountain, but who's to say what happens if this continues?

What happens if I don't die before I do serious damage?

The painkiller pushes back against the pressure. I know from experience that it doesn't take long, but it feels like the two forces are battling forever. I fight down the urge to be sick. I'm just not going to do it. I'm not going to be trapped here by my own body if Persephone is at the whorehouse.

It's Conor who comes over to me. He leans against my leg, giving his placid strength. With force, I unclench my fist and place it on his shaggy rump. He licks my face.

It helps me compose myself for a few minutes.

My mind clears. No more pain, but the clock starts ticking down the seconds until it starts again.

The door to my office opens, and I lift my head from my hands. Oliver frowns, concern etched on his face. It's my least favorite of his expressions. I'm not in need of his concern, or anyone else's.

I'm in need of Persephone.

At the very least, I need to assure myself that she's not getting fucked by some faceless man who has no right to touch her.

My blood pressure rises, and the beating in my veins causes an echoing pain in my head.

Calm.

The fuck.

Down.

"I'm going to the city," I tell Oliver.

His eyebrows pull together. "The train's gone. Do you want them to turn it around?"

"Get my car. I don't have time for the train."

Oliver takes another few steps into the office, rubbing at the back of his neck. "I've got a license," he offers, gruff, uncomfortable as hell. "I could drive."

"You need to be here to defend the mountain."

His eyes come to mine, and shame blisters down the back of my neck. I know what he sees. I've hated this kind of exposure all my life. There are times I'm helpless to prevent it. Unacceptable. Intolerable.

"Get the fucking car, Oliver. I'm not leaving her there another second."

SIX

Persephone

ZEUS IS A KING IN HIS OWN CASTLE, AND HE RULES FROM the ballroom.

He takes me neatly from Reya's arm. Everything seems too bright, too harsh. It's just candlelight and sconces on the walls, along with some lit-up centerpieces at the tables ringing the room, but it seems like the blaze of high noon.

"Tonight's a bit different," Zeus murmurs into my ear. "I've brought guests."

"You had guests last night."

"You're right. But tonight, I'm hosting an event for some local policymakers."

It's impossible to tell which men are clients from last night and which men are the local policymakers. They're all wearing dark suits. Zeus must like a dress code. All of them look weak compared to Hades. All of them look small. But they outnumber me by far. And they must know what Zeus does here.

No wonder my mother was afraid of the city.

If the people in power support this business, then they don't care what happens to me. Why would they? They're here to have a good time. I might be here to give them one.

Zeus mingles his way through the crowd, shaking hands, pushing me forward at every opportunity. He doesn't give my name, but he lets everyone get a good look at my face. I never checked the mirror after Reya was done with me. I could look like anything. I'm hoping I don't look like myself.

At one end of the ballroom, a low dais looks down over all the revelers. Two antique chairs perch in the middle. Oh, God. Zeus really thinks he's a king, doesn't he? He kidnapped me, and not a single person in this room will bat an eye. He can do anything. He can yank on the ties that bind him to my mother, toy with her, terrify her…

And he can do worse to me.

Whatever happened to Zeus must be what makes him scan the room so carefully. You can only tell when you're close enough to look directly into his eyes. Otherwise, he seems like any other business owner.

And what Reya said, about choosing clients…

Zeus and I take our seats.

A man dressed in simple slacks and a black shirt bends low next to Zeus, a silver tray in his hands. Zeus lifts the drinks from it with a nod and hands one to me.

I don't want to drink it.

Whatever it is, I don't want to drink it. My mind is trying to separate, to hide from whatever this situation will become, but my body knows the danger. My heart punches at the inside of my ribs. My vision sharpens, taking in hemlines and stubble and dappling on gowns.

The party moves around me, time slipping by. It gets

louder. More raucous. Men appear at the edges of my vision, watching.

"Drink," says Zeus, and his voice has taken on a sharp edge. His smile reminds me of predators in the woods. "Relax."

For what? I lift the heavy glass to my lips automatically and take the tiniest sip. Zeus is still watching. I take another sip. It's sweet. Light. The aftertaste is odd. I don't recognize it. It's not bad, though. I thought it might be bitter. Alcoholic.

"A sheltered girl like you could use some experience." His voice is a low lie in my ear. "Look around. You could take your pick."

This should scare me, shake me to the bone, but my heartbeat seems oddly slow. I don't recognize this calm. I'm used to the cold wash of anxiety. This feels warm. Too warm.

"What are you talking about?" My tongue feels thick in my mouth. "I thought you didn't want to return damaged goods."

"Getting fucked once or twice isn't damage when you've already been in Hades's bed. You can even get compensated for your time."

"I don't need that," I insist. "I don't want that."

"It doesn't have to be difficult, Persephone. A taste of freedom before I put things back together. Some experience…"

"I don't understand." I meet his golden eyes. "What you're trying to do."

"Wouldn't it all be better if you could stand on your own two feet?"

Yes. No. I don't know. "Why are you trying to put things back together?"

"So everyone stays alive, Persephone."

More suits, more men. More shadows. None of them is the shadow I want. It's hard to sit up straight. It's hard to stay on the edge of my seat.

Much too hard.

"Did you put something in my drink?" I can't even muster up a glare for Zeus. I'm thinking of Hades, and I'm thinking of how many men there are and how there's nothing between me and them. How Zeus could give me away with a wave of his hand. How he might do that. How it might be better for me if I just give in and let it happen. Let one of them take me upstairs. Let one of them—

My stomach twists, turns, but my body feels somehow distant and too close.

"Nothing to harm you," Zeus says mildly. "Just a pinch of something to help you relax. Something to help you enjoy the party."

What I need to do is get up and run. Get up. Run. I lift one arm off the chair. It only moves a few inches. I take a breath, summon more strength, and swing my feet above the floor. That's not running.

"See? You're having more fun already. Now. There are quite a few men who have expressed interest in meeting you while you're available. Some women, too, if you'd rather—"

I don't get to hear what I'd rather do, because there's a loud sound from the far end of the building. Toward the lobby. Toward the street. It beats back against itself until there are a thousand crashes all happening at once.

"Fuck." Zeus stands up inhumanly fast, too fast for me to see. I shake my head and try to focus.

It's chaos.

A chaos of bright gowns and dark suits sprinting away from one another. Men in vests with guns weave through the crowd, scattering people. Guns? Vests?

The police.

I've only ever heard about them from Decker. He says

they're not like my mother's guards. Police mean something bad is happening. Something terrible is happening for Zeus, and I'm going to get caught in the crossfire. Handcuffs glint in the light. There are so many officers in bulletproof vests. What goes on here that they think they need bulletproof vests? A fresh horror pinches and pulls at my skin, but I can't do anything about it.

And then, in the middle of the rush and the terror, I see him.

Hades.

Half a foot taller than anyone around him. Eyes black and cold. The other men in here aren't wearing suits. They're wearing rags. Hades wears black as deep as his eyes. Every step he takes creates more space around him. The policemen pull away. Women flee. He's not a charmer like Zeus.

He's here for me.

I'm holding my breath. I only discover it when my lungs start to ache. The first rush of officers arrives. I'm useless next to them. Nothing. Zeus steps out to meet them and they surround him, all talking over one another, or maybe it's one of them talking, his voice magnified by whatever was in that drink. I hear *human trafficking* and *prostitution* and *right to remain silent*.

They haul Zeus away, hands behind his back. It takes a lot of them to do it. Distantly, something shatters and cracks. Glass or something harder, or perhaps it's whatever twisted tie remained between Zeus and Hades.

The man who is here for me.

I'm relieved to see him, and I shouldn't be. He used me. He threatened to kill me. He doesn't want me, not really.

The officers drag Zeus toward Hades. I thought the two of them couldn't possibly be brothers, but as they come level with each other, Zeus leans out, using the grip of the officers for leverage, and says something to Hades. Zeus's charming grin remains in place. Hades answers him, jaw set, a casual fury on his face. Neither of them flinches or cowers. They're the same height. Two opposite forces. Power radiating from each one.

The moment ends with a yank from the officers, and Zeus walks with them, no resistance, head held high. He's still the consummate host of the party, and taller than the officers by far. He's letting them take him. He'd have to, in order for it to work.

It takes a long time—too long—to focus back on Hades. He draws nearer and nearer, and finally he blocks out the light from the ceiling.

He crouches down in front of me, if one could call it that. It's as elegant a movement as I've ever seen a person make. He looks so strange and different here. Too powerful for the room around him. Too lethal. Over his shoulder, I watch three separate officers change their minds about coming to talk to me.

Hades puts a huge hand on my knee. I feel like I've reached out and grabbed the only solid thing in a storm. The high winds stop tearing through the room, leaving it still. A dangerous energy arcs between us, as tangible as electricity. Whatever has happened here tilted the world on its axis. I just don't know how much yet. Maybe I'll never know.

"Did he touch you?"

The question drops from Hades's lips like he's asking about the weather or if I prefer chocolate or vanilla. The hairs on the back of my neck pull straight. I'm an ancient emperor at the coliseum, giving out a death sentence. Or a life sentence.

If I lie to him now, then Hades will kill Zeus, never mind the police and the other people. I can see it in his eyes. There would be consequences for that—consequences I can't see, no matter how long I look.

Zeus was complicated. And he was more forthcoming than

his brother. I'm not completely convinced there wasn't some good in his motivations for doing this.

He didn't hurt me.

"No." It seems important, crucial, to be clear. "Zeus didn't touch me."

Hades's shoulders relax a fraction of an inch. He does not let relief show in his face. Maybe he doesn't feel it. Maybe there's no relief to be had when you're in a war. And he is, isn't he? Zeus has started one. Or they've been locked in battle for years. I didn't know. I just didn't know.

It's the police who circle now, held at bay by Hades. He hasn't said a word to any of them, and he doesn't now as he takes me in his arms. He's solid rock, untouched by the wind, and I can't help myself. I put my arms around his neck and hold tight. He says nothing, but his heart beats hard and fast.

SEVEN

Hades

THE EYES OF ZEUS'S PRIVATE SECURITY NEVER LEAVE ME.
I can feel them burning into my skin on the way out of his
whorehouse. It's elegant for an evil man's business. Not to
my taste, of course, but not a hellhole.

This is a mistake. Zeus was so casual when he said it.
Smiling. That motherfucker. He only has himself to blame for
what I've done tonight.

His security team declines to shoot me. It would be easy
enough to do it now, when half the city's police force is in here
arresting prostitutes and clients. Easy enough to foist responsibility on the trigger-happy cops. But they don't. They're likely
in shock. What I've done is shocking, if only to our fucked-up
little family.

There are lines we don't cross. The most important one
is that we do not interfere with each other's businesses. Zeus
only skims off Demeter's products in the agreed-upon amount.
I keep his company on my payroll, a fiction of numbers and

spreadsheets. And Demeter makes the things we need and sells the rest.

All of that is rubble now. Demeter is past understanding. Her fields still burn, the smoke rising in thick curls to the sky. And my decision has been made for me. It's no longer possible to consider returning Persephone.

I'll have to make do with threats.

It might not work.

I might have killed us all.

It isn't for love. It's baser than that. More animal. Persephone belongs to me, and Zeus took her. He tried to hide her from me. Keep her from me.

Light batters my eyes on the way out of Zeus's building. The painkiller I took at the mountain is already wearing off. I have a single one left.

"Where are we going?" Persephone murmurs against my neck.

"Home."

She relaxes. Where else did she think we'd go? I'm going to close the doors to the mountain and bar them for good. I'll keep her locked in forever. I'll figure it all out later, when my heart stops racing like a runaway train car.

The upset I've caused at Zeus's business has spilled out onto the sidewalk. Some of his whores cry and argue with the police. A few of them are walking away as fast as they can in high heels. I don't care. Persephone—her warm, alive, untouched body—is the only thing that matters to me right now.

A car waits at the curb. As a rule, I don't drive. These are special circumstances. I pass by five additional officers running into the building, open the passenger door, and drop Persephone inside. She rests her head against the window.

Pressure mounts at the back of my neck. We need to get the fuck out of here before Zeus's people get themselves together.

The steering wheel feels unfamiliar in my hands, and the streetlights are knives boring into my brain. No time to dwell on it. I pull Persephone's seatbelt over her and click it into place. Then we're headed for the train platform.

The train is making an extra stop in the city tonight.

I abandon the car at my private platform and take Persephone in my arms. The train whistle sounds, echoing over the city. Persephone stirs against me.

The scent of her, hidden underneath a perfumed soap that's wrong, so wrong, has set my heart back into rhythm. And it's a dangerous one. It knows no boundaries. It's wild with pain and anger and something like love. It thrashes with things I've spent my life trying to keep at bay.

Trying, and failing.

The train rolls to a stop, hissing, clanking. It's in motion again the moment I close the door of my private car behind us.

Thank fuck.

The lights on the train are tolerable, but it's too late by now to ease the worst of the pain. I don't care. I had to come here. I had to retrieve her myself.

I put Persephone on the sofa. Her head lolls back and my lungs squeeze. If Zeus hurt her, I'll kill him.

But Persephone doesn't die.

She blinks, waking up, her huge gaze focusing on me. He's dressed her up like one of his whores—red lipstick, smoky eyes, all the things meant to attract the kind of men Zeus wants favors from. I've ruined his plans for her.

"He put something in my drink," she whispers. Then she focuses hard on me and clears her throat. "I want you to let me off the train."

"I won't do that."

Her expression changes. That lost, confused look should soften me. Instead it has the opposite effect.

I thread my fingers through her hair. Someone's changed it. Straightened it. It feels different when I pull her head back. If Zeus has done anything, it'll be on the slim line of her throat. There's nothing at first glance. It's her eyes I'm concerned with.

Yes, Zeus has put something into her drink. Persephone's pupils are wide and black, almost like mine. I shouldn't touch her. I should tuck her into bed and let her sleep it off.

No fucking way.

Her pulse beats at the side of her neck, breaths shallow between parted lips. Persephone arches her back for me.

That's proof she's all right.

It's not enough.

I stand her up, brace her hands on my shoulders, and rip the dress away from her. My skin is on fire. My heart's not beating, or it's beating so hard I can't contain it. I need to know. I am not a man who needs. Who gives into desires. For her, I am. *This is a mistake*, Zeus said. It wasn't a mistake. It was an escalation.

A killing rage blends with animal desire in a mix so potent it almost carries off the driving pain in my head. My father tried to stamp these things out of me. I tried to let him. I didn't try hard enough. These feelings take the form of Persephone, a living woman, here in my train car.

She's wearing lace underthings I've never seen, and the hot spike of jealousy that roars through me at the sight of them touching her skin is enough to melt the train to the tracks. Persephone gasps when the panties come apart in my hands, then the bra—shredded, nothing.

I put my hand around her neck where it belongs.

Need overwhelms. Overruns. I tip her head back and inspect her with eyes and tongue. Jaw. Neck. Breasts. Her nipples peak, hard and wanting. If there's so much as a scratch on her, I will turn this train around, find Zeus in his jail cell, and crush the life out of him. My hands ache. She smells so pure, so innocent, and she is not. I have fucked her, I have made her mine, and my own brother tried to take that from me.

It's searing hatred and equally searing relief that drives me on. I haul her off her feet, pull her to the desk, and force her open. I need to see every inch of her. I need to feel it too. I shove three fingers inside her, my hand still around her neck, and find her wet. Wanting. I stretch her, punish her, look into those big, black eyes, and let her see me.

"You signed a contract," I growl into her mouth. "That contract does not include letting you out of the train so you can wander off." I pull my fingers out and deliver a sharp twist to each of her nipples. She whimpers, cries. I can feel the vibration through the palm of my hand. It's mine now, that sound.

I open her wider, lean her back, expose her. Humiliate her. It's too far. There's no way she can hold this position, but she will. For this, I need the light. It's a rare occasion. She sucks in a breath. One silvery tear falls to the desk. Yes. Fuck. Yes.

She can't hide from me. With her legs like this, pinned, I see everything.

Everything.

Persephone squirms in my grasp. She doesn't try to cover herself. She knows better than that. I bite back the urge to praise her for it.

This time, when I lick her, she lets out a wail that's pure embarrassment, mortification. I do it again, and again. She tries to stop me, using only the force of her muscles. It's laughably impossible. I will never let her close herself to me. I won't do it. I will lick her in this place until she has no choice but to submit to the fact that I own her.

"Not there," she begs. "Not there, please, you can't—"

I lift my head from her, an act of supreme self-control, and put two fingers where she doesn't want me to go. Persephone writhes, trying to get away, and it is the sweetest torture I've ever known. She's still begging when I push those fingers inside.

She's tight here. So unbelievably tight. Her begging cuts off into a series of small, pained gasps that have me straining against my own pants. I'll die if I don't fuck her soon.

"Leave me again, and there will be worse punishments than this."

Persephone tenses, mouth open, shadows falling around her face. "Your fingers are too big. And I didn't leave. It was a trick. You know it was."

"You'll take them. You deserve them." Something cracks inside me, and anguish pours out, acrid and cold. I pull my fingers out, bend over her, and kiss her. It's savage enough to draw blood. More pain, deeper pain. I need her to feel it too. She will, and she'll finally understand. "You don't know what you've done to me."

She can't know the depth of what she's done. She can't, because there's no way for me to tell her. There's no way to describe the sensation of having your heart ripped out by two small, delicate hands. Admitting it is an arrow between my ribs and a knife in the back. There is nothing more terrible and wounding, but I can't be wounded. I will never allow myself to be wounded.

Except here. Except now.

Her eyes glisten with tears. She narrows them, slightly, hazy hurt in her expression. "It's not the same for you, is it? You know what you've done to me."

I undo my pants with one hand and shove inside her. I'm half-gone. Merciless. Feral. Whether it's punishment or pleasure makes no difference. Those distinctions are for people, and I am nothing but a raw nerve. She's so fucking perfect, panting and arching and crying.

"I came to take you home," I say.

"I don't want to go."

But she doesn't push me away.

Persephone grips the sides of the desk, trying to stay on. The world narrows until the only thing remaining is her and the way I'm fucking her, vicious and hard. Like she's property. Like she belongs to me. Because she does. I'm the only man in the world who gets to fuck her until she cries. They'll never get to her again.

EIGHT

Persephone

FOR MOST OF MY LIFE, I THOUGHT KNOWLEDGE WOULD make me feel better. Safer. I tried to get it wherever I could, which wasn't easy. My mother didn't want me to have it. And now I know why.

I don't feel safer.

The world seems enormous. Sprawling. Dangerous. It seems sharp as it goes by outside the train window. There's so much I didn't know, and everywhere I turn, another web is waiting to catch me.

I spent so much time making plans. I never thought I'd learn anything new about my mother. Like the fact that she has brothers. Or had brothers. Three of them. And if Zeus and Hades are any indication, they're all dangerous men.

What does that make my mother?

I'm parched for more information, the way I've been dying to see the lions at the New York Public Library for as long as

I've known they existed. All those things come with a cost. Going to that library isn't free. Knowing things isn't free.

Secrets glitter in the shadows all around us, never quite showing themselves. They've been there all along. Of course they have. It's only now that the curtain's been ripped away.

I was so naïve.

Hades didn't appear from nowhere as a full-grown man with cruelty in his hands and pain in his eyes. There was a life. A family. It made him who he is, but I've been imagining him as a dark gash in the middle of the world, independent of everything else. I've been imagining him as the one-dimensional evil that my mother whispered into my ear.

She didn't tell the truth. He's much more than that.

My mind struggles to untangle all those lies—all those omissions—all the way back to the mountain. All the way through the soaring rotunda. All the way up the elevator. All the way back to Hades's private wing. I can't quite get there, because wounded anger fills every breath I take.

I pad along next to him, barefoot and wrapped in a thick blanket from his train car. The pillars surrounding his open living area are like silent guards.

At the door to the guest suite, I turn without thinking.

His hand comes down hard on my shoulder. "No."

It startles me out of the half-dream I've been having. It's very late, or very early, and time seems unstuck from its usual pattern. I blink up at him. "Why?"

"You'll never sleep there again. Walk or I'll carry you."

He clips off the words, his impatience stinging my skin. Bone-tired. This is what bone-tired means. But when he tugs me toward the big doors at the other end of the hall, the urge to sleep falls away.

He has never, not once, taken me past those double doors.

My teeth chatter gently against one another with the adrenaline rush.

I try to tell myself it's only a bedroom.

I fail because it's not.

It's more important than that. I can't express why, not exactly, but when he opens the door and goes through, I hesitate.

I hold my breath.

Hades has done unspeakable things to me. Things I could never talk about in the light of day. For all he's made me show him, he's never shown me anything.

If I see it, there's no going back.

I draw the blanket tighter around my shoulders. The truth is that I want him, and I'm not supposed to. If I close my eyes to what he really is, then at least I can pretend I'm not falling for a monster. That part of me isn't hungry for the cruel things he does. Hungry and wet, even now.

Hades comes back into the hall, puts a hand on my elbow, and drags me inside. I hear echoes of my own screams from the first day I was here—*I belong to you, I belong to you*—and press my lips tight to keep them from coming out all over again.

He starts to drag me across a sitting room. Of course, it's not just a bedroom. Of course—

A shout from the hallway stops my heart, and the door bursts open again behind us. Hades's grip hardens on my arm, and he shoves me behind him. How did they get here? How could they follow us so quickly?

I don't want to go back.

Please don't make me go back.

"I'm sorry," someone calls, and I get up the courage to look out from behind Hades. The man who apologized holds the doorframe to keep himself steady while he holds Conor's collar. Conor, who is normally at Hades's side. He must've thought his dog would be in danger. "Couldn't hold him back."

The man curses, and Conor breaks free from his hand, his nails clicking on the marble tiles.

Conor comes to us as fast as he can and pushes his nose into the palm of Hades's hand. I tumble to my knees and put my arms around Conor's neck. He seems almost frantic to see us. I'm the only one close enough to see the tentative way Hades touches Conor's head, stroking so lightly between his ears.

A heavy silence passes between the two men, so heavy it gets my attention. The other man is red-haired and stocky with a scar running down most of his face. He sticks his hands into his pockets, the fabric rough like workmen's clothes, and looks across at Hades with a frankness that surprises me. They know each other. He probably knows Hades better than I do. Fear shivers down the back of my neck.

Or maybe it's jealousy.

Conor licks the side of my face and nuzzles into my shoulder. He's a huge dog, big enough to look normal standing next to Hades, and his affection pushes me off-balance. It gives me something to concentrate on other than the breathless tension in the room and the scar on the other man's face.

"Persephone, this is Oliver Callahan, my head of security. Oliver, this is Persephone." Somehow, Conor manages to lean into Hades's leg and my body at the same time.

Oliver pulls a hand out of his pocket and gives me a small wave. He wears an olive green shirt and sturdy pants. He looks like he could work in the mines, or anywhere else. "Pleasure to meet you."

I wish it were more of a pleasure. I wish I wasn't angry. But it's not Oliver's fault. "Hi, Oliver."

"You'll see him around my rooms," Hades continues. "If I'm not here, he'll deliver my messages."

"Messages?" I ask.

"You're not to go downstairs."

Anger pushes up from the soil again. Hurt I've been too tired to weed out. "Fine."

Hades straightens, shifts, and Oliver is his mirror. "Keep everyone out. You know what to do."

"Of course." Oliver disappears through the double doors at a quick pace. Through them, I can hear other doors closing. If this were any other time, any other place, I'd be terrified of a man who looked like Oliver. The only reason I'm not is because I'm here with Hades.

Right. We were about to go into his most private room. There will be no more hiding from the truth of him.

And the truth of me.

I bury my face in Conor's shoulder. I know he's a dog, but he's the most comforting thing here. After a minute Conor strains gently against me. He wants to follow Hades.

So do I.

I get up and hook my fingers into his collar. Conor pulls me along with him toward the bedroom, the blanket slipping down over my shoulders. My lips tingle, on the verge of going numb, but Conor is not afraid.

The bedroom door is open.

A massive window, floor-to-ceiling and nearly as high as the ones overlooking his factory, displays the night sky in such perfect detail that it must be fake. Breathtaking, but fake. There's no possible way the stars are so close, so bright. But the stars don't compare at all to the man standing next to a massive bed, all the sheets and blankets the color of that midnight sky. The window gives off enough light for me to see the dips and shadows of his face in profile and not much else. The light from the sitting room falls off behind me, and as I step into true darkness, they switch off completely.

The stars get brighter. He gets darker.

Hades went ahead. He must be expecting me to follow, but it doesn't look that way.

He looks lonely. He looks *alone*.

Like nobody could ever be watching. He's half-turned away from the door, the muscled lines of his body statuesque and carved from the stars behind him. If he were a statue, it would be called Pain. His chest rises so lightly it's hard to see the movement.

It's the hand over his eyes that gives him away.

It steals the last of my breath, and when Conor leaves me to go to Hades, I sway on my feet with a light-headed rush. Conor settles by his side and leans against his leg, insistent. I want to go to him, and I want to turn around and lock myself in the guest room. I want to demand answers, but I don't want to shout and cause him more pain. This is like finally being inside my library, not just out front but inside, and not being able to touch the books.

A new need hums into being and wraps itself around those deep instincts for his hands, for his mouth. It's not just the future I need to know about now. It's him. It's all of him. The thought of being inside his mind, with his thoughts, sends a fresh pull of goose bumps over my skin.

Hades takes his hand away from his eyes, and the movement startles me out of my emotions and into the reality that he means for me to sleep here with him. Here. With him. In his bed.

"Come here?"

"Why?"

He glares at me. The effects of whatever Zeus gave me are beginning to fade, but I still feel compelled to go to him. It's easier not to resist this. To just... carry my own pain with me. My lungs feel tight as I cross the room, cutting off the air I need for reason and logic. There's only a starlight anger, crisp and clear, in a constellation with no name but that I recognize intimately. Conor moves away to curl up by the fireplace.

Hades pulls the blanket from my shoulders and drops it to the floor. Air floods back in, my vision sharpening. I'm ready. *Do you know what you did to me?* His voice when he said those words. So ragged. So raw. I'm certain that what happened on the train isn't the end of my punishment.

I'm certain that I won't give in. Not this time. Not after what he's done.

"Get into the bed."

I know what comes of arguing, but here, in this night-painted room, I dare it. "Why do you want me here?"

"Don't be tedious, Persephone. The whorehouse was no place for my—"

"I'm not being tedious." His eyebrows raise a little at the interruption, but I press on, my throat starting to close and ache. "I don't know why you want me in your bed. I'm nothing to you."

"If you were nothing, you wouldn't have been able to sign a contract with me."

"I saw the note you sent to my mother."

Hades's eyes narrow. He destroyed every stitch of clothing I had from Zeus. He wouldn't let me put anything else on. In his rooms, the air is perfectly heated for my naked skin.

His hands go to the buttons of his shirt. The fabric whispers to me as he pulls it from his shoulders and lets it fall. Belt buckle next. Hades picks up his pants and shirt and tosses them both over the back of a chair.

And then, edged in starlight, he sits on the edge of his bed. Hades yanks me into the space between his knees, where I belong.

No. I don't.

Deliver the poppies, and I'll give her back. Destroy them, and I'll kill her.

My breath catches again and again, struggling to start in the middle of this cruel intimacy. My heart beats in a painful pulse. Hades slides his big hands over my waist. Over my hips. He pulls me closer.

I put my hands at my sides. "Are you going to answer me?"

"No." His tone is rough. Sharp. Pain grows through it in ivy strands. It's in the air between us. I'm so angry with him. I'm so hurt. My hands rise anyway. I put my palms at the sides of his face, by his temples. The softest, most gentle touches I can manage.

He closes his eyes.

Hades lets out a quiet breath. Every tiny movement is magnified by the night, and by the closeness, so I feel it when he relaxes. Not a lot. Not enough to fall to the side. To sleep. Enough to let his face tilt toward mine a fraction of an inch.

Better.

He doesn't say the word out loud.

He doesn't need to.

I rub my thumbs in slow circles over the skin there, and a tension in Hades's shoulders lets down. I didn't notice how he carried it until he put it aside.

Both his hands rise to curl around my wrists. Not to pin them. Just to rest there.

"Don't push me tonight," he says. "I'll punish you if I have to."

I'm stunned to hear the suffering in his voice. It's as intimate as him pressing his fingers into me while I writhe and beg. More intimate.

Through the storm of hurt in my chest, I trace patterns on his forehead, draw my fingers down his cheek. Run my palms around to the back of his neck. Anything I can think of, until my own eyes are closing and my body sways in his hands.

"You don't even want me here," I hear myself say.

"Come to bed."

This time, Hades's tone leaves no space for me to argue. I'm glad for it. He guides me out from between his knees so I can scramble into the bed. It's high off the ground. Hades doesn't seem to notice how awkward and exposing it is to climb this way when I'm completely naked.

I slip under the sheets and stretch. They're so soft, light and strong as silk, but burnished, like cotton. Hades climbs in after me.

The starlight dims in a slow fade, easing away with every breath he takes. I discover I'm jiggling my feet, tense and waiting, trying to breathe through the painful closeness of this and fight off sleep at the same time. I want to fight with him, but I need to rest. I want to feel every breath, but I need to dream.

A hand comes down on my thigh, low enough that I take it for what it is—a warning. *Stop moving your feet, Persephone.*

"Sleep," he says. The last of the light fades away, leaving us in total darkness. I can only feel the sheets, his hand, the rise and fall of him breathing next to me. It's too much to ask, that I fall asleep because he said so.

But he's not asking, is he? His touch is a command. And I have no choice but to obey.

NINE

Persephone

MORNING COMES.

I'm freed in one way, and bereft in another. Hades turned over in the night to the other side of the bed. Sleeping was easier when he made me do it. Now, in the filtered glow from the window, I still can't decide if I'm seeing any real light at all.

I test the boundaries. I wriggle my toes, then my feet. He doesn't stir. I've never seen him breathe so evenly and deeply, and it makes me feel… protective of him.

It's a foolish feeling. He was going to trade me for flowers.

Sleep cleared my head, and now it's like a freshly tilled field. I can't live like this. I can't sleep in his bed when he's just waiting to hand me over to my mother.

I watch the window over Hades's shoulder. It brightens so slowly. It must be an imitation of a sunrise with all the color stripped out of it. The thought of a real sunrise makes my heart ache.

The only thing I miss about my old life is being outside in the summer. Wandering through a lush field with a basket in my hand. Feeling green shoots of grass under bare feet. A flower's stem pulling up from the ground. This life with Hades is carved and polished. It's expensive. Even if I manage to get free and go to the city, there will always be a part of me that longs for summer. For blue skies and clouds and flowers in bloom. For wind in the leaves and a breeze in the middle of a hot day. Morning dew. Evening lightning bugs.

Part of me will always be bruised by what he did, and how he lied.

Deliver the poppies, and I'll give her back. Destroy them, and I'll kill her.

I turn over and start to sneak out of bed.

My head is three inches off the pillow at most when his hand glides around my throat and pins me. The early morning clarity I had disappears as if a cloud had rolled over the sun. Hades looms over me, tracing a path up and down my neck with the pad of his thumb.

"Where do you think you're going?"

The fact of him—tall, unbelievably strong, unbelievably dangerous—never gets less shocking. It thrusts me underwater and drags me out again, dripping wet and shivering. Hades is rumpled in a way he never let me see before. I'm not sure anyone has seen him like this, with a hint of bedhead and one cheek slightly pinker than the other.

I steel myself against him. Imagine thorns over my heart. Pinch my lips closed. My heart beats faster when his eyes are on me.

I know what Hades is capable of. That's why it's hard to fight with him. The kind of battle I'm inviting will be electric and painful. I'll want it in spite of myself. Fear rolls over me again, icy and taunting, but I imagine it melting in the summer heat.

"I asked you a question." The warning comes with a squeeze. It reminds me that he owns every breath I take.

I want him to touch me, to take me, and at the same time, my heart pounds out a warning to shrink away from him. To hide. He's a terrible man.

"I'm going back to my bedroom."

"You're not going back there. We've already discussed this."

"No. You just… gave me an order. I'm not going to follow them when you've done nothing but lie to me."

Hades scowls at me. When he's just woken up, the thread of blue around his eyes is slightly thicker. It's a sky-like, soaring blue. His body over mine throws off heat like a summer day. It lands on my skin and works its way through, rough and inescapable.

He has perfect lips. Every time my eyes drop away from his eyes, they land on those lips, those teeth. Every glance is like seeing him the first time. I feel like a fawn caught in torchlight.

"And what was I untruthful about?"

"You didn't tell me you had brothers. You didn't tell me that my mother is your *sister*." My heart beats against his hand. "You were *always* lying."

"I've never owed you a family history."

"I guess not, because I had to get it from your brother. Maybe I should have stayed with him. At least he was honest with me."

"Was he?"

"Oh, yes." Tears sting the corners of my eyes. "He told me all about you. He told me about your father—"

Hades lowers his mouth to my breast and bites, sinking his teeth in around my nipple until I cry out. He keeps his hand locked around my neck. Then he repeats the process on the other side. Pain scatters like new roots, and I find myself panting, struggling to keep the tears in.

"Would you like to continue discussing the past, Persephone? Or have you had enough?"

To my complete humiliation, my body is still searching for him. I can't stop thrusting my hips. I cannot stop searching for him. I can't stop wanting.

Well, I can fight with him at the same time. "You should have told me."

A cold laugh. "Would it have made a difference?"

I'm so angry, so hungry. But it's not rational, this want that takes me over. It's in my muscles and bones and the hot flush of my face. Anger burns through me, and fear chases along with it, and the mix is so intoxicating I don't know if I'll ever get over it.

"If I'd known what you came to the fields for, I could have hated you."

His smile is vicious and beautiful. "Who's the liar now? I recall you making your hatred clear several times."

"I didn't mean it. And I didn't want to hurt you." Tears fall faster. "I wanted to *help* you. I believed you when you said you cared."

"When did I say that?"

My hips meet air again and again while he watches with detached amusement. He's holding his body away from me, the way he holds the truth away from me.

"You said it," I insist. "I felt you say it. And you said that I should stay free. You're the one who tricked me. What was the point?"

He shrugs, expression unreadable. "To keep you compliant."

I let out a frustrated groan. "Why won't you just let me go? If you don't care, why won't you just let me *leave*?"

"Because I don't want to. You're a good fuck."

"Stop it." It hurts, to hear him dismiss this. To hear him go back on his word. It hurts, and it's all tangled up in embarrassing desire. I feel like flowers are going to burst out of my skin. Invasive plants that will take all the space until there's none left.

"You asked for honesty."

I bite back another sob. "You meant what you said in that note. You said you'd send me back there if she gave you the poppies."

"And I said I'd kill you if she didn't."

"What are you waiting for?"

He moves so fast I can't anticipate him. Hades drags me off the bed and pushes me to my knees on the floor. He strokes my hair back from my face, leaving no strand to distract me. The gentleness of this one touch takes my breath away. It takes the next breath too, because it's another trick. A trap. He doesn't care at all.

"Open your mouth."

I close it tighter.

He only needs one hand to force my jaw open. He uses the other to show me how hard he is, how huge. I'll never stop learning it, trembling on my knees on carpet so plush it reminds me of untouched grass. The air in the room slides between my parted thighs and strokes me where I wish he would.

His free hand comes back to my face. Hades brushes a thumb over my cheekbone. He skims his fingertips over my lips. Like I touched him last night. Except it's mean. It's terrible. It's a mockery of care.

Hades tests my teeth with the pad of his thumb. "I'm going to fuck your mouth now, Persephone. I've waited long enough."

"You'll choke me."

His cock bobs in front of my face, but Hades makes me look up into his eyes. "Yes, I will."

Hades puts a hand on the back of my head to steady me, and I get a burst of angry courage. "What do I get? Will you admit you care?"

He tips his head back and laughs. "You'll get what I give you."

Hades silences my last-gasp attempt at an argument with the full length of him. It shouldn't be a shock at this point. I should not be surprised. The night he took me for the first time, I thought he could never feel bigger than when he was splitting me apart. Everything I think turns out to be so, so wrong.

Except for the choking. I was right about the choking. It happens almost immediately, because Hades isn't kind or gentle or any of the things I'd expect from another man. He's himself. He promised he would fuck my throat. He's following through. I gag on him, and no amount of self-control can keep my hands down by my sides. The skin of his thighs turns pink under the sharp moons of my nails.

Hades groans.

He works his fingers through my hair and holds me in place, tugging at intervals to keep me close. Tears gather and spill onto my breasts, all down the front of me.

"Yes," he says, almost to himself. His fingers swipe at the tears, and I swear I hear him lick them off his fingers.

Hades pulls out long enough for me to gasp in a breath. There is no other reprieve, and I don't expect one. The shocks come one after the other in a relentless roll. Thrust. Gasp. Breathe. Try to keep my head above water. Cry around the hard length of him. Another thrust. Another gasp.

It's not long, or maybe it's hours later, that his rhythm

breaks down. His fists curl tight in my hair, and I flatten my tongue, trying to give him room. There's no more room to take. He holds tighter. Begging with your mouth full is a wordless, shameful experience. It pushes Hades right to the edge. He loses all sense of his strokes and shoves in deep. He's going to kill me, and the darkest, dirtiest part of me is going to love it.

"Fuck, Persephone. Hold still."

I have to hold still. I can't go anywhere else. My toes are already braced into the carpet, and if I hold his thighs any tighter, I'll draw blood. Air—air. I need air.

What he gives me is the hot spill of his release. There's so much to swallow, so much, oh my God. A cloud pushes in at the edges of my vision, and I can't tell if it's because I'm dying or because I'm dying for him.

He pulls away, and I fall forward onto my hands and knees. I'd crawl for him right now. I'd do it, if he would touch me. I would do anything. But he casually steps around behind me and lifts me in his arms. Hades carries my gasping, glassy self to the wide sill set into the window. I wait for him to bend me over it, for this to escalate into something that will erase the pain of that note.

Hades crowds me from behind, crushing me to him, and hits some hidden switch.

The window becomes an actual window.

It's green out there. Green and summery and gorgeous.

"What is that place?" More details come into focus. A small house at the edge of all the green. Tiny white flowers. A small figure in the distance. This place should be impossible. It shouldn't exist.

My throat feels bruised, and my balance is gone. I'm a light-headed mess. I can't do it, but I will if that's what it takes.

The space between my legs is molten and raw, and he hasn't even touched me there.

"This is what you get for being good while I fucked your throat." Hades scrapes a nail along each of my ribs, taunting me. His hand moves down only an inch at a time. "The sun. You can have it if you stop fighting."

"That's it?" I'm indignant, but inside, I'm in awe. Sunshine. Greenery. Up here. And my heart aches. "That's all?"

"My relationship with Zeus and Demeter is a technicality. The same with our brother Poseidon. There's nothing to know about them, except for one thing."

"What?"

"I hate them all," Hades says into my ear, his voice calm and measured, the opposite of the fever dream I'm currently living. "Just like real siblings."

TEN

Persephone

THE LAST WORD HISSES OUT OF HIS MOUTH, AND HE DROPS me.

Drops me.

Hades steps back and I catch myself on the windowsill. A reflection of the room comes into focus. The bed. The scattered clothes. Hades, rubbing a hand over his mouth.

"That's all you're going to say to me?"

Hades drops his hand and straightens. "You're correct. I don't care about you. This was never about love."

I round on him. "Fine. Then it's not about sex, either."

Hades narrows his eyes. "You're planning to deny me?"

"No." I'm a mess, on the inside. I still want him. But he'd changed before I left the mountain. He gave some of himself to me. Having it taken back hurts too much to take. "But I won't like it. You won't be able to make me."

He blinks, closing his eyes for a second longer than

necessary. The thorns around my heart retreat, then slam back into place. "We'll see about that."

Hades turns his back on me and leaves. Somewhere down a short hallway, a door closes. Water runs a minute later.

I crawl back into the bed and pull the sheet up. The sound of the water blocks out everything else. I don't bother following him to the shower. He can keep me locked up in here while he's on some power trip, and I can lock my heart away.

I follow the path of his hand with my own fingers and squeeze my eyes closed. He fills my mind like he's there in bed with me. The only impressions that matter are his hands on my skin and his cock filling me. The small release I get doesn't compare to what I might have had if he'd given it to me, but it's enough. It's enough to let me breathe but not enough to settle my racing heart.

He hurt me. I want him.

I throw back the covers and go to the hallway, where I find another door that leads to a walk-in closet three times the size of the one in the guest suite. This one is all man—all pressed suits and sharp black shirts, a neat row of polished shoes. All of it smells like him.

All of it except the new row of clothing, which is mine.

I recognize it from before I left.

I choose a blue dress that feels like home and yank it over my head.

The small library in the guest suite is just as I left it. Not a speck of dust out of place. Hades's people have been through here cleaning, the way they always do. The real comfort is taking a book from the shelves and curling up in the chair with it. No fire necessary. The temperature in here has been adjusted so I don't need more than the dress, and I'm not overheated.

I pick up several books and put them all down again.

The words don't hold my attention. My own heartbeat is too painful.

All he had to do was say he cared, but he doesn't.

I spend several days withdrawing from the world. I'm as silent as possible. As invisible as possible. I sit in the library all day. Sometimes I pretend to read, but really I'm just flipping the pages.

Every night, Hades takes me to bed with him. He says almost as little as I do. He barely touches me.

In the mornings, I wake up, get dressed, and go back to the guest room.

It feels colder on the mountain. The summer should be warming up, but I'm freezing.

One afternoon, Lillian brings in a tray with lunch on it. I barely glance at the food, and she frowns. "Did you want something else to eat? I can go back down."

"No." My smile feels frozen, too. "I'm all right."

Out in the hall, I can hear her talking to Oliver in a low voice. A little while later, she brings in another pot with fresh soil and new plants. They're sprouts, just peeking above the surface.

"Bad idea," I tell them when she's gone. "You should have stayed below. There's nothing good up here."

I mean to take a few bites of lunch, but it slips my mind. My thoughts run in slow circles. What's Zeus going to do when he gets out of jail? Maybe he's out already, and I don't know about it. Maybe my mother is already forming another plot to steal me back. Maybe she's here right now, hidden somewhere on the mountain.

Maybe it doesn't matter.

Maybe all of this is just a natural reaction to being kept prisoner by a man who just wants to use me as a bargaining chip. I wonder how he's planning to do that, if there are no poppies.

If there *are* poppies, they could arrive any second, in which case he'd just hand me over.

He'd have what he needed.

I'd be happy for him, if he didn't have to hurt so much. Less happy for me.

The sun sets slowly, gold on blue, and I watch it. There's nothing to distract me here.

The light is almost gone when Hades steps into the room. The wash of cold from his presence is muted, somehow. I don't turn my head away from the window.

"You're finished playing games," he says.

"I'm not playing games." Pain burrows through my heart, the roots thick. "I'm doing what you wanted. I'm staying here, and I'm not fighting you."

"You're not eating. It tests my patience, Persephone. I have spoken to you about eating."

"Honestly, you don't have the right to be mad about me. You don't care. That means you don't get to care if I eat or not."

I turn my head to look at him. The undisguised frustration on his face causes a distant pang of surprise. It's almost as if he *does* care. Conor pads to his side and starts to come into the library, but Hades grabs for his collar.

"Oh," I say. "Right. What you care about is keeping me alive so you can trade me for the poppies. How is that going, by the way? Did my mother accept the deal?"

"Get up."

I look back toward the window.

Hades doesn't give me enough time to be surprised. He's

across the room in two steps, his fist in my hair. I gasp at the pain, reaching for his hands, but he pushes mine away. He uses my curls to drag me out of the guest room.

Conor whines.

"Quiet," Hades snaps. "She's fucking fine."

"Why?" The question has more to it, but the words are lost in the pain. Frankly, it's a relief to feel it. I've been so cold, and the screeching tug of my hair is hot. "Why are you doing this?"

"I'm done. Finished with this bullshit. You're welcome to lie in my bed like a statue, if that's what gets you off, but you won't starve yourself."

Hades stalks down the hallway faster than I can keep up. I trip over my feet, over my dress, and he catches me by the hair.

"I get it," I manage. "You can't use a dead woman."

He makes a sound that's very nearly agonized. He's in pain, probably. The ache in my heart for him is so far away that it might as well be nothing. I do want it to stop. I'm not a monster. I'm just numb.

He drags me into his office. The big desk waits there, and Hades puts me in front of it.

"Conor, guard," he says.

Conor huffs. His big, dark eyes look from Hades to me. He doesn't want to leave.

"Now."

His dog goes back out into the hall and sits. Hades closes the door, shutting him out. For the first time since he stepped into the library, fear prickles at the back of my neck.

"Why did you send him out?"

"I don't need him to interfere in your punishment." Hades's expression is hard, diamond-like, but there's a tension around his eyes that would break my heart if my heart weren't frosted over.

I swallow hard. My body is nervous, even if I can't feel it. "You want me to cry?"

"Yes. And I'm going to be the one to make you do it."

Good, I think. *Fine. Make me feel something.*

"So I'll eat?"

"So you'll understand that you don't have a choice. You don't get to waste away because you feel like it. You belong to me."

ELEVEN

Hades

I will never get tired of the way Persephone's face reddens when I speak to her like she's property.

It happens even now, when her silver eyes are distant. Hopeless. I can see in her face that she genuinely didn't expect for this to happen. She really thought I'd let her go to pieces in that room.

This has been a rare miscalculation on my part. I thought she'd follow me. Fight me.

She hasn't.

The words stick in my throat along with humiliating fear. The sensation of caring for her feels like the sun in my eyes. If I cared for her, if I was open about it, it would be an exploitable weakness.

I can't afford to have two of them.

Not when Zeus and Demeter have gone silent. Not when dread screams, shrill and constant in my mind. I've increased security on the mountain in anticipation of an attack. I'm

having my people search every train twice. The rest requires patience, which is killing me. I need news from Demeter's farm, and I cannot appear anxious to get it.

This is a problem I can solve.

Persephone, blank-faced and silent, won't stay that way for long.

There are more ways to hurt her. More ways I will *hurt* her. Getting close to her, even when she's shutting me out, is like stepping into a hot room in winter. My skin is super-sensitive to my clothes. My head throbs with a splitting pain. It's been like that since I woke up this morning, but now the sensation is intensified a hundredfold. My hands ache to touch her.

The only way to make her see is to make my pain hers.

What I can't do is let her know how precarious this little game is. For me, not her. While she watches me, tears glistening in her eyes, I swallow the urge to admit how weak I am. How much I care.

I've never been so reckless. I know how vulnerability ends.

It ends the things you love struggling for a final breath in the hands of a person you hate.

But I can't let her sink into nothing like this. I'll play this game, because Persephone wants to, though she doesn't know it. Because her eyes get so wide and hopeful. Because her body loves being bent and punished. But even in this game, I can only give her scraps at a time. My better instincts will prevail.

My better instincts need her now. They need her to be present, not distant. Not lost.

She glances guiltily down at her feet. Persephone can pretend she's not that linen-clad little thing, fresh off her mother's fields, a new flower waiting to be plucked. Yet she is. We have much further to go before she turns into an autumn bloom. Before she disappears into the chill of winter.

I go to her, and she doesn't run. She only trembles like the angel of air and sunlight that she is. Persephone knows there is no escape from this darkness. She's brought it on herself.

"I'll eat," she says urgently as I bend her over the desk with a hard shove that doesn't leave room for argument. Persephone finds the crack in the wall of me. One errant tear flees down the bridge of her nose. "I just don't think it's fair to make me."

I take a fistful of her hair, digging in until she whimpers.

Fuck. I thought I killed and buried the hurt and the fear and the pointless jealousy. Persephone is a conduit for those feelings. They radiate from her, drawing them out of wherever they'd gone to hide. She can never discover how helpless I am to her—to the need to come back to her over and over again.

"You wanted to know about my business. You were in tears over it." I take a pen from the drawer closest to her and slam it shut, which causes a cascade of movements. She jumps, pulling harder against my hand, and lets out another half-cry. I wanted to fuck her long before I stepped into this room, and now I want it so much that my practiced denial is crumbling under an onslaught of feverish need. "Are you paying attention?"

Persephone's eyes flick up toward me. With my fist in her hair and her head turned to the side, she has no choice but to pay attention. I want to see those tears in her eyes. Her mouth forms the word *yes*.

I draw an X on the calendar page that takes up most of

the desk. As a rule, I never keep appointments on it. It's only there so I can mark the passage of time. Every day gone is one less day I have to live with myself.

"This is my business on the mountain." A few inches below the X, I scrawl a rectangle. "This is your mother's operation."

"Wedding flowers," Persephone whispers. "And your poppies."

"But most of all, drugs."

Persephone stiffens. "She makes bouquets for people."

Demeter kept her daughter prisoner for years. I know she wasn't kind. My sister hasn't ever been kind, despite the earth mother bullshit she uses as a front for her brand.

I study Persephone, study the quiver in her chin and the way she worries at her lip. She can't resist this. I should have dragged her out of that room earlier. Told her all this useless information earlier.

"A front for the majority of her business." Beyond the mountain, to the left, I draw another box. "And here is Zeus's whorehouse. He had you dressed up as one of them. Did you enjoy pretending to be a whore?"

She shakes her head. For a moment, I consider making her say it out loud. It would turn her on.

Persephone is already wet. I don't have to reach beneath her skirt to know it.

Around all three marks, I draw a circle then throw the pen into the corner of the room. It hits the wall and clatters down. With infinite restraint, I move Persephone's head over the collection of marks and stab a finger onto the paper. "Be a good girl and tell me what the circle is."

"The train." She tries to get up but only succeeds in

arching her back in a way that's going to take me out at the knees. "It's the train."

"What else?"

"I don't know." She can't get my hand out of her hair, and more than that, she's rocking back toward me. Slowly coming alive. I push her all the way flat on the desk. Persephone barely turns her head in time to avoid getting her nose in the ink from my pen. My most fervent wish is that I could fuck her right now, like this, but there are punishments to be meted out first.

She can't get into the habit of taking herself away from me.

I lean down next to her ear. "Money. Drugs and whores are frowned upon by the federal government. They need my diamonds to make their money legitimate." It pains me to stand up, but I do it anyway. "Our father was a titan of illegal businesses. Once he was gone, it made sense for Zeus and Demeter to take over what they could."

I let go of Persephone's hair. I need both hands free, and if I keep talking, I'll tell her too much.

I'll tell her what she wants to hear.

"What happened to him?"

"We ate him alive."

"You killed him?"

"Yes."

I take her wrists and pull her forward before she can ask another question. She grips the other side of the desk. A small glass figurine of a poppy waits on the corner of my desk. For years, it's been a reminder of the deal that kept me alive. I turn Persephone's hands palm up and make her hold it. Her fingers explore the shape.

"A poppy," she whispers.

"You will eat," I tell her. "You will not sit in that room all day. You will spend time in the valley, or elsewhere in my private space. You will hate me where I can fucking see you."

I step back behind her, and the sun catches in the paperweight. It shouldn't be possible, because of the windows, but the light seeks out the perfect angle to refract into my eyes, a stab straight through the head. It causes a brief loss of control in the form of a curse under my breath. I unbuckle my belt and slide it through the loops, test it in my hand. I shove the skirt of her dress up to her waist. She's naked underneath.

Persephone looks back at me. "I don't hate you."

I'm not thinking anymore, with heated blood and a pounding heart. "Ten if you can obey. Twenty if you drop the glass."

I bring it down onto her skin, and Persephone howls, throwing her head back.

She keeps the statue in her hand and stays bent over the desk, offering her ass up to me. I take what she's offering.

The stripes are so red, and the sound of her cries is so cleansing. It focuses my mind. It's a release and a torture at the same time, because—two more—it's not enough to claim her with leather. I want flesh too. Need it.

Four.

Five.

Six.

"You're here because this is where I've decided you'll be." *So I can fuck you. So I can protect you. So I can see you, while I can still see.* "Don't fuck this up. Don't disobey me."

Seven.

Eight.

Nine.

She sobs, tears flooding down her cheeks, face red. The sound of it hooks into my hidden places and drags me toward her. I lean down close. She needs to hear this next part even though she's sobbing. Especially because she's sobbing. And because I need another opportunity to breathe her in, to put my lips close to her skin.

"Don't ever try to escape me again."

I drive the last point home with a final strike. Persephone screams, her knees buckling, but she holds onto that damn paperweight like it's a lifeline. The belt falls to the floor first, and I follow it with my knees. Force her legs apart. Drink her in.

She is wet. I was right. And she tastes so sweet that an old springtime explodes in my mouth. A clear day, my first dog still alive by my side, before summer was a killing pain. One breath. That's all it takes for her screams to turn to moans.

TWELVE

Persephone

'M NOTHING BUT THROBBING, HEATED FLESH AND THIS delicate poppy statue. Nothing.

Hades's punishment has left me a blank slate. Everything is chased away from my mind except the bruising pain on my ass and the slick, hot pleasure between my legs. If I didn't know better, I'd think I was drunk. That's how it feels with Hades's hands between the desk and my hips, pulling me back to his mouth. That's how it feels, staring into the light captured in the statue. He didn't say when I could put it down, so I'm going to assume the answer is never. I'll hold onto this statue for the rest of my life if he keeps doing what he's doing.

It feels so good. Not the crack of his belt. That felt bad. Very bad. But every single stroke drove my desire deeper between my legs. He knew I was ready for him. I heard the sound he made when he knelt down behind me. I heard it, unless it's part of a grand hallucination I'm having. The statue is what

grounds me. It was real before this started, and it's real now, so the rest of it must be real.

My hips have nowhere to go. He holds me in place, trapping me against the hard boundary of the desk. There's nowhere to go, so I open myself to him. He wants more than that. His fingers dig in and spread. I can't hide anything. I can't—and I don't want to. All I want is to come.

His tongue takes me there. The rhythm is too fast. I try to scream, but nothing comes out except an anguished moan. His answer is another series of punishing licks. I'm getting hauled toward a vicious orgasm by a machine of a man. Crying makes no difference to him.

It's unbearably sexy.

My orgasm winds and winds until it finally snaps, so powerful that I'm begging for him to stop almost as soon as it starts. He doesn't stop. He keeps going and going until he's devoured it, until I'm hanging limp over the desk. Still holding onto the glass poppy. I won't let go. I won't earn myself another ten strokes with his belt. I won't. I won't.

He stands up behind me, and one hand comes down on the desk then the other. Without the desk, I wouldn't be standing. Without the desk, I wouldn't be here, a sacrifice under the braced body of this man, this god. The hard crown of him demands entrance, and Hades takes me with one strong thrust of his hips.

This time, I'm not the only one breathing hard.

He's a wild thing, all his muscle and power concentrated into fucking me. It forces the air from my lungs every time he enters. I have to hold on to the poppy. Hold on, hold on. My ass smarts from the extra contact. Oh, it hurts. I need it to hurt. I needed to feel it. A bolt of anger goes through me—why punish me like this? Why make me hold this statue when I could be digging my nails into him? Why not tell me how he feels?

Because it's better this way. Because I like it better this way. Twisted. Terrible. Mean.

Light. Caught in glass, where I wouldn't expect it to stay, but it does.

Pleasure and heat lock themselves together between my legs, skimming over a layer of pain that heightens everything until another orgasm sneaks up and pulls me under.

Far under.

He says something I don't hear, because all my energy is focused on his cock inside me and the statue balanced on my palms. If I hold it as tight as he's holding me, I'll break it. That will be enough for him to punish me. Of course it would. This is a precious object.

Then he pushes himself inside, so deep it makes me cry out again, and his superheated release paints my insides.

"Fuck," he says. "Fuck." His hands tighten on my hips, freezing me to the desk. Aftershocks roll through Hades's powerful body. I can feel them everywhere. My face flushes. He just fucked me over a desk, and I'm the one blushing. Why?

Hades banishes the thought with a final sharp slap to my ass, which layers itself on top of the burn and sinks in deeper. A shadow falls over me. I brace for more, fleetingly think of begging for it, but he only plucks the statue from my hands and puts it back on the desk.

It was the statue holding me up, then. I slide off the surface of his desk unceremoniously, landing heavily in his arms before I hit the carpet.

No, I'm going to tell him I can walk.

But I can't.

Hades carries me somewhere else. Light and shadow go by as he walks.

He knows how much I need him. He must know. He has to need me to.

Please, let him need me too.

I only know we're back in the bedroom when he tips me into the sheets. The window's gone dark again, but I curl up on my side and look toward it anyway. Hades stands at the edge of the bed. It's not like him to take so long to decide. I'm already drifting off, letting go of the aches in my body and my heart, when the mattress bends. It's another long while before he runs his fingers through my hair.

"You do that to me," he says a while later.

My mouth doesn't want to work, but if he's inviting me to have a conversation, then we will have a conversation. "Do what?"

"Make me lose control of myself."

I think it through, my mind hazy from whatever that was. Punishment. Pleasure. Both. "You make me sad."

His fingertips come down on my naked hip, and then he pulls the blanket up over me. "Something is better than nothing."

"I don't think—"

"What gives you the idea that I care what you're thinking about?"

"You're still here," I whisper. "You came to see me. All I have are new thoughts."

"That's ridiculous." He's silent for a long time. "Give them to me."

I'm on the edge of drifting off, but I haul myself hand over hand back to enough of a semblance of consciousness that I can talk to him.

Deliver the poppies, and I'll give her back. Destroy them, and I'll kill her.

"I used to dream about buildings. The New York Public Library." The taste of the words is so familiar. An old dream. "I used to dream of walking by the lions out front on 42nd Street." I was never allowed to go anywhere large enough to have a forty-second street. He's never going to let me go, either. That's why it's a dream. A fantasy. It doesn't compare to his fingers in my hair. "Going inside. There are so many books there."

"I gave you a library stuffed with books, you ungrateful little brat."

"So?" I prompt, like an ungrateful little brat. "I wanted to go to the New York Public Library. That's where I've always wanted to go." I can't open my eyes. My eyelids are far too heavy for that. "If I couldn't go there, I wanted to go to school."

"What do you dream of now?"

My eyes fill with tears behind my eyelids. I let one or two escape. My throat tightens, but I swallow it back. I'm not going to cry over this. If I cry, it will be because I'm wrung out and ragged and angry at him. I'm past my limit from being taken over Hades's desk. I get full control of myself before I answer him.

"Being outside." That was my last burst of energy. I tumble down into sleep. Hades's hand slows in my hair. His hand is a calming warmth. "I love to be outside."

"Picking flowers in your mother's fields." He sounds so far away.

Stay. I need to stay. If I do, he'll come back to me. He'll tell me the truth.

I drift away before he can.

THIRTEEN

Hades

I'M AT THE VERY LIMIT OF MY TOLERANCE FOR THIS situation.

Persephone falls asleep while I stroke her hair, and I'm left with the pain of her absence. With the pain of wanting her. With the unholy, battering pain in my head.

I have one painkiller left.

One.

I have to delay taking it for as long as possible. I'll have to shift to another source of pain. Like the hurt in her eyes. I've been refusing her out of a self-protective instinct. It remains dangerous for Persephone to know how I feel. It remains dangerous for anyone to know.

The pain outweighs everything.

When I was fucking her, it was all right. We were close. She was close, the way I need her to be. Alive, the way I need her to be.

But when I tucked her into the bed, her eyes shadowed.

Persephone wrapped herself in sadness. The light in her silver eyes disappeared.

I simply cannot lie to her anymore. I can't find her with that blank distance on her face, not eating, hardly getting up from her chair. She refuses to put on the diamond necklace I gave her. Persephone hasn't touched it since I brought her back to the mountain. She won't so much as look at it.

She needs more from me.

The usual gifts will not be enough. Flowers would be a cruel joke. Food would seem like an order. More jewelry would be meaningless.

I watch her sleep for quite some time, running my fingers through her hair. A thin, slicing pain enters my temples and threads through my brain.

I close my eyes and imagine the earth. Imagine the pressure displacing, if only for a moment.

For her, I request of a soulless universe. *So I can make her see.*

The pain doesn't end, but it does crystallize into the back of my head.

Fuck you, I think to that universe. It doesn't hurt any less. However, it's easier to compartmentalize. It allows me to leave her sleeping and go down to my office.

I spend three hours there choosing the items I need and contacting sources in the city. None of them have news about Demeter or Zeus. Others are available for rush deliveries to the mountain.

Persephone needs to have this before time runs out. She needs to know it.

And time is running out.

By midnight, Oliver is with me, directing the deliveries.

A modest sitting room near my office transforms, piece

by piece, through the night. My body burns with the pain in my head by the time we're finished. My stomach knots and threatens to revolt.

I've pushed too hard, but there is no other option. No other way.

I make it to the bedroom as my vision goes dark. It means I don't get to see her hair spilled over the pillow. I'm reduced to crawling onto the bed next to her, moving by feel until I can collapse onto the pillow.

I do not dream.

I'm aware, in a distant sense, of a lurking seizure. A few minutes more in my office and it would have happened. I focus on Persephone's even breathing and manage to follow her into sleep.

She's gone the next morning. The air in my rooms feels tentative, as if she's waiting for me. Waiting to see if anything has changed. It's foolish to assume it hasn't. Everything's been different since the moment I saw her in that field.

I get dressed, conscious of every movement, and then I go to find her. Conor hovers at my heels. I can hide the nature of the pain from most people. Not my dog.

Persephone has retreated to the small library off her former suite, like I expected she would. She's showered, though. Changed her clothes. A book is open in her lap. Relief tumbles through me like a rock fall when I realize she's actually reading, not pretending.

As I step into the room, the tag on Conor's collar *clinks*.

Persephone jerks her head up from her book. Her eyes go wide. For a split second, she's happy to see me... and then her gaze shutters again. She doesn't know what to expect.

I can't take it.

"Come with me."

She frowns a little, and I wonder if she'll fight me on this. It would be better than staring blankly at the sky. Better still to punish her to reassure myself that she can still feel.

That's not what she wants.

"Okay," Persephone says. Soft. Sweet. Mild, like a flower. She closes her book and puts it gently on the table. As she rises, her shoulders go down, and her head comes up. The idea she has of being a prisoner is obvious in the way she holds herself, no matter what happened last night.

I don't think of her that way.

I think of her as precious. More than diamonds. More than poppies. So precious that I can't allow harm to come to her. Not unless it's from me. Not unless she likes it.

The silence from the city seems to surround us as we leave the room and move down the hallway. It imbues every moment with more meaning. This could be the last one we have before they attack. This one. This one.

I pause at the door that hides her gift and push it open.

Persephone tilts her head, peering inside, suspicious.

"What's this?" she asks.

"Go in."

Her eyes search mine, huge and luminous. A spark of curiosity lights there. Persephone takes a delicate little breath, steels herself, and steps through the threshold.

I'm nearly overwhelmed with dread and anticipation. Hope is an unfamiliar feeling, but my veins are flooded with it.

Persephone takes another step into the space and turns in a slow circle. Her eyes move over the furnishings and all the new things I've bought for her. New books fill the shelves on the walls. Notebooks. Pencils. A shining, top-of-the-line laptop sits in the middle of the desk. It's so new that I'm half-certain it came out of the factory mere minutes before my contact in the city arrived to pick it up.

She touches the books first, then moves to the desk. Persephone runs her fingers over the edge of the laptop, then jerks her hand back like it bit her.

"Persephone."

She whirls to face me. "What is all this?"

I slide my hands into my pockets. "You mentioned something to me before you went to the whorehouse."

Persephone bites her lip. "I mentioned a lot of things."

"You were upset because you thought I had gone to school, and you hadn't."

Her eyebrows draw together, and her cheeks pink up. "I didn't think you cared whether I'd gone to school or not."

My oldest instincts shy away from revealing anything about myself, but it's what she needs. "I didn't go to school, either." Persephone's mouth drops open. "I couldn't be in the light long enough, even if Cronos had let us go. He never did."

"But you own a business. You know all kinds of things."

"We were educated through correspondence courses. We did the lessons by hand. There was no escape the way you were imagining."

The corners of Persephone's mouth waver. "I'm sorry."

"It was an education nonetheless." I'm circling the heart of the matter, and it can no longer wait. "I can't give you the things you missed. I can't let anyone come here when the situation is so volatile. But I can give you school, if you'd like."

Her eyes go wide. "School. Like college?"

"There are people available to you. Tutors. You can reach them through the computer, and they'll teach you whatever you want to know. Take any course that captures your interest. Learn anything you want. The books here are only a starting point." My chest is tight. A matching pressure circles my head. "The one thing I can't do is let you leave."

"Why?"

"Because I care too much about you to lose you to the city."

I see the words hit her. I see them land. "You wrote that note to my mother."

Persephone's voice cracks, releasing the pain she's been carrying. Tears line her eyes. It wounded her to see it. I'm going to kill Zeus.

"I didn't take you because I wanted a hostage." The pressure increases. If I put my palm to the wall, it could buckle into diamonds. "I took you because I saw you in that field, and I wanted you. In your dress, running through the flowers..." A laugh escapes me. "You seemed like a person I'd already known, though it was impossible. I had to have you. That's why I brought you here."

"You didn't—" A shaky breath. "You didn't change your mind?"

"No. The pain got the better of me. When I heard that Demeter was burning her fields, I sent the message to try to force her hand. I had no intention of returning you. I had no intention of harming you." I take a step closer. "I couldn't. It was a lie made out of desperation. All I wanted was to find a way to keep you here. To get the poppies without having to give you up."

Her chin dimples. "You care about me?"

"Yes." The burden lifts. The weight of this secret agony disappears. "I can't stop thinking of you. Nothing feels right unless we're together."

Persephone's mouth quirks. "You're pretty mean to me when we're together."

"You like it," I shoot back. "You like the pain and the

control and the release. You *love* it. It makes you so fucking wet. But that's not all I want you to have. I want to give you everything. I'll give you everything that's in my power to give." There's one more thing I have to say. "I do not have the power to set you free in the city."

"Because you don't think I can handle it?"

"I couldn't survive it." The naked, unvarnished truth. "I'll learn to survive without the flowers, if necessary. Not you."

"You can't." More tears. "You need them."

"I need you to stay with me."

"There's nowhere else for me to go." Something shimmers in the air between us. Light without pain. And then, softly: "There's nowhere else I want to go."

Persephone comes to me, rushing, and throws her arms around my waist. She hugs me hard, like I'm not the creature who stole her in the night. Like I'm not the one who caused all this strife in the first place.

"I can read any of the books?" she murmurs against my chest.

"Any of them." I fold my arms around her and let her body take some of the pressure from mine. "They're all yours. Everything is for you."

FOURTEEN

Persephone

I DON'T KNOW WHERE TO START, SO I START WITH everything. I take down one textbook after the other. The pages are smooth and shiny. They smell…

They smell so good. I've never been able to press my nose into a new textbook before. He's given me books about history and math and science.

For the next few days, Hades leaves me in the new space to study. To think, really. I've never had a chance to think about what I wanted to learn before. I took whatever scraps my mother would give me. Mostly fiction, but you can learn from novels, too.

Hades said he was going to his main office to work, but I think he's mostly going there to worry.

My mother hasn't sent a single message. Neither has Zeus. They're both dangerous in their own ways. They both have reasons to retaliate against Hades. I wouldn't be surprised if

he wanted to whisk us both to some secret safe room on the mountain and barricade us in.

Instead, he's giving me space. There's nothing normal about learning to use email when you're twenty, I don't think, but he's doing his best.

I look up maps of New York City. Photos of the New York Public library. I make plans in my notebooks. Email my new tutors with endless questions. I have no idea what I'm doing. It's not so much college as swimming in new information, at this point.

Formal classes will come later.

If.

If we can survive the battle with my mother. Or Zeus. Or both. If we can find a way to get or grow the poppies he needs. Dread creeps in constantly. It makes it hard to breathe. But I push it aside, because Hades gave me this gift, and he wants me to enjoy it.

It feels good to have new notebooks. It feels good to have time.

The outer door to his rooms opens, then closes again. Probably Lillian with coffee or lunch. I go back to making a list of things I want to learn about, by subject.

It's not Lillian I hear coming down the hall a moment later.

It's Conor, with the soft metallic *click* his collar makes and his breathing. I turn around in my chair in time to catch a glimpse of Hades walking past.

"Hades?" It feels almost right to call for him, like this is our home, and we live here together without fear of my mother or his brother. Like nothing complicated has ever happened between us.

He doesn't answer.

I put my pen down and follow him. The double doors leading into his rooms are open. He's not in the sitting room.

"Hades," I call, my voice softer. "Is something wrong?"

No answer.

I find him in the bedroom, sitting on the edge of the bed with his face buried in his hands. Conor presses anxiously against his feet.

"Get out." I flinch at the sharp tone. Pain. That's what it is. Nothing to do with me.

"No." I cross the room and stand as close as I can. Conor edges sideways to make room. "You're not all right."

"It's nothing."

"It's not nothing." I tug at his wrists until his hands come away from his face.

There is no blue left in Hades's eyes. Not even the smallest thread. He's pale, and his hands are trembling. The motion is so slight that I know he must be working hard to hide it. His breath hitches, but he doesn't look away. Shame flashes through his eyes, but then his expression hardens again.

"It's nothing," he repeats. "I spent too long in the light."

"Here." I reach for the switch by his bed, and the room dims. I leave just enough light for me to see him. He's mostly in shadow then. It's enough.

Hades lets out a slow breath, then another one.

"How bad is it? Is there someone I should call?"

"No." A harsh laugh. "It's bad, Persephone. I don't know how else to describe it."

Guilt washes over me. I've spent hours over the past couple days looking at textbooks. I should have been working on this. It's all that matters.

"How many painkillers do you have left?"

He doesn't answer me.

"They're gone?" What was I thinking? I could have been focused on him, not studying. I could be trying to grow the poppies. He showed me that green valley. It would get enough sun.

"I have one left," he admits. His next breath sounds shaken. Almost weak. It terrifies me. Hades is strong. The strongest man I've ever met. But he could be crushed by this pain.

"I think you should take it," I decide, sounding more confident than I feel. "I think you should rest for a minute."

"I'll sit in the dark."

"The pill—"

"I can't take the fucking pill," he snaps. Hades reaches for the switch, and the room plunges into complete darkness. The only light comes from a crack under the door. It's faint. Almost nothing. "I need to have one in case there's an emergency."

This feels like an emergency. Shaking hands? A pale face? I don't know what happens next if this escalates. I don't know what I'm supposed to do if he has a seizure in front of me.

I reach for him. Find the front of his shirt. Trail my fingertips down to his hands, and take them in mine.

"I'll try to grow the flowers. I'll go outside and try right now," I promise. "Please. Just take it."

"If I do that, they're gone." Hades squeezes my hand. "That means there's no more time. That means it gets worse."

Until he has a seizure. Maybe more than one. Maybe they don't stop, and the mountain turns to diamonds and caves in.

"I'll fix it." There's no other choice. "I will. Please. Take it and rest."

I'm accepting the consequences for this in advance. If I'm wrong, and we end up needing this reprieve later, I know it'll be my fault. But I can't stand this pain for him.

Hades's hands tense on mine, and then he releases one

of them. I can feel his trembling movements as he reaches for his pocket. There's a *click*, and then he lifts his hand. Swallows.

I feel every second now. Every heartbeat.

It's time to go to work.

"Outside, in the valley," I begin. "There was a building."

"It's Eleanor's house. You know her. She'll give you anything that's available on the mountain."

"Who?"

In the dark, Hades puts his palm on the side of my neck. "She came with me from the farmhouse." He sounds cautious now. "She was our nanny growing up."

"Have I met her?"

Hades sighs. "She cared for you for a period of time when you were younger. Your mother was sick."

"She was away." I'm pretty sure it's the only time I've ever been separated from her. It must have been distressing. "I don't remember much about it."

"Eleanor hasn't changed." His voice holds an undercurrent of affection, carefully guarded. "She'll be helpful to you."

"I'm going to try everything." Hades's thumb brushes my jawline. "I won't give up."

"Don't waste your daylight in here."

"No. I'm staying until you feel better."

"The valley has full sun." It sounds like it hurts him to say it. To picture it at all. "It has good soil. The plants behave a bit differently at this altitude. It's nothing you can't handle."

"I don't want to leave you."

"Just go, Persephone."

Try.

I put my arms around his neck, keeping my grip loose in case it hurts him. What I want is to press my face against his skin and breathe him in forever, but I press a kiss to his cheek instead.

Hades shudders.

I leave him in the dark. Oliver's pacing outside in the hallway, worried.

"Make him rest," I tell him. "Don't let him go back to the office."

A smile lifts the corner of his mouth. "I'll do my best."

"I'm going out to the valley. Which way is the exit?"

"I'll show you."

He leads me down a shorter hallway. The flowers I missed so badly have always been closer than I realized.

The next door I find clearly leads outside. It's an all-weather door. Reinforced. I'm nervous as we approach. Almost like I'm heading toward a reunion with my oldest, best friend.

Oliver pushes the door open, and summer bursts in. It's green and gold, blue sky and clouds, and so much sun. He's wearing a plain gray shirt today, but it looks beautiful in this light. It looks warm.

I take a deep breath. The air is sweet and fresh and it makes me feel like I'm blooming myself. All that gold light floods my veins.

There's hope. We have hope.

I step toward the light.

"Do you want me to go out with you?" Oliver asks.

"I'll be fine." I'm more certain with every breath I take. "You stay here and stand guard."

FIFTEEN

Persephone

OUTSIDE IN THE SUN, I RUSH THROUGH THE GREEN GRASS of the valley toward the house on the other side. Eleanor. That's who I'm looking for. She'll help me.

I'm running across the jeweled green when she steps outside of her house. My heart skips a beat. She looks like a mother, but she's not *my* mother. This is not the woman who cut me with thorns. Who kept me inside on the strength of her anger and her fear. Who kept the world from me.

Eleanor is older than my mother. Even from a distance, her face is kind. She wears loose, flowing clothes and a sun hat.

The valley is extremely steep. One wrong step could send me tumbling down into the ravine at the center. That would not make a great impression.

And.

Having a grandmother is my oldest, silliest, most impossible wish. The characters in the books I read had grandmothers. Big, sprawling families. From what little I've learned from Zeus

and Hades, I don't think a big family is less complicated than a little one. Maybe it's worse.

But a grandparent? I can't imagine it.

Eleanor waves to me, a bright smile on her face.

She's familiar to me. I recognize something about her, though I can't say what. Maybe her eyes, or her wave.

She'll help me.

"Hello," I shout across the breeze. When the wind dies down, it's plenty warm and summery, but the moment it picks up again, it reminds me that we are on the top of a mountain.

Eleanor bends to pluck one flower from the grass, then another. I don't know how to have this conversation with her. It's urgent. The situation is dire.

Best not to think about that now.

Best to just breathe in the clean, fresh air and feel the sun on my face.

Up here, it's like the summer is on a delay. No humidity hangs in the air. The world on the mountain is just waking up. It's real earth. Not a fantasy.

Real.

I come level with Eleanor and fold my hands into my sleeves. The blue sky is an upside-down bowl above us, the jagged edges of the mountain keeping us in. That's for the best. If I could see down the side, I'd get vertigo and fall.

"Good morning, Persephone." Eleanor straightens up and smiles at me, and her smile is warmer than the sun. She has a cute, crinkled face. She's not as old as I thought she was, though her hair has gone softly gray. It's tied back in a loose knot. "Do you remember me?"

Now that I'm closer, I know I've seen her before. Many years ago. I didn't understand what was happening then, so I tried to forget. I did a good job of forgetting.

"A little," I admit, and reach out for a hug anyway.

She hugs me back.

"Thank you," I say into her shoulder. "For taking care of me."

"Oh, honey." Eleanor pats at my back. "I was glad to do it."

I pull back from her embrace and look her in the eyes. "I have to ask you for something else."

"Step inside and tell me what you need." Eleanor heads back toward the cottage, and I walk beside her. "We can talk while I work."

I expect her to head around the back of the cottage. Work with flowers happens outside, unless you have a greenhouse. Eleanor opens the front door instead and gestures me inside.

The space reminds me of my mother's cottage. Same white-washed walls, same braided rug. Simple wood furniture. A bright kitchen with a faded dishrag hung on the stove. I close the door on a breeze and head through the kitchen and living room, following the sound of her voice.

I find Eleanor in a back room. A huge back room. It's a smaller version of the rotunda by Hades's train station, with the same marble. When I get far enough in, a hidden door glides closed behind us. Eleanor flicks on a light, but the light comes from the wrong direction. The floor. It's a luminescent glow under our feet.

What is Eleanor working on in here?

"Your house looks a lot smaller from the outside."

Her eyes twinkle. "Doesn't it? Hades insisted on a direct connection. I wouldn't call that warren of hallways direct, but you can see where his space begins and mine gets bigger." Eleanor laughs at her own joke. Oh, I like her. It's an instant, comfortable affection. It's probably not allowed, to like someone so quickly, but too late. It's happening, in spite of everything.

Eleanor looks down into a planter in front of her, the top edge at waist height. Seeing the first one makes the rest of them come into focus. There are forty of them, maybe fifty, set into slots along the outside of the circular room. And what's in the planters makes perfect sense, except for the weird lights.

Plants.

Flowers.

"This is your work?"

"I grow flowers." She laughs softly to herself. "As you can see."

"What are they for?"

Eleanor moves to the next planter, which has pretty spring beauties. Waters. Pats down the soil.

"Hades likes flowers."

The things people tell me about Hades seem like little bombs, meant to explode what I thought I knew. My mind does a hasty struggle between my assumption—that Hades only cares about poppies—and what Eleanor knows, because she's known him a lot longer than I have. Jealousy pricks at my heart.

No. I refuse it. I'm not going to be jealous of Eleanor, even if she does know something about Hades that I would never have guessed.

"The flowers here have to be resilient enough for the lights." The watering can flashes in the light at the next planter down. "If you ask me, it's more a problem of timing than anything else. Everything must be exactly right." She snaps her fingers to indicate *exactly right*. I understand her completely. "Otherwise, they can't stand up to the environment. Between you and me, I'm not often successful."

"But you keep trying? Is it a contract with him?"

"No, no." Eleanor's fingers move down into the dirt. A sprouted plant comes up, and she moves it a few inches to the right. "He gave me something to do. He thinks I'll be lonely without a project."

I think of Hades with the pomegranate. Of the fury in his face when he discovered I wasn't eating. The way his fingers soothed my hair after he punished me.

"Are you? Lonely, I mean."

"How could I be lonely? I'm getting constant visitors. Hades visits me at least once or twice a week. And the others are in and out for the things they need."

"You talk to the people here?"

"Don't you live on this mountain too, my dear?"

"I know there are other people, but I haven't met many of them. I've been preoccupied."

Pressure accumulates at my breastbone. She's going to tell me something else that rocks the world off its axis, isn't she? I brace myself.

"Ah," she says.

The urge to explain rears up. Whenever my mother was angry, I had to choke out this same compulsion. Explanations never made her less furious. Explanations didn't convince her to take the lock off my door or send me back to school.

"What are they like?"

Her gaze goes to the shadowy gloom at the end of the room, where those hallways connecting her to Hades's fortress must be. "Most of the workers on the mountain are like him, in one way or another."

My head shakes in spite of myself. "That's impossible. Nobody's like him."

Does she not know about the diamonds?

"The light hurts them too." Eleanor's glance at me is weighted.

The blood drains from my face. "All those people can't be like him. Someone would have done something by now." The way his body relaxed under my touch, as if he had been holding in pain and tension all day. If everyone here was like him, there would be a drug. A treatment. A cure.

"They don't share his physical reaction to light," she says, her tone reassuring. "What I mean is that many of his workers find it intolerable for other reasons. Not the sun, but the world. They sign their contracts with him, and then they don't have to go back." A little shrug. "The rest of the people on the mountain are not like the two of you."

"Did you know about me? When I was younger?" I have a job to do, but the urge to know about the past is powerful. If I don't have to explain to Eleanor, that will make things easier.

She smiles, like the memory delights her. "Oh, yes. You didn't think to hide your gift from me."

The poppies.

"I have to use it now," I tell her. "He's in pain, and he doesn't have the flowers he needs. The poppies."

Eleanor lowers the watering can to her side. "I've been afraid of that." Her hand goes to her mouth, and then she drops it again. "His condition wasn't so bad when he was younger. Most times, I could keep him out of his father's way. Not often enough, I see."

"No." I put my hand on her arm. "It wasn't your fault."

She nods. "What can I get for you, honey?" It sounds like something a grandmother would say. "Name it, and it's yours."

SIXTEEN

Persephone

THE VALLEY BECOMES MY LIFE.

I spend hours outside in the green grass. Hours in Eleanor's darkened rooms with the lights that approximate the mountain.

I spend hours growing flowers.

I've never put so much effort into it before. Gold flows constantly through my fingertips and into the plants. It hurts, actually, like running all day in the fields.

Everything I can think to do, I do it. I send a team of people out to the natural areas surrounding the mountain and have them bring back the flowers my mother uses to create the hybrids. They won't be the exact strain she has in her fields. Those were bred over generations of flowers.

I use what I have.

One of the necessary plants is a poisonous flower that blooms at night. I'm sure my mother didn't think I was paying

attention when she told me about which plants made the hybrids. I was so young.

I'm old enough now to understand the value of her words.

Gathering the three species of flower is only a fraction of the battle.

Coaxing them to create the hybrid Hades needs is the bigger fight.

I try everything.

I bring bees to the flowers, held in the palms of my hands. I will the root systems to intertwine. I think of those poppies as I touch the petals. I picture them as clearly as I can in my mind.

I grow the flowers in full sunlight.

I grow them in the dark at Eleanor's.

I get down on my knees, summon all my energy, and let it pour into the earth. I let it stream through me until there's nothing left.

I grow them faster. I grow them slower. I whisper prayers to the sun. Prayers to the poppies themselves.

The valley blooms.

Eleanor's garden overflows. Every errant seed in the soil pushes up toward the sky. The flowers are the size of my fists. The petals lush and bright. The most vivid colors I've ever seen. It looks like my mother's fields grown wild and joyful.

I can't make the hybrid poppies.

What I need are the seeds. Even one of the original poppies from my mother's fields. But I don't have them. I can't will them through the soil to me.

Eleanor comes to me, picking her way through the blooms. "You should rest, sweetheart."

I sit back on my heels and tip my face to the sky, panting. My wrists ache. My hands ache. It feels good to grow flowers. Gold and light. But even the most gentle rush of power can be painful if it lasts for days. I've never understood Hades better than I do right now.

"I can't. He needs these flowers. It's hurting him."

This is true. Hades spends more and more time every day in the bedroom with the lights turned all the way off. He forces himself to go to his main office and check on his people. When the painkillers run out, he can last three hours before he has to be in the dark. Then two. Then one.

"He'll be all right if he rests." Eleanor puts her hand on my shoulders. "If he has time to close his eyes, he'll—"

"What will he do when Zeus comes?" I shade my eyes with my hand and look into her face. "What if my mother comes? He'd be defenseless."

"He has his people. And if Zeus visits the mountain, they'll come to an understanding. They always do."

"It doesn't..." My laugh sounds disbelieving. "It doesn't seem like that."

"They're brothers. They share a close bond."

"I don't think that'll be enough." I don't think she's right. I bow over the flowers, searching for another reserve of gold.

It doesn't work.

I try new strains of poppies. New locations in the valley. More water. Less water.

I repeat all of it under Eleanor's lights.

Every day ends with my hands aching and my muscles worn through. I feel like I've run a thousand miles, but I keep going.

I bathe my hands in ice water and keep going.

More flowers. Bigger. If I just give them the energy to be more colorful, maybe I can encourage them to become what I need. They spill across the ravine in the valley. I can feel the root systems under my feet reaching into the soil.

Eventually, they'll hit rock. Eventually, they'll reach a dead end.

I refuse to be a dead end.

Petals flutter to the ground. Daisies bow their heads to the grass under the weight of their petals. I start again and again and again.

Eleanor has the most brilliant red poppies brought to me. I grow them with all my concentration. All of my heart. I grow them next to an orange strain of poppy in case that can make the gold filament appear, but it only results in an orange band in the middle of the red petals. I grow them at night next to the poison flower. One palm over the night blooms. One palm over the others.

They refuse to combine.

I wish I had instructions. But as much as this is part of me, as much as it's a biological fact that I can do this, there's no science to it.

There's only hope.

When the sun sets, I go to Hades.

There's dim light in the bedroom. For me, because my eyes have adjusted to the harsh sun, and I lose my bearings completely.

"Persephone."

I walk straight into his arms. Never mind the dirt on my dress. Never mind the ache in the soles of my feet and the palms of my hands. I push my face into his shirt and close my eyes.

He runs his hands over my hair. It's escaped from the braid I had it in this morning, and is now running as wild as the flowers.

"I shouldn't have done it," he says. I feel the words over the beat of his heart. It's a little too fast. Otherwise, he hides how much pain he's in. I can't hide anything from him. I'm so exhausted that my legs tremble. My abs. After this long, it's a whole-body exercise to make the flowers grow.

"You shouldn't have done what?"

"I should have saved more painkillers. I shouldn't have taken the last one."

I try to detach myself, but he holds me tighter. "Turn the lights all the way out. I don't need them."

"You haven't eaten."

"I can't—" I clear my voice to force the tears away. "I can't eat until I've had a shower. I'm covered in dirt. I'll just be a minute."

Hades lets me go. I turn the lights off, then feel my way to the shower in the dark. I hold my breath while the water gets hot, then step in underneath the stream. I let it soak through my hair, but the thought of raising my arms to wash it is too much.

The bathroom door opens. I can't see Hades. I hear the soft fall of his clothes hitting the floor. He steps into the shower without a word.

Just having him close makes me feel like my lungs are filled with flowers. Blooming. Pushing out at my lungs. I could choke on them, but I can't make the damn things grow.

"It's not working," I admit, and burst into tears.

Hades pushes his fingers through my hair and tips my head back into the water. "It's all right."

I don't know how he can say that to me. It's not okay at all. He's suffering, and I'm letting it happen. I can't make the argument through my sobs. Hot water runs over the dirt on my skin. It gets absolutely everywhere, though I'm clothed the whole time.

He runs the pads of his thumbs over my face, wiping away the stuck-on streaks of soil.

"The valley looks beautiful," he says.

That only makes me cry harder. The valley looks so ridiculously beautiful. It's gorgeous. If I had my own garden, that's how I'd want it to look.

"Beauty doesn't matter. The poppies matter, and I can't make them grow. I don't know how she does it."

Hades washes my face. My hair. He feels for what he wants with light brushes of his fingertips. There's no hesitation to the movement. He's at home here in the dark.

He has to be at home here.

There's nowhere else for him to be.

"I like them." Hades smooths conditioner through my hair.

"How?" A laugh escapes. It sounds slightly bitter. It sounds exhausted. "They're all pointless."

"They're gorgeous. And you made them. Anything you make is a treasure. You should know that. You should know..." He steps away, returning a moment later with a washcloth. "You should know it's a joy to see you in the valley. Even if I can only watch from the window."

"Oh, no." Heat paints my cheeks. "I'm not at my best out there. I look..."

Ridiculous. On my knees, begging the ground to give me the poppies. Glaring at the sky, like it's the sun's fault that I can't do what my mother does. Frantic. Panicked.

"You look like a summer queen." Hades uses the same wondering tone he used to talk about the flowers on the first night we met. I'd been so afraid of him then that I couldn't hear it for what it was.

"A summer queen?" My tears are slowing, but his words cause a new pain in my heart. A warm one. A flush of pleasure. "A real summer queen would be able to grow the poppies. Nothing would stop her."

"Have you stopped?"

I shake my head.

"My point stands."

"I'm going to try again." My eyelids feel so heavy. I could curl up on the shower floor and go to sleep.

"Don't exhaust yourself." An edge comes to his voice. "I'm not losing you to this."

"You can't make me stop," I point out. "I'll just wait until you're sleeping to try again."

"Do you honestly think I'll let you stay awake once you've eaten? Do you think you can steal away from me in the night?"

"No." I wouldn't fight him, in the end. If he caught me. If he kept me. "I don't think you'd let me get away."

"That's right, summer queen. Don't bother trying."

SEVENTEEN

Persephone

'M DELIRIOUSLY EXHAUSTED BY THE TIME HADES HAS gotten his way about dinner. I've eaten it mainly in the dark. Good thing, too, because my muscles are so sore my hands tremble.

But I could still try. I have enough energy left to try.

Hades offers me his hand, but I don't take it. "I'm going to go back out."

"You will do no such thing."

"There's time," I insist. "I could have a breakthrough."

"You could collapse outside on the grass. Is that what you want, summer queen?" It gives me a thrill of pure, starlight pleasure to hear him say that.

"If it works, then I want it."

"You've forgotten your place." He's made entirely from stars now, or else I'm so tired that my eyes are playing tricks. Shadows and stars. Hades is not particularly gentle when he takes me to the bed. "I'll remind you of what it is."

My nightgown is the first casualty of the evening. Hades tears it away from my skin. My panties next. The only thing he leaves on is my diamond necklace. Tired as I am, I feel awake for him.

"If you did this outside—"

"Eleanor would hear you scream."

That lights up every nerve in my body. All of them, a fiery gold. He knocks my knees apart with his free hand and twists his fingers into me. I'm sensitive from all the work and the effort, and I curl toward him on instinct.

He's pretending to be cold. Uncaring. Harsh. Nothing makes me hotter than when he's like this. He curls his fingers, and I clench down on them with a gasp. Hades does it again, and I try to close my legs. He reminds me to keep them open with a mean slap.

"Maybe that's what I have to do." I'm already panting. Already hot. "Maybe I have to do this out in the valley to—to—"

The first orgasm hits me mid-sentence, and I lose the rest of it.

Every time I think nothing can ever be more humiliating, nothing can ever turn me on more, Hades finds a way.

His fingers are still inside. Working. Twisting. Curling. "Go ahead, summer queen. Tell me how you think a punishment will make the poppies grow."

"I'd try anything."

"Do it here, and maybe I'll make you cry out in the valley."

"What—" I can't think, so I reach for his face. His fingers are vicious inside of me, and it takes a lot of focus to touch him gently. But I have to. If I can't make the poppies grow, I can do this for him. "What am I doing?"

"Have you ever stared into the sun?"

The inside of me is so sensitive. Another pleasure bomb ticks down a warning. I'm pinned in place by his body and by his hands. There's nowhere to escape from his fingers.

"No. It's dangerous. You're not supposed to look—"

He strokes harder, and I swear I can feel the tip of his fingernail touching a part of me that feels like a live wire. Like a spark, a cascade of sparks, a wildfire. Hades watches me while I come again, short and hard.

"You're not supposed to look at the sun," I finish.

"And if you were a fool, you might try it." Those fingers. Again. Again. I can't even begin to get away I can't begin to want to. My breath is becoming a sob. "If you stared long enough, it would feel like knives in your eye sockets. It would feel like an icepick through your temple. It would feel like jagged rocks boring into your skull."

He makes me come a third time, and when it's almost over, he adds a thumb to my clit and rubs in slow, easy circles.

Slow.

Easy.

Relentless.

Until I scream. Hades shudders at the sound.

"See how it works? How quickly pleasure turns to pain?"

"I do. I do. I see."

The rest of what I'm trying to say turns into nonsense. Whimpers. Cries. His thumb is unforgiving. I had no idea a light touch could feel so good or hurt so much. His fingers twist again, and I can't resist him. I couldn't stop myself from coming even if I tried. It tears through me on a knife's edge. I can't catch my breath. Beads of sweat gather on my collarbone.

"If you start with pain…" Hades curls his fingers, deliberate, slow, torturous. "It turns into more pain until finally all pleasure is consumed. Until the hurt could swallow you whole."

The orgasm he's punishing me with is all thunder and heat. I'm barely alive at the end of it, hanging on by a thread. "That's what light does to me. That's how the pain builds. I won't allow you to torture yourself like that."

My heart breaks for him while my body breaks apart under his hands. The beginning of a scream bursts out of me, but I bite it back. If I scream again, I might not stop, and I'm getting what I wanted. I wanted to know more about him. I know it now down to the marrow.

"I'm not," I gasp. "I'm not doing that."

"You are wearing yourself to the fucking bone. There are consequences."

"It's worth it."

He offers me one moment of reprieve in the form of tracing his thumb around the outside of my pussy. It's not enough to get a full breath, not with his fingers in as deep as they'll go. He's going to do it again. He's going to do it a—

His fingers curl.

This isn't so much an orgasm as a wretched, screaming peak. Words fly apart into senseless sounds, and the universe narrows to his hand. Curling. Stroking. I have to fight my way out of it, out of darkening vision and not enough oxygen.

Hades is calm. My hands are on his face. I've managed to stay soft with him.

I take the biggest breath of my life. "What else can I give you? Let me give you something else. Is there anything else that makes you feel better? Any other flower? Anything?"

I don't realize he pulled back until his hand slams back into me, his fingers ready to destroy me. Hades gives no mercy. He drives me into another electric burn. I feel it up to my fingertips. I'm not trying to pull away, not trying to wrench my wrists away from him. It's my base instinct. If I am the universe, then this is also the end of the universe. It's the end of me. It rushes up in a tall wave, inescapable, and I take one final breath before I go under.

It's a long while before I resurface. How long, I don't know. My hearing comes back first. Wind plays on the narrow window, testing the glass. Hades breathes nearby. Vision is next. The starlit shadows move across his face.

He's watching me.

When I blink up at Hades, he eases his fingers out of me. Even that small movement is too much, and I arch back on the pillow, jaw locked tight, making small noises I won't let into the air.

He takes a deep breath.

Lets it out.

"Only one other thing has that effect," Hades comments. His lips are an inch from mine. He brushes a kiss to them. All of me is so sensitive I could die. Hades nudges at my opening with his tip. He feels enormous.

"What is it?"

Hades thrusts in. Oh, pain. Oh, pleasure. When he's buried to the hilt, he leans down to brush a stinging kiss to my cheek. He whispers one word in my ear. "You."

EIGHTEEN

Hades

"**W**HERE THE FUCK IS THE BOY?" I SNAP at Oliver. It's past our usual meeting time, and I am at my wits' end. Persephone is killing herself in the valley. I can't allow it to continue. At this rate, I'll have to start going out into the light myself to bring her back inside, and that's a dangerous prospect.

Less dangerous than what she's doing, putting her own life into the flowers. She swears that's not what it is. I know better. The explosion of growth and beauty in the valley doesn't come without a cost. I wouldn't tolerate it even if it was simple. Even if she was just exhausted at the day.

Persephone cries when she thinks I've fallen asleep. She insists on smiling for me, though the poppies are not forthcoming. Every morning, she brightens up with fresh hope and tries again.

Her frantic optimism is like having another source of pain outside my body. I can't live with the competing pressure. My

vision is already shadowed at the margins for most of the day. There's very little to be done about the relentless diamond pain cutting through my skull unless the boy has news.

"Missed the early train. The next one's almost here."

"Go down to meet him."

Oliver leaves.

I sit down at my desk and push the heels of my hands into my eyes. Conor pushes his body close to mine and nudges at my leg. He's making a futile effort to convince me to leave the office. I'm making a futile effort to contain the pressure. It cannot be contained. I had to close off one of the sections in the mines late last night after the shaft became unstable. Two backup teams are on permanent standby to reinforce the tunnels. Structure failure, I call it. Movement on account of rock stresses and deformation.

I have not told Persephone what happens in the event the seizures chain themselves together, which is that Oliver will have to shut down the mines.

In the worst-case scenario, he'll have to shut down my brain.

Where the fuck *is* the boy? Decker is not particularly intelligent, but he is reliable. I find it unlikely that Demeter has kept her operations on lockdown for this long. It wouldn't be profitable. Beyond that, resuming her usual routine would provide cover for the other plans she's making.

The train whistle filters through the rock on the mountain. Any minute now.

I should never have taken the last painkiller.

I should never have allowed myself to care so much for another person that I'd let them influence me in that way. Persephone has made it impossible to ignore the pain. I can see it reflected in her face. In her eyes. That's the fatal trap of getting close. I can't let my weakness hurt her.

And, at this moment, I have no fucking choice.

The pressure increases.

I sit very still.

As a boy, I used to imagine that if I could slow my heart rate enough, keep my muscles from moving, the pain would cease to notice me. I believed it came from a vindictive god that I had displeased, embodied in my foster father.

It took years to understand that I was the source. That the pain and I would never be separated unless death intervened.

Imagine my shock when it was my sister who intervened instead.

Our father would be proud of what she's become.

It seems nearly impossible that she could be responsible for the creation of her own opposite. Persephone shares her mother's determination, but not her disconnection. The summer queen in the valley doesn't see people as inhuman creatures to perform experiments on.

Or perhaps the reverse is true. Perhaps Demeter is searching for proof of her own humanity in all her torture games.

I laugh into my hands. Pain ricochets between my temples. Cronos stamped out Demeter's humanity long ago. Same for the rest of us.

That's the argument I should be making to Persephone. That failure on her part would only rid the world of one more monster.

My summer queen shouldn't care so much. She comes into my rooms every evening with dirt smudged across her face. The muscles in her hands cramp from all the life flowing through them. When I see her in the light, her eyes are red.

Her hope is wasted on me. If the pain kills me, it will only

313

be the inevitable conclusion. I should have died long ago at Cronos's hands, but I didn't.

Conor makes another attempt.

"Not now."

I was forced to keep living against my will. I've hated Zeus for that for so long. That bastard can pretend his driving motivation was altruism, but I suspect it was entertainment.

A knock at the door. I lift my head. One of the men from my distribution team comes across the office at speed, as if he had to gather a significant amount of courage.

"For your signature." He pushes the paper across the desk to me.

I sign it.

This collapses if I die. The business would be dismantled, unless Persephone wanted to step into my shoes. She would be horrified at the idea of digging the evidence of my existence out of the ground and selling it for money.

The man leaves.

Some distant part of my mind disagrees about Zeus. That part is shoved down into a pressurized dark and crushed. Childhood has no bearing on what happens now.

However.

If I hadn't survived it, I wouldn't have been able to steal Persephone for myself.

Fuck.

I'll pay for it. I know. I can feel the fallout coming like I can feel the mines and the diamonds. Like I can feel the unsteady nature of my own mind. Like I can feel the threadlike tendrils of power up in the valley.

Persephone is there now, out in the sun. She is carpeting the valley with blooms. It's a tangible reminder of how much of herself she's putting into the ground. I can't help but think of it as death by slow increments.

I'll go to her now. Make her stop early. I'll make her understand that her life is a limited force. If she succeeded in growing the poppies at the cost of herself, there would be no point. I wouldn't live.

I stand up at the same moment Oliver returns.

His face is set. Hard. "I think you'd better come."

I'm in too much pain to ask questions. To have a conversation about this hell we're living in right now. We leave my office in silence and cross the rotunda. Conor follows close.

The train idles at the platform. It's still running. There's a schedule to adhere to even when my siblings are likely launching a covert attack.

Some of my men have gathered around one of the cars.

Conor tenses, sniffing at the air. He hesitates. Only for a moment. He's loyal, and he won't let me continue without him. But he comes along with a worried snuffle. He doesn't like whatever's waiting for us.

Oliver waves the rest of the men away and stands at the door of the train car. Goose bumps follow cold dread down the back of my neck.

I step through the threshold. This is one of the cargo cars. There's nothing here except a wooden bench, some steel shelves to strap crates to if necessary, and a body.

It's the farm boy.

He slumps against the wall, his head tipped into the corner as if he'd climbed on alive and sat down to rest.

I know he didn't. Demeter sent him this way. She put him here in this parody of a stowaway. His hands sprawl lifelessly in his lap. He was still recovering from the burns. She wanted them to be convincing, and she succeeded. No doubt she enjoyed his torture, too.

Now they'll never heal.

I crouch down in front of the body. Conor trembles at my side, a whine in his throat. I'm familiar with the sensation.

Decker's eyes are closed. There's no mistaking his stillness for sleep. His chest does not rise, and does not fall. I reach for the side of his neck anyway.

His skin is already cold.

Demeter has replied to my message.

Over your dead body.

Oliver's footsteps draw closer. "Do we send a response?"

"No." There's nothing to send. There is no bargaining with Demeter. "Take him out and have the body prepared. We'll need to send someone to the farm to locate the family."

I leave the train car, and Oliver stays behind on the platform to carry out my orders. Conor brushes against me on the way up to my private space.

The lights go out as I move through. It feels better to be in the dark, but I can't stay. The sun is out. It will be excruciating in the valley.

Persephone hears me open the door, or else she feels me step onto the ground. Her head snaps up, silver eyes going wide. My summer queen scrambles up from the blooms and runs to me. "You shouldn't be out here."

She is correct. I shouldn't. The light is like fire. The flames lick into my brain.

"There's something I need to tell you."

"Let's go in. Hades—" Persephone grabs for one of my hands.

"Hear it first." When I move again, it'll be to walk straight to the bedroom. I won't be able to talk to her.

"Okay…" Persephone's so worried for me. It makes me sick to see it. Or else the seizure is coming on faster than I anticipated.

"Decker is dead."

She gasps. Her hand goes to her heart. "What? When did you—how do you know?"

"Your mother sent his body on the train."

Persephone turns her head, staring out at the flowers. She nods, almost to herself. Tears glisten in her eyes. "Why would she do that?"

"She wants us to be afraid. On edge. She wants us to spend whatever time we have left dreading her arrival."

My summer queen glances down at her feet in the grass. The flowers have almost reached the boundary of the mountain. I have no doubt that Persephone could grow them from the rock, if she wanted.

Her chin quivers.

But when she looks back up at me, her eyes are clear. "That's not going to work. I'm not afraid of her. I won't be." She rises on tiptoe and kisses my cheek, smelling like sunlight and flower petals. "Go inside. I still have work to do."

NINETEEN

Persephone

DECKER'S DEATH CHANGES EVERYTHING.

We weren't really close. I know that. He was working for my mother, and he was working for Hades. When push came to shove, he wanted money more than anything else.

He never told me why. Decker didn't talk about his family. Now I'll never know the reasons he had for what he did. Whatever they were, I can't find it in me to blame him. He must have been desperate.

I know what that's like, because I feel desperate now. I push every bit of myself I can into the flowers. I work with my newest generation of poppies until the sun sets.

Hades is waiting for me in his rooms, the shower already running. Afterward, I pull a fresh dress over my head with aching arms. I slip on soft shoes.

"I'd like to go see him," I tell Hades in the sitting room as he strokes Conor's head by the window.

"I'll go with you."

I don't bother arguing.

The lights adjust as we move through the mountain, dimming ahead of Hades. It's not enough. He's gritting his teeth against the pain by the time we approach a room on one of the lower levels of the mountain.

At the sight of it, my stomach turns. I know about death. My mother's business hangs on the seasons and the cycles of plants blooming and withering. Returning to the earth. It always seemed warm to me in the soil. When I pictured my own death at Hades's hands, I imagined being buried in summer warmth.

It's cold down here.

Hades pauses outside the door. "Decker's body has been cared for and dressed. He looks like he's sleeping."

I want to protest that I don't need the warning, but I do. I've never seen a dead person before.

Hades has.

He takes my hand and we go into the morgue.

It's even colder inside, and it smells sterile. There's no hint of summer here. Conor huffs his displeasure at being in the room, but he won't leave Hades.

It's just bright enough for me to see the shape on the table. It's almost like candlelight.

I mostly saw Decker in the sun. Early morning. Late afternoon. He was tan from all the time he spent outside. He's pale now. The difference strikes me with every heartbeat. His skin is colorless, and he's still. So still. I half-expect him to wake up.

Someone has dressed him in new clothes. A blanket has been folded down over his chest. His burned hands rest at his sides. I reach for the nearest one without thinking.

"Oh," I burst out. "He's so cold. He's going to need another blanket. And he never—he never liked to wear shirts with a collar."

"I'll have someone change it."

"He wasn't my friend. He was just talking to me so he could spy on us."

"When it comes to grief—"

"That's not what this is." I put Decker's hand back onto the blanket. "I'm sad. I'm—" The weight of what my mother has done makes me sick. "He shouldn't have died for this."

"No."

Anger and fear and determination reach through my veins like roots. Every one of my heartbeats tangles them together. That's time ticking away. My mother's warning is a sign that we don't have much left. It's like the first frost. A sure sign that winter is coming soon, like it or not.

Decker is proof that my mother has lost her mind. It's proof of how far she's willing to go to have her way.

Only Decker was nothing to her. He was as disposable to her as a piece of paper.

If she thought this would scare me into coming back to her, she's wrong. I won't break down over this. I won't give in.

Because I'm not letting her get to anybody else.

"I'm sorry," I tell Decker, though it's far too late. And then I turn back to Hades. "Take me back upstairs."

Hades pauses in the hall to talk to Oliver, and I go into his rooms ahead of him. Wash my hands with warm water. Twice. A third time.

I'm stepping into the shadows of his bedrooms as he arrives.

Conor is tight at his side, pushing against Hades's legs. The window shifts into muted moonlight and trailing stars. Hades closes out the rest of the world with a click of the door. He leans heavily against it and tips his head back.

His eyes catch the stars and meet mine.

Desperate energy pulls tight through the air.

This could be the last time.

Every moment could be the last peaceful one we have together.

Hades closes his eyes. It breaks my heart. His pain. The flowers I can't grow. Everything.

Conor is on alert at his side, his tail beating at the floor in a rhythm that's more warning than greeting. Hades strokes his head with a hand. His fingers play over his dog's collar.

He doesn't speak.

His hand tenses on Conor's head, and he takes a quick breath. Another. Lets it out slow. Hades doesn't want to tell me how much it hurts. He doesn't have to. I've been watching it get worse every day.

My dress is over my head in an instant. Hades hears and turns his head a fraction of an inch, but he doesn't open his eyes.

He keeps them closed as I move across the soft carpet. Closed as I lift my hands to the front of his shirt to feel the hard muscles underneath, rising and falling with breaths that are too fast for a man who is almost never out of breath.

Closed as I sink to my knees in front of him. Undo his belt. Set him free from his pants.

The first tentative lick around his crown drags a noise out of him that I'm sure he wouldn't make if the circumstances were different. It's a sound of deep lust and deep relief. Hot pride brushes down over my spine. Hades moves his hand from Conor's head to my hair.

He sinks his fingers into the curls and holds. Pulls until the threshold of pain. Stops at the edge.

I take a few inches of him into my mouth. He's huge, hard as steel, and it's entirely different being the one with a scrap of control.

I use this new power to explore him. Every small fact is burned into my memory. The curl of my tongue that makes his hips jerk. The soft suction, followed by harder licks, that pulls more noises from his lips. He tries so hard to hide them, just like he hides his pain. But he can't. One by one, I add links to the chain of knowledge like the bracelet around my wrist. Each one is delicate by itself, but together—

Together they make him groan, both his hands in my hair. "Summer queen."

He says it in a voice like stars, a voice like the far side of forever, and my whole body responds to the words. I light up like the dawn. My core clenches, empty of him, wanting him.

In return I take him so deep tears run down my cheeks. I give him my own air, my own breath, my own frantic sounds. I choke on him until I'm mindless, given over to him, blushing despite the extreme vulnerability of him right now.

It doesn't make him less powerful.

No.

It makes him more powerful.

I think he's about to come when he pulls me up off the floor. Into his arms. It's only a few steps to the bed and when we're there he sets me down on my knees. "Bend."

A single word, pure command, and I bend. I lower my head to the covers and offer him everything.

Hades climbs on after me, clothes abandoned. Thrusts into my swollen pussy with hard, possessive strokes. I come on the first one and the sound he makes—the sound—

He pulls out and a whimper drops into the covers. *Don't leave*, I mean to say, but he's not leaving, he's turning me over onto my back. Pushing inside me.

Taking my mouth with his.

Hades kisses me like I'm his last tether to the earth. He fucks hard and kisses softly until his body takes over and he's all hard man, all teeth and tongue, all nip and bite. He spreads my legs with both hands and pushes my knees up and up and up until he's settled between them, driving in with enough force to rattle me.

I won't let anything happen to you. I say it with every touch. *I won't let her keep hurting you.*

I'm too much his summer queen to do that.

He's a king, and even a king in pain needs a queen. I'll be a warm night for him. I'll be the summer moon. I'll be the fresh soil where flowers grow.

Hades licks across my lips as he comes, another sound escaping him. His hips pump in an old, old rhythm, and mine match him. I'm not fragile. I can take him. I can take anything he has to give.

His head drops onto my shoulder and he takes a long breath. Another. And then we're moving across the bed. He pulls me to him like I'd pull on a blanket, hitching my leg over his hip so he can touch me where I'm wet from the both of us. So he can find my clit. So he can coax an orgasm out of me with my mouth against his neck, my cries on his skin.

Aftershocks roll over me, smaller and smaller, but I won't give in to sleep yet. "I won't let you go," I tell the warm skin below his jaw.

I'm drifting to sleep in his arms when he takes a breath and says *I know.*

TWENTY

Hades

I HAVEN'T MADE A HABIT OF WAKING PERSEPHONE IN THE night.

Since she began her relentless pursuit of the flowers, it's been the opposite. Me, startling awake to find the other side of the bed empty. Several times now I've found her on her knees in the moonlight, her fingertips brushing the petals of a night bloom.

Persephone whispers to them while they grow. I can't hear what she says. From the pleading hope in her eyes, I imagine her words are either encouragement or praise, despite how they've disappointed her.

Tonight, I can't sleep.

She's the one in a restless sleep.

I've been lying next to her for several hours, bargaining with the pain.

It has retreated, for the moment.

Pain affects my experience of time. It makes minutes last

for hours. It makes days last weeks. I've lived several fucking lifetimes against my express wishes.

Now we're rushing toward fate like a runaway train.

The arrival of Demeter's message could mean anything. It could mean she's moving her people into position around the mountain. It could mean she's decided to wait until she thinks I've let my guard down. The team I sent to the farm found nothing.

Not her normal operations—nothing.

Not a worker in sight. No bodies, either. That doesn't mean Demeter hasn't killed them, though we can't be certain without the physical evidence.

The only thing I learned this evening after Persephone went to sleep is that Zeus is no longer in custody. No one could confirm how long he's been out. They might not have held him for more than a few hours.

Tonight, Olympus is open for business.

Another piece of non-information. It's not an indication that he's decided not to retaliate. It's not even an indication that he's at the whorehouse. Zeus prefers to micromanage the situation, but even he has people who can take over for the evening.

I've been waiting for him to make his move since I walked out with Persephone in my arms.

My mind wanders aimlessly through my options. I've doubled security on the mountain. I'd triple it, but a full lockdown will cause disruptions that I won't be able to manage.

Persephone stirs in her sleep. "Grow," she whispers, coaxing some dream-flower to life. "So easy."

I slip out of the bed, put on pants, and go down to my office. Conor uncurls himself from his place on the floor and goes with me. He stands close, alert and guarding. It would be quite something if he could intimidate the seizures out of my brain.

Oliver appears at the door a few minutes later. "One of our people got confirmation that Zeus is at Olympus hosting the party."

"Has he sent his people ahead of him?"

"Not as far as I can tell."

"Demeter?"

"Quiet on the farm. There was a light in her window an hour ago."

I rub my hands over my face. We are reduced to telling fortunes based on lights in windows and party attendance. I briefly consider going back to the bedroom, getting my phone, and sending a message to Zeus.

Just do it already.

Instead, I take a seat at my desk. Conor wedges himself between my desk and the chair and rests his head on my leg. The warmth is a small comfort in a cold situation. "The mines?"

One of the muscles on the scarred side of his face twitches. "All in order."

"Don't fuck with me, Oliver."

"I'd have come to you if I needed you. It's quiet down there. No trouble this shift."

There will be trouble. It's only a matter of time. I can't leave those responsibilities to Oliver. We're quickly reaching the point where I won't have a choice. Old shame tastes bitter and sharp-edged, like swallowing a raw diamond whole. It was never supposed to come to this. My weakness was supposed to be a contained disaster, never reaching outside my body.

"Nothing of concern in the tunnels, either." Oliver crosses his arms over his chest. "I reviewed the reports before I came up. Everything is quiet right now."

"If you have something to ask, ask it."

"Are you planning something?"

I glare at him. "What the fuck does that mean, planning something?"

"You're spending half the time on reinforcing the tunnels and the other half closing out contracts like you're not going to be here long."

Oliver is a tough bastard. I've never seen his face quite like this before. The shadows erase most of his features, but I can still see the worried lines in his forehead.

"I didn't hire you to fret about me. I hired you to keep the mountain secure and ensure my operations continue to run."

"But—"

"Even in the event that I am... incapacitated. Especially in that fucking event. But if I am, it won't be because I chose it."

Oliver nods, glancing down at the floor. "It's warm out tonight."

"What?"

"One of those pockets of heat in the valley."

It's cooler on the mountain in the summer than it is in the surrounding countryside. Sometimes, however, a warm front catches on the rock and stays a day or two, warming the night air in the valley. I thought it was too early for that to happen.

A shiver goes down my spine. It's like Persephone brought the summer with her. Then I crowned her queen. My mind goes to her, sleeping in my bed.

Oliver leaves me to my ruminations.

I haven't made a habit of waking Persephone up in the night, but I don't know how many nights we have left. I don't know how many hours we have left.

The prudent thing to do would be to sleep. To spend as much time as possible unconscious so I can make it through another day. There's a certain pleasure in denial, but I can't deny myself tonight. Not when every breath I take says *last, last, last*.

It's not necessarily accurate. The way this scenario plays out is yet unknown to all of us. I'm still unable to shake off the feeling that this night is set apart. I want her in it with me.

Last, last, last.

Conor accompanies me back to the bedroom.

"Sleep," I tell him.

He pushes his nose against my leg one more time. I stroke his head. His soft ears. When he's had enough, he shuffles back to the fireplace and lowers himself to the floor.

I gather a blanket. A spare pillow.

At the side of the bed, I look down at my summer queen.

She sleeps with her hands curled protectively in front of her, holding them close. My throat closes. I'm a selfish asshole for wanting to disturb her sleep. She spent all night in the valley, exhausting herself for me, and then she had to confront the reality of her mother's obsession.

Persephone doesn't stir until I put my hand on her shoulder. She turns toward me at my touch and opens her big, luminous eyes. Her thighs part automatically under the sheets. I slide my hand up and over her mouth just to feel the way she gasps against my palm.

"Come with me."

My summer queen makes a noise into my hand that's not quite a laugh. It's sexier by far. Filled with so much frustrated want that I almost abandon my palm.

Last, last, last.

I let her up. Help her out of the bed.

Persephone's footsteps are soft on the floor next to mine. I drape the blanket around her shoulders as we go. She doesn't ask me where we're going. There's a certain pleasure in shared silence.

Last.

She was angry with me for not telling her every last truth about me.

If she could, I think Persephone would press her forehead against mine and go exploring through my memories. She sees something worthwhile in the story of my life.

We don't have time for me to tell her everything. I don't know that I'd have the strength. What we have is this night. This hour. This minute.

Persephone stops at the door leading out to the valley and looks up at me. The moment takes on a sacred character. My vision hasn't been this clear in days. I use it to study every line. The shape of her shoulders underneath the blanket. The way her chest expands when she breathes. The fall of her curls over her shoulders.

I could swear she's doing the same. Which makes me pity her. She has to look at freakish black eyes in the face of the man who might be taken from her by his own weakness.

Finally, when I've memorized her there in the shadows, I push open the door.

Warm air from the valley sweeps in over us. Persephone sighs. "That feels good. I'm out in the sun all day, but I'm not tired of the heat."

I put my hand on the small of her back and guide her across the threshold.

The night air is perfumed with hundreds of flowers. Persephone looks out over her work, the smile fading from her face. She's a moonlit goddess against the black background of the mountain. The warm breeze plays through my hair and breathes into her curls. It toys with the hem of her nightgown.

Last.

"You don't like it outside," she says, her voice as soft as the breeze. "You can't stand it."

A hundred excuses present themselves for why I haven't told her. Why I haven't whispered every fucking thing about myself into her ear. I ignore them all.

"I love to be outside."

Her eyes turn sad as the admission reaches her on the wind. More moonlight catches in her hair. It lights her from the inside. She belongs out here, in the grass and the breeze. Among her flowers.

I put my hands on her waist the moment she's close enough.

Another wall crumbles and blows away into the summer night.

"You love it," she repeats. "Because it's dark."

"Yes."

Persephone closes her eyes like I've done something unbearably intimate. I bend to lick the hollow of her throat, fierce need beating through my bloodstream. What I feel for her is made from the truest parts of myself.

Bringing her here is a painful contradiction. I want to give her everything she wants, but I'm not a kind man. I'm a terrible man.

A monster.

The most monstrous thing I do will be to take myself from her. It will be entirely against my will. I don't know how to stop it.

Last.

"Hades," Persephone whispers. "Maybe I could hurt instead."

TWENTY-ONE

Persephone

H E HISSES AT MY WORDS, AND I KNOW I'VE ANSWERED some question he won't ask. I can feel it in the energy around him. Hades will always have jagged edges, and I want all of him. The parts that look refined and expensive and the parts with sharp teeth. The parts that hurt. The parts that want.

The parts that are afraid.

I'll never ask him to admit it, but I can feel it. A heavy sense that something will end when the sun rises. Or something will begin. Change will settle over the mountain like the heat settled in the valley.

Maybe I could hurt instead.

Hades wraps a big hand around my arm and pulls me through the valley. He sweeps me up in his arms and carries me across the ravine. Some of my newer flowers are here, and Hades is careful not to step on them as he goes. We stop at a flat place in the grass, hidden from Eleanor's house by the slope of the earth.

Goose bumps bloom on my skin. My mind wants to race forward into the future, into all the problems we have to solve in order to survive, but my heart wants to stay here, with him.

Hades spreads one blanket on the grass and tosses the other down at one end. A pillow lands with a quiet thud. He moves me to stand on the blanket and strips off my nightgown. Warm air brushes across my skin. Across all the exposed parts of me.

With his usual cold precision Hades takes one of my nipples between his fingers and pinches. Slowly. Deliberately. Until a cry comes to my lips.

I pinch them shut so it doesn't escape, but this only makes him pinch harder. The other nipple next.

He makes a sound that's pure dissatisfaction. He wants to hear me whimper. "Fine, but it would be better to watch you writhe from clamps."

The thought of his metal and diamonds biting into my nipples makes me moan.

Shamelessly. Awfully. We're out in the open air, under the stars, with nothing between us and the mountain. Anyone could come out and see us.

It doesn't make a difference. I would still moan for him.

Hades puts a hand around my throat and it's a familiar gesture now. It's as if he'd stroked my cheek. A softness hides beneath this show of possession and cruelty. He slots his other hand between my legs, pushing my thighs apart.

"Wider." His tone is frosty now, and I get wetter from that single word. "Now, Persephone. Spread wider. Do you think that's far enough? More."

I spread my legs until my thighs shake and burn. My body reacts. Thoughts tumbling into dark possibilities. Into the cruel things he could do to me. It makes me pant. It sets my nerves on fire.

It clears my head.

It washes away the heavy feelings of yesterday and puts the future at a distance.

I don't know what to do with the waiting and the terrible, sexy fear that grows with each second. A thrilling fear. One I've chosen.

Hades's grip tightens, his thumb adding pressure to my neck. The hand between my legs draws back, giving him a few inches of space. He swats it against my pussy. Ice pours into my gut. There it is—that instinct to freeze. I can't move. Can't close my legs. I don't want to close my legs.

He laughs. "I'm going to punish your pussy, summer queen." Hades sounds like the night around us, warm and dangerous at the same time. He's threat and promise all in one. "And what are you going to do?"

"I'm—" I'm desperate to please him. To hurt for him. My body fears the pain, but it's nothing compared to the fear I feel at losing him. At failing him. "I'm going to keep my legs apart and let you."

"If your toes leave the ground, it's ten with my hand on your ass and we'll start over."

It feels good to give myself over. I'm safe in his hands. He'll only hurt me as much as he wants. As much as I want. I can feel him loving me through his hand on my throat and the coaxing pressure at my pussy. Hades strokes his fingers through my folds, making sure I want this.

I shouldn't.

I do.

"How many?"

"Five," he says, and then he draws his hand back and delivers the first slap.

A fiery pain erupts between my legs, and now I see. Now

I see why he said my toes couldn't leave the ground. My heels come up in spite of myself. I'm starved for air, struggling for breath. The second slap comes. I arch in his hand. The only thing keeping my toes on the ground is his hand around my throat. The only thing keeping my knees from collapsing is that same grip.

On the third, I burst into tears from the pain and the mortifying pleasure. I might come from this. I might die from this.

But I don't close my legs.

Hades leans down and kisses the salt off my lips in a hungry bite. "Would you rather I finish your punishment with my hand or my cock?"

"Hand," I sob. "Please. Now."

A low growl escapes into the night. The next two slaps are fast and hard, and when they're over, he takes me to my back on the ground. Sheds his clothes. Then he's between my legs, pushing himself into my wet, hot center. I sob out pleasure and pain.

Hades fucks me hard, hips working, the pain and frustration of the day whipping away from him and into the night. Into me. He's driving me into the ground. Into the earth. Summer glides between us. Covers us. Touches every inch of my skin, and his. I grab for the blanket and end up with a handful of grass. A bloom pushes up from the earth beneath my fingertips. I breathe him in. Hades's scent reminds me of a cold snap. Clean and new.

I curl my legs around him and pull him in closer. It goes against every instinct. His strokes are dangerously hard. They're too much. But when I hook my ankles around his waist—

Something breaks inside him. He lets out a sharp breath, his shoulders relaxing.

He gentles.

Slows.

The force of him is the same. The power is the same. But they take on an almost unbearable tenderness. A hand on my face. A tilt of his hips. It brings me to the edge of my first orgasm and pushes me into it.

"You love punishment," Hades murmurs into my ear as I come, crying out. "I felt how wet you were. You almost came on my hand while I slapped your pussy."

"I know," I gasp. "I know."

"Come now."

I do it. It curls into me like lightning and I clench on his cock, again and again and again. When it's over Hades spreads my knees wide and fucks into the new angle he's created with my body. I can't stop clenching down on him. Can't stop fluttering around him. It's beyond my control.

Beyond his, too.

He makes a noise that I don't recognize as surprise until he's coming. There's so much liquid and heat, so much movement in his body. He bites down on my shoulder as he comes.

And then he lets his weight rest against me. He folds me up into his arms, his lips brushing my ear.

"When I was younger, I would sneak out during the summer. There was a lake at the farmhouse, where my brother Poseidon taught us to swim. I would go there at night." He pumps in and out in a lazy rhythm. I know it won't be lazy for long. "One night I went to the lake, and I swear, Persephone, there were a hundred falling stars. I loved them until I wasn't capable of love."

"You love me." I'm half-senseless with him.

He says nothing for a long time. He's hard inside me. Still fucking me. The night is nothing but stars and Hades and one more whisper into my ear. "I do."

TWENTY-TWO

Hades

FOR THE FIFTH TIME IN AN HOUR, CONOR TRIES TO CLIMB up into my lap.

"It's a desk chair," I tell my dog. "There is not room for both of us. You're not a puppy. And I'm fine. Please stop acting like I'm dying."

He declines to believe me, but the situation is not as dire as he's making it out to be. After I fucked Persephone under the stars, I carried her to bed, and we slept. I was careful about the lights this morning, and so was she. There's a single, dim night-light on in the office.

It's early in the morning. Too early for the night to have ended already.

Persephone is working in the valley, and I am being a useless fucker here, holding off the pain.

It takes most of my effort to do it. I'm sitting very still. I am not letting my heart rate rise. I am keeping my mounting frustration in check. None of those things are enough to stave

off a seizure, or even the worst of the pain. In the absence of the poppies, it's all I have.

One of the outer doors in my foyer bangs open. Its echo sends a spike of pain through the center of my head. I close my eyes and will it away. I force down the jolt in my pulse. It's not possible to send the door flying. Both its weight and the soft-close mechanism keep it from doing battle with the wall.

It is, however, possible to run into it at high speed.

Running footsteps in the hall announce Oliver's presence. He throws the door to my office open before the hallway lights can adjust. I slap my hand over my eyes.

"Fuck." He's breathing hard. "Sorry. Closed now."

I put my hand down as Conor launches a renewed attempt at climbing onto my lap. Oliver's eyes drop then flicker to my dog and back. I narrow my eyes at him. "Is there something you need to report?"

"News." His shoulders go up and down. "From the city."

My blood runs cold, but I hold tight to my composure. "No one is going to scale the mountain and burst through the window, Oliver. Not in the next fifteen minutes. Sit down."

"I can't." He crosses his arms over his chest, and I get a glimpse of the man he used to be. The man I forced onto the train by his shirt collar when he tried to run back to the city the first time. "Zeus is building an army."

"Sit the fuck down."

Zeus hiring an army is not a welcome turn of events, but it's not a death sentence, either. *Army* could mean a variety of things. It could mean an increase in private security. It could signal that Demeter has turned her attention to him instead of me.

"I have to be ready to go downstairs."

"And what, have a heart attack? Sit down, or I'll end this conversation now."

Oliver stares off into the shadows, his jaw working. No doubt he's taking stock. The fact that I'm sitting here in the dark, insisting on calm, does not bode well for my performance during an assault on the mountain. If I'm weak, then the mountain is weak. And if I die… well, I don't want to think about what happens to the mountain then.

He rolls his shoulders back and approaches the chairs across from me with the air of a man who's about to undergo interrogation. Oliver sits on the edge of one, his back straight, and meets my eyes.

"Continue."

He takes a deep breath. "Zeus is gathering an army in the city. He's been doing it quietly, which is why it took our people longer to find out. He's keeping them away from the whorehouse."

"If he's being so discreet, how did we come by this information?"

"One of the new recruits had too much to drink at one of the dive bars near where he's stationing them. Zeus is paying them well. The worker showed off a pay stub."

I raise an eyebrow. "And my brother's name was on it."

"One of his shell companies."

"Fuck."

Conor puts both paws on my lap and pushes me bodily away from the desk.

I take his head in my hands and stare into his eyes. "Calm *down*, Conor. I'm. Fine."

He looks back at me. Only the faintest catchlights illuminate his eyes. I'm not imagining the concern I find there. I ruffle his ears.

Last.

My dog agrees to sit at my feet with his head on my knee. He won't go any farther.

When I look back at Oliver, I discover he hasn't bothered to hide his fear. He hurries to wipe it from his expression.

"What is his new army made up of? Private security?"

"Russian mercenaries."

"What the fuck."

Mercenaries. I suppose it's one way to react to my visit to the whorehouse.

However, mercenaries are in a different league from law enforcement. I gave explicit instructions that no one at the whorehouse would be killed in the raid. The officers responded well to the threat of consequences if that were to be the case.

Hired guns only have one purpose, and it's not to make arrests.

"I don't know how many he has." Oliver folds his hands on the desk. "I have people looking."

"Heavy weapons?"

"The asshole with the pay stub ran his mouth about machine guns."

In one sense, it's reassuring. A braggart would be compelled to name the largest weapon available to the army. In another sense, machine guns could do quite a bit of damage. Particularly if my people panicked and ran into the line of fire.

"I don't imagine he outlined any of the battle plans."

Oliver grimaces. "No."

I stroke Conor's head and consider my choices. The list is limited, and my thoughts keep returning to Persephone. My summer queen is on the mountain, and she won't agree to go into hiding. It's unlikely that I could secure a space that would be tolerable for me without access for painkillers. Even if she would agree, and I didn't need painkillers, the idea of abandoning my people is offensive.

Oliver summons the courage to speak again. "You crossed a line with him."

"Do you fucking think so?"

Silence.

"I can't uncross it. I can't un-send federal agents into his illegal whorehouse. It's not my fault he chose to follow in our father's footsteps."

"You were justified," he says. "In going to get her. I'm not arguing that point. I'm just… is there any chance he'd talk to you? That you could get him to stand down another way?"

I don't know. Zeus is the one who kept me alive at the farmhouse. I was unconscious for most of his rescues, but I remember enough to blame him for it. I can't speak to his motivations. The end result was that Cronos got to continue with his campaign of torture and pocket the money.

No, whispers a summer voice. *The end result is that you got Persephone.*

That's up for debate. After all, I might not be able to keep her.

"Zeus will take any offer for negotiation as a sign of weakness." I can't risk letting him know that I'm not in a position to fight. Not for long enough to chase him from the mountain. Not for long enough to kill him.

"Then what?" Oliver grips the edge of the desk. He's looking to me for an answer, and all I can think is that I was right about last night. We won't get another moment of peace. Conor huffs, sounding anxious, and I pet his head.

"No one leaves the mountain."

"What about the trains?"

"We'll keep them running. If we stop them, Zeus will know we found his man. And we need more people in the city."

"To find the rest of his army?"

"There are a number of people here with family members in the city. They'll be safer here."

Oliver looks skeptical. "He has machine guns."

"Better machine guns than people to hold hostage."

"Christ," he says under his breath.

"Send a separate team back to the bar, and any other gathering places you think Zeus's people might use."

"What are they searching for?"

"Nothing. They're going to buy drinks for people and talk."

"Gossip." Oliver's hands relax, a signal that this is enough planning to keep him from losing his fucking mind.

"To reinforce the idea that there are women and children here."

Because, of course, there are.

"I don't know if Zeus cares about women and children."

"He cares about his image as the city's most benevolent pimp. Storming the mountain and murdering innocent women wouldn't play well with his clients."

Innocent women reminds me of Persephone. An image of her in the valley, surrounded by all those blooms, springs to mind. Persephone, windblown, her hair a beautiful mess. Persephone, encouraging the flowers to grow. Persephone, reaching for me in the starlight. A fist squeezes my heart. My summer queen spends all her time trying to save me. I can't fuck or punish that desire out of her. I'll never be able to.

Not even if Zeus does his worst.

Not even if he drags me to a bloody, hollow death.

Persephone is not a creature of death. She belongs in green fields. In sunshine. The hem of her dress lifting in the breeze.

A vision of a clear blue sky appears in my memory, and when I look at her, it doesn't hurt at all.

I stand, and Conor rushes to my side. Oliver scrambles to his feet. "Where are you going?"

"Downstairs. So are you."

"You should stay here," Oliver says, even as he follows me out into the hall. "Persephone says—"

"You don't work for Persephone. You work for me. And if you want her to stay alive, you'll shut the hell up and do your job."

Oliver shuts the hell up, and we go down to my office together and set our plans in motion.

Our last plans.

TWENTY-THREE

Persephone

SPEND TWO DAYS IN THE VALLEY, ON EDGE EVERY MINUTE. It's hard to concentrate on the flowers.

Eleanor comes out to worry over me, a basket for collecting flowers in her hand. Her sun hat casts a round shadow over me.

"Any luck?" she asks.

"No." I sit back and wipe my forehead with my sleeve. I probably look like a mess, but Eleanor doesn't. Her gray hair is neat, and her clothes are clean and flowy, like always. "And Hades says Zeus is hiring mercenaries. He's making all sorts of plans to fight back."

She nods, serene. "How is he?"

"It's getting worse," I admit, getting to my feet. "Conor seems tense all the time."

"The dog has a sixth sense." The corners of her mouth turn down. "If the situation changes, I hope you'll keep Conor with you."

It makes the hairs on my neck stand to think about separating Hades from Conor during some kind of battle. "Hades will need him when it's over. He warns him, doesn't he? About the seizures."

"Yes," Eleanor says. Her thoughts seem far away. "But I don't think he'd survive the loss of another one of his dogs. Not right now."

"Another one?" Hades has never once mentioned owning another dog.

She sighs. "He loved one other pet. Rosie. He tried to keep her out of harm's way." Tears come to her eyes, but she dabs at them with her knuckle. "Cronos killed her anyway. He never had another dog after that. Not until after Cronos died."

His foster father.

No wonder he was so cold. No wonder he wouldn't admit that he cared.

I breathe out the deep ache in my chest and look Eleanor in the eye. "If anything happens, I'll keep Conor with me."

She pats my elbow. "All of you stay safe."

It doesn't occur to me until later that Eleanor never seemed concerned about herself.

In spite of Hades's plans, I can't relax. Defeating Zeus won't solve our biggest problem, which is the lack of poppies.

"Just stay where it's dark," I whisper to him as I'm falling asleep. "I'll make them grow."

On the third morning, I only make it an hour in the valley. I need to talk to Hades. I need to be with him. The sense of impending doom is so strong that my bones ache.

Except Hades isn't in his bedroom.

He isn't in his office.

I search the rest of his home as quickly as I can. In the process, I discover a small gym with a hot tub attached. I discover a room with glass ceilings and one huge glass wall. From that room, I can see the ocean.

The *ocean.*

Where is he?

On my way back through, one of the main doors opens, and Oliver comes in. His eyebrows go up. He looks guilty as hell.

"Oliver. Where's Hades?"

"I don't know."

I give him a patient look. He does know.

He grimaces. "He's down in his office."

"*Why?*"

"There are plans to make. Things he needs to put in place before—"

"He can't be in the office. It's too bright. The factory floor is right there, and none of those people can work in the dark." I've been begging him to stay where it's safe. I can't believe he's being so reckless. "I'm going down." Oliver moves to step in front of me. "Don't you dare try to stop me. I'm going."

Oliver does his job well, and I can see how much it pains him to even consider going against Hades's orders. "I'll call him," he offers. "I'll call him and tell him to come back."

I draw myself up to my full height, which is still quite a bit less than Oliver's. "Get out of my way."

Something shifts in his expression.

In this moment, I don't feel like a prisoner or an asset. I feel like a queen. They're equals to their husbands or wives, and they don't let the staff stop them from living their lives.

Oliver steps aside.

I go out the doors and down the long hall to the elevator. The rotunda is filled with people huddled in the alcoves and whispering to each other. They're nervous. I think that's normal when you're waiting to be attacked at any moment.

I'm nervous, too, but I force myself to smile at them.

People move out of my way as I get closer to Hades's office. I should've worn different shoes, but it's too late for that kind of regret. I should have done a lot of things, like changed my clothes or put on makeup, or brushed out my hair. I should have checked in the mirror, since five minutes ago I was out in the grass and dirt.

But here I am.

Nobody stops me at the giant doors to Hades's office. At the last minute I pick up the pace so I'm almost at a run when I go inside, heart beating out of my chest, pulse singing with blue skies and indignation.

Hades stands silhouetted in front of the windows that give him a panoramic view of the factory floor, his head bowed over a tablet. The blue light catches his face as he raises his head. Oh shit. He's not in a good mood. His shoulders are all tension, his hands tight on the sides of the tablet.

"What are you doing here?" Hades glances behind me, like he expects Zeus's army to come in next.

I put my hands on my hips. "What are *you* doing here? You're going to hurt yourself."

His jaw tightens. There's no color in his eyes. His frustration is a heat wave. It's extreme pressure. I can feel a hint of it in the air, I think.

"I told you to stay upstairs, Persephone."

"I said the same thing to you."

Hades strips off his jacket while he crosses the floor toward me. I rock up on the balls of my feet and come back down. Adrenaline washes through me. I don't run, but I have the energy for it. The jacket falls. One of his buttons comes off when he shoves his sleeves up. Then he's breathing over me, an icy cold front. From this close, there's no denying his fury, or his fear.

He's wordless with it. Another first that's terrifying in its uniqueness. He always has something to say. Not this time.

I'm bent over the desk before I have time to catch my breath or my balance, the glass surface coming up to meet me and crushing the air from my lungs. Hades takes a breath. It steadies him enough to speak while he pulls one arm behind my back, then another. A familiar tension around my wrists. His tie. He's binding me.

"I told you to stay upstairs."

I struggle out of instinct, and his large palm pushes me back down.

"That wasn't for my fucking health. It's to keep you safe."

He pushes my dress up. Shoves my panties down. A drawer opens. A drawer? All of me goes tense and hot. I'm already bound. I already want this. But it doesn't stop the chill of not knowing what's going to happen. This is, in a way, what I wanted when I came looking for him.

"Punish me, then," I tell him breathlessly.

"What the fuck do you think I'm doing?"

He spreads me apart next, perfunctory, humiliating. Wide. And then something cold and slick makes contact. A vicious, visceral flashback to the train rears up and slaps me. I know exactly what he's going to do. He can't do it. He can't. He can't. It'll never work.

"I think you're teaching me a lesson." I think he's buying time. I think he's as desperate to be near me as I am to be near him. I think he can feel the storm in the air, just like I can.

"That's right, summer queen. You should pay attention."

His finger comes next, pressing inexorably into that secret, virgin place. I have no way to stop him, and it's terrifying and wonderful—it's what I wanted. But the pendulum swings toward terrifying, and I squeeze tight, trying to keep him out. Not there, not there. No, no...

Another finger. There's just not enough room. My lungs flatten, refuse to take in a breath. It's so wrong, what he's doing. This is worse than when he made me come over and over. This is worse. Two fingers in a tight space, and I can't get used to him. I rock uselessly against the desk in the half-inch of leeway he's given me. I'm getting nowhere. He won't stop.

"You can grow your flowers. You can push yourself to the brink of exhaustion. But you're not going to put yourself in danger. I won't allow it."

He takes his fingers out and pushes them back in. I discover I've been crying. *He's* in danger. Just from standing in his office. I couldn't grow the poppies. And his fingers. They're too much. Too much. More lube, cold and slippery. More fingers. His other hand pins my wrists to my back. It's so sexy I can't catch my breath, and so embarrassing, so awful. Wrong. Wrong. Wrong. *Wrong* is a drumbeat that makes my face red and the tears come faster. It makes wetness gather between my legs, where he won't touch.

Another panicked tear splashes onto the desk, and the next moment, the fingers are gone. Something much bigger is pushing against me. It's him. It's him, and he will never, ever fit. Hades lets go of my wrists and strokes his hands down the outside of my hips. Is he going to force it? The answer is almost certainly yes.

"Open up for me." The command filters down through my ugly, wheezing sob, but I hope he doesn't stop. He follows with a sharp slap to my ass.

"I don't know how." I don't know how to solve any of this. "Please, wait."

Don't wait.

He strokes across my back—*easy, easy*—and then that hand moves around to the front of me and delves between my legs. I cannot fathom how I got to this place in my life that this situation—this, here, now—has me on the edge. It's not right. It's so terribly wrong.

"Open. Relax." The pressure intensifies. He's going to do this no matter how much I struggle and cry. So why struggle? I can't help crying, but I can let go.

I can let go.

I fall onto the desk, letting it take all my weight, and he murmurs things to me. *Summer queen. You don't know what you do to me. Good girl.*

He pushes the head of his cock inside. It's a painful stretch. Too big and too much and not enough. Hades plays gently with my clit. It's the polar opposite of what he's doing to my ass. My legs shake. I'm up on tiptoe, trying to get a good angle, trying to relieve any of this intense pressure, but nothing works. The trembling moves up and takes me over. I'm at its mercy, and his.

Another inch. Another.

"Good." His voice is stretched thin. "Good, you filthy thing. You're such a pretty summer queen. You're doing so well. Hold still. Yes. Hold still, that's it…"

My mind splits away from the rest of me. He is so huge, and I am so small. Another inch, and then another. He keeps me from falling. That, and the desk. One by one, my memories fly away. The things I wanted. My name. I'm no one. I'm his.

When he's fully inside me, I know it's the end.

The end of me, the end of the world, the end of everything.

If he moves, I'll die. The stretch is too much. The struggle to keep letting go is too much.

Hades doesn't move.

He makes me do it.

His fingertips on my clit have gone still, and I only notice because he starts moving them again in an infinitely soft circle.

"No," I howl into his empty office. "Don't make me."

"Oh, summer queen. It's far too late for that."

One final stroke yanks me down into an orgasm so filthy and powerful that my eyes go dark from all the tears.

"Please, please." I sound like I'm underwater, drowning in him. "Please."

Please, don't hurt yourself. Please.

What I get is Hades dragging himself back out and pushing himself back in. He sets his own deadly rhythm. I twist in his tie, searching for his hand, and hold his tight.

Hades holds on tight while he fucks the breath out of me, and then the tears, and then, finally, lets himself go.

"Fuck," he says, so softly I could be imagining it. I could be hallucinating. "Fuck, I love you."

TWENTY-FOUR

Persephone

HADES LIFTS ME FROM HIS DESK AND FIXES MY CLOTHES. The second my hem drops into place, I turn around and throw my arms around his neck. My heart is going to beat out of my chest. My heart is going to burst into bloom. He kisses me so hard I end up perched on his desk, one of his hands braced behind me.

"I love you," I say into his mouth.

He pulls back to look into my eyes, a hopeful astonishment on his face.

"Yeah." I can't quite catch my breath. "I heard you. And I love you."

A flicker of joy crosses his face, and I smile back at him.

Except his smile never materializes, so I'm smiling at him like a fool when his expression freezes. On the other side of his desk, Conor barks. The dog races around the desk to Hades.

The momentary happiness on his face disappears. The

muscles around his eyes tense. I'm too close for him to hide the pain.

Hades leans harder against the desk. Conor pushes at his leg. He's gentle, then insistent. He barks again. He barks again. I don't think I've heard him bark quite this way before.

"Oh, fuck," Hades says.

Conor flies around his feet on the way upstairs, herding Hades as fast as he can. My gut twists. This is bad, and I'm powerless to stop it.

Hades holds it together until we step off the elevator. As the doors slide shut, he covers his eyes with both hands. Conor presses the side of his body to Hades's leg and stays there, perfectly still, until Hades reaches down for his collar.

Conor leads. I follow until we're at the sitting room, and then I rush ahead and turn all the lights off. The door closes behind me. Hades is through.

I can't see anything. It's pitch-dark. Hades brushes past me, heading toward the far corner, away from his bed. I hear him slide down the wall to the floor. I hear Conor's collar *clink* as he sits next to him.

Silence.

It's loud enough to hear my heart beat.

I go to Hades.

He's shaking, his head in his hands. The air around him feels thicker. Pressurized. I get a sense of him in the dark, skimming my fingertips over his wrists. His shoulders.

I put a hand on his knee. "We have to get the poppies."

"There isn't a way to get them."

"We have to, Hades. There's no other choice."

I almost say *look at you*, but there's no point. I don't need to see him to know how much this is hurting him.

It's killing him.

"You can't keep living like this."

"This is how I live, Persephone. There's no alternative." Every word out of his mouth is strained.

"We know where the poppies are. I grew them in my mother's fields myself. I can go back and get them."

"No."

"There's enough for me to work with," I insist. "She can't have burned all the roots. I only need a scrap of one of those poppies, and I can grow them here. One seed deep in the ground. That's all I need." I get to my feet and pace in the dark. I bump into a chair almost immediately. "We also need to send out a search party. There has to be another source. My mother isn't the only one who can grow flowers, and you're not the only person she sold them to. There has to be someone else."

"Do you think I haven't looked?"

"How hard did you try? Maybe you missed something. Maybe you thought you deserved this, and you didn't search everyone."

"Trust me." A hollow laugh. "I do. I deserve all of this and more for taking you."

"That's not true." I go back to him. Drop to my knees. Take his hands in mine. He's shaking harder now. "This is too much pain for any person to stand. That's why you're trembling."

"I'm trying to stop what happens next. You shouldn't be burdened with it."

"You're not a burden. Don't try to convince me that you are."

"I'll be dead weight, Persephone. I'll hurt you."

"If you have to be moved, then I'll get help. I'll be fine. You're the one who is not fine. I won't let you keep suffering like this."

"Have you ever considered that suffering has a purpose?"

Hades's teeth click together. He forces a breath through them. "Have you ever considered that some people suffer because they deserve it?"

"That's not why this is happening to you."

I take his face in my hands. His skin is hot. Almost feverish. A few moments later, he's gone cold. All of him is tense. Wracked with pain. I can't tell if he's stopped hiding it because I can't see him or because he can't do anything else.

"Hades, this has to end."

"Then kill me," he says drily.

"No." I squeeze his hands harder. "And that's not funny. I need you here with me."

"Why, summer queen?"

"Because I love you." My heart thunders with how much I love him. How much I need him. "I told you that before. I'm not going to let this happen. What we have to do is make a—a contingency plan. There is another way. I've tried the valley. I've grown everything I know how to grow. Do you have any other ideas?"

His silence is his answer.

"I can't sail around the world and hunt for seeds, but I can send people."

Hades scoffs. "I'm not sending anyone out there. My sister is fucking unhinged. Zeus will make his move soon enough. I'm not sending people out there to die for me."

"What happens to me, then?" My voice catches. "What happens to me if you're in too much pain to handle things here?"

"There are people to help you." Hades takes one of my hands and runs the pad of his thumb over my knuckles. "You won't be alone. You'll just have to live your life slightly separate from mine."

My throat closes. Salt tears swim in my eyes. "I don't want to be alone if we can't be together. How am I supposed to be happy if I can't see you?"

"You can't see me now."

He doesn't have to say the rest. That this could be the rest of his life. That darkness might be all we have.

"I'd rather stay in the dark with you for the rest of my life than know you were hurting like this."

Silence settles between us. Hades works to control his breathing. The pressure around him increases. He's trying to get it out of his body and into the ground. It'll win, in the end. He told me that.

I didn't know how fast he'd fall without the painkillers. Now that I do, the answer is clear.

"I have to go back to the farm."

"Absolutely not."

"Not in secret. Not to hunt through the fields for a stray seed. I need to go back to speak to my mother. I can make her send the flowers. I can convince her to do that. I can trade myself for them, the same way you offered to do in that note."

Now he's the one squeezing my hand. "You hated that note. You were furious with me for making the suggestion."

"Yes. I was angry. But if this is the way to save you, then I'm going to do it. I'm happy to do it. That's what makes this different from last time. That was your choice. This is mine. I'd willingly go back to her to spare your life."

"No," he snaps. "You're not sparing me anything."

"If you had the poppies, you wouldn't be in pain. You would feel better."

Hades pulls me closer to him, locking his hand around the back of my neck. His fingers work through my hair. "There is no pain greater than losing you. It is a fucking joke to say I'd feel better, summer queen. If I had the poppies but lost you, then all I'd have done is traded this pain for a worse one. Why the fuck would I want that? I don't want to live without you. When are you going to understand?"

His voice rises, but he doesn't shout. Hades restrains himself. I'm afraid for the moment when he no longer can. I'm afraid for the moment when his pain takes over completely and I can't reach him.

"I understand," I say softly. "I do."

I might never understand the magnitude of his pain, but I understand the depth of his desperation. If I don't fix this, we'll never have a chance to know each other without a looming threat. I will never know him when he's not being tortured by my mother.

But if this is how I get to know him, then I accept. If I have to trade myself for those poppies to keep him alive, I will.

My mother can't take this time away, no matter what. If I get one season in the sun before all this withers away, then it's been worth it.

That's what love is.

It's not locking someone in a farmhouse and forcing the world away. It's doing what's best for them, even when it hurts.

I would never compare my pain to his, but it hurts like hell to think of leaving him. It hurts less than imagining him cold and still on that table downstairs in one of his beautiful black shirts. I'd rather be locked in my childhood bedroom forever than have someone tell me that he looks like he's sleeping when I know it's a kind lie.

"I'm going back. I'm going to bargain with her. I can do it. You just have to trust me."

His grip on my neck turns aggressive and hard. So hard it hurts. "You're not hearing me."

"Yes, I am." I can hardly breathe for how much I love him and how much I want to stay. For how certain I am that I have to go.

"You are not going back to that place."

I lean in, because I am compelled. I can't be this close without kissing him. I brush my lips over his, and Hades kisses back. He can't stay soft. He doesn't. He kisses like he can punish me into agreeing with him. He kisses like he knows it won't work.

"I have to."

"Fuck no." He winds his fingers through my hair and pulls. "You're staying here with me."

I brace for him, because I know what happens now. He takes me one more time before I leave.

One last time.

Someone pounds at the bedroom door, and Hades holds me tighter.

"They're five minutes out," Oliver calls. "There was a meeting point outside the city. We got the intel just now. They're moving on the mountain."

I rush to the door. Oliver stands in the hall, a shadow against a dark backdrop. "Both of them?"

"Zeus and Demeter," he says. "They're working together. They're almost here."

TWENTY-FIVE

Persephone

I'M OUT OF TIME TO WORRY.

I'm out of time to plan.

And I discover, as the news sinks in, that I don't need to do either. My decision is already made. No part of me wavers. I know this is right.

"Five minutes?" I ask Oliver.

"Zeus and his people are coming from the west. Your mother from the south. First count says they each have about a hundred people with them."

"The mercenaries."

Hades comes to stand next to me. He slides his hand across the small of my back. Conor brushes against the backs of my calves. "Have all our people been ordered to their stations?"

"Before I came up," answers Oliver.

"Close off the mines. Cancel the shifts. Keep everybody inside."

Oliver nods. "And you?"

"If I come down, we'll have to shut off all the lights. It will create chaos. I'll stay here until everyone gets where they need to be."

"I'll be back with a report."

Oliver rushes away. I hear him break into a run.

Hades turns away from the door like the faint hallway light was full sun. Conor crowds him over to the bed. He sits down on the edge and breathes.

I go to the space between his knees, lean in, and kiss his temples. His forehead. His cheeks. His hands come up to cover his eyes. I kiss his knuckles, too.

And then I go to the bathroom. Wash up. The closet next, where I strip off my dress. I hunt for leggings by feel. A shirt that's more of a tunic. Shoes. I gather my hair into an elastic. I'm not sure if I'll have to run, or how far I'll have to go.

I wish for weapons.

Unfortunately, the only weapon I have any skill with is poisonous plants. I'd be just as likely to hurt myself with a knife or a gun. And anyway, I'm going in the spirit of peace.

Bargaining, at least. I don't think I'll be very successful if I'm trying to hold Zeus or my mother at knifepoint. I'm the valuable commodity now, not violence.

The last thing I do is check for my necklace. At the end of its chain, the black diamond has been warmed by my skin. It's a small comfort that I'll be able to keep it with me even if I can't come back.

But I *will* come back.

I will.

I go back out into the bedroom. Hades hasn't moved from his spot on the bed. I can hear him breathing. It sounds uneven, as if his pain has become unbearable.

Moving past him without touching him is the most painful thing I've ever done.

I slip out into the sitting room.

"Persephone."

I don't know what to say. We don't have time to argue. I need to get out there before all those armed men reach the mountain. Before anyone starts shooting. I'm the only one who can make any difference.

"*Persephone.*"

"I love you," I whisper, and break into a run.

I sprint down the length of the hallway, my breath loud in my ears. I hear Hades connect with the doorframe of the sitting room. Any other day, he'd be faster. I've taken advantage of his pain. I hope he can forgive me.

A string of curses follows me down the hall. "*Stop.*"

I don't stop. I get to the foyer and cut right, to the double doors. I'm halfway to the elevator when he reaches them.

Strips of emergency lights are on in this section of the hall. The light hits him like arrows. His entire body flinches back, but he throws himself after me.

I hit the button to call the elevator. If it's not here, I'll be screwed. He'll drag me back into his bedroom and I won't get another chance. My heart beats in my fingertips. In my toes. Everywhere. A gold, powerful feeling suffuses my chest. It's not the power that I use to grow flowers. It's just my own determination.

I've decided this. Like I told Hades before, the note he sent? That was his choice. This is mine. I can sacrifice myself for the man I love, and that makes me more powerful, not less.

The elevator doors open.

I jump inside and stab at the button to take me down. My mother and Zeus will be waiting outside, poised to attack. The five minutes are up. The rest of our time is up. All that's left is the future I'm about to make.

I straighten up and press myself against the back wall of the elevator. I did that on the very first day I came to the mountain. I was afraid of Hades and Conor.

I'm not afraid anymore.

I'm choosing this.

It's not like the night I left with Decker. That was against my will. It was being kidnapped. This time I'm leaving of my own volition.

Outside, the world is bathed in sunlight and summer. It's the one place Hades can't go, so I'll go for him. I'll be the one to decide how this ends.

Hades runs down the hall, picking up speed as the elevator doors move. Conor is in his way. Barking at his feet. Circling him. Trying to get him to go back.

"*No.*"

"I love you," I tell him. "I'll come back to you. I promise."

He reaches for me, too far away. That's the last I see of him before the door closes between us.

He'll be safe in his kingdom. I'll make sure of it.

MIDNIGHT KINGDOM

ONE

Persephone

THE ELEVATOR DOORS OPEN ONTO THE ROTUNDA, AND I come face to face with Oliver.

He's out of breath, the scar on his face white against the active flush of his skin. It hasn't been fifteen minutes since he left us upstairs, but he's completely transformed. He's traded his usual outfit for black pants and long sleeves and body armor. A rifle is slung over his back, held by a strap that crosses over his chest.

We stare each other down.

He has orders from Hades to keep me upstairs. I have orders from myself to keep Hades alive and stop this situation from becoming a massacre.

Oliver has the advantage when it comes to height and strength, but I have determination, bright and gold like growing the biggest, most beautiful flower the world has ever seen.

I draw myself up to my full height. "I can climb onto the

train tracks and follow them out of the mountain, or you can take me to a more convenient exit. Your pick."

He narrows his eyes. "And what's your plan for when you get outside?"

"Negotiate a cease-fire."

"Nobody's shooting yet."

"And how long do you think that will last? I think it would be the best, actually, if nobody died today, including Hades."

Oliver scowls. Not long ago, I would have been frightened by his expression. Now I lift my chin.

"You're going to get me fired," he says. "Or worse."

"You're not going to get fired. I promise."

"You promise," he mutters under his breath.

But he glances over his shoulder at the rotunda. Workers move quickly across it, splitting off from people in business suits. They're all part of Hades's business. All part of his home. None of them need to get hurt because my mom didn't get her way. "I'm going with you. He'll kill me if I let you go out there without any cover."

"You can't shoot anybody. I'm serious. I'm going outside to have a conversation, and if you start shooting, they'll shoot back, and none of this is going to work."

"I won't shoot unless they shoot at you."

"Fine."

"Fine," Oliver says.

"Let me out of the elevator." He steps out of my way and we move across the rotunda, Oliver a half-step ahead of me. "Where is everybody going?"

"Home," he answers over his shoulder. "Either their permanent homes on the mountain or guest housing. They'll all shelter here until this is over."

The pressure of that responsibility is heavy on my

shoulders, like a summer downpour on sunburned skin. Lives depend on me. Lots of lives. The girl who spent her days in her mother's fields would have buckled under the weight, but now I find I can carry it.

"This way," Oliver says. We switch directions, heading for another hall branching off the rotunda. It angles down and turns into a hall I recognize. It's the one Lillian led me through when I went looking for Hades in the mines. We pass the entrance to the underground city.

The hallway branches again, and Oliver hesitates. Then he turns left.

The hall dead-ends in a huge metal door and part of what must be Hades's own army. Five men with more guns and armor.

"Open it," Oliver calls as we reach them. "We're going out."

"That's against protocol," says one of the men.

"We have new fucking protocols," Oliver snaps. "Open the door."

"Our instructions—"

Oliver puts his hands on my shoulders and moves me in front of them. "Persephone wants to go out. *Persephone*. Do you need Hades to come down and tell you himself?"

They do not want that.

It takes two of them to open the door. Oliver and I step out onto a gravel strip, baking in the warm summer light.

"We'll be coming back through," he says. "Be ready."

The men agree to be ready, then shut the heavy door behind us with a ringing metallic *thud*. There's a finality to the sound. No turning back.

I square my shoulders. "Okay. Show me where they are."

The mountain looms over us, looking a thousand times bigger and more intimidating from down at its base. Oliver takes his rifle off his back and leads the way across the gravel strip. The ground stays flat for a little while, but then it slopes into a rocky hill. I keep an eye on my feet as we go. Breaking my ankle right now would not make me look like a confident queen.

It feels a lot like walking in my mother's fields. The breeze in my hair. The sun on my shoulders. The new, green scent of summer.

"Persephone."

I look up from the rocks and into Oliver's steely expression. And then past him.

Far down the slope, against a line of trees, is my mother. Her dress is pure and white, nearly radiant. Her hair glints in the sun. I could almost believe she'd come to see me, that she'd just wanted to talk, if it weren't for the men gathered in groups around her.

She sees me.

I know it, though her features aren't clear at this distance. She's looking right at me. One of her arms lifts from her side in a little wave, or a reach.

"She's not who I'm here to see."

A pause from Oliver. "What?"

The forest curves across the land, hugging the hilly ground below the mountain. Around to the west, another army has gathered at the trees.

I turn away from my mother and go toward it.

From far away, I think I hear my name on the wind.

If I were going to run back into her arms, this would be the moment.

A tiny part of me wants to do that. To give that to her.

I still love her, but it's a painful, disappointed love. She can only be what she is. I can't rely on her to keep her word.

If I'm going to save the mountain, I need to deal with a different devil entirely.

Oliver curses under his breath and follows. He keeps himself between me and my mother's army. I don't look to see what they're doing. I just keep walking. Faster and faster until the army resolves into individual men and I can see its leader leaning against a Jeep, a cocky, infuriating smile on his face.

Zeus is dressed in black slacks and a white dress shirt, the sleeves rolled up to his elbows. Other than his bulletproof vest, he looks like he could be hosting a party at his whorehouse. His eyes brighten as I plant my feet in front of him.

Oliver hovers a few steps behind me.

"Fancy meeting you here," Zeus says. "Did you come to have your soldier fire the opening shot?"

"I thought you'd like a chance to explain yourself."

He's golden and comfortable in the sun, and I hate him for it a little. He can be out in the light and his brother can't. "Explain myself?"

"Explain why you're such a twisted asshole that you'd kill your own brother. Why would you do that?"

Zeus's smile dims. "He's been a thorn in my side for decades, and it's time I put an end to it."

"You saved him before. Lots of times, according to you."

"That was before he raided my business." Genuine anger flashes through the gold in his eyes. "That's a line we don't fucking cross."

"Yeah, because you were keeping me prisoner there. And people who own whorehouses don't have the moral high ground."

"I don't give a fuck about the moral high ground. I give a fuck about the women who work for me. Their livelihoods were put at risk by his little stunt. They were terrified."

A breeze kicks up through the trees, and I get a lungful of forest and summer along with the hint of something gold, like champagne. It's the scent of a party invitation.

"And they're not terrified of you? You're unkind to every woman you meet. You use them."

"Thank you for noticing."

"Those women deserve better than you, Zeus. All you do is sell them for your own benefit. If I were one of them, I'd spend the rest of my life cursing you every chance I got."

Zeus covers his mouth with his hand, eyes dancing. "I like when you do this. It's like being punched by a butterfly."

Frustration tries to push its way up through the soil, but I imagine it blooming into confidence instead. Into calm. Zeus is pretending to laugh off what I said because it got to him. He really does believe he's doing a good thing, running Olympus the way he does, being the benevolent brothel owner.

"I didn't come out here to discuss your business."

He slips his hands into his pockets and purses his lips. "No. You wanted to discuss my brother."

"I want to negotiate terms."

Zeus's eyebrows go up. "Terms? What is it you think you're going to get from me?"

"Stop this before it goes any further. Call off your army. Don't attack the mountain."

He looks around at his men. Oliver was right. There are lots of them, and more vehicles back in the trees. "But we've come all this way."

"Don't hurt Hades."

Zeus rolls his eyes. "Fuck that guy. He's always been a little bitch."

"You love him."

All the charm drops off Zeus's face. For a split second, he

looks young. Wounded. Tired. Like he doesn't want to be out here in this field wearing a bulletproof vest and waiting to destroy his brother's house.

"And furthermore, he loves you."

Zeus scoffs. "Don't insult me with bullshit."

"He does. Eleanor told me that the two of you are close."

"Ah, yes. Close as can be. That's why he felt so comfortable bringing the cops to bust up one of my parties."

"And was anyone hurt? Was your business even really damaged, or are you already having parties again?"

"That's beside the point."

"Eleanor also told me about Rosie."

Zeus looks away. With the dappled sun behind him, the light in his hair, I get another glimpse of him the way he must have been all those years ago. He's put a lot of work into the appearance that he doesn't care. That the past can't touch him. But the past isn't like the orange marigolds we planted every spring at my mother's farm, dying away at the end of the season like they were never there. It's like peonies or lavender. Once planted, it keeps coming back, year after year after year.

"He can't come to you. Because of the sun, obviously, but also because he knows better than to admit what he loves. He thinks it'll be stolen from him."

Zeus huffs a breath and looks me in the eye. "He kidnapped you."

"I love him." My eyes fill with tears, but I refuse to acknowledge them. I let them dry in the gentle breeze. "And how can love be wrong? Don't do this."

He rolls his shoulders, the illusion of ease coming back to his posture. "What would you have me do instead, Persephone?"

"Help us. He has people on the mountain just like you

do at Olympus. People who are frightened. And even if you don't care about them, and you don't care about me, then just help *him*."

Zeus stares above my head, exasperated. The moment stretches out like a long summer evening. I hold my head high and pretend I'm not afraid of my mother's army or all the men with guns surrounding Zeus, waiting for the order to move on the mountain.

"Fine," Zeus says, standing up tall. "Take me inside, and I'll talk to him. But only because I want to prove you wrong."

TWO

Hades

I CAN'T STOP HER.

I can't fucking stop her.

I get to the goddamn elevator, and the door closes in my face.

My own elevator, and I can't get it to stop. I slam my hand into cold metal, and that's it. That's all I have.

Running after her spiked my heart rate, and the increase in blood pressure is all through my skull. It bears down on my brain. My vision falters. Blacks out. Conor barks, and the sound is murder. Absolute fucking murder.

I'm reduced to holding myself upright with a palm on the wall and digging through my pocket for my phone. The light on the screen sinks claws into my eyes.

"Callahan."

"Stop her," I snap. "At the elevator."

I shove my phone into my pocket. If I drop it, it's gone. Fuck me. Fuck this. Persephone looked so determined,

standing there at the back of the elevator, her chin up. I'm furious at her disobedience, and I'm reluctantly, angrily proud.

How dare she run from me.

How dare she leave me.

How dare she love me enough to do it.

"Where does she think she's going?" I say to no one. The act of speaking increases the pressure in my head. "Out into a fucking battlefield?"

Conor barks again, and I put my hands around his muzzle. "I'm fine. Stop. For fuck's sake, stop."

This is the worst idea Persephone has ever had, and the bravest one. I'm helpless to stop her. I am fucking helpless to do anything. I cannot defend the mountain. I cannot protect my people. I cannot get her back.

Conor pulls his muzzle out of my hands and circles me, pushing at me with all the strength in his body. I reach blindly for his collar and find it. The world narrows to the collar in my palm and the sensation that my heart has been torn out of my chest. I've lived for years under the assumption that it had long since turned to ash and earth, compressed into a raw stone. I am astonished to discover that I was wrong. That it still beats. That it was free for the taking for one summer queen who has now escaped with it.

My dog leads me back to the bedroom. How dare she do this to me? The obliterating pain in my head is nothing compared to the idea that she's in danger. To the idea that I can't protect her.

I told the truth when I said I needed her more than anything. Her absence is the most excruciating pain I have ever experienced.

The mines are going to be overflowing if I survive this. The tunnels will collapse in on themselves. It won't be because of the headaches or the seizures. It will be from losing her. It will be from watching her walk away.

No. Watching her *run*. She ran toward the elevator like she ran across her mother's fields, only there was no fear in her. Persephone wasn't running away. She was running toward something.

A false hope. A suicide mission.

Please, no.

I'm being chiseled in half by hope I can't crush and terror that the world won't bend to her will. That it will pull her up by the root and crush her in its fist.

Conor tugs me directly to the bed, and my knees give out. My balance can barely support my weight on the edge of the mattress.

She's not back yet, which means she's outside.

I should be out there with her. I should have gone in her place. I should have accepted my own death rather than allowing her to bargain with her life.

Fuck, it hurts.

Then what's the difference? I can die outside, or I can die in here. Weapons. I need at least one weapon if I'm going to go after her. I fucking hate guns. They're dangerous on the mountain. Too much opportunity for ricochet. And tunnel collapse. But a gun might be my only option. I don't know if I'll be able to get close enough to Zeus or Demeter for a knife to be of any use.

I gather my strength and begin to stand.

My head splits. It feels like my skull is shearing off.

I can't fucking do it.

I need her. I've finally found the limit of my endurance, and she is it. Unlike the pressure of the headaches, there is no mechanism to offload the pain of not knowing whether she's safe.

Impossible. She cannot be safe. Not out there, where Demeter could reach her. The moment of reunion crashes into my mind like a rock through glass. Persephone would hug her, because that's what she's like. She's soft and beautiful to the core. A flower in bloom.

Afterward, Demeter would drag her back to those goddamn fields. To that prison of a house. To those thorns. I can see the marks on her skin.

My stomach constricts, but I force back the urge to be sick. It's not the thought of thorns. It's a seizure. Coming on fast. I can't let it happen now.

I'll come back to you. I promise.

Will she? All I can think about is her body devastated by thorns. All I can think about is a metal door sliding shut between us. All I can think about is the relentless, killing light keeping me from her.

I've never hated the sun more than in this moment.

I can't sense my body in space. Only Conor's collar grounds me now, and I hold on tight. His powerful body quivers next to the bed. No doubt the pressure is intolerable for him, too.

I'm dying without her. My pulse won't stop racing. It feels like a diamond beating inside my body, pushing its cut edges into the wound where my heart used to be mine. If only I were a part of the mines. Made from unfeeling rock. If only I didn't have to feel this.

But.

Feeling this is better than not having her.

Isn't it?

Isn't that fucking true?

My thoughts compress under the pressure and heat. I brace them again and again. Reinforce them. I'm worried sick, but I refuse the sensation. I will not give into that vicious cycle. I will not. I will not. I will not.

I make my demands of my body with every empty heartbeat. The pain is massive. It flattens everything in its path, including time.

It's consumed with missing her. Made unrecognizable. There are no landmarks in this darkness. No anchors. I don't know how long it's been.

I'll come back to you. I promise.

Come back to me.

If she does...

What will she find?

I think of her face in the morgue when I took her to see the body of the farm boy. I saw her imagining me in his place.

Conor edges closer.

I sit very still. I keep my eyes closed, though there's nothing to shut out but the dark. I claw back control over my breathing. Suffer through each heartbeat. There. That's how time passes. It hurts.

It settles.

I can think.

I can *hear*.

Somehow, through force of will alone, I manage to pull myself up. I reach for my phone. Oliver doesn't answer. Probably because he knows I'll kill him. Instead I reach a guard who works under him, but still manages a team. He'll have resources. And unlike Oliver, who must have helped Persephone do this, he'll be obedient. He answers on the second ring.

"Persephone," I manage to say, my voice hoarse.

"She went out, sir. I'm not sure how."

I already know how. "Get her back. No matter what. Don't

let her stop you. Pick her up and throw her over your shoulder. Even if Oliver is there. Even if he tries to stop you."

The briefest pause, where the full import of my words hits him. "Yes, sir."

I hang up the phone, but I don't wait for him. Instead I'm pulling on my boots. I'm forcing one foot in front of the other. I'll die, first. I'll collapse and die. That's the only thing that will stop me from getting to Persephone. Since I'm not dead yet, I keep going. That's the logic that sustains me. That's the logic that pierces the intense pain and exhaustion and blinding light.

I find myself in the bathroom. I scrub my face with cold water and soap. Again with colder water. It'll have to be enough.

Conor puts himself in the way when I go for the door. I push him aside. He settles for sticking so close to my side that he's practically on top of me.

Sitting room.

Hallway.

It's a thousand miles to the elevator.

I haven't reached it when the doors open.

My vision is fucked, so it's mostly outlines and shadows. The hallway lights come up a little.

The pain is worth it, because I see her.

Persephone.

My summer queen.

I'm flooded with relief, like starlight, like new flowers, until I realize she's not alone.

Zeus steps into the hallway after her.

No fucking way.

Rage goes straight to my head. "What the fuck are you doing here, Zeus?"

"Persephone asked me to come."

"Why?" I snarl. A few seconds ago I was terrified for her

safety. Her mother would have hurt her. Would Zeus hurt her? I don't like to think that way, but he's definitely not good for her.

A smirk. "She wanted me to help you."

"No," Persephone says, her voice sharp. "I want you to make peace with him."

"Never."

"Hades—"

My gaze is locked on Zeus. The enemy. "He's the one who brought an army to the fucking mountain."

Fiery anger flashes through my brother's eyes, but it's Persephone who answers. "He thinks you kidnapped me, Hades. And… he's not wrong. That's why he helped my mother smuggle me out. That's why he believes her when she tells him you're a threat."

"I am a threat," I mutter, which isn't precisely true. I've managed to stay standing throughout this encounter but it's taking its toll. There's no harsh lighting near the elevators, but I'm far from stable.

"Right," Zeus says, faintly mocking as he strolls past me, into my home. I have no choice but to follow. "I know what you look like when you have a headache."

"Of course you do." The words taste like poison. "You watched me die a thousand times. And then you were there, bright as the fucking sun, demanding that I come alive again."

A pained noise rips from Persephone. "You can't be mad at him for saving you."

Perhaps I'm not. I spent so much of my life in agony that I'd forgotten there were reasons to live. Reasons like Persephone. If he hadn't forced me to survive through that hellish childhood, I would never have met her. "I still can't trust him."

"Can we stop talking like I'm not in the room?" Zeus asks.

"He kidnapped you," I continue speaking to Persephone

while keeping a steady gaze at my brother. "He didn't take you back to the farm. He took you to a fucking brothel."

Zeus grins, cocky and insufferable. "She had a good time there."

My skull nearly gives way under a new rush of hate.

"I did not," my summer queen says, stepping between us, her chin held high. Regal. Beautiful. Indomitable. "And this needs to end. If you want to bicker like two schoolboys, fine. I don't care, but don't you dare let the people in this mountain hide in fear because you don't want to admit you actually care about each other."

What the fuck.

I break the stunned silence. "Schoolboys?"

"Harsh," Zeus says.

I turn to him. "Demeter? Really?"

He sighs. "You knew it would come to this. You knew she would lose her fucking mind. I warned you. It might be a better option to stop being such an obstinate fuck and let me—"

"I don't need your help."

"I think we do." Persephone puts her hand on my arm. "If we work with him, we'll be able to protect the people on the mountain better than all your soldiers and guns."

Fine. Fuck. I glare at Zeus. "If you want to switch sides, then you deal with me. Not Persephone."

It's not because I don't believe in her power. It's because this is still too new. Too tenuous. Too dangerous. I can't risk her again, not with the terror still fresh in my body.

Zeus smirks. "But you picked a lovely plaything, Hades. Why wouldn't I want to deal with her?"

"Don't," Persephone says. It's not clear whether she's talking to Zeus or whether she's telling me not to punch my brother in the face. Because it's a close fucking thing.

"She walked around in full sight of two armies for you," he continues. "It's a shame you're planning to keep her here. She would've made a beautiful whore."

Pain cracks across my temples, and my body explodes into motion. I'm only dimly aware of leaping at Zeus, but my knuckles make contact with his face.

"Stop," Persephone says. "Hades, don't."

It's too late. The momentum was enough to take both of us both past the living room.

"Fuck you," I spit into his face. "And I'm supposed to trust you when you say shit like that?"

"I don't give a fuck if you trust me." He tackles me into the hallway. "I came here because you deserve this. You fucked up my business. You scared all my women. You don't fucking care. You've never cared. You've always been a selfish piece of shit. Fuck you, too."

He rolls away from my next punch and hops to his feet.

I go after him.

Zeus grins, a bruise blooming on his cheekbone. He's spotted the door to the valley. "Come on, Hades. Let's do this outside, like civilized people."

He's baiting me. I know that.

He's staying just out of reach.

I rush him one more time, colliding with him against the door. He falls through and out, into the sun. The light is like knives. It's like hell itself. But I gather what's left of my focus. If Zeus wants a fight, he can fucking have one. I pull my fist back and punch him again.

THREE

Persephone

THERE'S NOT ENOUGH SPACE TO STOP THE FISTFIGHT. Hades and Zeus are too tall and too committed to even think about putting myself in the way. Conor bolts after them, and I run, and the two of us meet Oliver in the hall.

I try to push past Oliver, who tries to push me behind him, resulting in a brief scuffle that ends when Hades tackles Zeus into the valley. Then I cut and run, Oliver on my heels, Conor slipping past me in the gap between my body and the wall.

We tumble out into the sun.

The fight is worse out here. More vicious. It's as if the extra room has given them permission to let loose on one another.

"Stop," I shout. Oliver catches my arm before I can throw myself into the fray.

He has Conor by the collar. Conor strains, growling, and I drop to my knees next to him and put my arms around his neck.

"They're hurting each other, Oliver."

Hades will never forgive himself if the two of them crash

into Conor. My heart is the size of the valley. It pounds so hard that every beat shakes the earth.

Or it's just the force of the blows.

I've never seen two men fight like this before. I've never seen such hard punches and cruel tackles. Every time Hades hits the ground, my heart breaks a little more.

He can't be doing this. He can't. He's already in so much pain.

But nothing seems to stop him.

They're killing each other on top of my flowers. I feel the plants breaking as they land. I feel each impact. Each crushing hit. Stems snap. Petals tear. There's supposed to be value in beauty, and in softness, but it does nothing now.

It just provides a colorful backdrop for violence.

Up on the slope, Eleanor's cottage door opens. She comes out onto the grass, her eyes wide. Three steps down the hill, she comes to a stop. It's too dangerous to get close.

Zeus throws Hades off of him, stands up, and laughs.

The sound echoes off the ravine. It's a bitter laugh, painful, and Conor strains against my arms with a choked whine.

"No," Oliver says. "Stay."

"Why the fuck did I bother keeping you alive all those years?" Zeus is shouting, but he doesn't seem to be aware of it. He's like a pot boiling over. All the energy he usually contains and focuses is breaking free of him in fists and taunts. "Why are you like this?"

"Why *did* you bother? I'd rather die than look at you."

"Then come here and try to kill me. See what happens."

"Fucking gladly."

Hades goes for Zeus with all the precision of a soldier, but the precision doesn't last. I can't make sense of their bodies. Fists fly so fast they're blurred. Zeus's head snaps back so hard I think it's over. It must be over. But he recovers like it's nothing. He drives an elbow into Hades's stomach. Hades takes him down to the ground.

Nobody's clean anymore.

The sunny day has cracked open, spilling a storm onto the mountain. It's been a long time coming. Life has made these two men skilled at fighting, and watching them—

It's like they've been waiting for a chance to settle this forever.

One of them could die.

Hades could die.

He's already at a disadvantage. Already buckling under the pain. He couldn't follow me outside. What I did to him was awful. And then I made it worse.

I didn't have the chance to apologize.

My mind scrambles for a solution, but Conor struggles so furiously that it takes all my strength to keep him with me. I lose a few seconds. Lose track of the fight. I don't see how they stand up, and I don't see how they go back down again, falling toward a rock.

Hades gets a hand on the side of Zeus's head and cracks his head on the stone.

Dizzy.

I'm getting dizzy, sick with how awful this is. How real. Not like it is in books. This is personal. With a hit that hard, Hades might've killed him.

Zeus spits blood onto the grass and gets to his feet.

"You didn't have to do any of this," he growls. "You could have let me help you."

Hades laughs, an agonized, terrible thing. "Don't you think you've done enough? Congratulations, asshole. I'm still alive for you to fuck with."

"Oh, that's fucking rich, Hades. Tell me. Which one of us kidnapped a woman in the middle of the night? Which one of us *knew* that it would set Demeter off?"

"I didn't care," Hades snaps. "I did not give a fuck about Demeter. But you do. Is that why you're here? Did she send you in here to kill us? Did she slip a little poison into your pocket?"

Zeus blanches, and then his face goes red. "You're not worth the hemlock."

But the look on Zeus's face. *Poison.* I asked my mother once if she did something to Hades. I didn't know to ask about her other brothers.

What did she do to Zeus?

Who did she kill?

"So lovely to finally agree on something," says Hades.

Zeus wipes at his mouth with his sleeve. "You're so goddamn selfish. You'd bring the world down on your head just to keep your plaything."

"Of course I would. I'd bring down a hundred worlds for her." Hades's tone is acid venom. "You wouldn't know what that's like."

Zeus leans in, his face incandescent with rage. He looks so hurt that it reminds me of Hades. "You don't know what you're talking about. You're going to pay for that, motherfucker."

"Perfect. Hurry the fuck up so I can stop looking at you."

"I could have *helped* you."

"I never asked for your help." Hades grins, and it's terrible. "I never wanted it. I don't want a fucking thing from you. If you're going to kill me, stop waiting. Take your revenge."

"Since you asked," says Zeus, and they're on each other again, blows connecting.

The sun comes out from behind the mountain's peak and lets its full force down into the valley.

It's warm on my face and on my shoulders. A sweet relief.

Only it's not. It's not, because it's going to kill the man I love.

Someone is screaming and that someone is me, but I can't stop it. They're past the point where stopping is an option.

But they have to stop. They have to.

Conor snaps at Oliver, howling, his tail a frantic beat on the ground, and his collar tears loose from my fingers. "Fuck," Oliver says. "I can't hold him—"

They're both upright again.

Zeus takes a big step toward Hades.

Hades doesn't react.

My nerves fray, splitting, ripping. And I know, with a certainty I've never felt before, that this is it. This is the moment when I watch Hades die.

He can't see.

It doesn't show on his face. He would never let it. But Zeus takes another step and Hades does nothing. He just stands there, his hands at his sides.

The sun is killing him, and his brother will finish the job.

Zeus wears a lopsided smile, teeth red with his own blood. A fresh breeze ripples through the wildflowers at their feet. Conor pants, digging his nails into the grass. I feel every wretched heartbeat.

"In front of you." It's not going to be enough. Screaming is never enough.

Hades turns his head, only an inch, toward me.

Zeus hesitates. The rage on his face is replaced with a fleeting second of confusion.

They both move toward each other, and I brace myself for more blood. Hades draws back one of his fists and snaps it neatly into Zeus's face.

Zeus rocks back a step, his hands to his nose.

The mountain holds its breath.

All at once, I become aware of other people in the valley. Workers from the mines, crowded by a door into the mountain I hadn't noticed. I think they felt Hades react to Zeus's arrival. The fight must have sent wild energy all through the rock.

I get up off the ground, tasting metal in my mouth. Oliver locks both arms around Conor.

"Go back inside," I tell the workers. They glance at me, then back to Hades. "Go in," I insist.

"Is this really how you want to die?" Zeus's voice carries on the wind. "You hate me that fucking much?"

I turn back and find him staring at Hades.

No answer.

Hades wipes at his face, and when his hands come down I'm looking at a king. A battered, broken king, but a king nonetheless. Shivers trace down my spine. There's something new in his eyes.

Fear.

FOUR

Hades

I can't let them see me.

This is going to be a bad one. I can feel it. It's going to kill me. The premonition rips through the air.

The shadow that Zeus has become ignores me. Or he leaves. I don't know. He fades out into a pitch-dark background. My vision fails, and it doesn't come back. It's been flickering in and out since we landed on the grass outside, and now it's gone.

Everything is gone.

There's nothing left in my head except a searing, hot pressure. My mind is breaking beneath the force. It comes from everywhere. The ground. The air. The sky. There's too much to transfer into the rocks below the mountain. It's difficult enough to direct under the best of circumstances, and this is a disaster.

Something warm and strong slams into the side of my legs.

"Rosie," I say.

She came back.

But no, she can't. She's dead. This dog is taller than she was. Taller. Heavier.

Conor.

I drop a hand down to make sure it's him. I feel like I'm reaching forever. A gnawing fear suggests that I'm reaching toward nothing. That I'll never make contact. That all of it was a dream. A nightmare. No Rosie. No Conor.

No Persephone.

My hand meets Conor's collar. The sturdy fabric touches my palm but the connection is on some distant horizon, beyond the devastating pain.

He pulls, and for a moment I'm rooted to the ground. My feet are wedged into the soil like concrete. Like diamonds.

I can't move.

He pulls harder.

I should have died. All those years ago, I should have died. All those useless breaths have brought me to this point when I could have been buried in the dirt at the farmhouse. But Zeus was a stubborn bastard. He wouldn't let me die. He condemned me to this merciless existence...

Until now.

I don't think I'm going to get back up. Not this time.

Doesn't matter now. I'm moving through inky, unbroken black that feels like sunshine. It feels like the summer breeze. I'd laugh if it didn't hurt so much. A lifetime of this. Days of this. Weeks. And it still surprises me. I keep hoping it won't.

My God, it hurts.

Time to be done with all this. Time to die.

Time to stop fighting with Zeus. Time to stop wishing he hadn't seen. Time to stop feeling so desperately alone.

I knew it would be terrible when the painkillers ran out. I didn't know it would go on so long.

There's no mercy in it.

No one would envy this death.

My thoughts disintegrate. I'm surrounded by voices, but I can't be. Who would approach me now? No one, no one. Old shame opens its jaws and bites the sounds in half.

Hades. Is the gardening done?

The hairs on the back of my neck stand. Cronos is coming. He'll be here any second, and the gardening is not done. My feet drag through miles of flowers. They'll be choked off by weeds. He'll have a hell of a time digging out the diamonds. I hope there are so many thorns.

No. He's dead. As dead as Rosie. We killed him. It's my own traitorous brain that will murder me now. It's the sun. His hands have nothing to do with it. He won't be able to sell the diamonds I'll leave in my wake.

Somehow, it does not comfort me.

There's someone I need. Someone I didn't want to be without.

My summer queen.

I can't go back to find her. There is only moving forward into the dark, Conor's collar biting into my palm. I need to get out of the sun so I can die without being burned alive. Would be better if I didn't have any witnesses. They don't want to see the house of cards tumble to the ground.

"They're going back inside," someone says. From behind me or beside me, I don't know. "Persephone's getting them to go in."

I don't know who he's talking about or why Persephone is not with me.

Where did Zeus go? Fuck him, though. I never wanted to know him in the first place.

Definitely never wanted to call him my brother.

And I don't want him to save me now. I don't want him to rescue me.

Just end it. Just make it stop. He could make it stop. Any means necessary. He said I was ungrateful. I didn't appreciate my life enough. I didn't appreciate being eaten alive by my own brain.

Older memories crowd in, burrowing into my skull like so many diamonds. Zeus, with dirt on his face. Zeus, with a shovel. Rosie. Rosie's at my side. She came back. She wasn't dead, she was only missing, and she found me again on the mountain.

She's a good dog. She'll take me with her this time. We'll go through the gates together, and it won't hurt.

"Tell Persephone to take the mountain." I don't know if the voice is still here, or listening. I sound so cool. So practical. But I'm being buried alive. Crushed and crushed and crushed. Knives in my eyes and a throbbing pain on one cheekbone. Is it broken? "Tell her it belongs to her."

My vision returns and light pummels me. Oliver's face forces itself into view, but the light blinds me again. Please. I need the dark to stay. It's so painful in the light.

"You're going to be okay," says Oliver.

Why isn't she here?

"She'll be right back," he promises, but I'm sure I didn't ask a question. "How are you doing?"

"I'm fine." The oldest lie I've ever told. The very oldest one. I've been telling it and telling it until a facet of a diamond tore through the cloth of it. I've never been fine.

This is all right. I haven't fallen down yet. I haven't been sick. I've avoided this for so long, but I can die in the shadows.

"Zeus," I say.

"He'll leave you alone," Oliver answers.

That wasn't what I was going to ask.

I don't know what I was going to ask.

"You're not far from Eleanor's."

A colder fear grips my spine. Eleanor lives at the farmhouse. She works for my father. I can't do it again. I can't let him take me outside. Even if it's the last time.

Last time, last time, last time.

The ground shudders under my feet. I don't think the diamonds are going to the right place. I don't think they're going into the rock, down below in the dark. They're crushing Persephone's flowers. They're doing irreparable damage to the roots. She won't be able to make things grow.

I'm sorry about that.

Conor pushes me again.

I take another step, then another.

My bones are crumbling. Soon I'll be nothing but diamond shards. They'll suffocate the flowers. They'll catch the sun and set the valley on fire.

The hem of her dress would spark and burn. A summer breeze could carry an ember into her hair. Persephone can't be here for that.

"Make sure she's not here when it goes up."

No one answers me.

My heart beats in a rhythm that sounds like her name. It's a melody. Or a hallucination. My knuckles brush against the infinitely soft petals of a flower. I didn't know I was so close to the ground.

Someone is making a sound of such pain and grief that I reach for them to cover their mouth.

They can't do that. Not on my mountain. It's killing me.

Everything is killing me.

A doorframe sprouts up underneath my hand and I fall

through an open door. My knees meet warm wood. The palms of my hands find it, too.

Eleanor's house.

It smells the way it always did. There are plants somewhere near. Plants she's growing. I gave her something to do, so she can pass the time when Cronos isn't here.

He's never been here. It's just something to do.

Fear bubbles up. The plants smell green and fresh, but Persephone isn't here. An explosion blooms and dulls behind my eye sockets. Another one. Mine shafts collapse. They bulge with diamonds. I can't keep up.

I love her. My summer queen.

I hurt her.

I have to tell her.

Tell her what? I don't know. I reach for the words and can't find them. Only that I love her. Bring her to me. Why did I ever walk away?

So she doesn't see.

So she doesn't see me die.

Someone's singing. It's so soft. So far. A lullaby. An old song about a train car. My stomach turns itself inside out and I'm sick on the floor.

Hands on the back of my neck. On my forehead. The hem of a skirt clutched in my fingers.

"It's all right," she says.

"Eleanor, it hurts," someone else answers, the words garbled and rough. Tortured. Me, I think. I could be six, I could be sixteen. My body is too huge, too unwieldy, too difficult to move. "I'm sorry. I couldn't get away."

She murmurs soothing nonsense. My body doesn't shake this close to the end. It locks down. Locks up.

"Where's Rosie?" Grief puts stress on my skull. It'll make a million diamonds.

"She's not here, Hades."

"Cronos?"

"He's dead." Her palm presses flat on the back of my neck. Cronos never did that. "He can't hurt you anymore."

More soft hands. Everywhere they touch the pain is less but not gone. Not nearly gone enough. Shut it down for repair. Do it quick before you lose anything else. Before the mountain is a diamond rockslide.

It would bury her, and she belongs in the sun. She belongs in the fields. Not choking on diamonds.

Persephone.

Please.

"Eleanor," Persephone says. "What do I do?"

Oh, summer queen. This has happened before. Don't look. Cover your eyes. I don't want to leave you.

A delicate hand slips into mine, soothing bruised knuckles.

"Get Zeus," Eleanor answers.

Yes, get my brother.

See if he can save me one more time.

FIVE

Persephone

HADES HAS ONE HAND ON CONOR'S COLLAR AND THE other one in Eleanor's skirt.

He's on the floor, on his knees, and every muscle in his body is so tense that he's hardly breathing. He does not look up at me. I don't think he can.

Eleanor's words sink in, and my hands freeze on his shoulder and the back of his neck.

"Zeus?"

"Yes." She looks past me. "Run."

I hear Oliver bolt out the door. Zeus brushed by me while I was in the middle of ushering the workers back inside. I knew Hades wouldn't want them to watch, or worse, follow him.

Zeus didn't say a word on the way out. I didn't have time to talk to him. I'm responsible for what just happened. I asked him to come here. I owe him a conversation. Maybe even an apology.

I don't know.

I don't *know*.

I never imagined that Eleanor would ask me to get him back.

My nerves stretch thin. Zeus is not going to be in any mood to help Hades now. He can't be. But if he's the only one who knows what to do, then we need him. I need him.

"Can he stop this?" I ask. Hades leans forward another inch. "Eleanor."

"Hades," she says softly, her hand resting on his head, almost like a blessing. "You have to go back to your room. It's time to lie down inside."

"I am." His fist balls up in her skirt. "Inside."

I don't know how he's supposed to walk all the way across the valley like this. I don't know how Eleanor can trust Zeus to help after the fight she just witnessed.

I have no one else to trust. If she trusts Zeus, then there's no other choice.

The adrenaline from the fight hasn't faded. It beats harder now, but there's nowhere for the tension in my muscles to go. I want it to have a purpose. I want to be able to help Hades.

Let me help.

"Eleanor—"

Zeus bursts through the door of her cottage. With both the brothers inside, it seems like a playhouse. Zeus pushes between me and Eleanor and leans down to look into Hades's eyes. Then his golden gaze meets mine.

"Why didn't you tell me?" he snaps.

"Tell you what?"

"Why didn't you tell me it was this bad?"

"I thought you knew," I snap back. "You were working with my mother. Maybe you liked what she was doing."

Zeus glares. "Why the fuck would I *like* this, Persephone?"

He pushes his sleeves higher up his elbows. Zeus abandoned

the bulletproof vest in the rotunda on the way up, and his white shirt is covered in dirt and grass stains. There are streaks of color from broken flower petals. He moves around to Hades's other side and reaches for him, but I put out my hand.

"Don't hurt him."

"I'm not going to hurt him, for fuck's sake. It's time to go home," he says to Hades. "Come on."

Zeus takes one of Hades's hands and loops it over his shoulders, then walks him out into the sun at a steady clip.

Conor and I are at their heels. Oliver close behind. I pick up speed to match Zeus's pace.

"He can't be out here. It's too bright."

"He can't stay in there, either." Zeus's jaw is set. He's determined. He's practically dragging Hades, whose knees keep going out from under him. If it weren't for Zeus, he'd be on the ground. "Go first and open the door."

I hurry ahead of them, heart in my throat. It's awful to see Hades like this. In so much pain. So far away.

The last of the workers, the ones who tried to stay behind, disappear when they see Zeus coming. They fade back into the mountain like ghosts. There's no one left when Zeus and Hades reach the door and go past me.

"Cronos," Hades says.

"He's gone," Zeus answers. Then, to me: "I don't know the way."

A nervous chill trickles through my veins. Zeus has never been here before. That means there's a weight to this visit. Maybe it's fate. If Zeus hadn't come back, would Hades have died?

Conor pushes at both their legs now, but he seems less panicked than he was outside. It has to be a good sign if Conor is relieved. I should be relieved, too. Instead I'm caught in the strange tension of the moment. I'm seeing into the past, I think.

I'm watching what it means to be brothers, even if neither of the men admit it.

Calm determination settles over my shoulders like a mantle. I've never worn one in real life. I've only seen pictures in books. I swear I can feel it anyway.

I wonder if queens were also this torn between fear and hope.

In the bedroom, Zeus puts Hades on the edge of the bed and sits down next to him. Conor rests his head on Hades's knee.

"Water," Zeus says to me. "Quickly."

The lights in the bathroom come up as I reach the sink and grab for one of the glasses on a small shelf by the mirror. I've never once thought about the glasses before, but I'm deeply, passionately glad for them now. When I take it back to the bedroom, Oliver's adjusting the lights. Making them brighter.

"We have to keep it dark," I say.

"And I have to be able to see. It'll be dark soon enough. And it's too fucking late anyway." Zeus doesn't so much as glance at me. My queenlike confidence is slipping. What would I have done if Zeus wasn't here? Would Oliver have known what to do? Judging from the wide-eyed expression on his face, this is beyond what he's seen before.

The water rattles in the glass. My hands shake. I think of flowers and sunshine and a poppy blooming underneath my fingertips. I think of everything being all right.

Zeus props Hades up with one arm around his shoulders. The pressure in the room is pulling tight at my ears. All the tiny hairs on my arms stand up. It's wrong for this sensation to be in the room with us. It was never this intense before. It was practically nothing.

I'll be dead weight, Persephone. I'll hurt you.

Too much dead weight to be moved by anyone but his brother. Too much pressure in the room for other people to withstand. The reality is so much worse than what I imagined. It's so much more terrifying.

And the expression on Hades's face.

It breaks my heart for how little pain it shows. He's had too much practice hiding it. He could be staring into nothing except for the agony in his eyes.

My ears pop from the pressure, and my pulse speeds up.

Zeus digs in his pocket. "You don't have people in the mines, do you?"

"They're all out," Oliver says.

A pill bottle appears in the palm of Zeus's hand. He flips the top off with his thumb. The top falls to the floor, and he sticks the bottle in his shirt pocket so he can take one of the pills out while he keeps Hades upright.

The air feels thin. There's a gossamer layer between the past and the present. Zeus looks like he's done this many times before, and I don't know whether to be heartbroken at how much Hades has been hurt or grateful that his brother has had enough practice to save him. He tips the pill into Hades's mouth.

"Water," Zeus says. I bring the glass, and Hades doesn't fight Zeus when he makes him drink.

I've just taken the glass back when Hades squeezes his eyes closed, his muscles going tight. Zeus braces a hand on his chest to keep him from falling to the floor.

Conor whines.

The pressure is everywhere. My eyes. My ears. My temples. It makes me want to scream. Makes the urge so powerful that I can't believe Hades doesn't.

Oliver backs toward the bedroom door.

It goes on and on and on. I'm frozen in place. Oliver, too. Conor pants, but the sound of his breath is muted by a wall of crystallizing pressure.

Hades gasps, like he's been underwater and finally managed to break the surface. The pressure in the room drops. His expression doesn't change as he turns his head toward Zeus.

"Leave," he orders.

"No." Zeus's tone is light. "I'm an invited guest."

"Hate you," says Hades.

"You can't hate me if you're dead."

Hades glares at him, but the expression disappears in a heartbeat. His black eyes are emotionless again.

"What did you give him?" I ask Zeus.

"Something to interrupt the seizure. There's no way to stop them from starting. Believe me, I've fucking tried. Only thing that does that is the poppies." Zeus looks over his shoulder at me. "I didn't know, or I wouldn't have taken the bait."

"He ran out of painkillers days ago."

Regret flashes across Zeus's eyes. I don't know what to say in response. I didn't think I could tell Zeus, otherwise I would have. I didn't think they'd end up tackling each other into the valley.

Hades grabs the front of Zeus's shirt in his fist. I expect Zeus to react, even if it's just to brush Hades's hand away, but he doesn't.

"Don't do this to me," Hades says.

"Has to be done," Zeus answers.

And then Hades's eyes close, and he's gone. Unconscious. Zeus stands up and lifts Hades into place on the bed. It looks easy for him, and I'm struck by how hard it would have been for me. How impossible.

Hades's breathing evens. Conor curls up on the floor next to his bed.

Oliver curses and leaves the room.

Zeus rubs his hands over his face. "Is this why you strolled through a fucking battlefield, then? This is what Demeter's been doing?"

"Yes," I admit. I had no idea how much pressure was in the air until it was gone. My lungs feel supersized. "I've been trying to grow new poppies in the valley, but I don't have her skills."

He glances at me. "You have to know that this isn't over."

"Between you and him?"

Zeus scoffs, an impulsive smile lifting the corner of his mouth. "He'll never stop hating me completely. But it's not over with Demeter. She'll have her people move on the mountain."

"What about you?" I meet Zeus's golden eyes in the half-light of the bedroom. "Is your army going to attack, too?"

Zeus looks at Hades, bruised and unconscious on the bed. They're both equally battered. For a fraction of a second, guilt flickers over Zeus's face. Like he could take all of this back if he could. The fight. The army. Everything.

I'm not sure Hades would have let him help if it hadn't come to this.

His brother sighs. "No. My army is not going to attack, but Demeter's is going to get bigger."

"How do you know?"

"Because she is... convincing." Zeus's eyes darken. "Some of my men will go over to her side. I'll have as many as possible defend the mountain, but she'll get more people. She'll be determined. She saw you come back in here with me."

My stomach does a slow, nervous flip. "What do we do now?"

About my mother. About the mountain.

About Hades.

"Wait until he wakes up," says Zeus. "Then we make plans."

SIX

Hades

Twenty-two years ago

"**W**AKE UP."
Night draws soothing fingers over my eyelids. Humid air presses against the burnt-out pits where my eyes were before and cools them back into existence. It does little for the aching throb in my head that makes me feel like a floating skull.

I'm not floating, and I'm not a fucking skull. My life would be easier if I were nothing but bone.

Chilled grass imprints on the back of my shirt.

Where did I end up this time? Outside, somewhere. I could be anywhere, except I'm not near a road. No headlights sear across the red web of veins that must still exist in my eyelids. No tires hum across pavement.

I haven't been run over, which is a shame.

Something hard makes contact with my ribs and sends

pain spidering across muscle and bone. My ribs are intact—I can tell from the dull, full-body throb. Broken ribs are sharper. More insistent. The piercing pain I feel is courtesy of my own eyes conspiring against me. It's courtesy of the sunlight. And courtesy of my foster father, Cronos, who dragged me outside to let the sun do the torturing for him.

My stomach curls a fist around its empty center, and the back of my throat burns. I've been thoroughly emptied out. I was sick hours ago when the pain reached its peak. All the better if I'm not lying in it.

Another nudge and a voice. I don't catch the words, and I don't care. Just leave me here 'til morning. Let the sun do what the sun does best. Let it burn me alive and turn me to ashes.

Cronos would be thrilled. He'd have hundreds of diamonds.

I sense the kick before it lands—the space left in the air where the shoe will be—and try unsuccessfully to curl up on my side. A glancing blow. A jolt.

They're not trying to kill me, whoever it is.

Opening my eyes reveals nothing at first. My vision is still fucked and blurry, and the night has painted everything in deep shadow except the stars. They hurt too, but they're pinpricks compared to the sun. The light of other suns, farther suns, can only scratch at me, not stick a knife between my ribs.

The sky. The stars. A shadow tears across Pleiades, almost covering the Seven Sisters. I hate Cronos for doing this to me—for making the night painful too. The night is supposed to belong to me. It's the only time I can go outside without fear. If the stars turn on me, there's no reason to go on living.

"Are you alive?" asks the dark figure.

My brother Zeus. Not my born brother. The golden boy in the same foster home, the favored one, light where I'm dark.

He'd be better off minding his own business. A passing cloud lays the moon bare and lights up his face. Even the moonlight is too bright this early on, but now that I'm conscious, I can swallow down the pain so it doesn't show. Hard, though. Fuck, it's hard.

"Unfortunately."

It's agony to get up on one elbow. To sit up and rub my hands over my face. My head is a giant brick at the top of my neck—a brick that's been beaten to within an inch of its life.

We're by the barn, a monstrosity that our so-called foster father likes for the purpose of making this place look charming. He has it repainted a cherry red every year. I've landed two feet from the outer wall, close to where a shovel has been propped.

That's where the shade would have been in the daytime. Not that the shade would have saved me from anything. As it stands, my face is only badly sunburned and not viciously so. So are the backs of my hands. Obviously, when my brain shut down, it didn't care about saving my hands. It only cared about crawling away from a killing pain that can't be crawled away from. Or walked away from. Or run away from.

The monster is inside the house.

Zeus has a sheen on him like he's been running. Maybe he has. Our foster father likes to punish me, then collect the diamonds for profit. He brings Zeus with him to play golf or to sign business deals or to fuck prostitutes. Meanwhile I'm left to endure the sun until my brain seizes. Toss of the coin whether he'll beat me before I'm unconscious or after.

I spit out a bitter taste. "What time is it?"

"Almost four."

So I've been out here for what—twelve hours? Fourteen?

"Bastard cost me another day of my life." It's not the prettiest thing, getting up after you've been lying on the ground for so long, but I get to my feet. The rough side of the barn meets my palm. The bruises twinge. I forget myself and wince at a pain in my ribs. Maybe they're broken after all.

"Two days." To his credit, Zeus manages to look mildly uncomfortable.

"What do you mean, two days?"

"It's four on Wednesday."

More than fourteen hours.

Much longer and the crows would have started to pick at my flesh. Fuck. Maybe they already did, and that's why my entire face feels wrecked and swollen. At least I can look forward to a dark room. I sleep in the crouched attic on a thin straw pallet, but I don't care. As long as it's blissfully, blessedly dark. Eleanor says I've always been this way—sensitive to the light. It's gotten worse the more my father's beaten me. The more he's left me in the sun.

My hand searches for something else.

My dog.

A month ago I snuck out and went looking for a party. A fight. Something to feel alive. What I found was a dog pit. Took one look at the German Shepherd mutt shivering in the corner and bought her for too much money.

Her name's Rosie. I'd have changed it, but she won't come to anything else. That dog hasn't left my side since. She doesn't understand the limitations of a straw pallet when you're as tall as I am. The only soft spot left in my heart is for Rosie. And she has a soft spot in her heart for Zeus, though she's supposed to be mine.

It's odd that she's not here with me.

The night is alive with cricket calls and the wind slipping through cracks in the barn's shingles, but there are gaps in the sound. No paws on wet grass. No clink of a tag against a collar. No huffing breath.

Turning my head feels like dying all over again, but I do it anyway.

The farmhouse is a historical building with a wraparound porch, renovated to its countryside glory. I'm certain Cronos bought this place for the looks. Our foster father has no love of nature. No desire to live off the land. He has too much money to live so close to open fields, nice as this place purports to be.

The house could be beautiful, if it weren't painted with so much resentment and rage.

"Where's Rosie?"

Zeus sticks his hands in the pockets of his dirt-stained jeans. "I set her loose."

"Why the fuck would you do that?" Rosie can't be set loose. The reason she was for sale in the first place is that she wasn't mean enough for the purposes of the asshole who owned her. They wanted her to fight. Her talent is sleeping on my pallet and knowing when my brain is teetering on the edge of a seizure before I do. Before I'm willing to admit it, anyway. She's probably the one who dragged me into the shade.

My brother squares his shoulders. "She tried to get someone to help you. Hours of howling at your side. When we brought her inside she scratched at the door." He looks to the side, jaw ticking. "I tried to get her to calm down."

But he couldn't. That's the part of the sentence Zeus has left off. Our foster father would have no patience for a howling dog. He won't tolerate noise that he's not making.

"Where did you take her?" Something rips tiny gashes in the soft, unprotected flesh of my throat. I swallow at it reflexively, trying to get it to go away, trying to get it to release the grip around the middle of my chest, where my heart still beats in spite of everything.

I wish it wasn't beating now.

"Somewhere safe."

The problem with moonlight is that it makes it too easy to see everything. The dampness at Zeus's forehead. A swipe of dirt across one cheek.

The shovel propped against the barn.

He's lying. Zeus didn't take her somewhere safe. Our foster father did not patiently wait for Rosie to settle down. He beat her, like he beat me.

He's lying, and Rosie is dead.

"Why are you out here?" I can't live with the anguish. It's worse than dying. "This isn't worth ruining your safe little place at the whorehouse."

"There's no such thing as safe where Cronos is concerned."

"He never beats the shit out of you anymore."

"No." The edge in his voice would be shocking if I weren't on the verge of collapse. "I wish he would. Trading places would be easier than—"

My stomach heaves, but there's nothing left to bring up. I want to rage at the sky, find my so-called father, and squeeze his neck until there's no more breath in his lungs. But the house is far, and the night is deep, and Rosie is gone.

I put a hand to my face, and my fingers come away wet.

Disgusting.

I flick the moisture away, my own blood rebelling from it in a cold wash. A pressure at the edges of my consciousness sounds like an approaching storm. If it's going to happen again, I should sit down. But there's no warning pain, only a sick, hollow pit at the base of me. I am a building, and the pit eats at the foundation with gnashing teeth that leaves only emptiness. A cloud crosses over the moon. By the time it's gone, I'm a collection of walls and blown-out windows. No heart. No soul.

A light touch on my shoulder.

"He's asleep now, if you want to—" I move to wrench Zeus's hand away with enough force to break bone, but he must see it coming, because he yanks his hand back at the last second. "You can come inside now, anyway."

"Get away from me."

"Where are you going?"

"Why do you care?"

"He'll kill you if he finds you gone." Zeus's footsteps follow me. Fast. "Wait."

I turn around and shove with all the strength I've mustered so far, sending him sprawling into the cobblestone pathway with a *crack* that must be his head on rock. But Zeus hasn't been lying on the ground for two days. He leaps back up and drives his hands into my shirt, curling it in his fists, twisting it tight. He backs me up against the wall until my skull makes contact, a fresh wave of hurt radiating through my head.

"You're going to get people killed," he growls into my face. People like Zeus. Or Poseidon. Even Demeter, God damn her black soul. Our not-father's rage can burn up anyone in his path. "Even yourself, you fool. Do you want to die? After all the times I've kept you alive?"

"Yes."

"Fuck you." He slams me back against the barn one more time, then lets go and wipes his hands down the front of his jeans. The shovel loses its purchase and falls. "Die if you want. Just don't do it in front of me."

He stalks toward the house and goes in.

The night expands around me, bird-calls getting louder as we creep toward dawn. If I stay out here another day, I *will* die, and then I'll never get my revenge. Zeus will be the one to make it out. I don't care. The last of my compassion, the last of my empathy, bleeds out of me in wet streaks on the ground. It soaks into the earth and disappears like it was never there at all. Maybe it wasn't.

Maybe I'm an urn for the ashes of what little love I've known.

SEVEN

Hades

MY BROTHER IS STANDING IN MY BEDROOM.

He's on my fucking mountain.

And the most astonishing, terrible part is that I don't entirely hate it.

The fight we had in the valley was like a storm that had been hovering for years. Lightning and thunder. Close enough to see. Too far away for any resolution.

It's a pity I feel so awful.

"You don't have to prove anything." Zeus leans against the wall by my window, looking out into the valley. I've been able to tolerate small amounts of light today, filtered through the glass. "We can talk to you if you're in bed, you know."

I glare at him from my chair at the side of the room. "I'm not lying in bed all day. I was there all fucking night."

All of yesterday, in fact. The entire afternoon, into the evening, and through the night. The blackout would probably have lasted longer if Zeus hadn't intervened. I am begrudgingly

grateful to him for sparing Persephone the long hours of additional worry.

He studies me. "You should. You're going to end up there anyway if you push yourself."

"I am not pushing myself."

As if sitting in a chair is going to set off another seizure.

Fine. It might. I haven't gone this long without painkillers in years. None of us knows whether the episodes will chain themselves together. The pain so far this morning has been intense, but steady enough that I felt foolish being tended to in bed. It got worse when I showered and dressed. Stabilized again when I sat down.

Conor is curled at my feet, lazy but awake. I have no doubt that yesterday was an ordeal for him, too.

I find Zeus's presence here both infuriating and reassuring. Infuriating because he keeps looking at me with knowing concern, which I loathe, and reassuring because Persephone is glad he's here to help her.

She comes in with a tray balanced in her hands, sets it on my console table, and hands off a coffee to Zeus. Persephone puts hers on a coaster, then brings a third mug to me.

"Beef broth," she announces. "You should drink some."

"No. I shouldn't."

My summer queen leans in close and touches my cheek. She smooths my hair. Embarrassed heat goes to my face. There's no need for all this fuss, especially now that Zeus is participating. But it feels so good that I can't brush her off.

"Drink it." Her voice is low and beautiful, like the hush before dawn. "At least some of it. Please?"

"Don't be a pussy, Hades." Zeus grins behind her like the obnoxious prick that he is. "Have your soup."

If Zeus's worry is justified and the seizures continue in

waves, the broth won't matter. But Persephone's silver eyes are so hopeful, and her face so pink and pretty, that it's less painful for me to argue.

I sip at the broth. It's salty as fuck.

"There," I say to Zeus. "Am I less of a pussy now?"

"No."

Persephone rolls her eyes. She goes to get her own mug, then sits down on an ottoman near my chair. I'm forced to resist tackling her to the floor when she purses her lips to blow on the coffee.

"Well." Zeus shifts from the window and sits on the edge of my bed. The mood in the room sobers. "Demeter went back to the farm to regroup, but she'll be back."

My summer queen makes a face. "Why? Yesterday didn't work out for her."

No, indeed. After we finished trying to crack each other's skulls, he moved his people into position at the base of the mountain. And Demeter went berserk. She divided her forces in two and sent half of them to destroy the fortifications at the entrance to the train platform.

The other half started shooting at anything that moved.

Thankfully, we were prepared for her antics.

"Because she knows Hades is weak right now." Zeus glances between me and Persephone. "And by the fucking way, you two should have told me."

"There was nothing to tell you that you didn't already know."

Zeus purses his lips, the picture of skepticism. "I assumed you and Demeter were having some petty misunderstanding."

"What misunderstanding with Demeter has ever been petty?"

"I thought you were demanding more and more of the

poppies so you could sell them. Because you were a greedy motherfucker. In that case, I thought she was partially justified in keeping them from you. I didn't know she was withholding all of them. I didn't know there was no emergency supply."

A foolish, irritating part of me wishes I'd said something. If I had, we might have been able to sidestep this particular outcome. But I could not. It's only now, with Zeus standing in my goddamn bedroom with bruises on his face and knuckles, that I can be open about it.

I sip at the broth and get a mouthful of salt. "An emergency supply of Demeter's poppies wasn't relevant to our business arrangements."

Zeus's eyebrows go up. "You think this has to do with our business arrangements?"

"Yes."

He gazes at the ceiling, doing an admirable impression of a long-suffering man who has done his best in a difficult circumstance. "It has nothing to do with our business arrangements, fucker. If I'd known she was keeping them from you, I'd have put pressure on her earlier."

"It wouldn't have stopped her. She was retaliating."

"Because you stole Persephone?"

"No. For an encounter we had before I assisted Persephone in making her escape."

My summer queen blushes. She pretended to be terrified when I took her. No doubt she was, but she also loved what I did to her. It must have been such a frustrating contradiction to hate me and need me at the same time.

"What did you do?" Zeus asks.

Persephone watches me, her brow furrowed, mug gripped tightly in her hands. Demeter cut her with thorns, but she kept the murders from her daughter. The farm boy's dead body was the first one Persephone had ever seen.

"Two years ago, I got a report from the farm that she'd started using her workers for experiments."

Zeus's face falls. "I thought she'd given that up."

"She gave up animals and moved on to people."

Persephone stares down into her coffee, face pale. I can't tell whether she's going to cry or rage.

"And you stepped in?" Zeus asks.

"It wasn't an option to let her continue."

Zeus shakes his head. "Fuck."

"I don't understand." Persephone's voice is soft. She traces a fingertip around the lip of her mug. "All of this…" The corners of her mouth turn down, beginning to tremble. "She made it seem like we were the only two people in the world. She never told me she had a family."

"The word *family* might be an overstatement," Zeus says, his words dry. "We were more like a collection of fucked-up foster kids that her father accumulated."

Persephone's silver eyes meet his, and I'm struck by how much she looks like Demeter. There's something fundamentally different about them, however. A sweetness in Persephone's features that I can't remember seeing on Demeter's face. My sister's behavior has been, and continues to be, inexcusable.

And yet.

She managed to guard her daughter's sense of goodness.

Persephone's brow furrows. "Someone has to stop her. How are you going to do it?"

My head throbs. This nonsense causes Persephone pain, and I hate it. "We've secured the mountain. We didn't lose any men to her army. We're repairing the fortifications near the train platform."

"It's a waiting game," Zeus says. "You're sure she doesn't have spies among your people?"

"Of course I'm sure."

"You should find out."

Persephone glances between us. "We don't have unlimited time to interview people. Or however you get them to admit that they're a spy. We don't have unlimited time for anything."

I'm the ticking clock. The one whose brain is under imminent threat of collapsing. Every day we spend defending ourselves against Demeter is another day that we can't concentrate our efforts on getting the poppies.

And then there is the matter of the train.

If Demeter disrupts our supply lines, the mountain will suffer.

"Surviving yesterday isn't a victory. We'll lose people if she keeps attacking the train platform, or we'll lose the platform. It's guaranteed she'll grow her army, and she won't be shy about sending them on suicide missions." Pressure builds at the back of my neck and crawls up and over my skull. It hurts to look at Zeus when he's so close to the window. "You should go back to the city."

"*Fuck* no."

He stares at me for several long moments while I try to decide what the expression on his face could possibly fucking mean.

My first instinct is that Zeus is being a stubborn prick for the express purpose of annoying the fuck out of me.

But, given everything, he might actually care.

He's refusing to leave the mountain because of *me*.

Because, like all those hellish years at the farmhouse, he's invested in keeping me alive.

I can't even make the argument that I'd be fine were he to

fuck off back to the city. I'm clearly not fine now. It's patently not fine to be walking a line between brain damage and death.

And I don't relish the idea of Persephone being left alone in danger.

It's a strange feeling, wanting him to stay. I don't like having to rely on him. I like it even less that he's perhaps the only person on the face of the planet with the means to change anything at all.

And I loathe the fact that he went out of his way to research these interventions. I didn't know he'd gone so far as to find drugs to turn seizures to sleep.

I should have known.

I've spent years being at odds with him. Being wary of him, though this isn't the first time he's saved my life.

It's the first time I've wanted him to.

The pain at my temples abruptly crashes through its boundaries, rising from the repetitive *thud* to a screaming peak in a matter of seconds. Black crowds out my vision. A storm. In my head. Thunderclouds and lightning. Electric pressure. I see the shadowed facets of a diamond, a thousand diamonds, and it's too much.

My stomach rejects the beef broth. It lands on the floor, followed by the mug.

"Fuck." Zeus's voice comes first, then his hands on my shoulders. Another pill in my mouth. I swallow it dry and think of the dark. Of the pressure relenting. Of the pain going out like a wave. Just once, could it fucking *recede*, instead of turning my head to solid rock? My spine is going to be next, cracking under the weight of so many diamonds.

We were having a fucking conversation. I'm not done talking to Persephone. My last attempt to hold on slips through my fingers. I tip forward into the dark. I never hit the ground.

EIGHT

Persephone

THE MOMENT ZEUS GETS HADES INTO BED, HE DRAGS OVER
a chair and falls into it. He doesn't say anything. It seems
like a private moment, so I go to Hades, kiss his forehead,
and leave them alone.

Mostly alone, anyway. From the sitting room I call for
Lillian, who brings me what I need to clear away the remains
of the beef broth.

Then I really do leave the room. I don't want to stand there
staring at Zeus and probably making him feel weird. Even if
he is in my house.

It's strange to think of the mountain as my home, though
that's what it will be if we can get through this. I can't imagine
living anywhere else. I would have every season here.

I don't mind the idea. I thought all the rock would cut me
off from what I loved. Flowers and sunshine and the golden
hum of making things grow. I was wrong. Hades has summer

up here, too. He has dirt and grass and thousands of flowers, if I needed proof that I could survive here.

More than survive.

Rule.

A nervous laugh bubbles up as I wander down the hall and into the big living room by Hades's foyer. Queens don't sit around waiting for teatime when they have people to take care of. If I lived here, Hades wouldn't be the only one. There's a city full of workers and their families. If we're both on the mountain, if we're both together, we should both be involved.

That's a decision for later. Maybe much later. In the meantime, though, I'm confident in the knowledge that my life won't be an endless winter. Spring will come again. Even on the mountain.

I spend several minutes in the glassed-in room, looking out at the ocean. I never thought about the waves when I was in my mother's fields. I thought about the black rock rising above the green. I thought about New York City, out of sight but never far from my mind. The ocean is bigger than both.

The world is so much wider than I imagined.

It looms larger outside the mountain while I go back through the halls to the living room, with its pillars and muted window light. It's a less intimidating space once I'm down in the sunken part of it. The furniture is normal enough, even if it was clearly made for Hades. I drop onto one of the couches and stretch out my legs. I feel protected in here. Maybe because the main part of the room is lower than the foyer. There's a boundary between me and the world.

I wonder what Hades imagines for this room. It would be a nice place to spend time with other people. Conversation. A movie, maybe. But I've never seen anyone but Oliver here. Oliver, and other people who work for Hades. My heart squeezes at the thought of Hades sitting here with only Conor for company.

Footsteps pull me out of my thoughts. Zeus has a more relaxed stride than Hades. Not slow, but approachable. Like he's making the rounds at a party.

"Persephone." Zeus comes down into the living room and takes a chair across from me. He's tall, but the furniture was made for his brother. It fits him. He leans forward, resting his elbows on his thighs. When he looks at me, I'm jolted by the dark, undisguised worry in his eyes.

"Did something happen?"

I'm halfway out of my seat, but Zeus waves me back down. "No. He's still sleeping. He's fine for now. I need to talk to you."

My heart races. Quick footsteps, like the night I ran across the fields to the train platform. Like the night I found Hades there, standing in my path. That was the first time he ever touched me.

"Okay." I smooth the skirt of my dress over my legs. I pulled it from Hades's closet this morning after he'd gone to shower. He insisted, and I didn't argue, even though I thought it would be too much. "About what?"

Whatever Zeus has to tell me can't be worse than watching Hades suffer like this.

"I'm not sure that anyone has had a chance to explain the situation we're in."

"I know what situation we're in. Half my mother's army is still waiting outside."

"No." The utter seriousness of Zeus's expression makes my stomach go cold. There's not a hint of the charming brothel owner now. "It's much worse than that."

"Why?"

"Because we're going to be under attack soon. That's a

guarantee. Demeter won't stay away for long. My sister is not going to decide to accept defeat. There's no such thing for her." Zeus's eyes go distant. "She's tried to kill Hades many times. She used to do it with blueberries."

"Blueberries?"

"He's allergic." Zeus blinks, and he's back in the room with me, not looking into his memories. "She would wait until he'd had a seizure, then put them in his mouth."

Shock shudders through me. "What?"

"Most of the time he wouldn't know. He wasn't conscious when I took them back out. My point is that she's persistent, and she's made up her mind to take you back. She'll want retribution now."

"Why?"

"Because she's not right in the head."

I swallow hard, because I know this is true. I've had the bruises to prove it. But this is brutality on another level. "Has she always been like this? Even as a child?"

"Always. She belonged to Cronos. That's enough to fuck up anyone. So was she born with it? Perhaps. But everything that happened after was because of him. He didn't beat her the same way he beat us, but there's a lot of ways to hurt someone."

And not all of them leave physical scars. But they changed her. "You have to stop her."

"I'll be helping to defend the mountain. But Demeter could still disrupt the railroad. I'd be surprised if she hasn't done it already. We're not going to be able to get food and supplies from the city fast enough. There are too many people here to sustain operations without the train, not to mention basic necessities."

Those people are part of the reason I came out to meet Zeus.

"You're right." There's nothing else for me to say. He *is* right. The mountain depends on the train. "And you probably can't have anyone else come from the city. Not enough people to bring what we need."

He shakes his head, watching me. A sense of anticipation whispers through the air. I'm not sure what he's waiting for. Maybe for me to cry, or offer up some other proof that I really do understand the danger we're in.

But of course I do. I understood that before I took the elevator down to the rotunda and ordered Oliver to take me outside. I wouldn't have done that if I didn't understand.

Who knows? Maybe I would have. Maybe I would do anything for Hades. Even provoke my mother and bargain with his brother.

There has to be something else.

"What is it you're not telling me?"

His golden eyes search mine, and the corners of his mouth turn down. When I met Zeus, I knew for sure that he was a terrible man. Disingenuous. A liar. Someone who would pretend to care for the women who worked for him if that's what it took to make more profit.

The concern on his face now reminds me of a wilting flower. It's the way I felt when I thought I might not see Hades again.

"Zeus?"

His jaw works. Whatever he's about to say, he doesn't want to say it.

He must not have any choice, because he steels himself, looking me directly in the eye. "We have to get the poppies."

I let out a heavy breath. "I know that, too. I've known that for a long time. Since before my mother sent me to you."

"You might know it, but…" Zeus glances toward the

window, but I don't think he's seeing it. He faces me again. "If we don't get that medicine, it's not just pain that waits for Hades. It's not just seizures, though they're horrifying on their own. It's death."

Every hair on my body stands. My heart comes to a painful stop. It's anticipating the moment when someone, probably this man, with his golden eyes and easy smile, looks me in the face and tells me that Hades is gone.

That he's downstairs in that cold, solitary room.

"No," I say.

"You felt what it was like in that room."

I did. I felt the pressure rising until I wanted to cover my ears with my hands. I felt it get more intense, more unrelenting, until I wanted to scream. I felt it compress the space around us until I needed to run away, to escape, but there was nowhere to go. It was everywhere around Hades.

"So it can get worse than that." Inside, I'm pure panic, a thousand flowers popping open in a mad rush for the sun. I don't let that reach my voice. I can't be the one who bends to this. I can't be the one who hears this news about Hades and cowers.

I knew from the moment he told me about his pain that it was serious. He wouldn't have told me if it was something he could hide.

"I know it can." Zeus's eyes fall to his folded hands. The hands that have saved his brother time and again. "He's been close before, and I held him back. If this continues, I don't think his body will be able to handle it."

"Because it hurts too much?"

He sighs. "There's no way to know the exact mechanism for things like this."

"No."

"I think he has to be inhabiting himself for the pain and the pressure to go into the ground. If it keeps getting ahead of him, then it will just stay... contained."

Contained. It sounds so simple. Like putting flowers in a vase. You cut the stems and drop them in. A pretty arrangement.

Contained.

That's not what Zeus is talking about. *Containment* means all that extreme pressure stays in Hades's flesh and bone. It stays in his head. I don't have to have gone to school to understand what that means.

"It could crush him." I name the fear out loud. It's already hanging in the air between us. I won't run from it.

Zeus looks away.

For the third time in two days, I feel like I'm seeing a younger version of Zeus. The one who must have come to this conclusion many years ago, before I was born. He's been carrying this weight with him from the moment he understood.

That's what he doesn't want to admit out loud.

Not that his brother is a burden, but that Hades's life means something to him. Losing him wouldn't be as simple as cutting a diamond out of the ground. He wouldn't be able to make it into a business transaction. There wouldn't be any profit. Only loss. Only the worst kind of defeat, for a man like Zeus.

"If we don't stop this." Zeus's voice is soft, but the words have a sharp edge. "He'll become a black diamond, Persephone." A shadow crosses his eyes. Sorrow and fear. A future he might not be able to prevent. "You could wear him around your finger."

NINE

Hades

I'T'S THE MIDDLE OF THE NIGHT WHEN CONSCIOUSNESS returns.

I search for the pain first, automatically, keeping my body perfectly still.

Oh, thank fuck. It's at a distance, at least for now. The quality of that space suggests I might have a few hours before it's out of control again.

I know better than to count on it.

I know better than to think this means the situation has improved.

It hasn't.

The first episode was like a rockslide. With nothing to keep the pain at bay, the whole system is unstable. I shouldn't have had another attack so soon. There's no telling how long I have before the next one.

Even so, waking up like this is a staggering relief.

My eyes adjust to the dark. The window hints at starshine. It's the dimmest the light can be without being off.

Persephone sleeps next to me, the covers pulled tight around her and clutched in her fists. She's huddled as close to my pillow as she can get without taking it for herself.

I don't want to wake her, but I have to touch her. I've been away in the dark for too long. The blackout from whatever drug Zeus carries around in his pocket lasts for no time at all. And, simultaneously, I'm drifting for days. Any amount of time is too long to be separated from Persephone.

I run my fingers through her hair, winding my way through her curls. They're soft as petals. I think of her outside in the valley, surrounded by flowers. I haven't spent significant periods of time in the sun in years. When Demeter stopped shipping the painkillers, and then the poppies, I had no choice.

If I had them now, I'd sit next to Persephone in the sun, where she's happy. I'd watch her grow flowers. Watch her cheeks get pink from telling me about her books and her studies. I'd carry those books outside for her. Make her read them to me.

I don't care what's in the textbooks, but I love the sound of her voice. It's expressive, the way her eyes are. When we're alone in the dark, the sound makes the room seem brighter.

In a *good* way. Not a fucking excruciating one.

I need a way to survive this, even if there's no deal to be had with Demeter. Even if there's no victory. I have to survive to keep my summer queen with me. On some level, I've known that since I saw her for the first time, running across the field, taking care not to crush the flowers beneath her feet. When she lowered herself to the floor of my train car and crawled to me, something snapped behind my heart.

I would rather die than give her back. Demeter would rather die than give me the poppies.

So. Until another solution presents itself, I am fucked.

I roll onto my side, and one of my healing bruises calls attention to itself. I put a hand over it and get closer to Persephone anyway. Zeus didn't hold back during the fight. I wonder if he's been so attentive because he feels guilty about it.

He shouldn't. I tackled him first.

It occurs to me, with my fingers in Persephone's hair, that I should be more concerned about getting a status report from Oliver. I need to know whether the trains are still running. I need to know where we are on supplies. I need to know if everything's all right.

I'm almost certain, however, that he's been giving Zeus the reports instead.

My throat feels strangely tight. Shining the light from my phone screen into my face would be a terrible idea. Oliver and Zeus will have come to that conclusion. And if I'm in bed, and Persephone's with me, with Conor sleeping by the fire...

It's all right.

For now, everything's all right.

Because of my prick of a brother.

I let all these thoughts fade into nothing.

What matters is Persephone. What matters is that she's breathing peacefully. Every gentle rise and fall of her shoulders is a small gift. Like a flower just beginning to bloom.

Losing this battle against Demeter, and against my own mind, would be a fucking tragedy. Persephone has so much more to do. With me. In her life.

She could be happy here, at my side. And not like a prisoner. Like an equal. The people in the city would love her. How could they not? Persephone looks like springtime. She sounds like a summer dawn. Her silver eyes remind me of a watchful moon.

The mountain breathes around us both. Tonight's quiet isn't an illusion. Aside from the men standing guard, everyone else is sleeping. Or talking. Or fucking. Whatever they like to do best when they're not working in the mines or elsewhere. Only a few stripped-down shifts are on through the night for food and medical care.

All of which is at risk.

Work in the mines can't resume until my brain stops trying to kill me. Food and medicine are going to run out. I stockpile what I can, but unfortunately for me, there's not endless storage capacity on the mountain. Just endless opportunities for me to collapse into rubble.

I can't do that.

I can't leave them defenseless.

I can't leave Persephone.

An ache in the middle of my chest seems like it might be a heart attack, at first. Something dire. A side effect of that many fists meeting that much bone. But here, in the dark, with my fingertips skimming her cheek…

I love her in a way that makes oxygen and food seem insignificant. It makes pain a small price to pay.

Ever since the farmhouse and my foster father, I've done my best not to care about anything. Fondness is a trap, and one that would chew your leg off rather than set you free. But she's broken me wide open.

I'll never be repaired from this love. It'll be with me, always.

A hiss escapes me at the thought. My body still reacts as if it's dangerous. Cronos made it perilous to love anything. I learned that with Rosie. He took her away, and the part of me he broke didn't recover until Persephone.

It's not fully healed yet. I don't know if it ever will be. It's not the emotion I have to come to terms with. It's the way it makes me so open to attack. So open to heartbreak. I hate it. I can't live without it.

Conor huffs from his spot in the corner of the rug.

"Go back to sleep," I tell him. He puts his head back down on his paws.

The only feasible way to plan is to assume that the trains aren't running. Demeter will stop them in the next few days regardless. We'll be isolated here with a city's worth of people to feed. Some of them are children. A few of them were born on the mountain. This is the only life they've ever known.

Persephone sighs, rustling in her sleep. She murmurs something about poppies and turns over.

I take the opportunity to slip out of bed. Brush my teeth. Wash my face. I'm stiff as fuck from the fight, and from being in bed so long. I'm not meant to sleep this much. In the end, I find the idea of hot water too tempting to resist. It eases some of the stiffness, if not the bruises.

I didn't feel them quite this much before. Or perhaps it's worry making fists around my ribs.

It's my summer queen's fault. She made a beating heart out of the cold, black diamond in my chest, and now I can't return it to its previous state.

What wouldn't I do for her?

That's the only line in the sand of any significance. A month ago, I wouldn't have dreamed of asking for help. From anyone. Admitting weakness was only a guarantee that someone would take maximum advantage.

Persephone makes me think it could be different.

After all, I admitted it to her, and she made a thousand flowers bloom. She's continued to try, despite everything.

I finish the shower and go back to her.

My summer queen stirs when I readjust the sheets over her shoulders. She stretches delicate wrists above her head, and fuck, if all I ever get to do for the rest of my life is watch her sleep...

All the rest would be worth it.

Her eyes flutter open. It takes her longer to see me than it took me to see her. I'm so fucking glad for that. I'm so unbelievably glad that she doesn't have eyes like mine.

"Am I awake?" A little smile curves the corner of her mouth, like she's not sure. "You smell really good."

"You're awake."

She inches closer, her body warm against my skin. "Are *you* awake? Or did you sleepwalk into the shower?"

"I was thinking."

Somehow, she's angled herself all the way into my arms. Persephone reaches out, the movement slow, to touch my face. Her little smile disappears. "Are you okay?"

"For the moment."

She lets out a relieved breath. "Good. What were you thinking about? Tell me."

"You're very demanding. I thought I trained that out of you."

Persephone hooks her arm around my neck and pulls me down to kiss her. It's sweet and soft and slow. It's not a kiss for a bastard like me. It's not a kiss for the man who's causing so much grief and stress. She gives it to me anyway.

"I guess you'll have to try harder," she says when I resurface. "I guess I'll have to live here on the mountain forever."

"Did you have somewhere else to go?"

She shrugs. "Not really."

Laughing hurts. My bruises ache. My ribs ache. My head

aches. Fuck me. She's the most perfect creature ever to have wandered into my path.

Persephone is pleased to hear me laugh. So pleased that her eyes sparkle. For a moment, there's no mountain. No pain. No poppies. It's just the warm, sweet scent of her skin and her outsized joy at making me laugh.

It's like sand slipping through my fingers. The warmth between us remains, but reality returns. Time, ebbing away.

"You know." A voice like soft darkness. "I trust you."

"Do you?"

Persephone nods, solemn. "I know you'll decide the right thing."

"For what?"

"For whatever you were thinking about. You won't let anything happen to your people. And you won't let anything happen to me." Her expression is utterly sincere. Silver eyes wide. No tension around her mouth.

"What gave you that impression, summer queen?"

A little breath. "How hard you've tried to keep yourself safe. Aside from the fight with Zeus, anyway. You could have refused to rest. You could have kicked him off the mountain. But you didn't, because there are more important things to you than your pride."

"I *tried* to kick him off the mountain."

"You didn't mean it."

She's right.

"Our options are limited. More limited by the day."

"What are the options?"

"Move against Demeter at the farm. Request supplies from overseas." I trace the line of her face with a fingertip. "Ask Poseidon to intervene."

Persephone's quiet for a minute. "Would he come if you asked?"

"I don't know."

"Zeus said..." My summer queen's eyes go a little distant. "He said Poseidon spends most of his time at sea. Is that because of how you grew up?"

"He would always have gone back to the sea. He's connected to it."

"Like you're connected to the diamonds?"

"My understanding is that the connection is constant. He feels it always. And, of course, the farmhouse was hell. Probably more so for someone who needs to be on the ocean."

"So he wouldn't want to come back."

"He did enough at the farmhouse. Too much. He distracted Cronos when he was at his most violent, and it ate at him."

I think he viewed it as a kind of penance, though I'm not sure what he thought he'd done. He was the last one to arrive at the farmhouse. After we killed Cronos I swore not to bother him. I've already broken that promise more than once. I don't relish doing so again.

"What does Zeus do? If you and Poseidon and my mother..."

"Do you have a guess, summer queen?"

She thinks. "Influence?"

"Yes. He can extend an... energy across a space. Change the mood in a room. It's why his parties are so successful."

Her nod is slow. Thoughtful. She must have felt him do it at the whorehouse. "So... Poseidon might not come, but you're still thinking about asking."

"No. I'm looking at you."

Persephone looks back at me. I'm never going to take

seeing her for granted. Never. I don't care if her face is mostly in shadow. I can still see her eyes. How silver they are. How hopeful. The moment takes on a timeless cast. We could be in the distant past or the distant future. She'd still be my summer queen.

She swallows, then parts her lips. Her fingertips are gentle on my face. She traces up to my temple. This is how she touches the flowers when she makes them grow. It's soft, and she does it with exquisite care, but she's not tentative. Those flowers are hers.

A shock of gold moves through my nerves, head to toe.

I'm hers.

"Aren't you worried?" she whispers. "Aren't you afraid of what happens if—"

"No."

Because I'll do whatever it takes. I'll reach out to Poseidon, if it's necessary. I'll offer him anything.

I can almost hear him out there now, in the waves. It's dangerous to be at sea, with its swells and currents and storms. It's barely safe here, with my brain on edge and Demeter doing fuck knows what at her farm.

Luckily, Poseidon doesn't shy away from danger. He hunts it down.

TEN

 Persephone

I BELIEVE HIM.

Maybe I shouldn't. But Hades feels so warm and strong next to me. His eyes are clear for the first time in days. He doesn't seem afraid.

If anything, he seems determined.

He guides one of my curls away from my forehead, and at his touch the world falls away. His lips take mine, and then there's no world, only him.

A field of blooming flowers hums through me. Gold light and summer. Petals, opening to the sun. He kisses me like I'm honey. Like I'm pure sugar. And when he's licked off all the sweetness, the kiss edges into a bite.

I gasp, aching under him. He's bracing himself over me, held up by strong arms. "Hades."

"Yes?"

"We should—" I've *missed* him. His seizures have taken

the past couple of days, but it feels like a lifetime. "We should be careful."

"I'm being careful." He bites me again.

Oh my God, I love it. "But you have to rest."

He pulls back and slides his hand around my throat, his grip casual. It makes my pulse beat louder in my ears.

"I've been resting, summer queen. Now I want to do something else."

"We—" I can't think. Being close to him when he's like this is an entirely different kind of pressure. It's a hot, aching kind that covers my skin and beats in my heart and draws me to him like the force of gravity. "We really shouldn't."

His hold on my neck tightens. "You've forgotten your place."

"I just want—"

Hades silences me with another kiss while he steals more air from me. All I can taste is him. Cold and refined and powerful. I don't need air. I just need this. Him. Relief is a bruise across my heart. I was the one who was afraid and trying to hide it. I was the one who worried that he might not return to himself.

And I know, I *know*, that this doesn't mean he's healed. It doesn't change a thing about how much we need the poppies.

I need it anyway.

Hades feels like sheer power over me. He feels as all-encompassing as the dark.

He lets me up to breathe, black eyes searching mine. I lift my head and try to kiss him, but no. Hades pushes me back down and readjusts so that there's space between us.

"Turn over."

I scramble to do it, my cheeks burning. "But how should I—"

His hands are on me before I can complete the sentence. Hades strips my nightgown over my head. Goose bumps run down from my shoulders to my wrists. It's warm in the bed, but the chill of his power calls to all my nerves. He's unceremonious about ridding me of my panties. Then he pushes my cheek into the pillow and taps impatiently at my hips until they're up where he wants them.

I'm already panting when he settles behind me and runs his palms over my skin. My shoulders. My back. My waist. He makes his way up to my breasts and pinches one of my nipples. I jerk away from the pain, but he pushes me back down.

"Stay where I put you." His fingers spread out between my shoulder blades with a warning pressure.

Slowly, deliberately, his hand glides to my other nipple. He rolls it between his finger and thumb, and this time, he's methodical about it. It's hardly a pinch at first, and then it's rougher and rougher until I'm shaking. Struggling to stay in place despite his other hand on my back.

"Yes," he hisses. "Show me how it hurts."

I've wanted to cry since Zeus brought him into this bedroom after the fight. Letting the tears overwhelm me felt wrong. If I let myself cry, I'd be admitting how scared I was. Queens don't cry. That's what I thought.

They do when they're ordered to.

One tear streaks down my cheek, but I don't try to get up. I keep my cheek on the pillow. It's beyond me to stop my hips from moving side to side, just a little.

"Oh," I breathe. "Please."

Hades makes me hold on a few more seconds. I'm gripping the sides of the pillow in my fists by the time he relents.

"I fucking love that." His voice is low, like the starlight in his window. "Now I want to see you come."

If I was going to argue, it would fall apart beneath his thick fingers. Hades strokes between my legs, making a satisfied noise when he discovers how wet I am.

It's just as hard to stay still for pleasure as it was for pain. Harder, maybe. I want him with an overwhelming ache. He leans over me, lifting my head from the pillow with a hand on my neck. He kisses me while I'm up on hands and knees. When he pushes his fingers into me, a soft moan escapes into his mouth.

"Have you remembered yet?" Hades returns my cheek to the pillow. "This is where you belong."

He pulls his fingers out of me and delivers a stinging slap between my legs. I turn my face into the pillow in just enough time for it to catch my cry.

"Shh, summer queen. Not so much noise." Hades presses his palm over the ache he's made so I can't close my legs. I can't fight him. I don't want to.

Instead, I find myself pushing back into his hand. I'm on fire with embarrassment and need. I shouldn't be surprised that I love this. I shouldn't be shocked at all, but I am. It hurts, and it's thrilling. It's just like Hades to turn pain into something else entirely.

"Tell me." His tone is cold and casual, like we're sitting across from each other at his desk. "Do you need more training to be a good summer queen? More punishment?"

No. Of course not. I've been so good.

"Yes."

"I'm impressed that you'd admit it."

He works three fingers into me and drives them deep, finding the place that makes my hips rock across his knees. He twists them, toying with me, hissing his approval. Every touch feels new and raw and right.

It feels like reassurance.

If he can do this, he'll survive. Not tonight. Not this minute. Forever.

Hades swipes his thumbs over my cheekbone. "You were afraid for me."

More tears. I was. I've been terrified since Zeus sat in that living room and said he'd turn into a diamond. I've just been pretending not to be. I buried the fear as far under the soil as I could.

I don't have another *yes* in me. I'm too consumed by the moment. He's here now. He's awake now. He's sending an electric pleasure through that fear. It compresses the feeling. Makes it small.

I can't see him now that my eyes are closed, but I saw him before. He's healing from the fight. Hades's bruises are already beginning to fade. I'd never say there was a silver lining to the seizures, and his pain. The only good to come out of it is that he's had to rest. Hades wouldn't have let himself do it otherwise.

And he *has* to. All the damage from the fight has to get better. We have to do everything we can to keep his pain under control. To keep the seizures to a minimum. Because I need him here with me.

That's what he's doing now.

Telling me he's here. Telling me, with his voice and his touch, with his pain and his pleasure, that he won't leave me. Not if he can help it. Not now.

He guides my hands up near the pillow. *Stay.* His hands run over me again. Steadying me. There's more warm pressure in the air, or it's coming from how much I want him.

And then.

The reality of him.

Between my legs, thick and hard and insistent. He pushes in, shoves in several inches, and it's like we've never done this before. I struggle on instinct.

Not because I want to get away.

Because I want him to stop me.

And he does. His hands lock around my hips, and he pins me against him so he can take more of me. He makes a low humming sound. Sheer satisfaction. The farthest thing from diamonds. I wriggle down onto him. It's so hot, a real heat, a filthy wetness. Maybe it's bad to want him like this. To need him like this. Maybe it's wrong.

I don't care. Pleasure is a knife, a blade, and I need it to be tempered with something else.

"Please."

Show me. Prove it.

He stops fucking me and laughs. It undoes a knot hiding behind my heart. But his absence is too much. I'm too empty.

"Oh, no. That's not—come back. Please, come back."

Hades wraps a hand around one of my thighs and holds me in place. My fingers clench on the sheets, but there's nowhere to go. There's nowhere I want to go. He delves his fingers into the wetness between my legs and spreads up to where I'm still clenched tight, despite what I've asked for.

He does it again, and again, long enough that I have time to be embarrassed about how wet I am. Then he's bending over me, a hitch in his breath. His teeth meet the flesh of my neck and he bites like he could eat me alive.

"Be good, summer queen. I'm going to make you cry."

Hades starts with his fingers. Two of them in a very tight space. There's no coaxing this time, only that iron grip on my hips and his insistence. My breath turns ragged, but he doesn't let up. He pushes them in and in and in until it hurts. Until my hole is tight around them and I can't believe they fit.

It's dirty. It's wrong. I can't take it. It's all I want. I want to be a good summer queen for him, because I don't know how long we have, because any moment could be the last good moment.

"Focus," he snaps. He felt me getting distracted by those thoughts and tensing up. "Be *good*."

I'm as good as I can be while he pulls his fingers out and pushes them back in. Once. Twice. Three times.

That's all the patience he has.

His grip feels even more inescapable when he presses himself to my hole. I lean back into a splitting pressure. I know I begged for this. My body doesn't realize it. A cry tears loose from me, but I aim it into the pillow. Hades doesn't give an inch. He takes one instead. Then another.

It's not any easier than the first time. I don't want it to be easy. I'll do painful things for him. I'll take him where he doesn't fit. I'll force myself to relax, to accept. I'll do anything.

His thumbs rub circles on my hips. "It's all right." I can't tell if he's talking about the fact that he's fucking my tightest hole or the terrible situation we're in.

"Beautiful tears. Take a deep breath, Persephone. Yes. Another one. Relax."

He pushes himself the rest of the way inside me, and I lose all the air in my lungs. It *hurts*. And it feels so good to take him. Like growing all those flowers. I try to tell him, but all that comes out of my mouth are wordless sounds. Tears drip onto the pillow.

There's a seismic tremor in his thighs. He's holding back for me. Hades could do more. He could fuck me harder, but he's being kind.

In his way.

Which is possessive and territorial and cold. Relentlessly cold. When he moves again, it's to pull out and drive back in, over and over again. His hands hold me still while I thrash against him and sweat and curse.

"You're my perfect summer queen." Hades forces each word out through the force of his thrusts. "Look at you, taking me with those pretty tears on your face. I can feel how hard you're trying. Does it hurt?"

"Yes. Yes. It hurts so much."

"You love it."

"Please. Please. Please."

Anguished begging is the magic word. And because he's Hades, because he's alive and in control and not ever going to leave me, he waits until I'm at my limit to touch me.

It's the most painful, most perfect orgasm of my life. I take him with me over the edge into that pleasure, and then into the sheets, and then into the dark.

ELEVEN

Persephone

WE SURVIVE ANOTHER DAY. ANOTHER EVENING. HADES spends the day in the dark, pretending he's not tired. I spend most of it with him, emerging to meet with Zeus and Oliver about what's happening on the mountain.

Mainly nothing. The workers are restless. Everyone is uneasy. There's no news from my mother's farm, or from the city.

The main development is that the trains have stopped. Oliver's sent people to scout the tracks, but he can't send too many without drawing my mother's attention. Hades is adamant that we don't lose anyone on these missions.

I can't sleep.

I should be able to, given how tired Hades made me last night, but I'm too restless to lay in bed. When I'm sure he's asleep, I sneak out from under the covers.

Conor stirs by the fire, watching me with his huge, dark eyes.

"I'll be just down the hall," I whisper to him while I pat his head. He sniffs in the direction of the bed.

"What is it, Conor?"

He shakes, then settles back down.

I wait another minute, stroking his head. Was Conor's pause just then a sign that something's wrong, or a sign that it's the middle of the night? I've been making it a point to stay aware of the pressure in the room. It doesn't seem worse than usual. It feels steady.

Then again, Hades's episode two days ago came out of nowhere, and it happened fast. He's been living in almost complete darkness since then. No light from the windows. When we go in, we switch on a nightlight in the walk-in closet and close the door. What little light filters out beneath the door is it.

Hades is exhausted. I don't know how he could be anything else, with the constant pressure.

I'll be gone a few hours at most. It'll be okay.

I feel like a ghost moving across the sitting room. A ghost who pulls her robe tighter like it's battle armor. A ghost who needs to solve this problem.

I'm at the door to my study room when I hear soft footsteps behind me.

Zeus is being quiet on purpose, so I pretend I don't see him. It's easy enough in the murky light of the hallway. He doesn't glance in my direction when he slips inside the sitting room.

He's going to sleep on the floor next to Hades's bed. He does it whenever I slip out when Hades is asleep. I've stepped over him before. He's always gone when I wake up again.

So much for hating each other. Zeus might not admit it in the light of day, but he's afraid the pain will return in the dark. He's not waiting to be summoned by Conor.

Hades seemed stable today, which is the only reason I'm willing to leave him. Tired and wrung out, but stable. I can see the irony in being glad Zeus is here. They might come to blows if Hades discovers that Zeus is sleeping in his room, but I'd be glad for that, too. It would be a sign that he was healing.

In my study room, I turn on a soft lamp and shade my eyes while they adjust to the light. Then I wake up my computer and squint at the screen. I don't actually think I'll find the answers we need in my inbox or in the textbooks, but I keep looking anyway.

All this science business is out of my league, honestly. The few books that my mother let me read didn't come close to the level Hades needs. Still, I'm trying my best. Any knowledge about how the brain works is better than none.

But understanding won't be enough. Science doesn't include people like Hades. People like me, or my mother, or Zeus. Even if I had time to learn everything, it wouldn't take me far enough.

What I really need is people.

I've started making lists of people who could help Hades. Doctors are the hardest. I think of them as a last resort. We'd never be able to tell any of them the whole story. Judging by the pill bottle Zeus carries in his pocket, he's said as much as he can to the doctors he knows. I'm sure he knows a lot of good ones from the city. The party I saw at Olympus didn't look dark, or shameful, or sleazy. It was the kind of place powerful men could visit. Even doctors.

I've also looked into the places poppies grow, which is how I discovered exactly what my mother is doing to Hades.

You need a *lot* of poppies to make the painkillers he needs.

Less than if you were making the drugs made from different kinds of poppies, but much more than what she's been sending to the mountain. Much more than she was growing in her fields.

They're also very different from the photos online. I recognize the shape of the pods, but the petals…

There are no others with the white and gold filaments. None. The hybrids my mother made are worlds apart from everything else I can find.

On top of all that, the closest ones are illegal in lots of countries. Hades is rich enough to buy his way around the laws, but those flowers won't solve his problem. The poppies my mother grew for him are so valuable because they're rare. More than rare. They're unique.

I had a little hope that she was bragging. Telling me stories so I'd take my work in the fields seriously.

She wasn't.

As far as I can tell, they don't exist outside my mother's farm.

But in the middle of the night, when I can't sleep, I can keep looking. Maybe there's a distant relative of her hybrid that was grown by chance in some faraway field. Maybe, if I find it, I can have it brought to the mountain.

Or maybe there's another plant that would have the same effect.

I don't know.

I just know that when my mind is quiet, it wanders right back to the conversation I had with Zeus.

He'll become a black diamond, Persephone. You could wear him around your finger.

My fingers go to the black diamond around my neck. It feels like a talisman. Hades gave me this, so he'll be all right. The seizures won't take him from me. I won't let that happen.

I hold it tight in my palm, close my eyes, and wish I could ask my mother for help.

If she were different, I could go to her. If she were different, she might grow the flowers herself, just because I asked.

But she is not different. Her life didn't make her that way.

I go back to my lists and my books until my eyes burn.

Until my head is tipping forward.

Just for a minute. I'll rest my chin in my hand, take a break, then keep searching. Five minutes, maybe. That's all I need.

I don't know how long it's been when the sound startles me awake.

It wasn't very loud. A voice? Maybe it was Oliver.

My eyes are still bleary when I get back into the hall. Rubbing at them does almost nothing, so I blink harder. There's no movement down by the foyer.

But down toward Hades's room, there's light.

More light than usual.

I run toward it on numb legs. Light can't mean anything good. At the sitting room door, I force myself to slow down.

The light's coming from the bedroom. Enough to see by, and not much more.

At first, I think they're fighting. Zeus stands in the middle of the room, his body tense. It would make sense if Hades woke up and stepped on Zeus, and now they're sniping at each other over it.

One more step, and I can see Hades, too.

They're not fighting.

Hades has both palms pressed against the wall, and he's leaning into it as hard as he can. He grits his teeth and pushes, as if it's the wall causing his pain and the only way he can think to escape it is to force it back with his own body. The pressure in the room feels the way he looks. It's heavy. Inescapable.

Conor is as close to him as he can get, his body curled around Hades's feet.

After a few seconds, Hades takes a breath and bangs his forehead against the wall.

"Manners, Hades." Zeus doesn't move from where he's standing. I don't know what he's waiting for. I don't know what I'm interrupting. Only that Hades is in pain.

I open my mouth to ask.

Before I can, Hades draws his hand back and hits the wall with his palm. The loud *crack* almost covers the pained groan that slips between his teeth.

Zeus moves in and pulls Hades away from the wall. Hades resists, but it's a blind resistance. I know that as soon as I see his face. I've known it since I came to the door. There's no presence in it, only pain. Fear feels as cold as the morgue. As cold as winter.

Hades would never react this way if he could help it.

He's splintered the wall.

No.

He's put a diamond into it. A glittering, black diamond.

Zeus holds his brother's hands together, then pulls Hades's arms toward his own body. He doesn't seem to care that Hades might fight back and hurt him without knowing. Conor follows, staying close. He pushes at both of them.

"I know, Conor." Zeus's tone is so easy and gentle it shocks me. There's no stress in his voice, though the pressure in the room is going up. "No," he says to Hades. "I can't let you do that."

"No," Hades says. "No, no, no. That's all you ever fucking say."

I step inside the room, moving toward him because I have to. I should have been at his side already.

Zeus glances over at me, his brow furrowed with concentration. This is taking more effort than he's willing to let on. Hades is still trying to pull away from him, but he won't let go.

"Stay out of the way, Persephone."

"I could—"

"You can't." He uses the same calm voice with me, too. "That's not a judgment. You don't have the muscle."

"For *what*?"

"I just need you to understand—" Hades yanks at Zeus's hands, interrupting his sentence. Another groan escapes through Hades's teeth. It's a horrible sound to hear. Hades wouldn't allow himself to do that unless his pain had made it impossible to stop.

"You have to relax," Zeus tells him. "You're going to knock the whole fucking mountain down."

"What do I need to know?"

"That he doesn't know what he's saying." Hades throws his whole body into the escape, but I'm not sure whether it's Zeus he's trying to escape from or the pain. Probably both. "He doesn't know, and he won't remember. Okay? Tell me you heard me."

"I did, but there has to be something I can do."

"I've got him. Just don't get close."

"Zeus—"

Hades's eyes narrow, rage darkening his face. He snarls at Zeus like he could kill him. There's no control in the sound, and it's frost, straight to my heart. Hades never loses control.

"You motherfucker," Hades spits. "I hate you. Hate. You."

"But you're so affectionate," Zeus says.

"Get out."

"I don't think I will."

"Get *out*," Hades snaps. "Go the fuck inside."

Now they're fighting. Zeus to hold on. Hades to get away. Conor tenses, but he doesn't bark. He keeps moving, circling, staying out from under their feet but unable to leave Hades.

"We're already inside."

Hades leans close to Zeus, his expression fierce and blank and terrible. A mask of pain. "Do it."

Zeus cocks his head to the side. "Sorry. I have other plans."

"Kill me," Hades demands. "Kill me. You're taking too long."

"Not tonight. No—" Zeus nearly loses his grip on Hades's arms. "Not tonight. You'll feel better in the morning."

"Kill me," Hades shouts. "End it."

This was meant to sound like an order, but I know better than that. Hades doesn't shout to give orders. He hardly has to raise his voice on the mountain.

He's not ordering. He's begging.

"I can't," Zeus says.

"Kill me *now*." Hades's eyes are wells of pain. "I hate you. I hate this fucking place. Get out of my way. Get. *Out*. Of my way. There's nothing here for me. There's no one here. *There's no one here*."

My hand goes to my chest.

There's no arrow, just raw heartache. The pressure in the air drags it out across my lungs. Shoves it back into my spine.

I know he doesn't mean it. I know Hades isn't aware of the words. They don't sting.

What wounds is that he doesn't know I'm here.

The pain is taking him away from me.

Hades struggles harder against Zeus's hands, and I take an involuntary step forward.

"Kill me." Hades's voice rises. "Do it. Please. I don't want this. Put me down in the ground. I want to be in the dark, motherfucker. I—"

His words snap off, and Hades crumples toward Zeus, pushing his forehead into Zeus's shoulder. Zeus braces himself to stay upright.

"Not tonight," Zeus says. "I won't. I'm sorry." His eyes flicker to mine, and they're so sad. This isn't the first time he's had to do this.

Hades digs his feet in, and Zeus tenses. It's so much pressure now. My head aches. My chest aches.

We're out of options.

"Persephone. The bucket," Zeus says.

I bolt across the room, my nerves on fire, my heart broken, and pick up the bucket at the side of Hades's bed. I'm there just in time for Zeus to turn Hades around.

He's sick, and then he's gone. Knees going out from under him. Zeus angles him onto the bed. Conor follows, whining, the sound desperate. Hades's eyes are closed, but it's still happening. More pressure. More and more—

Oliver rushes into the room.

"What took you so long?" Zeus snaps. He snatches something out of Oliver's hand. A syringe and a vial. Zeus takes the cap of the syringe off with his teeth. His hands flash over the vial. One more second to hold it to the light, and it's done. He sticks it into Hades's arm like he's done it a million times.

It takes almost a minute for the pressure to let up.

It's the longest minute of my life.

Zeus curses under his breath when it does. Then he looks me in the eye. "We have to get those goddamn flowers."

TWELVE

Hades

THE PAIN ISN'T CLOSE WHEN I RESURFACE, BUT THAT DOESN'T mean anything. It can return whenever the fuck it wants. I don't know whether to be grateful that it gives me these moments of reprieve or frustrated that there's a ticking clock on peace.

Conor is the only one in the room, curled up on the bed next to me. Sitting up is a process. I'm a human bruise, and my balance is off-kilter. It takes several seconds to catch up with my movement.

Standing is possible, at least. Walking to the bathroom.

I shower in the dark. Conor follows me and bumps his heavy body against the outside of the shower door, standing guard while I'm here. The hot water can't erase the knots from the attack. From all the attacks. It's an impossible battle. My body tries to protect itself by locking up my muscles. It tries, over and over, to force me to my feet. To force me to walk. To get inside.

The body can't always overpower the mind. There's very little to overpower the pain. I don't remember how it ended last night. I only remember that I woke up into a shocking, excruciating peak that seemed to stretch out forever.

I can only assume that it wasn't pretty.

It takes an obnoxious amount of effort to towel off. Every move I make seems suspect. Will lifting my towel to my face be the thing that starts another seizure? Rubbing it over my hair? Who the fuck knows.

In the closet, I choose clean clothes by feel and pull them over my head. All the hems feel rough against supersensitive skin. It adds insult to injury. Quite enough that this weakness is embedded in my brain. To have it take over everything else is a needless reminder of its existence.

The bedroom door opens as Conor and I go back in. A low wash of light from the hall outlines my brother. He closes the door behind him and blinks into the dark at me.

"You're up." I'm not used to hearing undisguised relief in his voice. "And dressed."

"I should hope so." I take the chair by the window. Conor snugs himself close to the arm, and I rest my hand on the top of his head. "Where is Persephone?"

"Talking to her maid out in the foyer. We need to discuss last night."

"We don't." My abs tense. Legs. I'm not interested in an accounting of how weak I was, or how desperate I seemed.

"Hades…"

"Zeus. It's a waste of breath. I understand the risks of—"

"No, I don't think you do." His voice is charming and warm, almost as if he's amused. That's how I know he's serious. "Persephone was white as a sheet. And you were asleep in the dark when it happened."

He doesn't have to elaborate. I've never had a seizure start while I was sleeping. I've had the pain make it intolerable to stay awake, but it's never crept up and attacked in a dark bedroom while I was dreaming. Shame is hot, and crawling. Fear is cold. They fight one another, brawling in my rib cage.

"What are you suggesting? Surrender?"

Zeus huffs a breath. "No. It's time to call Poseidon."

"I know."

"He likes a fight, and he hates Demeter. You need to reinforce the mountain and get supplies before they start to run low, not after. Since he's coming by water, he won't have to cross—" A minuscule flicker of window light catches in his eyes. "What did you say?"

"I know it's time to call him. There's no guarantee he'll come."

And there's no guarantee it will do me any favors. Zeus could change his mind at any time and go back to working with Demeter. Poseidon could be in any mood ranging from vindictive to gleefully violent.

"He will," Zeus says. "Because you're going to tell him you're out of time."

Calling Poseidon with the news that I've found myself in this position isn't the last thing I want to do, but it's fucking close.

A concerned tension fills the air. It's not from me. It's Zeus, and he's not bothering to hide it. There's nothing I loathe more than admitting I'm no longer self-sufficient, and I never would have before.

Things are different now. I have Persephone. She's made her position clear. So has Zeus. Every word he says is carefully modulated. It doesn't matter. I could hear his worry even if I couldn't feel it.

I'd be shocked if I had the energy for it. Zeus rarely allows the illusion of the rich, charming bastard to crack. Here, on my mountain, he's done it for days.

The image of gates appears in my mind, fully formed. As if they're close. As if death is close. Only a few steps away.

Persephone comes in, light on her feet, the door opening and closing in a heartbeat. I get a flash of her curls, of her silver eyes, and then she's across the room. Then she's with me.

She doesn't say anything. She just folds her body into my lap, wraps her arms around my neck, and holds as tight as she can without putting any real pressure on me. Her cheek brushes against mine and I inhale cool springtime and warm summer and sweet blooms. It's very dark, but I close my eyes against the urge to see.

There are other sensations to memorize. Her hair under my hand while I hold her close. Every relieved breath. The weight of her. *Here.*

She stays like that for so long that I expect Zeus to leave, but the mood in the room doesn't feel particularly impatient.

"How are you?" she murmurs against my neck.

"The usual aches and pains. I'm fine."

This is the truth. My body feels bruised, but in comparison with the height of the pain in my head, it's nothing. Bruises can be soothed by my summer queen in my arms.

Persephone lifts her head, and her silver-eyed shadow looks at me. "For now?"

"Yes. For now."

"Then I'll stay with you while you eat. You should have something."

I lean forward and kiss her. "You have other plans."

My summer queen tenses. "What other plans could I possibly have?"

"I need you to go visit the workers and their families."

"Oliver can visit them."

"Better if it's you," Zeus says. "You'll be more comforting to them, given that the trains have stopped running. A symbol that everything is under control."

"That's right." I'm forced to take her mouth again, kissing her with only a fraction of the need I have for her. Persephone stifles a whimper. It sends heated desire searing down my veins nonetheless. "It's not Oliver's strong suit. It's a job for a queen."

A little shiver of pleasure. "Fine. What do you want me to do, exactly?"

My throat goes tight, an unfamiliar feeling. Loving her with this intensity—fuck. I hate it a little. The physical way it affects me. But I need it more than I hate it.

"Tell them that things will be all right. See if anyone needs food or medical attention. Quite a few of them had family members come from the city, and the incident in the valley unsettled them." *The incident.* When I almost died. "Make sure there's nothing they need. Reassure them."

Persephone sits up tall, brushing her hair back from her face. "I'd rather stay with you."

"I won't be alone. I'm sure Zeus will be here to bother me every moment you're gone."

"Every fucking moment," Zeus agrees.

"Take Conor with you," I tell her.

She shakes her head. "No. He can't be away from you. What if something happened?"

I give her face a shake. Persephone's body melts against mine. Fuck, I want her. And she wants this from me. It's all I can do not to banish Zeus from the bedroom and have my way with her.

"Take him with you," I say instead. "No more arguments."

"Okay." She brushes a kiss to my lips. "But I'm not leaving for long. You'll just have to live with it. Come on, Conor."

My dog presses his nose into my hand, then follows her out.

Zeus takes my phone out of his pocket and passes it to me. I shield it with my hand and turn the brightness all the way down on the screen.

"Why did you send her out?" Zeus goes to lean against the wall near the window.

"My people need reassurance. And I have no fucking idea what Poseidon's going to say."

I dial the last number I had for Poseidon. I didn't think I'd use it again, and I'm half hoping he won't answer. Then I won't have to ask him for help. I won't have to call him back to the land he hates.

The call connects.

Someone answers in Arabic. I give my name and tell the man I need to speak to my brother.

There's an abrupt silence, followed by a clattering like they dropped the phone. The wait stretches out for five minutes. Ten. I listen to the sound of wind and shouting.

"Did that motherfucker put you on hold?" Zeus says with a laugh.

"I don't know. They didn't hang up." I rub the back of my hand over my eyes. So many nagging issues, and all I want is for Persephone to come back to me. I wasn't lying when I said the people needed her reassurance. They do. But I'm a selfish bastard who wants it for myself.

On the other end of the line, there's a loud *bang*.

I put the phone on speaker in time to hear Poseidon say, in a voice like high seas, "You're garbage, you know that? You only ever call when you want something."

"And you only ever answer when you're not busy being a

war criminal. Last I heard, you were still sinking ships for fun off the Persian Gulf."

"Sinking ships." Poseidon has a big, echoing laugh that sounds like sea salt and pirate treasure. "Is that what they call it these days? You know, you big fuck, there are rumors about you in the Persian Gulf too."

"All good things, I hope."

He laughs again and it wouldn't surprise me if he revealed he was on the deck of some slimline historical reproduction with heavy cannons and a death wish. "What do you want, hellraiser?"

"Supplies for the mountain. We're in a bit of a siege situation."

"Who the fuck is *we*?"

"Hello, Poseidon," Zeus calls.

Another silence. "The fuck are you two doing?"

"We had a score to settle."

"Well, did you?"

"Yes."

"And then what? You invited him to stay for a fucking tea party?"

"No." I don't know what to say. "There hasn't been an opportunity for him to leave."

"Demeter's lost it because Hades took her daughter for his very own," Zeus cuts in. "She's disrupted the trains. And she hasn't sent Hades his painkillers in months."

Poseidon lets out a string of imaginative curses. "I don't want anything to do with her."

My throat goes tight. "Neither do I. The more pressing issue is that I have people who are going to starve. Or die of various causes that could be prevented if you take some of my money."

"What about you? Are you going to die too if I don't save your ass?"

"Probably."

Poseidon sobers. "Is he fucking with me?"

"No," answers Zeus. "Unfortunately."

"What about you, prick? Is this just entertainment for you?"

"Yes. Demeter's games are always delightful, as I'm sure you remember."

More cursing from Poseidon. "You don't just need supplies. You need weapons, too. And men."

"The more ruthless the better. We might need to move on the farm," Zeus says.

I expect Poseidon to flatly refuse this, even if it's only a hypothetical. A gull screeches in the background. A steady *clank* beats against the wind and the waves. It would be hellish, standing on the deck of Poseidon's ship. Full sun. Miles of reflective ocean surface. I've never wanted to be a sailor, but the idea that the rest of my life might come down to the dark of this room or the silence of death inspires bitter envy.

I recognize it for what it is. A distraction.

"Do we have an agreement or not?" I ask Poseidon.

"You'll owe me, you know."

"What, money's not enough for you?"

"Please, Hades, your life is fucking priceless. You can owe me or you can die. Take it or leave it. Choose quickly. I've got a ship coming up on the portside." Poseidon's voice rises with excitement. "Never know what might happen."

I know what might happen.

"It's a deal. How fast can you get here?"

"Five days. Four, if I push it. Try not to die before then, or I'll collect my favor from your corpse."

THIRTEEN

Persephone

IT'S QUIET ON THE FACTORY FLOOR. IT WAS LOUD WHEN Hades brought me here and made me grow the flower on the balcony. Noise, from down in the mines. It must run in cycles. Nobody could stand that much sound for hours on end. But right now, only a few people work at their stations, their heads bent over their projects.

Oliver catches me looking at them. He walks on my left side, and Conor walks on my right. "They insisted on coming to the floor."

He keeps his voice soft so it doesn't carry over the empty worktables and stools. There's more variety than I noticed from up on the balcony. Different kinds of chairs, some with backs and some without. One person has a red clay mug at the corner of their table. It holds pencils and other tools.

"They make jewelry, right?"

"Production and some simple designs." Oliver goes past the mine shaft opening. I follow him to the other side of the

room and through the door he holds open for me. It's part of the hallway system in the mountain's lower level. "Jewelry and other luxury items. He can hire more people that way."

"And they didn't want the time off?"

"Some people don't. Gives them too much time to think."

I take a deep breath to calm my nerves. Where are all the diamonds going to go? The jewelry? Without the trains, all of it is stuck on the mountain. Hades has enough money that it won't hurt him to take a break from selling, but this place thrives on a routine. It must. There simply isn't endless space to store everything.

Unless we run out of food. If that happens, nobody will be worried about making shipments.

My mind follows those worries like a train out on the tracks while we follow the hallway down. It narrows, then widens again. Oh—it wasn't the same hallway after all. We pass under a wide, open archway in the rock wall, and there it is.

The city.

That glimpse I had through the window didn't do it justice.

We stand at one end of what must be the main street. A row of buildings stretches down either side. Three stories, one stacked on top of the other. Balconies out front. The ceiling soars above us. Lillian said there was a way to get outside. The interior of the mountain's base is *way* bigger than I realized. Even looking at it from the outside didn't prepare me for the scale.

"Couple of branching streets." Oliver points. "More shops and houses."

"Is this where you live?"

He cracks a smile, and the scar on his face moves with it. "I've got a place to use on my off days. Usually, I sleep upstairs.

When I sleep." Oliver rubs his hand across the back of his neck. "I don't do much of that. Never have."

"Oliver. You should sleep."

He waves me off. "Don't worry about me. Worry about them."

I turn back to the street. The *city*. It's alive down here. Small groups of people have gathered at tables outside a café. Two women skirt the tables, chatting to each other. A man comes out of a store with a paper bag in his arms. He crosses in long, loping strides and disappears down one of the side streets.

When Hades told me to come down here, the people seemed faceless. Like a field of identical flowers. But now I'm seeing...

Families.

A mom sways with her baby close to her chest next to one of those café tables. A dad hurries down the street with his small son. There's a whole world down here with its own rhythm and pulse.

But it came from Hades.

This is his heart.

It's the one he's kept hidden and safe, even while he pretends that there's nothing in his chest but a lifeless black diamond. The rumors he cultivates outside the mountain are a shield as much as the rock itself. He plays the nightmare so the people here can sleep at night. He keeps them from being threatened by the outside world.

Tears line my eyes, and I blink them away. Hades did this despite the fact that he couldn't do the same for himself. He had to stay connected to the outside world through his deals with my mother. And all this time, he's done it for his people.

If anything happened to him, they'd be at the mercy of the world.

Just like he was.

"You okay?" Oliver's gruff concern makes me want to cry even more, but I pull it together.

"There are so many people. I guess I didn't understand just how many."

"Should we go talk to them?"

"You don't have to stay, if you've got other things to do."

"I don't." I narrow my eyes at him, and he laughs. "This is my job for the next little while."

"Does he think I'm not safe?"

"No. He thinks you don't know anybody's name."

It's risky to stand inside someone's living heart, and Hades didn't want me to fumble over it. My own heart melts a little more. It's going to be made of honey by the time I go back upstairs.

"Is he always right?"

"Usually." Oliver shrugs. "Let's go meet some people."

Our first stop is one of the tables outside the café. Oliver introduces me, and I'm looking into five surprised faces. It seems like many more. So many that I immediately forget all their names. Nobody's ever paid attention to me like this. The people at Zeus's party barely glanced in my direction.

"I wanted to make sure you had everything you needed. And make sure you were okay."

I wasn't this nervous running away from my mother's farm.

"What about you?" A dark-haired woman at the table gives me a kind smile. "You're so—you seem so young."

"I'm not *that* young."

"And she's steely," Oliver puts in. "Don't piss her off."

"*Oliver.*" I can't believe he'd say that.

"It's true. She went out to meet Zeus's army."

More wide eyes. "I thought that was a rumor," the woman says.

"Hell, no. I had to go out with her. She never flinched."

"Please." My face burns. "I just came down to meet you. Is there anything I can get? Anything you need fixed?"

The dark-haired lady reaches out and squeezes my hand. "We're okay. Everybody's helping each other out. There's enough food."

"You'll let me know, though?"

"Yes," she promises. "It was lovely to meet you. Now go on. People are waiting."

She's right. They're starting to gather. Oliver stays at my side until people are introducing themselves, and then he falls back. I promise to keep them updated about the train. I assure them that the mountain is safe. And, most often, I repeat that Hades is okay.

They're all worried about him.

"We saw some of the fight." The man telling me this lowers his voice. "But he usually doesn't stay away for this long. His brother's been coming down instead. Is Zeus taking over?"

"No. He's just here to help."

Thankfully, people accept that Hades's brother would do that for him. I guess that's what brothers are like. They throw punches, then spend the rest of their time keeping each other alive.

After an hour, I've made my way down the street. I stop outside a jewelry store to talk to a younger man with a quick, shy smile.

A *jewelry* store. People buy jewelry for each other here. They get engaged. Get married. Have children.

All the rumors about the mountain being worse than hell were just stories. It feels like a million years ago that Decker and I talked by the poppies. I was right, but I didn't know it yet. Hades can be cruel and ruthless. That's true. And it's also true that people come here and never leave.

Because they're happy. Because they're safe.

"Will you show me the rest?" My face hurts from smiling. I need to rest my voice.

"Of course."

Oliver takes me slowly through the other streets. It's clean here. Comfortable. A man comes out of a house ahead of us. It's not until we're level with each other that I see his eyes. They're too black for the glow from the ceiling, but green enough to tell the color.

He is the first person I've ever seen who has eyes like Hades. But Hades's are hardly blue at all. They're almost always black. Far more damage has been done to him, and here he is, stopping it from happening to other people.

Someone sniffles on the side of the street, and Conor stops, leaning out toward the noise. "Stay with Oliver," I tell him.

It's a girl. A little blonde girl in a blue dress, a matching bow in her hair. She can't be more than four. When she sees me looking, her eyes go wide.

I look up and down the street. She can't get hit by a car, but she's alone. It only takes a few strides to cross to her.

"Hi." How do you even talk to small children? I have no idea. My life is one surprise test after another. "My name is Persephone, and I live here on the mountain, too. Are you lost?"

She sniffles again, and my heart breaks for her. This girl is adorable. It's unreal, how cute she is.

"I've never seen you before." She swipes her hand over her eyes.

"I live on another floor." That's accurate. "What's your name?"

"Jill," she answers, and her lip quivers. "I don't know where my mom is."

I fight back an awkwardness so intense that I want to run back to Hades and demand to know what he was thinking. I'm completely out of my depth.

"Is she at work, maybe?"

"At home. I came down because my ball rolled across the street." Jill opens one hand and shows me a pink ball the size of an egg. "And now I can't find her. I can't read."

"We'll find her together." I offer Jill my hand, and she takes it. The buildings are numbered. Businesses are mixed in with apartments. I don't see any single houses. Doors for staircases, front windows with curtains. "Which way did you come from?"

She points. We go past a little bakery, and I knock on the next door. No answer. The second door opens on a man who tells me that Jill's mom lives five doors down. In a place like this, a ball could roll pretty far before it stopped.

It turns out that Jill's mom isn't at home. We knock on the door at the same time the next one opens, and two women come out into the hall, faces set. They're on a mission. One of them, with the same blonde hair as Jill, drops to her knees and pulls her close. The other gives me a quick wave and disappears back behind the door.

"Jilly Bean, where did you go?" The woman looks up at me and startles. "I'm sorry. You're—"

She doesn't finish. She's nervous. About me.

She stands up and sticks out her hand to shake. "I'm Scarlett, and you're Persephone. Thanks for bringing my daughter back." A little flash of a smile, embarrassed and uncertain.

"Word went through the mines early on about who you were. I hope I didn't overstep."

"No. No, of course not." Oliver's introductions were always for me, not the workers. Hades took me onto that balcony, after all. In a place like this, secrets are probably hard to keep. "I actually came down today to see how you are. How everybody is, really."

Scarlett slips an arm around her daughter's shoulders. "We're doing just fine."

"Are you really?" She laughs at my question. "Everybody keeps saying they have everything, but I mean it. If there's something you don't have, you can tell me."

"I mean it." Scarlett has a pretty smile. "We have everything we need. Don't we, Jill?"

Jill nods, her eyes solemn. "Will you come back and visit?"

I could say many different things. Dodge the question, because I don't know what's going to happen next. All those options are very un-queenlike.

I'll find a way. For Hades, and for all his people. I'll keep trying until something works.

"Yes," I promise. "I'll come see you again very soon."

No matter what.

FOURTEEN

Hades

THERE IS A SMALL BALCONY, MORE OF AN OUTCROPPING, near the lookout. There's nothing between it and the sea, and the salt spray occasionally gets carried up here on the wind and hits me in the face. Every time it does, Conor barks. He's going to keep that water in its place, everything else be damned.

It's been four days.

Since we can't run shifts in the mines, no one has anything to do but talk and eat. We've already made a dent in the mountain's food supplies.

Persephone came back from her meetings with the workers and found me in bed. She pulled her dress over her head and climbed over me. We did not discuss the conversations she had with the workers.

Zeus is the one who insisted I rest. In any other circumstance, we'd have come to blows over how stubborn he's being. In this circumstance, I'm forced to agree with him.

I can't risk any more seizures.

The only way I could be on this balcony to watch Poseidon's ship come in was four days of acclimating myself to the light. Every night, Zeus produced some pill or other from his pocket, and I had no choice but to remain unconscious for the duration. It's not a long-term solution. They make me feel sluggish and slow, and I sleep longer every time I have one. It can't continue. I can't spend all day and night in bed.

At the very least, something will change today.

Poseidon is almost here. His ship made contact an hour ago.

When he's out at sea he laughs and kills and chases. He's a wild motherfucker. More so on the land. He belongs to the sea.

"You made it out." Persephone comes out on the balcony, a shawl around her shoulders. Conor nudges my leg like he agrees. The two of them are co-conspirators now.

"Sun's setting." I curl a hand around her shoulders and push it beneath the shawl, finding her nipples already peaked. What has this filthy thing been thinking about? She was probably wondering just how far she could push me without earning herself another punishment. And then she thought about how she could tempt me to come inside and shut the door on the world with her. I pinch one of her nipples, hard, and she makes a little noise at the back of her throat. That's essentially an invitation to spend the rest of my life in bed with her. "You've been such a good summer queen. Don't fuck it up."

She presses herself against me at the warning, which— fuck. I'm not even going to be able to watch Poseidon's ship come in if she keeps this up.

The ship is a shadow out on the sea, getting closer with every second. Persephone shades her eyes to look for it. "He's bringing everything, right?"

"Fresh produce. Meat. Medicine. Everything."

"That's a good thing. Isn't it?"

"It's not that simple with Poseidon. Everything is complicated."

For more reasons than one.

"So he's like you." She shivers. The wind off the sea is cold, despite the summer sun.

"You're mouthy today." I don't want to get too far into the past. Not when the future is so unstable. Poseidon has always been the wild card. Now he's a pirate with too much money and not enough to lose. He takes being outnumbered as a delightful challenge. "I don't want him to have to stay long on the mountain. It puts him in a mood."

I had the dock built for a ship the size of Poseidon's. Persephone was surprised, but I'm not dull enough to cut myself off from the sea. It'll be a windy walk from the ship. Hopefully it will settle him.

"You're worried he'll be unhappy?"

I shoot her a look that makes her blush. "I worry he'll be angry. Situations involving Demeter have that effect on him."

Persephone cocks her head to the side, but I reach over and cover her mouth with my palm. "No questions. Not now."

She sticks her tongue out and licks my skin, so I press my hand in harder until she bites. I pull her into my side, the playfulness of the moment drifting away in the wind. It might not be lighthearted when Poseidon arrives.

I keep my face angled away from the sun as much as I can. The light hurts like a motherfucker, but I want to see this. I want to know exactly when that ship makes landfall, which it does about ten minutes later.

It is not, as I suspected, an oil tanker. He's moved to a smaller ship. It's the most bizarre ship I've ever seen. Metal, like a shipping vessel should be, but the deck is wood. There are no sails where sails should be. Other than that, it looks like something out of the past, but with modern features. Knowing Poseidon, he paid for it on some illicit seafaring black market.

I should feel better when it pulls in at the dock and stops. It means we'll have food. It means my workers won't starve. But it also means that Poseidon will be here. Those are the terms. He can stay while we're under our agreement.

I've never been good at trusting my brothers. They know how to exploit my weaknesses.

"He's here," says Persephone. "Let's go in."

I want to stay out here, touching her, but I'm out of time. The moment slips away. I don't get it back.

It's almost an hour later when Poseidon meets us in the den upstairs.

While I've been standing here with Persephone and Zeus, waiting to play host, Oliver's put people in every corridor, making sure nobody from Poseidon's ship gets any brilliant ideas. Conor sticks tight to my feet, standing so close I had to move him off my shoes several minutes ago.

This is only the second time something of this magnitude has happened on the mountain. It's a tectonic shift, something on the scale of the earth's layers, and I can tell Conor feels uneasy about it.

Don't we all.

I test my knee and the fading bruises at my ribs. I hate new habits. I should be able to discard this one soon enough.

But I won't ever be able to discard Persephone. I might not even be able to leave Zeus behind. My life is like the rocks under the mountain, being shoved aside by the appearance of new diamonds. They can't be put back the way they were.

My focus now is on stopping bodies from piling up in the corridors. My people insisted they were fine. If we stretch our food supply, we could last weeks. But then fights will break out. Tensions will rise. My own brain will work against me.

Voices in the hall. Oliver. Poseidon.

"Do you think he's in a good mood?" Zeus wears his cockiest smile, as if this hasn't been hell.

"No." I step closer to Persephone. "He's on land."

She frowns. "Should I go somewhere else and let the three of you talk?"

"Why would you do that?" Zeus teases. "This is going to be fun."

Poseidon bursts into the den, a fist to the door. It was built for me, so it holds. Any other door would be off its hinges. He's as tall as Zeus. As tall as me. My sea-obsessed brother is all muscle and glittering blue eyes. He has dressed for the occasion. No jacket, but nice enough pants, and a white shirt with a collar. Poseidon's lean and hard from spending all his time swimming.

Oliver sees him in, then pulls the door partway shut. "I'll be here in the hall."

Poseidon looks me and Zeus up and down, his eyes narrowing.

"What the fuck were you two thinking?"

"You'll have to be more specific." It's never *hello* with Poseidon.

"You assholes decided to beat the shit out of each other, and you didn't call me to come watch?"

"It was a spontaneous meeting," Zeus says. "And you're here now."

Poseidon rolls his eyes. "I'm always last on your mind unless you want something."

An undercurrent in his voice sounds like dark, genuine

hurt. And… guilt. I'm forced to hide my surprise. He wanted us to call him earlier. He didn't want to be last.

That's at odds with everything I know about Poseidon, but I can hear it. All these days in the dark have made everyone's voices so clear.

Poseidon will never admit that out loud. And he doesn't have anything to be guilty for.

"That's not true, Poseidon." Zeus might be the only one who's successfully pretending to be at ease. "I'm always thinking of you. Especially when I hear you've hunted down another ship with a brimming cargo hold. With money in your pocket, you're a danger to my women at Olympus."

He laughs, but I can't relax at all. I don't want to. Poseidon was the most volatile one in the farmhouse. Always willing to throw himself into danger. He baited Cronos. Sometimes I would harass Poseidon until he fought me. He could be counted on to punch me into blessed unconsciousness.

Now he looks mildly suspicious, eyes traveling slowly over everything in the room. There's nothing particularly threatening here. A collection of furniture made to look like wood but reinforced with steel so it's harder to break. A bar, tucked into one end of the room, fully stocked. I had the glass bottles replaced with some that are made to shatter into dull edges. If Persephone knew, she would ask me why I take such measures in a den we barely use.

Persephone never met my father.

Poseidon considers the space. There's no way for him to know about what I've done, but perhaps he senses it. In his younger days he would have torn a place like this apart just to test the theory.

I wait it out.

That is a skill learned in my father's house, though it was

only successful part of the time. One thing I will never admit out loud—not to anyone—is that the man has caught me in a permanent trap, even after we sent him to the underworld. He's made us all inadequate in one way or another.

I'd prefer to forget my brothers' faces and everything that came with them, but I can't forget. A part of me needs to see them to know it was true. To know that my memory hasn't been destroyed beyond repair. A part of me needs them to stay alive.

But I feel sickening shame at having to ask. I wasn't strong enough to win against Cronos, and that means I'll always be weaker than I could have been.

I idly wonder if it bothers my brothers to see me. Demeter tries to kill me, but she won't come close enough for eye contact. She has, after all, broken our contract. She knows what she's done.

Poseidon huffs a breath and his shoulders move down an inch. A scowl twists his face. Something about this room is displeasing to him.

He steps forward and puts out a hand anyway. When I take it, he pulls me in and slaps my back.

"I didn't want to come, you bastard." He offers his hand to Zeus next. "But here I am."

"Yes. And I owe you for it." I put my hand on the small of Persephone's back. "Poseidon, this is Persephone. Persephone, meet my brother."

He does not offer his hand. The bastard sweeps his eyes over her like he's just noticed she's there. His expression darkens. "About that. What the fuck is Demeter's daughter doing at our meeting?"

FIFTEEN

Persephone

I KEEP MY CHIN UP, EVEN WHILE MY CHEEKS BURN WITH embarrassment.

Poseidon asked his question with such scorn and suspicion. About me. During our introduction.

What the hell?

We've never met before. I haven't done anything to him. And now new tension in the room overlays the low-level pressure of Hades's headache. He didn't bother lying to us when it started. He can't hide them anymore.

"Don't be an asshole," Hades says, his tone cold. "You knew she was here."

Zeus strolls closer to us at the same time Poseidon does. We could be standing at one of his parties, only the mood isn't casual. This isn't a celebration. Oliver edges closer, too. Poseidon's eyes are stormier by the second. Calm, light as air, flutters down over my skin.

"Knock it off, Zeus," Poseidon snaps. "No one's turned over any furniture."

"Hades might, if you keep glaring at Persephone like that," Zeus offers. "He tackled me for giving her a compliment."

The calm dissolves, but not completely. It feels like there are thin tendrils left. Maybe that's Zeus trying to keep himself calm.

Poseidon crosses his arms over his chest. "You said Hades took her. You didn't tell me she was being included in strategy meetings."

Hades sighs impatiently. "Where else would she be?"

A grin spreads over Poseidon's face and he regards Hades with an admiration that chills me. "I didn't think you'd take revenge on an innocent. I approve, of course."

"This isn't revenge." Hades's jaw works.

"Then how can you stand to look at her?"

Hades's eyes widen at Poseidon's words. I heard it, too. An emotion that's hard to place. It's pushed deep under the waves for him. An old wound.

There are many wounds between the three of them. That's why they fight. That's why they're snappish with each other.

That's why they keep showing up anyway. Nobody else understands.

Another fight would not be good right now. It would be a disaster. So I put aside my confusion, push away the sting of Poseidon's comment, and step into the space between the three men.

I pretend, as hard as I can, that I'm not intimidated at all. After a few seconds, it's real. I'm not. I can do this.

Poseidon stares down at me.

He doesn't look anything like his foster brothers, but there is a similarity in their faces. It's almost too subtle to see. All in the tiniest expressions. The pressure around us ticks up. It's hurting Hades to hold himself back.

"Thank you." I put all the sincerity I can into my voice. "I'm glad you came. There are a lot of people here who are grateful to you, and I'm one of them."

Poseidon's brow furrows.

"Demeter would never say a thing like that." I can see Zeus at the edge of my vision. He only sounds like he's smiling. He's not. "See? They're different."

I'm sure Poseidon isn't going to believe him, but I keep my eyes on his. I'm not like my mother, and I can't help how I look.

On top of that, I didn't lie. I'm glad he's here. We need him. Hades needs him.

Poseidon releases a rough breath. "You'll have to understand if I don't take Zeus at his word. You could be just like Demeter."

"Honestly? I don't care what you think about me."

He laughs. "No?"

"No. I want the people on the mountain to have what they need. And I want my mother to stop screwing with everyone's lives. You can be as much of an asshole as you want."

"You can't." Hades moves closer. "If you're a prick to Persephone again, I'll kill you."

Poseidon raises his eyebrows. "You tackled Zeus, but you'll kill me?"

"It was a compliment," says Zeus.

"You said I would make a good whore." I shoot a look at Zeus. "And don't kill him, Hades. He brought us food."

The pirate brother shakes his head, a light in his eyes. "I brought you more than food. I brought a fucking mountain's worth of medicine and paper products and these."

He pulls an envelope from his pocket and hands it to me. It's small, taped at both ends, and basically weightless.

"What is it?"

Poseidon looks at Hades over my head. "I didn't approve of Demeter fucking around with you, so I asked around to some of my contacts on the black market."

Hades's hand tightens on the small of my back. He's pretending to steady me, but I think he's the one who needs to feel grounded. "What are you talking about?"

"I couldn't get any of the flowers. Demeter's too good at finding leaks, which is a pain in the ass." Decker was one of those leaks, and he died for it. My heart aches for him. But the envelope… "Got my hands on a few of the seeds instead. Pretty sure they're the last ones on the goddamn planet that aren't in her fields. Won't help you now, but maybe in a few months…"

"No," I breathe. "Not in a few months."

Poseidon blinks. "What?"

"It won't take a few months. If these are the right seeds, then I can grow them. Today. Right now."

He curses under his breath. "You're like her?"

A shift in the room. In the air. The pressure from Hades has let up a little. I think this might be understanding.

"I'm not like her. I can't make hybrids like she can, but I can make them grow. I have to go outside."

Hades catches me by the arm. "Do it here."

There's no way he can go to the valley. Not after he watched Poseidon's ship come in. And I know from the look in his eyes that he can't bear waiting for me to come back and tell him if it worked. If they're right.

"Okay."

"Oliver," Hades calls. The door opens after a few heartbeats. "We need a flower pot with fresh soil. Eleanor will know."

He leaves, footsteps quick in the hall. It will be harder without the sun, but I can do it. All I need is the dirt.

"You're so fucking rude," Poseidon says. "I bring you the thing you want most in the world, and you don't offer me a drink."

"He *is* rude," Zeus agrees, striding across to the bar. "But he's always like this when he has a headache. You didn't feel it when you came in?"

Poseidon works his jaw side to side. "I sure as hell do now. What were you going to do if I had other engagements?"

"Well, Hades was going to die." Ice clinks in the glasses under Zeus's hands.

Hades doesn't say anything. He'd rather die than send his people to my mother's farm.

"You're always doing that, aren't you?" Poseidon looks at Hades, exasperated. From the way Hades talked about him, I didn't think Poseidon would care what happened to his brothers. Maybe I was wrong, the way I was wrong about Zeus. "Trying to die."

"Yes. That's why I called you." Hades's sarcasm is overwhelmed by exhaustion. "You're a witless motherfucker if you think I'm trying to die."

"Manners, Hades." Zeus comes back and pushes a drink into Poseidon's hand. He gives one to me, too. I take a cautious sip. It's sweet, with only a hint of alcohol.

"This is… really good."

"Don't sound so surprised, Persephone." Zeus ambles back over to the bar and gets his own drink. The air feels sparkling. It's pure anticipation. "No need to stand on ceremony. Plenty of chairs."

Hades takes me to a love seat by the fireplace. Poseidon sprawls in an armchair across from us. Zeus dims the lights, and a low fire springs to life in the grate. I'm the only one close enough to hear Hades's relieved exhale when the lights go down and we're left with the orange glow.

"Where'd you get them?" Zeus asks Poseidon as he takes his own seat.

"Traveling salesman."

Zeus snorts. "Be serious."

"Guy out of Australia. Deals in rare and illegal plants. He hates Demeter."

"Why?" I can't help asking. I've never heard of someone across the world hating my mother, but that's probably because she didn't tell me.

Poseidon pauses before he answers, like he's debating if he really wants to speak to me. "He tried to make contact with her several years ago to form some kind of partnership. She didn't like the message. Or the messenger, who was second-in-command. Rumor has it their conversation ended with poisoned tea."

"Oh."

"He'd been holding onto those seeds for a while. Waiting for some opportunity to fuck her over, I guess."

Hades makes a soft sound that's almost a laugh. "Yes. My continuing existence will certainly fuck her over."

A chill goes down my spine. If these seeds grow into the flowers we need, what's next? My mother might never stop trying to get me back. She might spend the rest of her life attacking the mountain.

And me, inside it with Hades.

I hold the packet tighter in my fingers. I have the feeling that if Oliver doesn't get back soon, it'll disappear in a puff of smoke.

"How many men did you bring?" Zeus asks Poseidon.

I don't hear the answer. I'm thinking of my mother's fields. The dishcloth that she kept by the sink. Flowers, everywhere. I think of Decker's cold body and poisoned tea. I think of diamond mines bursting at the seams and cloudless skies.

The door opens, and Oliver comes through, a ceramic pot balanced in his arms. The firelight glimmers off dark green glaze. He puts it on the floor at my feet, then glances between me and Hades. "Is it all right?"

I slide down to the floor and put my fingertips to the soil. It's damp and airy, and there's more than enough room for the roots to grow. "This is great, Oliver. Thank you."

He nods, his cheeks flushing, and goes out again.

Zeus clears his throat. "Should we step into the hall?"

"I'm not going anywhere." Poseidon sits up straighter in his chair. "I want to know if I need to pay that bastard a visit."

"It's fine." I put on a smile to cover my pounding heart. "I don't mind."

But my hands shake while I peel back the tape and open the packet. I tap the corner against my palm until a single seed slides down the angle of the paper and meets my skin.

It's barely a speck. So small, and so important.

I make a hole in the soil with my pinky finger, then drop the seed into it. Brush the soil back into place. My stomach drops when the seed disappears. Now that it's out of sight, was it ever really there?

I take a deep breath and hold my palm over the dirt.

There.

I can feel it. The seed is almost nothing compared to the soil around it. Like a single drop of water in a watering can.

Okay.

Simple.

Make it grow.

I close my eyes and think of sunshine. Of green shoots. Soft, new petals.

The seed resists, and a sliver of doubt wedges into my heart.

It's different with new seeds. That's all. Starting out is the hardest part. There aren't any roots yet. Everything has to grow. The whole structure.

I picture more gold. I picture the white filaments. The gold ones. The way the poppies bask in the sun.

The seed trembles, but nothing happens. No roots emerge. Nothing grows.

They're all watching me fail. Hades and his brothers. They're watching me struggle with this, and I shouldn't be struggling. I do this all the time.

I try again.

Trying this hard takes my breath. I can't open my eyes. I don't want to see how disappointed they are. I don't want to see how smug Poseidon will be. My eyes burn behind my eyelids. Is it me, or the seeds? Were they just a trick?

Hades puts his hand on the curve of my shoulder. He runs his thumb over the soft skin at the back of my neck. And then his grip tightens.

It feels like *trust me.*

And then there's something else. Something dark. I recognize it right away.

It's him. The pressure from the air all around us. He's directed some of it into my body. As much as he thinks I can stand. It's not comfortable, squeezing there at my lungs, but...

It's power.

That's what it is. This is the form his power takes. A dark, relentless pressure.

It's the opposite of what I do, and I don't see how it can help, until…

It's the *opposite*.

Roots need pressure to break the shell of the seed. They need pressure to push into the soil. They have to move it out of the way. Life is the sun, but it's also force, it's also movement, and taking up space…

The roots emerge, grabbing at the soil, and I suck in a breath. I wouldn't normally make anything grow this fast, but I have to. We have to know. We have to see.

Sunlight and dark reach down to the seed. The stem flies up from new roots. The shoot breaks the surface of the soil like a swimmer coming up from the water. It brushes my palm, green and gentle, and I give it room to grow.

I make it grow.

And grow, and grow, and grow.

The bud rises, green and fresh. I think I can see red petals. Please, let those be red petals peeking through. Poseidon and Zeus are staring, both of them leaning forward in their seats. Poppies normally take a long time to grow, but I put everything I have into this one. Everything and more.

The green bud trembles, and then it blooms.

It blooms a vibrant red. The color of the most valuable flower on the planet. Red, like blood, with gold filaments that sparkle in the firelight. With white filaments that remind me of moonlight. And a seed pod in the center, round with what it carries.

Hades squeezes my shoulder. "You did it, summer queen."

Zeus collapses into his chair. "Oh, thank fuck."

SIXTEEN

Persephone

I GROW POPPIES IN THE VALLEY UNTIL MY HEAD ACHES AND I'm all out of energy. All out of sunlight, too. I hand off the last of the plants to Eleanor, who has been taking them to a man who works for Hades. He's the one who processes the flowers into painkillers. It normally takes the better part of a day, even with state-of-the-art equipment, he says, but he's hurrying.

Oliver is leaving Hades's bedroom when I arrive, covered in dirt and bone-tired.

"First one." Oliver gives me a meaningful look and steps out of my way.

I find Hades standing by his bed, looking down into his palm.

"Hello, summer queen." He opens his hand to show me the pill, and I go to see the thing I've worked so hard to get.

"It's small, isn't it?"

"The usual size."

Tiny seeds. Little pills. They don't seem big enough to handle his pain, but they are.

I didn't think I'd be strong enough to survive being captured by Hades, but I was.

He tips the pill into his mouth and swallows it.

And then, as if it's not the biggest moment of our lives, as if it's not a miracle, he turns to the task of stripping off my clothes. Every dirt-stained piece of cloth, onto the floor. His own clothes go next. As we become naked, the medicine kicks in. I can feel the tension start to leave his body. He's shedding pain the way he sheds clothes.

Hades won't let me walk to the shower. He takes me there in his arms. I lean my head against his chest and listen to his heart. The fast, painful rhythm is slowing.

By the time he's washed my hair, the pressure is going out of the room.

It's gone a few minutes later, when he presses my newly clean body up against the wall of the shower and kisses the side of my neck. Slips his fingers between my legs. He fucks me, slow and hard, until I break apart over him and turn into a desperate, clinging woman begging for more.

"Is it right?" I pant as he sets me on my feet. "Did it work?"

He kisses me in answer.

Yes.

We go to bed. Hades pulls me close, up against his body, and turns down the lights. This time, he lets the moonlight in. I could stare at him all night. He's gorgeous in light like this. The moon loves him.

Almost as much as I do.

Voices carry down the hall. Zeus and Poseidon, pretending with all their might that they're getting along and there's no tension between them.

I run a fingertip over Hades's collarbone. I can barely keep my eyes open, but I still need to talk about what happened today. I need to hear his voice. It's the first night in almost a week that I haven't been worried sick about him. For the past four, he's been dead to the world for hours on end.

"Poseidon seemed angry when he got here."

Hades runs his hand down the length of my spine, then back up. "He's always angry."

"He was angry with me, though. For looking like my mother."

Hades is silent, like his thoughts have gone far away. Down the hall, Poseidon laughs. It's a rolling sound. It reminds me of a huge wave. The ocean can be dangerous, and now it's in here with us.

"We all have our reasons."

"The same reasons?" Hades looks at me, his gaze black and calm. He brushes his hand over my face, and I close my eyes. "Tell me."

"If I tell you…"

"If you tell me, you won't be keeping it a secret anymore."

"If I tell you, then you'll know."

"And what?" I point my toes, stretching sore legs. "You're worried I won't forgive her for it?"

Another pause. "I don't want you to think that Poseidon was right. You're not revenge for anything your mother did."

"I'm not going to think that no matter what you say."

He takes a slow, careful breath, then exhales. "When we were seventeen, Demeter accused the three of us of raping her in the barn."

My blood freezes. Ice, head to toe. It doesn't matter that I spent so much time in the sun. "She said that?"

"To the police."

"But…" My tongue sticks to the roof of my mouth. "But you didn't do that."

"No. We never touched her. They arrested us anyway. She looked young and innocent, and we looked like rough and tumble boys from the fucking farm. All of us except Zeus, who had to go to work in the whorehouse. Made no difference, in the end. They don't let you keep your nice shirts in jail."

I can't speak.

"In jail," Hades mentions, "the lights are always on."

"That's torture."

"Yes. It was."

He's quiet for a long time. Then he runs his fingers through my hair. "For me, it was torture because of the lights. Poseidon couldn't stand being caged. It drove him out of his mind. Zeus was…" He searches for the word. "He was heartbroken."

"He was?"

"He and Demeter were close. He went out of his way to take care of her. She liked—" He clears his throat. "She liked to play. She was only a couple of years younger, but she liked children's games. Tag. That kind of thing. Poseidon was too angry. I was too concerned with staying out of the sun. Zeus would make time for it. So the accusation blindsided him."

"And he's hated her ever since?"

"I think there was more. Some of the things he said…" I feel him shake his head, the motion quick and uncertain. "I don't know."

"Did you have anything when you were in jail? Anything to help? Or was that before the painkillers?"

"It was before." A shudder goes through him. "We only got out because Cronos made a deal with the judge. We had to stay at the farmhouse and out of trouble until we turned eighteen, and then he'd have it erased from our records."

I hold him closer. Living on my mother's farm wasn't all bad. I loved the fields and the flowers and the open skies. I've come to love the mountain, too. It has a dark, metallic beauty. A rougher beauty than the blooms I put in my hair.

Hades went from one hell to another.

"Was it any easier after you got out?"

His fingertips follow the curves of my shoulder blades. "Demeter came to me not long after with a proposition."

"The painkillers."

"She'd already figured out how to grow them by the time she made her offer."

It takes me a minute to realize what Hades is doing.

He's hesitating.

"What did she want?" I keep my voice softer than the dark. "Money? Diamonds?"

"She wanted me to kill a man for her."

My stomach turns over. "Who?"

"The man who raped her. He was on Cronos's security staff. Spent most of his time patrolling the boundary of the property, all the way across the woods. I don't know whether she went to him, thinking he wouldn't hurt her, or he found her gathering flowers. She had tears in her eyes when she told me. But I can't say if I believed her or not. I just wanted the pain to stop."

"You did believe her. You must have. Otherwise you wouldn't have done it."

"Maybe I would have."

Hades's breathing is lighter now. Almost like he's anticipating something. Dreading it, even. Tears prick the corners of my eyes. Understanding is like a new plant sprouting in real time, pushing slowly through the soil.

"The man she named." I swallow a strange ache in my throat. "Was he my father?"

"I can't know that for sure."

"But you think it was?"

"Yes. Sometimes…" I can almost picture Hades, young and in pain and without any other choices. "Sometimes I wonder if it was an act of mercy. Cronos must have been pressing Demeter to give him the name by then. And he wouldn't have made it quick."

Emotions sweep through me like petals on the wind. I didn't think much about having a father when I was growing up. He was never there, and my mother was, except for when I was with Eleanor. I read stories about people with fathers, though. In my imagination, the one I had was a decent man who couldn't be with us for a good, noble reason.

I didn't dream of meeting him. I didn't dream of the day when he'd swoop down and rescue me. I always knew that if I left, it wouldn't be because of that faceless man.

Now it's really true. He'll never show up and change things. I don't think I'd want him to. I'm disappointed in the dead man I'll never meet. And I'm sad for my mother, who was so young when she was pregnant with me. There's no question she hurt her brothers. She did serious damage along the way.

But she was hurt, too.

She could have blamed me for it. She never did.

I don't forgive her for the way she kept me trapped all that time. Not exactly. I understand, though. I understand how you'd do anything for a person you loved. I understand how you could get it wrong.

"I don't blame you," I tell Hades.

"Then why are you crying?"

"Because it's sad. What happened to her. What happened to you. None of you deserved that."

"Those years are dead." He wraps his hand under my chin and pulls my face to his. "They don't deserve your tears."

Hades has never considered himself worthy of sadness, but he is. Of course he is. That's an argument I won't win tonight, even if I could find the energy.

"Then give me a better reason to cry."

He laughs, the sound dark and relieved. "When I'm finished with you, summer queen, remember that you begged."

SEVENTEEN

Hades

Twenty-one years ago

THE KNOCK AT THE DOOR COMES AN HOUR AFTER MY father dropped a thick stack of papers on the kitchen table and ground his knuckles into the top while he explained in no uncertain terms that if any of us fucks up again, he won't be able to get the charges erased when we turn eighteen. Not fucking up means staying near the house and not killing each other. It was a condition of release, and now he's bartered it into something better.

Poseidon is displeased.

He's been in the basement since Cronos left for the whorehouse. Another *crash* comes from down there. Glass shatters. He prefers the antique medicine bottles we've dug up all over the property. They're more satisfying to crush against brick, or so he says.

"Go away, Zeus." This knocking thing is a new refined habit

of his. He thinks it does a better job of hiding that he's an animal, ready to sink his teeth into the nearest available warm body.

"I came to ask you something."

Not Zeus, then. I focus back on the reflection in the window instead of searching the yard for any shadows that could be Rosie coming back.

I know she's dead. I can't stop hoping.

Demeter stands in the doorway, backlit by weak light from the hall, and she looks wrong.

Really wrong.

I get out of my chair and stand up. It's always better to be on your feet when Demeter appears out of nowhere. *Nowhere* in this case means elsewhere in the farmhouse.

"You're not supposed to be here."

She narrows her eyes, defiant despite the fact that she is pregnant. Not slightly pregnant. Very pregnant. So pregnant it had to have happened before she accused the three of us of gang-raping her in the barn. This is the first time I've seen her since we were released, and now it makes complete sense.

This is worse than a lie. This is a truth wrapped up in a very fucked-up veneer. The hairs on the back of my neck pull up. She's small. Small enough to be easily overpowered by the three of us. But being small hasn't stopped her from being absolutely unhinged. She spends half her time in the greenhouse, growing things she won't talk about. I have no idea how she's kept them from Cronos all this time. Probably because he forces her to spend the rest of her time in her room. She's not allowed to go outside. Greenhouse. Bedroom. That's it.

The bedrooms are a recent development. When we got back from jail, our limited possessions had been brought from the attic. Cronos didn't give a reason.

Demeter rubs her hands over her belly, eyes enormous and silver in the shadows from the doorframe. "I wouldn't be here if I had any other options."

"It looks like you've had lots of other options."

She's gritting her teeth so hard her teeth clack together. "Hades."

"Demeter."

"I can't live with him in the world."

"That's not my problem." Cold? Callous? Maybe. But I've seen the bodies of the animals in the woods. Zeus doesn't care for hunting and Poseidon prefers fistfights. Demeter is the one who leaves them. She does it when Cronos isn't here, whenever she can slip away.

"You have other problems."

I glare at her. If she loses her shit entirely I'll have to throw her out one of the windows, which would probably be construed as *fucking up* by Cronos.

"What are you offering? It had better be good, Demeter. I'm not doing a damn thing for free."

Her lip curls. "You never do anything out of the goodness of your heart."

"What goodness could I possibly have in my heart after my foster sister sent me to jail for gang-raping her? What the fuck is wrong with you?" This is not a fair question, and I don't care. What's wrong with her is living here, same as the rest of us. And now she has an added difficulty. It doesn't make me hate her any less. "Get out."

"I made something to help you."

I lean against my desk, shoved up against the wall and rickety as fuck. "If I wanted to die, I wouldn't use poison."

"It's not poison."

"What, then?"

"Painkillers. Good ones."

"Don't fuck with me." The amount it would take to stop my pain is enough to kill a person, or make them an addict. At the very least, it would be enough that I wouldn't be awake after I took them. I wouldn't know when Cronos was coming.

"I'm not fucking with you. These won't give you a habit." She takes a forbidden step into my room, and for the first time in the conversation I get a real look at her.

She's desperate. Tears gather in the corner of her eyes, and her pulse ticks at the side of her neck. Her face is blotchy, like she's been crying for a long time.

Demeter doesn't cry.

"Explain to me how you've found some miracle drug out in your greenhouse."

"I didn't find it, I made it." Demeter sticks out her chin at me. "And I'll keep making it for as long as you want."

I run a hand over my face. It's still sore from when Cronos visited yesterday. I'm still an aching wreck. I'm still hiding it. "I don't like deals without clear terms."

"Choose, Hades. I'll give you painkillers for the rest of your life, or you can have another attack and die."

"I didn't die from the last one."

"Doesn't your throat hurt?" She cocks her head to the side, eyes suddenly clear and dry. "Even a little?" I stop myself from rubbing at it, but I can't stop my hand from twitching. Fuck. "See? He had his boot on it. Cronos has always liked theatrics. Boots. Necks." She giggles and a chill hooks into my spine. "Everybody saw. You're not going to make it out of here if you don't work with me."

If she's right, then that is the most seductive prediction I've ever heard. The certainty that I'll be dead, and this will be over. Good. Fine. Let it happen.

A competing impulse drowns it out. My foolish heart wants to stay alive. It beats fast and afraid, hiding its face from the towering gates that stand between me and death.

I scan the yard again. No sign of Rosie.

There will never be a sign. I can't stop looking.

"What, then?"

Demeter comes and stands next to the desk, close enough that I can see how tight her dress is over the bump. She tilts her face down to look at it. Curiously. Like she's continually discovering that it's there. Her expression empties out like a room at the end of a concert. Nobody's home. When she looks back at me, it's with something past emptiness.

"It's just one person." She rests a hand on the top of her bump, but decides against it and drops it to her side. Something flashes between her fingers. Something small and white, like a pearl. It shines in the moonlight, then disappears into her palm. "He's a lot smaller than you."

"No." I'm eighteen in three months. Cronos is powerful, but not powerful enough to erase a murder charge. Not right now.

Demeter gazes out toward the barn, moonlight skimming along the lines of her face. "Do you know what you looked like out there?"

Shame blows out a hole somewhere near my kidney, letting blood seep into the wound. There was nothing I could do about it. Nothing.

"Pathetic, I imagine."

"It was worse than that," she says. "You were defenseless." She meets my eyes again, a smile at the corners of her mouth. "Anything could have happened."

The love affair with easy death I've been flirting with blows away on the breeze. It's like all the times Cronos has held my head back and let the sun tear out my eyes. It lets me see clearly. An easy death won't be from Cronos or Demeter. I won't let them do it. I'll stay alive and do it myself.

"Who is it?"

She blinks at the question and purses her lips.

"The father, I assume?"

"There was a rape. I didn't lie about that." Demeter's chin trembles. "Things got out of hand, and then—" She must see on my face that I don't care to hear her explanation of why she sent the three of us to jail. "I can't use poison. It would make me a suspect."

"If it's Cronos—"

"It's not. It wasn't." She names a man who works for Cronos. He works the night shift, keeping watch on the road on the far end of Cronos's property. Past the lake. Past the trees. It'll take at least an hour to walk there.

"Fine."

"When?" Her voice rises with relief.

"Tomorrow night."

"Okay." She trails back to the door.

"I'll pay you for the painkillers," I call after her. "Once I have the money."

I don't know why I say it. For the child's sake, perhaps. So there's some official transaction to look back on later.

"They're made from the most beautiful red poppies, Hades."

I don't say anything.

Demeter furrows her brow. "You don't care?"

"No." I sit down at the desk, but I don't turn away. You don't turn your back on someone like Demeter. "I don't care about anything at all."

EIGHTEEN

Persephone

THE MOST VALUABLE FLOWERS IN THE WORLD ARE A DEEP red.

I'm growing them in the valley on the mountain, but they seem more precious, not less. In some ways, it was easier to worry about the seeds themselves. It's more complicated when you're dealing with the plants.

For one thing, I can't grow all the seeds at once. I don't have the energy to do it. I wish the sun would fill me with that gold light in an endless stream. I guess maybe it does. I'm not a sorceress, though. I'm not a magical being. I'm a person, and people can only do so much before they run out of steam.

For another thing, the poppies are difficult. They're not like the flowers that grew in my mother's fields. I'm not sure if it's the soil or the altitude or some hidden homesickness that makes them take more effort. More coaxing. More convincing.

And for a third thing…

Hades.

I love him. I'm past caring whether it's right or wrong. It's a fact. The sun rises in the east. Summer follows spring. I love Hades.

But his past is worse than I expected. Far more painful. What if he wakes up one morning, and all he sees in my face is what my mother did to him?

What if we can only be safe if she's dead?

I love him. But I don't know if I can watch him kill her. I don't know if our relationship can survive knowing that I agreed to her death. She's wounded, too. And I don't know if anyone has ever loved her the way I love Hades. I don't know if it would save her, or if she's too far gone already.

Above all, I don't know how to make her understand that she has to let me be. Look. I'm still growing flowers. I'm still safe and protected. If I wasn't drowning in worry, I could be happy.

The poppy sprout struggles under my palms. A thin, beating headache taps between my eyes.

What if Hades isn't happy? What if no flower in the world can take away the pain of his childhood?

I sit back on my heels, tip my face to the sun, and press the back of my hands to my eyes.

He insists that he loves me. The way he handles me, the way he kisses me, the way he lets me see him at his lowest— all of it seems like proof that what he said is true. His love is dark, like he is, and endless, like the night.

But my mother could be darker. That pain could be darker. It could crack the foundation.

The question folds into itself like a flower and refuses to reopen.

I feel light, careful footsteps on the grass. Eleanor. That's how she walks, even though she's not the one who filled the valley with flowers. She takes her time approaching, making sure she doesn't crush them.

I let my hands fall to my lap. "Hi, Eleanor."

"Too much time in the sun?" Her shadow falls over me, and maybe she's right. Maybe I'm baking in the heat. "You look like you're at your wits' end."

"Probably.

"Come in with me for a few minutes. I'm watering. You can help."

I get to my feet, brush the dirt off my hands, and walk with her to her cottage. Stepping into the shade makes me feel a thousand times lighter. I wash my hands at her kitchen sink with soap that smells like rose petals. When I'm finished, Eleanor hands me a glass of water. It has a light, lemony taste.

"Better?" Eleanor looks me over. Her gray hair is pulled back from her face in a loose braid, and strands catch the breeze moving through her kitchen window. Her eyes are clear and concerned. "No. Not much. Let's go to the plants."

We move through her house and into the higher-ceilinged space with the planters. Without a word, she hands me a watering can. Eleanor takes one side of the row. I take the other. We face each other over a neat arrangement of English violets. She's trained these to grow with the light coming up from underneath.

It feels better to be out of the sun. A vague fear drips into my mind like the droplets from the can. What if we do everything right and Hades still ends up stuck in the dark? Will I get used to it, too? Will I stop being able to tolerate the sun?

"What was she like?"

Eleanor tilts her head at the question, but she doesn't

look up from her work. To give me some privacy, I think. My voice rang a little loud and desperate. It wasn't really the question I meant to ask. "Your mother?"

"You knew her when she was young, didn't you?"

"Yes. Cronos brought her to the farmhouse not long after she was born. He wanted her away from the city."

"Who was her mother?"

The corners of Eleanor's mouth turn down. "I was all she had. Cronos never told me the name of the woman who gave birth to her."

"I didn't mean to say that you weren't... enough. I would never think that. What you did for all four of them—" I let out a heavy sigh that doesn't do anything to ease the ache in my chest. "I've been thinking about her. Trying to understand how she became the way she is. Or if she was always that way."

"Hmm." A thoughtful sound. "Demeter always loved the outdoors. She loved flowers, even before she could walk. As a baby, she was happiest on a blanket outside. Anywhere she could reach the grass. She was so gentle with the petals."

I can believe that about my mother. She's always taken the best care of her plants. "When did she stop?"

"Loving flowers? Never."

"Being happy."

Eleanor purses her lips. "There were times when Cronos wouldn't come back from the city for a week or two at a time. That was when I'd hear them laugh. Usually outside, where they thought I couldn't hear. Like they were practicing."

I water another of Eleanor's blooms. We move to the next planter at the same time.

"Ten, I'd say." Eleanor's brow furrows, and she looks

down at the blooms as if they're holding her memories for her. "Demeter had been afraid before then, like her brothers. But Zeus made it possible for her to hold on a little longer."

"Hades said they would play together."

"Zeus taught her everything he could think of. Tying her shoes. Writing her name. He helped her with the lessons that would come in the mail. But he wasn't enough for her."

"What did she want?"

Eleanor meets my eyes, and it's the saddest she's looked since I came to the mountain. "She wanted Cronos. Wanted to please him. She knew what kind of man he was, but she couldn't help it. She wanted him to approve of her, and I think that's what started her... cruelty." Her watering can pauses above the row of flowers. "Demeter was smart, and she was talented. She could make flowers do incredible things. Understood them in a way I'm not sure anyone else does. But Cronos never cared about that. He cared about ruthlessness."

"And she never got that attention from him."

"She did," Eleanor admits. "When she was a teenager. After you were born."

Goose bumps rise on the back of my neck. "Eleanor, do you mean..."

"He took advantage of her." She holds up a hand. "I don't feel right saying anything more about it."

"Okay." The plants I'm watering swim behind a sheen of tears. It was all terrible, then. It's what Zeus said at the whorehouse. A good seed can't grow out of bad soil. We can't go back and dig out the garden now. Zeus was talking about Hades, and about his siblings, but what does that make me?

"Persephone."

I look up into Eleanor's eyes. There's no sign of judgment on her face. No sign that she's looking at a stunted, twisted plant.

"Your mother loved the early mornings and going barefoot in the grass. She caught bugs in the house in her hands and took them outside to release them. Her favorite game to play was tag. She liked running as fast as she could."

I wipe my tears with the back of my hand. "She's hurt a lot of people. Three of them are here right now. What if she never stops? What if it's already too late?"

"Too late? You have the poppies."

"Too late to make her understand that she has to leave us alone." My real fear becomes a knot in my throat. "And too late for Hades to recover from what she did. Too late for him to be happy with me."

How can you stand to look at her?

If Poseidon feels that way, Hades could, too.

"You don't think he's happy with you?"

I take another painful breath. "He could decide that I'm like her. I could do something to remind him, and he—he could realize he made a mistake."

It hurts to say it. At least the ugly, roiling thought is out of my head and in the air, where it doesn't seem so huge and threatening.

"And…" I might as well just say everything. The words have been trapped behind my teeth for days. "Zeus said he couldn't be any other way. That none of them could. Because they grew from bad soil."

Eleanor snorts, and I stare. "I'm sorry. I'm not laughing at you." She sobers, reaching across the planter to take my hand in hers. "Zeus said that because he fears it about himself."

"Isn't he right, though? He owns a whorehouse."

She arches an eyebrow. "I don't know if it's so black-and-white. Hasn't he been here, taking care of his brother?"

"Yes, but that could change. It could go back to the way it was."

"The way it was?"

"Before Zeus agreed to help."

Eleanor moves on to the next plant. "It could go back to the way it was when they were young."

"Which was how?" More bad soil. Twisted plants, growing in poisoned air.

"Zeus was a charmer." She smiles down at the flowers blooming in good, loamy soil. "He had a smile you couldn't look away from. And Hades was sweet."

It's my turn to make a noise of surprise. "Seriously?"

"He loved the sun, even though it didn't love him back." Eleanor gives a little sigh. "He'd bring me wildflowers from the woods to put in a vase. He knew how I loved something pretty in the kitchen. On the morning he left, he brought me a bouquet of English violets."

The purple blooms in the planter reach into my chest and squeeze my heart. We've moved far enough down the row that the pattern has repeated.

"He'll never be soft," she says. "But there's some of that boy left in him. The people here are proof of that. And the way he looks at you."

"But one day…"

"After Rosie died, he claimed he didn't have a heart. It's never been true. Not for a single day. If he'd been heartless, he'd have found another dog that week. He waited years to take another chance. He waited until he knew that dog would be safe from Cronos."

"Conor."

"That's right. It will always be harder for him to lose one of his companions. It will bring back a painful past, every time. But he'll withstand it."

"Because he loves Conor."

"He loves *you*." She pats my cheek the way a grandmother would. "The past can never change that. It's done, Persephone. Written in stone. The past, and his love. Permanent."

NINETEEN

Hades

PERSEPHONE IS PRETENDING.

She's *hiding*.

I saw it in her face when she woke up this morning and again when she returned from the valley. Watching her attempt to conceal it is unfathomably hot. She lifts her chin. Squares her shoulders. Draws herself up into a queenlike figure, even when she has a streak of dirt on her cheek.

I also hate it. Very much. I'm not sure what possible emotion would make her think she had to hide it. From *me*, of all people. I haven't been able to hide a damn thing from her from the moment we met.

Worrying this much over her feelings is new and unbearable. My clothes feel too tight, and my skin feels like it's being sandblasted. She belongs to me. All of her. Including the thoughts she's ashamed of.

I've cautiously returned to my office, testing the new painkillers. So far, they're behaving as they used to before Demeter

started decreasing her supply. We've been able to resume shifts in the mines. Making shipments to the city is another day's problem. For now, my people are occupied.

I've been signing documents at my desk without reading them. Conor sleeps nearby. Oliver does laps around the office.

I'd rather claw my own skin off than feel this way.

"Oliver."

He stops pacing by the door. "We need to discuss your brothers."

"They're here helping to defend the mountain."

"What if they decide not to?"

"You think they're going to turn on me in the middle of a family reunion?"

Oliver shrugs. "A party's never stopped anyone from throwing a punch. We should make plans."

A party. Clever.

"And we will. For now, I need my business to continue functioning."

He folds his arms over his chest. "You might not be prepared."

I put down the pen and look at him. "Oliver, if you suggest that I'm in some sort of vulnerable state one more time, I will kill you."

"Fine." He goes out the door, closing it gently behind him.

He's right. Obviously, he is right. We have to plan for the possibility that my brothers can't be trusted. A not-insignificant part of me wants to trust them. At the very least, it wonders what it would be like to rely on someone of my own volition instead of against my will.

It's a dangerous idea. One that I can't entertain, not fully, until I get to the root of what's bothering Persephone.

I text Oliver with orders to send our best scouts to report

on what Demeter's been doing at her farm. We need to know the size of her army.

The last document in the pile presents itself for my signature. There. Done.

I could drag Persephone here and force her to tell me what's making her silver eyes so guarded. I've taken her places that way before. I've enjoyed it very much.

But there's something intoxicating about the way she holds herself lately. As if she's ruling on the mountain alongside me. That's the version of my summer queen who hides her feelings. Who attempts to push them aside in favor of the greater good.

I think of her white dress in her mother's fields. The angelic glow surrounding her.

Conor stretches at the corner of my desk and puts his head on my knee. Absently scratching behind his ears gives me no good ideas, but looking out at the factory floor does.

A queen needs a crown.

And she needs it from me.

There are pieces in my personal collection that have been worn at actual coronations, but none of them would be right. She doesn't need a hand-me-down relic of someone else's power. Persephone should have a symbol of her own.

The hum of activity on the factory floor drowns out all the competing bullshit in my brain. I don't know which of us Persephone thinks is not equipped to bear whatever it is she's trying to bury, but she'll be certain of my position by tonight.

My master jeweler has an office built into one of the alcoves off the factory floor. It's carved from the black-and-gold marble of the mountain, an ancillary altar to the gods of metal and stone. The man who works inside is their most experienced acolyte. He works on all my personal projects.

There is no more personal project than this one.

He does not look up from his table when I approach. The settings on his pieces are oftentimes extremely delicate until they reach their finished state, so he won't interrupt his work for anything less than a full-scale invasion. After a heartbeat, he pulls a cover over the piece and meets my eyes.

The corners of his mouth rise with a relieved suggestion of a smile that's gone as soon as it appears. I nod toward his project. "Put that aside. I need something specific for tonight."

Persephone sits in the chair by the window, the glass clear so she can see the stars. She's lost in thought. My heart lurches farther outside my body at the sight of her so still, with no book balanced on her lap. Heartbeats become tense pulls between the place where the organ is supposed to be and where it is, which is wherever she goes.

I balance the tiara in the palms of my hands. It's delicate, but strong. I pulled the diamonds from my personal collection and hovered near the worktable while it was made. If I didn't know better, I'd think this was a spray of stars pulled down from the sky and set in platinum.

My heart beats harder, blood pumping through all the still-wounded parts of me, and finally Persephone looks up at me in her regal silence.

"Yours." I let the diamonds catch the starlight, and her gaze follows the tiara's curves for a long time.

Then silver eyes meet mine. In the glow from the stars, they're the color of platinum. Platinum shot through with diamond light. "Those came from you."

"So did your necklace."

Her fingertips go up to meet the black diamond dangling from its chain. I've given her pieces of myself from the very beginning.

Persephone rises to her feet and comes to me. She's changed into soft black for the night, but she glows nonetheless. As if she can never scrub the sun from her skin.

She reaches for the tiara at the same moment I reach for her. My fingertips meet the wild fall of her hair as she touches the diamonds. I lift a stray curl from her cheek and tuck it into place.

"What if I'm my mother's daughter?" Persephone traces one of the diamonds in its setting. My master jeweler grew the platinum into petals and leaves, almost as if Persephone had done it herself.

I force a knot out of my throat. "That's not what you're really asking."

Persephone keeps her focus on the tiara. She touches it like one of her flowers. No part of me would be surprised if it grew in my hands. "What am I asking?"

"If I'm my father's son." I was right. Her eyes snaps to mine. "If the pain is permanent. If your mother's wounds can't be healed."

"I could remind you of the past." She swallows. "You could wake up one morning and be sick at the sight of me."

I'm going to kill Poseidon for what he said. I'm at least going to punch him. Perhaps throttle him until he takes it back.

"Summer queen, you've let your fears run away with you. I knew what Demeter had done before I met you. How could it change anything now?"

"If I had another face, I wouldn't be a living reminder of everything she did to you. And everything her father did to you." Persephone lifts her chin, though it trembles. Her bravery

507

shifts something in me. A spill of diamonds. A boulder rolling off my chest.

"You are a living reminder that I survived everything I suffered."

She lets out a breath that's half cry, and she puts her free hand on mine. "You didn't always want to."

The question she can't bring herself to ask hums between us.

"The moment I saw you in that field, I stopped wanting to die. Quite the opposite. I'd rather suffer every moment for the rest of my days than give up a single one with you. It's a permanent state, summer queen. More permanent than anything Cronos did, or anything your mother could do."

Persephone isn't responsible for her mother's crimes. And if Cronos did irreparable damage, then that was set in stone long before my summer queen was born.

This is not an issue of recovery. There is no going back to the person I was before Cronos. Before Demeter. Persephone has already unearthed what's left of him.

It's simpler than she imagines.

I lift the tiara and settle it onto her hair. Persephone takes a little breath. "What are you doing?"

"A summer queen needs a crown. And you need to understand your place here."

Her chin dimples. "What's my place here?"

"At my side. Always. No matter what happens. There will never be a sunrise that makes me want you any less."

I pull her dress over her head and drop it to the floor.

She's naked underneath. Standing proud, with diamonds in her hair.

"Sit down, summer queen."

She goes, lowering herself gracefully to the chair by the window. My chest tightens with the double-vision sensation that I'm looking into another time. Who taught her to sit like that? Who made her so perfect for me to punish and ruin and keep forever.

"Why?" she murmurs.

"You could call it worship."

I go to my knees in front of her. It's a head rush of unbelievable proportions. So intense that for a fleeting second I'm certain the painkillers have failed.

The painkillers haven't failed. It's something else.

It's still happening when my palms make contact with her knees.

Persephone gasps.

Gold. I can feel it through her skin. A sense of movement. A new bud breaking through spring soil. A sense of binding. That same gold, formed into a knot that winds around something fierce and unbreakable, like a diamond. It's directing the power I can't get out of my head into her body. The way I did when she was struggling to grow the first poppy. The difference is that it doesn't hurt. The difference is that she's doing the same to me.

The two forces meet.

And I understand, on a level beyond words, that they can't be untangled. It's as final as marriage vows.

I spread her legs.

Persephone tastes like honey. Like clear water. Like a summer berry crushed between my teeth. Her hands find their way to my hair and she pulls me in close. I can feel her desperation in her grasp, but I'm the one who's desperate. Who's undone. I'm the one who's starving for her. I have always been starving for her.

She hisses, hips rolling and bucking. I'm forced to pin her down so she doesn't throw herself to the floor.

Yes, this. Yes, here. Now.

There is no part of her I leave unexplored, no fold I leave unlicked. I suck her clit until she cries diamond tears to match her new tiara. Until she begs me to fuck her in sobbing whimpers that wake up all the pieces of me that I thought were sleeping or dead.

And then I fuck her on the chair with hard, deep strokes. Persephone digs her nails into my shoulders, and her teeth. Pain sparks under the half-moons of her nails and stings goose bumps into my skin, all of me tensing with it. With her.

I slow the rhythm, though the sensation of her cunt wrapped around me is so intense it thins the air. Persephone begs with her eyes. *Don't stop.*

"I would suffer it all again, every fucking second, if it meant I could keep you. You're everything." I bend my head and kiss the side of her neck.

"Hades."

"I love you. It's done. You know it is. You know we can't take it back."

She does. She felt it, too.

The night drops down around us. Nothing to see here. No mountain, no people, no looming threats. No brothers outside. There's only the sweet clench of her muscles around me and the soft sound of her panting, which gets louder with every stroke. She's pulling me in, trying to keep me there.

She doesn't want me to leave. Persephone doesn't count down the minutes until I'm out of her sight, out of her life. All of her is a plea to *stay, stay, stay.*

Stay here. Stay home. Never leave.

TWENTY

Persephone

THE TIARA IS ON THE BEDSIDE TABLE. IT'S THE FIRST THING I see when I wake up, glinting there in the soft morning light.

The *light*.

Hades let it in. My hand goes to my heart, pounding with relief. It's a good sign. The best sign I could have hoped for. The new painkillers are working, and last night was real. The tiara is proof.

It was all real. I know it down to my bones. Hades touched me, and all his darkness flooded in. Only... it wasn't painful, the way I thought it would be if we could trade places. That probably has to do with the painkillers, and the fact that we didn't trade places. Not at all. I felt the gold in my chest wrap around a dark diamond like a knot of ivy.

It can't be undone.

I know that, too. I'm sure of it. Just like I'm sure I couldn't

lay my palm on the earth and come up with a diamond. I didn't take anything from Hades.

I feel him, though. Nothing so obvious as a heartbeat. It's like the gold in my chest has a new dimension.

A shadow.

He's not here now. It was late by the time he was finished with me. *You could call it worship.* I fell deeply, dreamlessly asleep.

I pad into the bathroom, then come back for the tiara. In front of the full-length mirror in Hades's closet, I put it on just to see.

It looks good.

I look good.

Hades appears in the mirror behind me, and his eyes darken at the sight of me wearing only the tiara. I didn't realize how much stress he was under from the pain. Not until I grew the poppies. That expression is nowhere to be found on his face. There's satisfaction, and something else.

"Look at you, summer queen." His eyes meet mine in the mirror as his hands slide around my hips. He's so much taller. The difference is stark with both of us reflected in the glass, me with nothing on and him in pristine black. His left hand glides up to palm one breast then the other, but he doesn't break eye contact. Not even when he leans down to brush his lips against my neck.

"I will never change my mind about you," he murmurs against my skin. And then: "I'm going on a trip."

It's so strange to hear him say it that at first I think the mirror's cracked.

"You don't go on trips." He doesn't. He's never mentioned traveling. Even Zeus was sure he wouldn't come to the city for me. But things are different now. "Where are you going?"

"Poseidon got word that Demeter is attempting some opposition by sea. I'm going with him to intercept the ship and sabotage it. It'll never reach the mountain."

"When?"

"Tonight." Hades coils one hand around my throat and holds me against him. It's obscene, the arched line of me against the black fabric. I'm a jewel on velvet. He touches the tiara first. His fingertips meet every diamond and skim down over my eyes, my lips, each nipple. They both pull into tight peaks, and he cuts off a small noise that would have been begging with more pressure to my throat. Air transforms into a resource I don't have enough of, and every breath is a new reminder of his power.

What he said is important. My mother, hiring some sort of… battleship? Pirate crew? It's not good. My anxiety is overwhelmed by him. By how strong he is, and how beautiful, and how big his hands are.

He makes me watch while he nudges my feet apart with his, spreading me open for the glass and for his searching eyes. He makes me watch while he dips one finger into my folds and pulls it away again, glistening with me. Hades gives my head a shake—*keep watching*—and sticks that finger into his mouth, sucking on it like it's the best thing he's ever tasted.

Then somehow he's on one knee, shoving me back onto his leg, and spreading me even wider. Pushing one finger into me, two, three. And there I am, letting my head fall against his arm.

He jerks it back into place.

There I am, clutching his shirt in my fists while he

orders me to keep my toes on the ground and my legs open *wider, summer queen*. I obey him. He might have made me a queen, and the diamonds in my hair are a sign that I belong beside him and *to* him. In every way. Even if that way is to watch as he fucks me casually with his fingers, stretching, going deep. Pulling me apart so that all the pink, wet parts of me are on full display.

I'm close to a rough, electric orgasm when he picks me up like a doll and arranges me on my hands and knees. I have a closer view of my face now. Of how pink my cheeks have gotten, how wide my pupils are blown, how fast I'm panting. Short, sharp breaths. It's a new woman in the mirror.

Hades stays in the frame while he strips off his clothes, and even in the closet's soft light—designed for him—he's stunning. Even with bruises fading on his ribs and sides. Even with healing cuts. They all seem superficial now on his tight muscles and the taut planes of his body. How could I have ever thought he might die? It would take so much to kill him. More than life has already dealt.

A whisper of worry tries to fight its way in—*opposition at sea*—but Hades kneels behind me and drags my hips back, putting my pussy where he wants it.

The thick head of him nudges against my opening, and he pauses. He's on display as much as I am. Warmth stretches across my chest. This is a gift for me, too. People do not get to see him like this, tensed and ready, concentration furrowing his brow, his teeth digging into his lip. The muscles low on his belly are coiled because he's about to fuck me. His black eyes skim over my face in the mirror so coldly that I know he's on fire. When our eyes catch in the middle of the mirror, me already bracing my hands on the plush carpet of his closet, bending for him in small movements so that he can take what he wants.

And give me what *I* want.

His gaze pins mine to the mirror. *You*, I think. His lips and teeth ravage me until my skin is pink and raw. His eyes turn my belly to a keening, animal desire. And while I'm watching, while he's sure I can see, he gives a half smile that's so unguarded that it takes my breath away. It reveals his dark, jagged lust. The hard center in all that gold.

He's prepared me with his fingers, but the first thrust knocks the rest of the air from the room and the world, so vicious I try to crawl away from it. But I'm stopped, as always, by big hands hard on my hips. The pleasure of pain, of making room for him, of having to take him, arcs through me like gold made electric. I'm transformed again. A queen can be crowned and still scrabble at the carpet, still have her back arched in a begging angle, still struggle for breath while her king demands entrance again and again and again with punishing strokes.

It's so dirty. I'm knocked off-balance, and my nipples scrape against the carpet. He's beautiful with the shield dropped away from his face. An old fear tightens my muscles around him, and he laughs, the sound twisting into a groan.

"I love when your eyes get wide like that." He digs his fingers into my skin while he says it. "You look like prey."

"I am." It's work to get the words out, too much work, and I focus on not melting into the floor. "You caught me."

Hades slows his pace. His hand drops down to work between my legs, coaxing out the orgasm that's been waiting since he first put his hands on me.

"Watch," he commands.

So I watch while my mouth drops open and my eyes

flutter halfway shut, and I come while he's deep inside me. I don't look like myself. I look like a fallen queen and—oh. *Oh.* That's what I am. That's what I am now. I watch while the first cries escape me, and then I watch while I get lost in the curling, pulsing pleasure of being fucked by the man I love.

When he's finished, he gives me a desultory kiss on the neck and lets me collapse to the floor. His footsteps recede, and far away, the shower starts. I'm trying to catch my breath.

I'm going with him to intercept the ship and sabotage it.

That means a battle. At night. At sea.

Or it could mean something much, much worse.

TWENTY-ONE

Hades

"**T**HIS ISN'T SABOTAGE, YOU PIECE OF SHIT. THIS IS highway robbery."

Poseidon claps a hand on my shoulder on the deck of his ship. The *Trident* is fast and lethal. Weapons everywhere. Too many weapons for the skeleton crew he's brought with him.

"And here you are, helping me like a good brother."

"Oh, so we're brothers now?"

"Brothers-in-arms." Poseidon grins. This is what he lives for. Rain-soaked missions in the middle of the night. "Don't complain about a good deal, Hades. My best men are watching your place. You're just having fun."

Being separated from Persephone is not my idea of entertainment, but it's my mountain we're here defending. The ship is also carrying supplies for Demeter's people. She might have stopped the trains, but she cut herself off, too. This is a necessary evil.

However, the enemy ship is not nearly the caliber of the army she gathered on land. They didn't expect us. I'm not a connoisseur of maritime laws, but I'd bet pulling your ship up to another one and scattering high-powered bullets across the hull is fairly straightforward piracy. Given the size of the other ship, I doubt it rises to the level of naval warfare.

That's not for me to say. I'm just here to *have fun*.

"Do you feed your crew? Some of them look thin. You can't expect anyone to keep working for you if they're starving."

Poseidon ruffles my hair, sending droplets to mix with the rain on the deck. I won't snap his wrist, but only because I'm out here on his boat with him and drowning isn't a high priority for me. It's a good thing I fucked Persephone before I left. Otherwise, I might not have so much control. Spitting rain beads on our slickers and heavy boots.

"You've gone soft. And foolish, if you think I'm not feeding them. The thin ones are my newest crew members. They haven't had time to put on weight."

The moonlight is broken up in the oil-black sea, and down on the deck of the other ship, panic reigns. "How long do you think you'll toy with them?"

"Long enough that they know it's a personal matter." I glare at him, but Poseidon is too busy fucking the other ship with his eyes. "The captain needs to be relieved of his post. Anyone who works for Demeter doesn't belong at sea."

"Is that why you shot holes in the side of his ship?"

Poseidon holds up a finger, and a *boom* rings out from his ship. I don't see the ammunition, but it punches a larger hole in the ship below. Men shout over one another. "No. That was for fun. Time to go."

We're the only ones standing on the deck. "Nobody else is ready."

"Nobody else is coming. You're the only one I trust."

"What the *fuck*, Poseidon?"

A few of his people jog out with a gangway. They hook it to the railing and let it crash down to the other ship's deck. Poseidon starts down, and the whole thing tips sideways when an ocean swell lifts both of the vessels.

"Are you fucking with me?" I yell after him. This seems very much like a thing he would do, but we aren't seventeen anymore, and we could die.

He is not fucking with me. He raises one hand in the air and beckons me after him.

Fine. The gangway is slippery as fuck and not solidly connected to either ship. At the other end, I hold out my hand for a gun. Poseidon cracks his knuckles instead.

Wonderful.

The ship is fucked, with a hole in its side and water coming in, but the upper deck is curiously silent. The chaos of a few minutes ago has been reduced to nothing but the patter of rain and the slosh of seawater against the sides.

"One, two, three." Poseidon laughs, and all hell breaks loose.

The entire ship's crew has hidden themselves away for an ambush, which is apparently their only plan. They burst out from the captain's quarters. The first one slips in the rain and falls. One of his hands gets crushed under a boot and then, because my brother-in-arms is completely unhinged, they're on top of us.

"The ones who make it go up the gangplank," Poseidon shouts, his fist connecting wetly with a man's cheek. The guy falls to the deck in a beautiful, boneless arc. One of the other men rushes past him and overshoots, going overboard.

And Demeter spent all those years warning Persephone about *me*. She should have taught her to fear the water.

"I thought you said you didn't want her people."

"These fucks don't know what they signed up for. I'll keep them in the brig and see if they can change their ways. If they can't—" Another series of punches. "I'll drop them on the other side of the ocean."

My muscles protest, still aching from all the seizures. There's nothing for it but to ball my hands into fists and swing. The first man to reach me goes down hard, a pool of blood spreading underneath his head, but the second and third pose more of a problem. They've determined, correctly, that they have nothing left to lose. One of them gets a hit to the side of my head, and it rattles me. I suck a breath through my teeth and the split-second pause is long enough for the next man to land a punch to my face. Pain splinters beneath my eye, but it doesn't stop me from moving.

Never stop moving. Never become a target.

I am becoming a target.

They're looking for big moves, so I shoot the heel of my hand out, catching one in the nose and the other across the throat. They both go down, the first onto his knees, the second lurching for the railing.

A little reinforcement would be nice.

Poseidon is busy dragging a man over the gangplank. In the end, he picks him up by both ankles and throws him onto the *Trident*.

It's not elegant, but it gets the job done.

In the meantime, there are six more people to deal with. Judging by the splashes, some of the crew members have decided it's better to chance the waves. The last ones stalk forward as the rain throws sharp pinpricks into my face.

Poseidon wades into the fray. Demeter's crew has been reduced to clawing at us, one swinging wildly with a length of pipe. I find myself back-to-back with Poseidon in the middle of a screaming clutch of desperate men.

"A couple pistols would've solved this." I hate being cornered. It's the only time I find guns acceptable.

He laughs as he blocks someone's hand from tearing off my ear. They settle for yanking my hood off my head, sending water down the back of my neck. The cold shock of it makes me think of how warm Persephone was earlier. How tight.

"Bullet holes are harder to repair than broken bones." Poseidon's tone is infuriatingly sage. He is technically correct, which is why I keep them to a minimum on the mountain. Too many guns in plain sight and people get reckless. That, and the windows I had to install to survive can repel bullets and cause a ricochet.

I wish for a rifle now. Something I could use to back these fuckers up. A knife flashes in the rain and stabs through the side of my coat. There's a warm spill of blood. Fuck—that's a cut.

I grab the man who did it by his shirt and introduce his head to the side of a fiberglass lifeboat.

We're winning, but in the last throes of violence, I take a hit to one of my bruised ribs. A strained growl escapes me.

Two more down. Then three and four and five.

One left.

Poseidon gets tired of him and throws him across the gangplank. One of his men catches the bastard, but not before he hits his head on the railing.

My brother wipes his hands like he's just finished eating. He grabs two of the unconscious men and drags them toward the *Trident*. His crew comes down to help. They're getting prisoners today. Or new crew members. I don't care which.

The ship lists badly to the side beneath us, but Poseidon stops me at the gangplank with a hand on my chest. "One more thing."

"The ship is sinking, motherfucker."

"It's fast."

There's no time to argue, so I follow Poseidon down to the lower deck. He tears through the mess we find, upending bunks and half the galley kitchen. Four of his men sprint down the stairs behind us to rid the hold of abandoned weapons and Demeter's supplies. I put a hand to my side, and it comes away bloody.

"What the fuck are we looking for?"

Poseidon rifles through a trunk tucked under the bar.

"There you are." His voice is barely audible. The ocean threatens at the side of the ship, spitting through cracks in the hull. Poseidon wrenches something from the trunk, and his shoulders relax. The box looks small in his broad hands. Poseidon kisses it and tucks it gently into the pocket of his slicker. Then he heads back toward me, grinning. "Ship's going down." He catches sight of the blood on my hand. "Which one of them fucked you up?"

"I don't remember."

On the way up, the stairs tilt. The angle is all wrong. Poseidon's crew only managed a few trips down to raid the ship. Is there even going to be a deck when we get up there?

The deck still exists, but Poseidon's men are having a hell of a time holding the gangplank in place. Poseidon pushes me ahead of him. He's two steps up when Demeter's ship wails, metal screeching. The end of the gangplank plunges down into the water.

Some instinct makes me stick my hand out, and Poseidon

grabs it before his boots hit the surface. The ocean nips at his heels.

"Not now," he scolds, like the waves are playing with him. Some fucking game.

I'm half on the deck, half off, and the weight of him does something remarkably unpleasant to my ribs. Poseidon scrambles up, boots coming down with a heavy *thud* on the deck. Then he pats his pocket to make sure his precious box is still there.

"Hades, be careful. Don't hurt yourself on my account." This makes him laugh harder than anything else.

Next time, I'll drop him.

Water fills in the space where the other ship used to be. Poseidon surveys the deck of the *Trident*. Blood and rain, salt and sea. He puts one hand on the railing. If I didn't know him, I'd say it was a loving touch.

"Good." Poseidon pats the *Trident*'s railing and ambles toward the bridge. Halfway there, he turns back. "You sure you don't want to join the crew? Nice break from all that bullshit on land."

"Everything worthwhile is on land." I follow him. Mainly, I'm in search of a bandage and a dry shirt. My knees almost give out at the first aid station on the other side of the ship, but I stay standing.

I thought the ocean might take me away from Persephone. It's not going to get another chance.

TWENTY-TWO

Persephone

I'D NEVER HAVE MADE IT AS A SAILOR'S WIFE. NEVER. THE
waiting would have eaten me alive. Some of those women
searched the waves for their husbands' ships for months or
even years.

Hades has only been gone since sunset.

I can't sleep. Neither can Conor. He whined at the foyer
door when Hades and Poseidon left, then padded worriedly
through all of Hades's rooms.

Even Zeus had a part to play tonight. He went downstairs
with Oliver. They said it was to discuss the mountain's defenses,
but I know it's because Zeus doesn't like it that his brothers left.

He won't admit it out loud. Instead, he made a bunch of
noises about how separation leads to vulnerability. *If Demeter
senses an opening, she'll attack.*

Zeus is down there because he's going to fight if my mother
arrives. He won't sit in the living room while his brothers are
intercepting a ship.

I don't love the idea of *interception*. It sounds like knives and guns. It sounds like war. I'd rather let my mother attack the mountain than lose Hades.

In my study room, I find a book on the desk. A novel, not a textbook. It's the most beautiful book I've ever seen. It has a deep black cover, soft and leathery under my fingertips. And the edges of the pages are *silver*. They shine in the light.

It's gorgeous… and a bit worn. The pages fall open easily in my hands. A few of the corners have a slight wave to them.

There's a note.

I liked this in spite of myself. I'll be back before you can finish it.

—H

It's a story about a circus that only opens at night. Two people who are supposed to be mortal enemies. The first page gives me goose bumps.

Hades didn't like it. He loved it enough to read it more than once.

Conor sniffs, and I pat at his head. "All right. We'll take it with us."

I tuck the book under my arm, and we go to the lookout. Conor curls up on the floor next to one of the window seats. With the book propped on my legs, it's easy to imagine another kind of night on the mountain. A peaceful evening. One that didn't stretch my nerves so thin.

If swimming after the ship were an option, I'd do it. Better than waiting and watching.

It's impossible to read. I know I won't hear any sounds of battle coming from the lower part of the mountain. There's too much rock and space to travel through. I keep straining to listen anyway. I get bits and pieces of the story. Caramel popcorn and acrobats. A tarot card and a man who can change his face. A ghost. Someday, when everything is settled, I'll read the whole thing.

Poseidon's ship is nothing but a blur on the horizon when it first appears. A silvery smudge, far out in the water. I don't let myself believe it's the *Trident* until I can see it clearly. It's almost to the dock by the time I can make out the ship's features. Rain falls in translucent ribbons. Whatever they were doing to intercept my mother's boat had to be miserable.

Conor puts his paws on the window seat, peering out the window. He barks once, his dark eyes impatient on mine.

The walk back toward Hades's rooms takes forever.

Poseidon's ship is back, but are they safe? Are they alive? Dread weighs my stomach down.

They're alive. They're both alive. Someone would have sent word to the mountain. Zeus would have come to tell me if anything had happened.

Right?

I don't know who runs first, me or Conor, but we sprint into the foyer as the door opens. My hand flies to my necklace and I squeeze my eyes shut. What if it's Zeus, delivering terrible news? It's only a second of hesitation and I force them open again.

"*Hades.*"

He steps inside and lets the door close behind him. He's soaking wet, wearing a rain slicker I've never seen before, and there's a new bruise across one cheek. "Hello, summer queen."

I rush to him along with Conor, who circles and circles, checking to make sure he's okay. I brush droplets of water from his face. Stare into his eyes. "What happened?"

He cracks a crooked smile. "A little maritime warfare. It was nothing."

"You're all bruised."

"I might have a bit of a cut."

"What?" I lean back, and it's only then that I see the slash in the rain slicker. "Hades. We have to—we have to sit down. You can't just stand here in the foyer pretending everything's okay."

I put my hand on his back and attempt to nudge him along, which is like trying to nudge the mountain itself. Hades looks down at me, water droplets clinging to his hair, his eyes black and fiery. He wraps his hand around my chin and pulls me in. He's cold from the wind and rain, and his kiss tastes like night air and salt. He kisses me hard, then harder, and I lose my breath.

He hated it being apart as much as I did. I can taste that on him, too. The water from his clothes soaks into my dress. I keep the book he gave me wrapped tight in one arm, but my free hand goes to the collar of his jacket.

Conor whines, pushing at Hades's legs, and he breaks the kiss with a frustrated noise. I'm light-headed from relief and from falling headfirst into his touch. A flash of pain over his face brings me back to earth.

"Please." I take his hand, interlocking our fingers. "Come sit down. Dry off."

In his bedroom, Hades pauses by the door and shrugs off the rain slicker. I get him a towel from the bathroom, then go back for the first aid kit. I'll need a bowl of water, too.

When I return, Hades is sprawled in his chair by the fire, eyes closed. The warm glow of the fire illuminates everything that's changed since he left this morning—or yesterday morning, since now it's after midnight. The fresh bruise on his cheek. Red, swollen knuckles. He must have slipped into the closet for a new shirt. It's dry, but he has one hand pressed to his side.

He wouldn't do that for a *cut*. It has to be a wound.

I sink to my knees in front of him, my heart racing. "What happened?"

He opens his eyes, regarding me with something that starts out as amusement and turns darker. "Poseidon and I boarded Demeter's ship. He was looking for something down below."

"Weapons? Supplies?" I rest my hands on his thighs and look into his face.

"It was something else. I don't know what. All I cared about was getting back to the *Trident* before the damn thing sank."

A hot surge of anger blooms all across my chest. "You're bleeding. I can't see what I'm doing when you have your shirt on."

Hades leans forward and pulls his shirt over his head. "You're angry."

"Poseidon was going to let the ship sink while you were on it?"

"His crew disabled the ship, yes. We boarded to retrieve the members of her crew who could be salvaged." There's a constellation of bruises across the carved lines of his abs. Newly beaten skin. "Persephone."

"You were hurt." My pulse is an echoing drumbeat. "You could have been killed."

He takes my face in his hands again. "I was not killed, summer queen."

"Well, I'm going to kill Poseidon. He could have gone onto that ship without you." I try to stand, but Hades keeps me in place. "Where is he? Why didn't he come up here?"

"He sleeps on the ship every night. He's there with his crew." Hades meets my eyes, his gaze steady. "Your mother is unpredictable. I have no doubt he chose me to go with him because we have experience with Demeter. His men don't.

And I wanted to be certain that the ship never made it to the mountain. Everything that matters to me is here."

My cheeks are hot under his palms. "I love you. I don't want you to die."

He huffs a laugh. "I'll do my best to avoid it." Hades leans in and nips my lower lip. He's not gentle about it, and I yelp at the bite. "I love you."

Hades doesn't let go until I've blinked the frustrated tears from my eyes. When I've collected myself, he settles back into his chair with a hiss.

I lift some of the cloth from the tray and dip it into the water.

I'll start with his face.

A cut at his hairline is dark with dried blood and sea salt. Hades closes his eyes and lets me dab it away, the warmth from the fire at my back. I keep breathing through the shock of the moment. The ragged intimacy of it. The fear of losing him. The danger of loving him. The uncertainty and hope of having his brothers here. My mother, still trying to hurt us.

It all falls away as I touch him.

I'm in the right place. At his feet, tending his wounds. I need this moment, and I think Hades does, too. I'll always be grateful to Zeus for saving him. I'll always owe him for that. This moment is different. It's only for us, and just as intimate. Hades is *here* in a way that he can't be when he's having an attack. He's letting me see him when he's hurt. He's letting me care for him.

I drop the cloth and trade it for a new one, which I soak with antiseptic. "Were you afraid?"

Hades gives a deep sigh. "For a moment. When the other ship started to sink." Anger flares again. How *dare* Poseidon? Hades is mine. I press the cloth against the cut on his side, and

Hades balls up a fist on the arm of the chair. "If you're going to light my skin on fire, a warning might be appropriate."

"You don't like warnings." I hold the cloth in place, guilt replacing my anger. "And I'm sorry if it hurts."

"I'm not sorry."

I pause in the middle of reaching for the bandages. "No?"

"Better to be hurt with you than feel nothing at the bottom of the ocean. Don't you think?"

My cheeks flush. I bandage the cut, then take his hand. Hades stays still while I clean the bloody grit out of his knuckles. "Do you think she'll ever stop?"

If my mother doesn't give up, Hades will kill her. Or Zeus. Or Poseidon. It seems more inevitable with every breath I take. I don't want her to die at her brothers' hands. And I can't lose the man I love.

Hades leans forward, catches my chin in his fingers, and pulls me in for a kiss. He tastes metallic. "I don't know."

He gets to his feet and curls his hand around the back of my neck. Hades takes me with him to the walk-in closet, Conor following close behind. He takes a small key from one of the shelves and unlocks a drawer at the back of the room.

Then Hades turns back to me.

He has a gun in his hands.

It looks tiny in his huge grip, but he doesn't tuck it away to keep it with him. He brings it to me, turns my palm up, and puts it in my hand.

And then, in a gentle tone, a loving one, he tells me how to load it and shoot it and unload it when I'm finished with it. Hades goes over the parts until he's certain I have it right.

"Promise me that if Demeter attacks the mountain, you'll use this."

It's an order. "I promise."

Hades brings the gun out to my nightstand and puts it away. I swallow the sharp realization that it could be me. I could be the one who ends this. I've been worried about our relationship surviving if Hades kills my mother, but what if it's me? Will I be able to live with myself?

I try to hide my shaking hands. It's no use. Hades catches both of them in his. He towers over me, and even bandaged, even aching, he's still the strongest person I've ever met. His face shows no fear. His eyes are dark with lust and love and possession.

"We won't get any answers tonight, summer queen. Now come to bed. I'll make you forget I was gone."

TWENTY-THREE

Hades

OLIVER RUBS BOTH HANDS OVER HIS FACE AND LOOKS intently down at the schematics for the mountain on my desk. "We need more people."

He's seated in one of the chairs on the other side of the desk while I pace back and forth by the window. Conor keeps watch from his place by the fire. I left Persephone sleeping for this. It's not long to sunrise, and my summer queen doesn't need to sit in on every strategy meeting. Certainly not this one.

She was rattled by the cut on my side, which stings under the bandage. Persephone tried not to show it. I saw the fear in her face despite her efforts. Her anger, too. And a confusion that's growing too heavy to bear. A woman like Persephone belongs in a field of flowers or in her study with her books. The last fucking thing she should be doing is learning how to shoot a gun and worrying about everyone but herself.

"Anyone we hire from the city could be loyal to Zeus." It's difficult to keep my thoughts away from Persephone and

concentrate on the task at hand. I want to go back to bed. An uneasiness has settled over the mountain, like the air has been infused with nerves and anticipation. That won't be Zeus, unless he's lost control of himself.

I doubt that. He was in his element when Poseidon and I arrived on the *Trident*. After all, defending a city's worth of people is a social event with slightly higher stakes.

I've never seen Oliver look more skeptical. "I would vet them. Like I've vetted everyone on the security team."

"It's a fucking contingency plan, Oliver. If we need to recruit, then we have to look outside the city. I'm certain you've made this point before."

His brow furrows. "I thought things might've changed."

"Because I spent one evening on Poseidon's ship?"

Oliver shrugs. "They've never been on the mountain this long."

My brothers have never been on the mountain. Ever. Our meetings since the farmhouse have been rare, and usually take place in the city. Neutral ground, where they wouldn't be near my people. I told myself I was correct in keeping them away. Responsible.

Now that they're here, I can't shake the nagging idea that I was wrong. That my brothers are, in fact, trustworthy. That allowing them into my life might not present an existential threat.

But then what? I can't make a fucking announcement. My soul recoils from the suggestion of openly admitting to weakness, even if they've witnessed it firsthand.

Shame crawls up the back of my neck, and I rub my hand over it. "We need to be prepared for either of them to move against me. If you need more people, find them elsewhere. I don't want word to reach Zeus's people or Poseidon's crew."

Oliver nods. They can't know how far I'd go to protect the

mountain, or it would jeopardize the safety of everyone in it, including Persephone.

And…

I don't want them to know. For the first time since we left the farmhouse, I find myself in the outrageous position of giving a fuck about my brothers' feelings.

However, there is a more pressing issue at hand.

"What's the news from the farm?"

"She's finding people, too. We'll be competing with her." Oliver makes another note on the schematic. "And she's running low on supplies at the farm. Do you want me to make plans for Persephone?"

"What plans?"

"Have you thought about sending her away?"

Despite the painkillers, pressure drills into my skull. It doesn't stop there. My ribs. My stomach. It's excruciating, and it has nothing to do with the light. Nothing on earth could stop me from feeling this. "What the fuck kind of question is that?"

Oliver grimaces but presses on. "She might be safer somewhere else. Another city, in hiding. I could put a team together."

I cannot send Persephone away.

I can't.

The idea of being apart from her rends me in two. It starts at my ribs, prying them apart until my naked, beating heart is exposed to the corrosive air. It twists at my spine until my lungs fold in on themselves. Black encroaches on my vision. Send her away, and then what? Let Oliver's people stand outside her door until this is all over?

No. Not after what I felt the night I gave her the tiara. Not after I felt that gold under my skin. It did more than wrap around a lifeless diamond. She's completely surrounded my heart. The ship was fucking far enough.

Forcing her to leave me would be death.

"That's not a plan to fortify the mountain against my brothers." I stab a finger down on the schematics. "Build out the station. Have people start as soon as the sun is up. Add to the fence by the entrance to the mines. I want people at every door. Rifles and pistols."

"Are you sure you want her here?" Oliver has apparently slipped back into his own past, where he was a reckless fool with a death wish more extravagant than mine. I reach across the table and take a fistful of his shirt in my hand. He bumps the glass figurine of the poppy on my desk and knocks it to the floor.

"If you ever make a suggestion like that again, Oliver, it will be the last suggestion you give me or anyone else." My blood rages at the thought of Persephone away from the mountain, where I can't see her. Where I can't *reach* her.

"I understand." His voice makes me realize I've pulled the collar of his shirt so tight it's choking him. I toss him backward. His foot hooks onto the chair he was sitting in and it tumbles over. Oliver catches himself, pulling the chair back into place. "Do you think you'll marry her?"

It brings me up short.

We are already married. More than fucking married. What happened that night was beyond a ceremony with some priest. She's mine, and I'm hers. No further discussion.

Except Oliver's question has revealed a flaw in my thinking.

I've never asked Persephone how she feels about wedding ceremonies. If she's ever imagined her own. If she wants one. An image of her flashes into my mind. Persephone in a white dress. A beautiful one. Nicer than anything she wore at her mother's farm. In my vision, the dress does her justice until I rip it away from her skin. Until I tear the bouquet from her hands and let the petals fall. Spread her out on the bed on our wedding night.

Our *wedding* night.

I am not the kind of man who thinks about weddings. But I am the kind of man who thinks about Persephone in a gown that makes her pink with happiness.

She could want that. And if she does, I would give it to her. I'd give her anything.

"Hades," Zeus shouts. Footsteps approach in the hall.

"Where the fuck are you?" Poseidon, too. Perfect.

The two of them barge into the office without waiting for an answer. Both of them have rifles slung across their backs, and they've changed into clothes that can stand up to battle. Oliver jumps up from his chair.

"She's moving on the mountain," I say. There's no point in waiting for one of them to announce what's written on their faces.

Zeus doesn't bother to roll his eyes. "The report just came in. Guy was looking for you, Oliver."

Oliver curses under his breath. He makes a move toward the door. A single step, and he looks back at me.

"Go."

He pushes past Zeus and Poseidon, a string of additional curses trailing behind him.

Poseidon folds his arms over his chest. "Did he think we came here to take you out?"

"I'm insulted, Hades." Zeus's jaw is set, but amusement lights up his eyes. "You thought I'd orchestrate a coup after all the time we've spent together?"

"Now would be the most opportune moment." I feel a blistering uncertainty. Because, of course, I'm not wrong. If my brothers were going to turn on me, this is the perfect time.

Both of them know too much about me to believe the myth that I don't have any weaknesses.

One of them is sleeping in the bedroom down the hall.

Persephone, more than anything else, makes it difficult to breathe. If these fuckers prevent me from going to her, I'll tear them apart with my bare hands. A few bullet holes won't stop me. The pressure in my head increases. The last painkiller I took is wearing off. The first aching tendrils tap at my temples. It will take several weeks of consistent access for my brain to stabilize and the pain to retreat, which means I can't let it get any worse. My brothers are blocking the goddamn door.

"Hades."

Zeus hasn't made a move for his rifle. His hands are in his pockets, and his posture is relaxed. He's ignoring the tension vibrating in the air. It takes me a few moments to place his tone.

It's the way he says my name when I'm in the middle of a shattering seizure. On rare occasions, I resurface in the middle of the event. I can't see, so the memories from those times are all sound. Cronos laughing. Poseidon cursing. And Zeus, saying my name.

He shakes his head. "Not today."

I've heard that, too. It means he is refusing to let me die, usually against my will. My lungs expand, air flooding in. "But you're leaving your options open?"

Now he rolls his eyes. "We're business partners, you stubborn fuck. Moving against you now would only make my life more complicated."

Poseidon laughs like a wave rolling across dark seas. "I don't need your mountain. I need you two assholes to stay alive so I have some entertainment. Now." He claps his hands. "Let's figure out how the fuck we're going to win. Demeter's on her way."

TWENTY-FOUR

Persephone

I'M AWAKE BEFORE HADES OPENS THE DOOR.

I'd fallen into a dream, but at some point in the middle I reach for his side of the bed. I feel the emptiness and the dark, distant energy of him. Close, but not here. A wave of pressure rises and breaks over the mountain like a night breeze.

So I'm sitting up as he crosses the room. "What is it?"

"Your mother is moving on the mountain."

My muscles ache from missing him, but the hurt disappears under his touch. Hades takes my face in his hands and kisses me. It's a diamond of a kiss. Something sharp and solid to hang around my neck.

It's over too soon, and he's a shadow headed to the walk-in closet.

"Where are you going?"

"Downstairs to plan. All three of us will need to coordinate our people for when she arrives."

Drawers open and close. I throw off the covers and follow

him. Hades is dressing in the dark. When I step across the threshold, the lights in the closet come up. The glow is slight, gentle enough for his eyes, but I can still see him strapping on a bulletproof vest.

The sight of it makes my heart race.

"Do you think she'll send people inside? Can they get inside?"

"I think she's desperate." More drawers. He puts clothes into my hands. Leggings and a tight-fitted shirt. All black. "We should have enough people to repel her army, but it's hubris to ignore the possibility that someone could get through."

Hades puts a smaller, slimmer vest on top of the pile in my hands.

"Do we have enough of these for everyone?"

The low light catches the regret in his eyes. "Not everyone on the mountain, no."

"Then I'm not wearing one, either."

"Yes, summer queen, you are." Pressure surrounds me, but it's a light touch. A bedsheet instead of a boulder. "You'll wear it if I have to put it on for you myself. I'm entirely willing to punish you for refusing. This is your life." Hades hasn't raised his voice, not at all, but the intensity of his worry and his command is squeezing the air out of my lungs. "You are my life."

A shout from down the hall barely reaches us in the closet. Hades doesn't so much as blink. His eyes are locked on mine. He holds the vest in place.

You are my life.

It's not just worry. It's love.

"I'll wear it."

He leans down and brushes a kiss to my forehead.

"Get dressed and meet me downstairs. Your boots are on

the lowest shelf." Hades is at the door in two long strides, but he pauses with his hand on the doorframe. "Bring the gun."

The clothes are an exact fit, and so are the boots. In every way, the outfit is the opposite of what I wore on my mother's farm. In the bathroom, I turn the lights all the way up. Wash my face. Tie my hair back. The woman staring back at me from the mirror isn't a frightened girl running away from her mother. Not by a long shot.

Her hands shake anyway.

At the bedside table, I find a holster that buckles around my waist.

And, of course, the gun.

With the bulletproof vest and the black clothes and the *gun*, there's no sign of that girl left. Hades has prepared me for a last-resort situation.

It's about to arrive.

His rooms are silent. Empty. I ride the elevator down to the main floor.

The doors open on a peaceful rotunda. There's no panicked noise yet, which means my mother isn't here. She hasn't managed to invade the mountain.

Two men hustle across the space. All of their clothes look bulletproof, and the guns across their backs are enormous compared to mine. I follow them across the rotunda and down one of the long hallways.

Voices come from a room up ahead, which is a relief. I'm not following the guards for no reason. One of the men gets louder, and a lower voice interrupts.

Poseidon and Zeus.

The guards disappear into the room ahead of me.

I'm not going to go in at a run. I keep my pace even, though my heart pounds. This couldn't be farther from my mother's fields. The girl I was before would have waited upstairs with the door locked for Hades to tell me what was going to happen.

I push away a vague sadness for her innocence. It didn't help me, in the end. I had to move past it to be here with Hades.

The meeting room they've gathered in is relatively dark, like all the places he spends his time. A soft light in the center of the table casts a warm glow over a long meeting table. Hades stands at the head of the table, Conor by his side. He looks like a different version of himself, too. He's replaced his perfect suit with clothes like the guards were wearing.

He even has a rifle like theirs.

Zeus and Poseidon stand side-by-side facing the door. Poseidon leans over the table, pointing to something on a big sheet of paper. Zeus's eyebrows are drawn together, his golden eyes dark and skeptical.

Hades turns his head, as if he's sensed me standing out here.

The cold, impassive expression he wears when he's with other people melts away. Relief flashes across his face. He's glad to see me. His eyes flick down over my clothes. Over the bulletproof vest and the gun at my hip. Approval lifts the corners of his mouth. The dark echo of him stirs in my chest, twisting itself together with the gold that always hums under my skin.

I belong here with him.

My place is at his side, near Zeus. "What's happening?"

Hades leans down, letting the chatter in the room wash over us. "Your mother has been sending her people in small groups. Twos and threes."

"Why would she do that?"

"So our scouts didn't notice that they were leaving the farm. The bulk of her army is following."

I swallow bitter fear. "They're already out there."

"Yes."

"How many?"

"Between fifty and a hundred," says one of the men seated at the table. "None of them has attempted to approach the train station. They haven't come near the auxiliary entrances."

"We need to make the first move." Poseidon straightens up. "You're kidding yourselves if you think you can fuck around in here and still win."

"Ah. Is the *Trident* prepared to transport between fifty and a hundred bodies, then?" Zeus's tone is light. The mood in the room is steady. Calm. But it's not nearly as light as he sounds.

"To fucking where, the city docks? Her people are only my problem as long as they're alive."

"Do we know if she's with them?" Hades's question sends a chill down my spine.

A man at the far end of the table taps at a tablet. "We don't have confirmation either way."

"Then your crew will have to be patient, Poseidon."

Poseidon glares at Hades. "Are you afraid to kill her?"

"I'm not going to gun down a hundred people whose only crime so far is falling under her influence. There's no telling what kind of orders she's given until we capture one of them."

Zeus and Poseidon exchange a look.

"What do you think she did?" I hope I don't sound as nervous as I feel.

The conversation misses a beat. It starts up again around the table. Hades puts his hand on the small of my back. The warmth of his palm grounds me.

Zeus looks me in the eye. "There's a chance she's given her people instructions in the event she's killed. Those could include attacking the mountain or any given target in the city."

I don't think he's lying, but I look to Hades anyway.

He gives me a single nod.

"Defensive positions." The guards who came in before me are instantly in motion at Hades's words. "Everyone on the mountain needs to be in their homes or in one of the safe rooms."

Oliver leaves with two more men.

"What the fuck are you going to do when your defenses fail, Hades?" Poseidon's arms are crossed over his chest. "Try to negotiate?"

"They're not going to fail."

Zeus frowns at the paper on the desk. It's a blueprint of the mountain. I can see the arrangements of the tunnels and the factory floor and hundreds of other rooms. The one place it doesn't include is Hades's home. That's just a grayed-out area near the top of the sheet.

"Hades." Zeus steps closer to the table. His eyes fly over a tablet near the plans. "Are you prepared to lose the train platform?"

Hades narrows his eyes. "It's lined with charges. The rest of the mountain can stand without it. We all have people on the ground outside."

The calm in the room evaporates. It's like watching a light-bulb flicker before it dies. There's fear in the shadows, and something clicks into place. It must be Zeus, losing his composure. The calm returns, but it doesn't feel stable.

"What if she already has people in here?" I ask.

Zeus looks at Hades over my head. "The farm boy."

"She knew about Decker." My panic can't quite reach me through the calm. "She killed him. He might have told her how to get to someone who—"

A high, shrill scream echoes through the rotunda. It's a piercing, spiraling sound, and it startles everyone into action.

Poseidon leaps over the table, landing on the other side and sprinting out the door. Zeus is next.

"Go upstairs, to the bedroom. Lock the door behind you." Hades ushers me out into the hall.

"No. I'm staying with you."

"Persephone."

"I'm staying with you." I plant my feet and face him. "If she's already here, you can't send me up there alone. If we've already lost, then I'm not going to be apart from you when it ends."

Hades wraps me in his arms, lifts me off my feet, and kisses me. It's short and vicious and it tastes like dark and diamonds. Then we're both running after his brothers.

It's chaos in the rotunda. Workers are running for the train, obviously terrified. Zeus and Poseidon weave through them, out of sight in a heartbeat.

Hades runs in the opposite direction, toward the train platform. Conor flies after him. He won't be separated from Hades, and he guards the platform entrance along with him.

It takes my breath away to see Hades and his brothers like this. I've never seen anyone run faster. I've never seen anyone taller, or stronger. It's no surprise that Hades makes it to the platform before the bulk of the crowd. He charges in and returns a moment later, herding three people back into the rotunda.

"The train is not running." His voice cuts through the noise. "There's nothing outside but a hostile army. Someone tell me what the fuck happened."

A woman with tears running down her face struggles to catch her breath. "From the mines. They were from the mines, and they said—they said—"

"What did they say?" Hades is keeping six people from

running into the platform now, but he poses the question like he's at a business meeting.

"They said the whole mountain is going to come down. They said there were *bombs*."

Oliver enters from the other side of the rotunda. "Three of them," he calls to Hades. "She didn't warn them about your brothers."

"The train isn't running," Hades says. "The mountain is secure. You have a choice."

He stops and waits for the panicked hum of voices to subside.

"You can shelter in your homes until we've completed a second search of the mountain, or you can follow Oliver to guest housing. It was last swept five minutes ago, and I have a full contingent of guards waiting to escort you."

They appear at the far end of the hall. The woman who was crying goes toward them without another word from Hades.

Most of the others follow, but there are more people spilling into the rotunda every second. I get a flash of calm, but it's not enough to replace the growing terror.

Three men in the mines were all it took.

Three liars, unless they were telling the truth.

The only place I can stand to be is next to Hades. I go to him and reach for his hand. We only have a few seconds. People keep trying to get past him. They keep trying to reach the dead end of the platform.

He takes my hand and lifts my knuckles to his lips.

Seconds. We have seconds before he has to let go.

I squeeze his hand tight.

He squeezes back.

TWENTY-FIVE

Hades

I T'S FUCKING PANDEMONIUM.

Whoever Demeter chose to infiltrate the mines did a hell of a job. They've been here for weeks, because I cut down on hiring when I realized the painkillers weren't going to resume. No one new has been brought on since well before I took Persephone.

How Demeter gave them the signal is another matter.

It's one I don't have time to engage with. Not when all of my workers have lost their minds.

They're stampeding towards the exits, everyone cramming into the rotunda. People are hurting themselves trying to get safe. Stumbling over one another. Falling.

And for what? A bomb threat? We have every entry and every exit monitored constantly. But anything is possible.

I won't risk the safety of my people while we wait and find out.

"A complete search," I say to Oliver. "Bring the dogs out."

I hired a trainer months ago as the situation with Demeter deteriorated. Ex-military. His team works with German Shepherds who can detect bomb materials more accurately than a human and an x-ray machine. In minutes, we'll know if the threat is real or fake.

Persephone stays with me, gently helping people move along toward guest housing, holding a baby while a woman gathers up her wriggling two-year-old boys, their father nowhere in sight.

"All clear," comes the trainer's voice over Oliver's radio.

"You're sure?" he asks.

"The dogs are sure."

Fuck. Overall, that's a good thing. No bombs means no real danger, but my people are already in a frenzy. "Send out an alert. Tell everyone in the city."

The lie was a clever one. Most of the people who came here to find work have never seen an explosive firsthand. They don't understand how thick the walls are. They don't understand the effort it took to carve into the mountain in the first place.

"You can't leave on the train. It's not running. But you don't need to go, I promise," Persephone says to a woman with a little girl balanced on her hip. The child leans her head onto her mother's shoulder. "It's safe here."

"Is it too late to leave?"

My summer queen takes the woman's hand in hers. "If you want to leave when everything settles down, you can go. But right now, it's best to stay inside."

I can't watch this happen. Can't wait for the alert to filter out through panicked minds. I push through the heavy flow of people and step onto a crate one of the workers has been dragging with him.

"*Silence.*"

Most people slow. Some people stop entirely.

They look up to me. For assurance. For safety.

Persephone looks at me, too. She doesn't need me to make her safe. She's proven that. But she needs me to be a king worthy of her. My next breath feels made of the pure, shimmering gold that came to me the night I crowned her. It's pride and longing, inseparable from one another. I want to barricade us in my bedroom and fuck her until the world ends.

She'd never accept it. Persephone thinks of the people on the mountain as hers. She'd never abandon them.

Neither would I. They signed agreements with me, for one thing. And Persephone would never look at me the same way.

"The bomb threat was a lie." My voice carries through the rotunda. "We've confirmed that with an extensive search of the property. You're safe here."

There's some muttering. A bag slips from someone's hand. They don't all seem sure. Their eyes are clouded with fear. Now I understand why Zeus was pissed when I scared his women. These are my people, and they deserve to be secure in this mountain.

"Go back to your homes, or come through to guest housing. Stay there until I give the order."

Someone shouts from the back of the crowd. "What if you're wrong?"

Tension thickens. They're expecting me to have a temper, because I've been an angry person. Then Persephone came along. Persephone is all beautiful brightness, the only light I can bear to be around.

"It's not safe outside. I can't let you walk into a dangerous situation. But Persephone is with us. You can see her. My wife. My queen. I wouldn't keep her here if I didn't believe it was secure."

That seems to convince them. Voices rise as I step to the floor. Some people still want to go to guest housing. Others want to go back to their apartments.

Persephone smooths the little girl's hair back from her cheek. "Don't worry, sweetheart. Everything is okay now. You can go home."

Half of me is having the same conversation with a jittery, shaken man. He's the one I pulled out of the mines a few days and a lifetime ago. The woman he broke down about has her arm looped resolutely through his.

The other half of me is enthralled by the sight of Persephone smiling softly at the little girl.

This is the first moment in my existence that I've entertained the idea of children. Of a *child*. My child. Until Persephone, I was a wasteland. I could never have supported a new, innocent life.

Persephone takes exquisite care with her flowers. She touches the petals like she touches the girl's hair.

Can the child feel the gold sweetness in her fingertips?

Could ours?

The rotunda starts to clear as people filter out. They're safe… for now.

I can have my security staff sweep the mountain every fucking moment until dawn, but until Demeter withdraws her people and disbands her army, we'll be on edge.

We'll be under attack.

I'm getting reports. Text messages, one after the other. Every man I have is clearing hallways throughout the mountain. The same phrase comes in again and again. *All clear. All clear. All clear.*

Demeter's game is unfolding exactly as she intended. My

men are occupied with ensuring that the mountain is indeed secure, and her army is closing in.

There's a big *crack,* almost like lightning. It's an electric sound. The systems for the train are switching over to an emergency generator. It happens when the entrance locks down, which is rare enough that most of the workers have never heard it.

The rotunda descends into complete chaos.

People who had been heading home turn and run. A screaming surge rushes every available door. Every worker on the mountain, from the miners on up to the account managers. Their families. Their children.

Most of them head toward me.

Conor flattens himself to my side. I pull Persephone behind me moments before the crush reaches us. Any explanation I gave them now would be lost in the piercing echoes bouncing off the ceiling of the rotunda. None of my people are in any state to hear that no one has breached the train platform.

"Not this way." Simple instruction. "Down that hallway. It's safe. *No.* The trains aren't running."

This must be what it's like to direct a landslide.

Zeus flies out of a doorway on the opposite side of the rotunda and cuts through the crowd. He moves people out of his way with hands on shoulders, his face set. When he reaches me, he's a rock in a stream. People give us more space, but they don't stop screaming.

"She's outside. One of us has to go."

"Where's Poseidon?"

"Dragging the three motherfuckers who started this stampede to your holding cells. He's got part of his crew with him. The rest are with our people."

Persephone shoves her way forward. "My mother's outside?"

"Yes. And her people are already firing." Zeus meets my eyes. "Who's going to go?"

"What's your plan? Shoot her?" Persephone asks.

Another man, lost to panic, careens toward me. He almost knocks Persephone over in the process, but she doesn't take her eyes off Zeus.

"If that's what makes this stop, then yes," he snaps.

"I'll go." If anyone is going to kill Demeter tonight, it's going to be me. She's attacking my home. My people. It can't be anyone else. "Keep people out of the train platform."

"No." Persephone wraps her hand around my elbow. "I'm the one who has to go."

Someone barrels into Zeus at full speed, but he doesn't stumble. He pushes them toward the hall.

"No." I can't accept this.

"Hades."

"You really think you can talk her down?"

"I'm the only one who can stop this." Persephone looks into my eyes. My heart is a diamond that falls straight through the floor. "She wants to see me. She wants to talk to *me*. She won't stop until she gets a chance."

Fuck. "Then I'll go with you."

"It's almost dawn."

I've never cursed my weakness more. "I can go."

It's true... and false. I went too long without painkillers. My brain hasn't stabilized enough to stay in the sun. There's a decent chance I could have a seizure in the middle of Demeter's army.

"You have to be here," she says.

"I'm not letting you out of my sight. Don't ask it of me."

"You have to be here," she says again. "All these people—" Persephone ducks, narrowly avoiding an elbow to the side of the head. The situation here is about to boil over. "They're looking to you for leadership. You're the person they need right now."

"It's not fucking safe for you out there."

"I'll take Zeus with me."

This is the worst negotiation of my life.

Because she's right.

Demeter is here for her. And if I go out with her, Demeter will believe I'm pulling the strings. She'll see red. And the most important thing is peace.

"I'll go." Zeus is deadly serious. "I'll bring her back."

All I know is that we're out of options. "If anything happens to her—"

"You'll level the city and damn everyone in it."

I'll do more. I'll burn down the world.

I meet Persephone's silver eyes, and the thread between us tightens. It's made from spun gold and diamonds, and far away, I can feel the whispered beat of her heart. "Come back to me."

She rises on tiptoe to kiss my cheek. "I will."

Zeus leads her into the crowd, and my soul goes with her. My breath.

Outside, the sun is rising. But there's no light on the mountain without Persephone. There's no light anywhere. And I don't want to live in the dark.

TWENTY-SIX

Persephone

Zeus and I step out of the tunnels and into the new edge of dawn.

The sun crawls up from the horizon bit by bit, soaking the clouds in pink and yellow.

It makes the battlefield look beautiful. Like a garden, if the grass had been planted with soldiers instead of flowers. Their guns glint in the light. They've set up barriers to hide behind, and they're picking off shots at my mother's people.

Her army is huge, and it's advancing. A row of people with guns drawn.

They're already firing.

I duck on instinct, but no bullets hit. They're edging closer now. Step by step. A laugh echoes across the ground.

Zeus cups his hands around his mouth. "Demeter. I have your daughter."

It should be impossible for everyone to hear him, but they do. I see the sound ripple through them. The line of men comes

to a halt. The men defending the mountain crane their necks to look at me. A fresh breeze kisses the back of my neck.

"I know you want to talk to Persephone."

A man in the center of the row turns his head.

That's what gives her away.

My mother is behind her men, still hidden from view.

"Let me see her," Zeus says. Then he slips his hands into his pockets.

"They could shoot us right now." All around us, birds are singing the sun into a clear blue sky.

"She won't let them shoot. She's here for you. Remember?"

A shiver shakes me, head to toe. "Yes."

"Are you ready for this?"

No. Who could ever be prepared to have a conversation with her mother on a battlefield? I never imagined this would happen. Never thought I'd have the courage to leave at all.

"It doesn't matter. This has to end before anyone else dies."

There are bodies out in the field. They wear thin blankets of mist. I don't force my eyes away. Some of them were Hades's people. Some of them were working for my mother. I bear some responsibility for all of them, all because I wanted freedom. The disagreement is between my mother and me, not these armies.

A low murmur rises from my mother's men. It doesn't interrupt the birds. One of them soars above the rocky slope where Hades's army is defending the mountain. It sings as it does a loop, carrying it down the hill to my mother's people.

They take it as a sign, or else she gives them an order I don't hear.

The line of soldiers splits apart. Divides neatly in two. They were coming for us a minute ago. Now they're unsettled. Shifting from foot to foot. They came here to destroy

something. More than a few of them were probably here before, when Zeus's people turned on them.

Zeus unstraps his rifle from his back. He holds it as easily
as any of the soldiers. Mercenaries. Whatever they're called.
Zeus could have been anything, I think. He could have been a
ruthless killer for someone's army. The fact that he hosts parties is just a cover for how dangerous he is. Just like the rumors
about the mountain are a cover for how loyal Hades is. How
committed to his people. Both men learned to be lethal growing up, and both of them use it for different purposes now.

But at the core...

They're brothers.

"Did Hades give you the pistol?" Zeus asks the question
without taking his eyes off my mother's army. He's giving them
time to see that he's willing to shoot if they make the wrong
choice.

"He told me to use it if my mother attacked the mountain."

"Good for him."

"What does that mean?"

"He hates guns."

I blink at Zeus, forgetting the armies for a heartbeat. "He
does?"

"He insists it's because they're dangerous with all that rock
and reinforced glass, but I think he considers them cheap in
comparison to fighting with his bare hands. He's not taking any
chances with you." A quick inhale. "There she is."

Through the gap in the army, I see my mother.

She stands in the grass, nearly at the tree line. Her white
dress is alive in the breeze. A basket dangles from her fingertips. As I watch, she bends to pick a flower from the ground at
her feet. My mother tucks it into the basket. *There*, the movement says. *Safe*.

I take the first step forward, then another.

Zeus follows. We leave the gravel and continue down onto the rocks.

The sun keeps rising. Dew droplets cling to the grass, the fresh, clean scent carried up to us on a gentle wind. Zeus walks beside me and the earth itself makes the journey to my mother a simple one. All we have to do is choose our steps carefully on the rocks.

That, and watch my mother's army for movement.

I'm not afraid.

I belong on the mountain with Hades. That doesn't mean I've lost my sense of the earth. New flowers open for the day, their roots reaching down into the dark. None of them would mind if I stopped and touched the petals, giving them a bit more life.

The mountain is Hades's kingdom, but look what it's surrounded by.

Mine.

The two of them are one and the same. I picture wrapping a gold shield around the mountain. A heart beats inside, strong as a diamond. Alive in a way a gemstone can never be.

I won't let it die. Not as long as I'm living.

I set some of the gold free. It sinks into the ground, and purple forget-me-nots bloom beside my footsteps. Daisies that were crushed by the army stretch toward the sky. I hope the feeling reaches all the way back to the mountain. All the way back to Hades.

We get closer to my mother.

I can see her face.

She's crying.

Tears run down her cheeks, but her expression doesn't

crumple. It's a strange way to cry. Almost like she doesn't know she's doing it.

Ten more steps.

She doesn't recognize me.

I didn't think she'd be this wary. My mother is never this unsettled about anything other than Hades. I'm not sure she believes it's me.

My hands go to the straps on my bulletproof vest.

"Persephone," Zeus warns.

"Shh." I undo the straps. Shrug off the vest. Zeus catches it before it hits the ground and throws it over his shoulder. My gun goes next. I hand him the holster, which he wraps around his fist. I'm left wearing a long-sleeved shirt and sturdy leggings, so different from the white dresses I used to wear on the farm.

I stop about fifteen steps away from my mother. Flowers bloom between us. Maybe some of the gold can reach her, too. Help her understand.

"Hi, Mama."

Her eyes widen. Shock, I think. Shock that it's my voice, and not some false creature who replaced her daughter. Do I seem that different? "It's you."

"Yes. I came out to talk to you." The breeze ruffles my hair, then hers. "I came out to tell you that it's over. Please. Don't do this. Don't let anyone else get hurt."

She rocks back on her heels like I slapped her. "You're speaking for *him*?"

"I don't speak for him." I gesture behind me to the armies. To the mountain. "I speak for them. This needs to stop. The shooting. The killing. The attacks. You've gone too far. I can't let you do this."

A bitter grin twists her mouth. "Is that what Hades told

you? That I was responsible for all those deaths? He *lies*. That's all he ever does. He tortures and lies and—"

"No. He doesn't. I've lived with him. I know him. And he's nothing like you said."

"You would believe him over me?"

"That's the thing." I keep my voice as gentle as the flowers. "You never told me anything. If you had, I would have understood why you wanted to keep me on the farm with you. We could have talked about it."

"Oh. It was *details* you wanted. You wanted to know exactly what Hades did to me. And you." Her eyes snap to Zeus, and they're stormy with hurt and rage. It looks real.

"I never touched you," Zeus starts.

"I know you accused them of raping you, Mama. I know you sent them to jail." Her horrified gaze comes back to mine. She looks like a cornered animal. "I know how you hurt them. I know what you did to Hades. It happened in front of me."

"I did what I had to do." She swallows a sob. Another one takes her by surprise. "I've always done what I had to do to survive. And then I had to protect you. Can't you see that? Haven't you learned anything? The world is filled with monsters." Her voice breaks. "Come home with me. Please. It's all I want in the world. You'll be safe there. I'll take the lock off your door. You can go wherever you want as long as you stay in the fields. You can—you can spend the summer in the sun. You've always loved the sun."

Maybe in some other life, I'd shout at her. Make a list in one of my new notebooks of all her crimes and read them to her. Force her to see what she'd done.

But this woman, with her flower basket and her shaking shoulders, wouldn't hear a word I said.

"You're not yourself." She sounds thready now. Uncertain.

"You never dressed like this. He must have done something to you. I can help you. I can, Persephone. Let me take you home."

"No."

"Don't say that." My mother takes a step forward. So does Zeus. "Don't."

"I'm not coming home. I live here now. This is where I want to be. I love him, Mama. I love Hades, and I'm not leaving with you." I move around Zeus. A dandelion shoots up from the ground and blooms yellow. Five steps to her. Three. None.

I put my arms around my mother and hold her tight.

She always seemed so tall when I lived with her, but we're almost the same height.

"Come home." Her body trembles. I can't remember the last time she hugged me like this. I know she did, but was it months ago or years?

"You have to stop. You have to take your army and leave. Send them all home."

"I won't."

"Then I won't come to see you."

She goes still. So still she's hardly breathing. "You don't mean that."

I pull back to look into her eyes. They're just like mine. "I'll visit you every spring and every fall. But only if you end this. If you tell them to shoot, I'll never come back. You'll never see me again. All you'll ever see is the mountain."

Birds sing in the forest, filling the silence between us. It goes on for a long time. Heartbeat after heartbeat. I can feel Zeus behind me. He's tense and trying to hide it.

"Turn around and leave, and I'll come visit you. Stay, and you won't see me again."

The corners of her mouth turn down. "Swear."

I lean in and kiss her cheek. "I promise."

And then I let her go.

My mother can't bring herself to move. Not at first.

Not until I bend down and pick one of the forget-me-nots blooming at my feet. Then another. A third. I keep going until I have a bouquet.

I offer it to her with both hands.

My heart kicks to life, pounding with the razor's edge of the moment. She could decide not to go. She could order her people to shoot. I could die without ever seeing Hades again.

She looks down at the bouquet. A faint smile whispers over her face.

My mother accepts the flowers. "You'll come this fall?"

"Next spring. When I'm certain we're safe."

A shallow nod. Her chin dimples. "I'll be waiting."

"I'll be there."

The wind lifts, and my mother turns her head to follow it. She takes her basket and walks into the woods.

Zeus curses under his breath.

Beyond him, my mother's army is turning into a ragged group. They're all coming this way. The mountain gleams behind them, the gold in the rock on fire with the sunrise.

"This is your chance," Zeus says. He keeps his gun trained on the army. I don't think it'll be an army much longer.

"To do what?"

"To escape. Go to the city. Go wherever." He cuts a glance at me, then focuses back on the men straggling toward the woods. "You won."

TWENTY-SEVEN

Hades

L ETTING HER GO IS UNBEARABLE.

The unfortunate side effect is the rising pressure in the rotunda. It's not a seizure. I'm the only one who can feel it. It's the agony of being separated from Persephone.

My workers continue to panic. They keep trying to fight their way past me to get on the train. Oliver joins me in holding down the platform, along with half of the security team. We shout reassurances and orders, but the frightened energy of the crowd feeds on itself.

Even if I could leave, storming out of the mountain now would terrorize Demeter. Never mind that she's been terrorizing me for months. The sight of me coming to take my summer queen would break her, and I need her to leave.

Alive.

I need that for Persephone.

I've seen how much it bothers her to think I might kill her

mother. I imagine I would feel similarly if someone murdered Eleanor, though Eleanor has never been evil a day in her life.

"What do you need to keep them off the platform?" I snap at Oliver. "More people?"

"At least ten. For the next hour. They'll get tired, but—"

It's not efficient to pen people in like terrified animals. I understand why they're like this. Demeter likes people afraid. This is what she creates in the world. It can't go on. The panic has to be stopped. Not with barriers and shouted orders. I need to appeal to their humanity.

I stop resisting the crowd. The moment I step forward, they fall back, scrambling to get out of my way. Some of them grab for my clothes, begging for answers, but I brush their hands off.

Conor circles me, doing his best to keep them at bay.

I stand on the crate again. This time I don't shout to get their attention. Frantic energy would only be absorbed in the melee.

"Listen. It's far too fucking loud in here. I need your attention." It takes a moment for them to hear me, but one by one, they come to a stop. "I came here to run a business. You came here for work. I've always been clear about the terms. Haven't I?"

Murmured agreement.

"I've never gone back on our agreements, and I never will. Because you're not just employees. You are part of a family. This is your home as much as mine. And on the mountain, we're loyal to each other."

The workers hang on every word.

"I need you to do something for me now." Before Persephone, I hated to ask. To need. "Trust me for one more day. Trust Persephone. We'll keep you safe. You have my word."

There's some applause as I step down, some shouting, but I can't focus on that now.

My people are safe, but my queen is not.

I'm at my limit.

This is as long as I'm willing to let her be out there with Zeus. With *Demeter*. Poseidon will be enough for the mountain. He and his crew locked up the men who started the stampede, and they're making their way back to the rotunda.

Oliver runs to catch up with me. "If Demeter sees you, it will set her off. She could send her whole army to rush the mountain. She doesn't care that it's a suicide mission."

"I'm going to get Persephone."

"She might need more time."

"I don't care."

The ghost of a seizure slices into the center of my head. This is what torment will always feel like to me. The beginning of a blackout. But the painkillers hold.

I need her as much as the poppies. More than the poppies.

My heart races, the rhythm so fast and jagged I could be sick.

If Persephone wanted to leave, she could go. My summer queen could seize this moment and walk away. She could leave me behind and disappear into the world.

She'd deserve it, too. A life free from the mountain and the burden of my pain and the need I'll always have for the dark no matter how many poppies she grows. I can't be out in the light. Not all the time. I can't push the painkillers too far.

If she never grew another poppy, I'd still need her.

"—have to wait," Oliver shouts.

I break into a run. Throw myself into the nearest tunnel and take it down. Oliver chases. Conor runs ahead.

"You shouldn't go out there. You—"

I don't care. I don't care about anything but Persephone. Where *is* she? What have I done? What was I thinking, agreeing to let her go out there? The mountain is surrounded by assholes with guns. One of them could be aiming at her now.

Or she could be gone. Back to her mother's farm. Back to her fields and her flowers and enough sun to blind a man. Without the painkillers, I'd have to wait until it was dark to search for her. I'd have to wait until fall. Until winter. I'd have to wait, and I can't.

The guards at the tunnel exit scatter as I approach. One of them rushes to open the door. A crack of light shines into the hall, growing wider and wider. I put my hand on the door and shove.

Oliver grabs for my arm. "Wait—"

I shake him off. Too hard. He hits the doorframe and stumbles back, and I walk out into the light. Conor barks, sticking with me. He hates this. I do, too.

My eyes refuse to adjust. The dawn is a yellow wash, and I can't see anything. I can't see.

"Persephone." I bring up a hand to shade my eyes, and the closest shadows start to resolve. My people. The ones defending the base of the mountain. They're all on their feet, looking toward…

A retreating army.

And coming through the center of it, her vest and gun abandoned, is my summer queen.

Mine.

Wearing only clothes I've given her. Clothes that don't hurt to look at. Dark clothes that show me the lines of her body. She's whole and safe and there are no shining patches of blood. No one shot her. No one hurt her.

She came back to me.

I don't know which one of us runs first.

What I know is that she's an angel, sprinting up that hill. This time, she sees me. She's chosen me. Her hair comes loose from its tie and flies over her shoulders, the curls shining in the sun.

We meet on the hillside and she leaps into my arms. Her heart beats hard under her skin. Persephone is sweetly out of breath, her face buried in my neck. "I love you. She's leaving. I said I would visit her if she left."

"I don't care what you promised her."

"But—"

"Are you staying?"

Please stay.

Persephone lifts her head. "Did you think I would go?"

I don't have the words to admit it out loud.

Persephone doesn't need them.

"I'm staying." She kisses me, her arms tight around my neck. "I'll never leave you."

"This is all very sweet." Zeus's voice comes from somewhere nearby. I don't bother to look for him. I'm looking into Persephone's eyes. "But let's take this inside before you fall over like a goddamn fool."

TWENTY-EIGHT

Persephone

HADES TRACES A FINGER DOWN THE LINE OF MY SPINE, edging over each one of the bones. He's been touching me like this for what feels like forever. Could be minutes. Hours.

He brushes his fingers down over the curve of my ass and the backs of my thighs, all the way down to my ankles, which are tied to the posts of his bed. Same for my wrists, up in front of me. I can barely stay up on elbows and knees like he's ordered me to. My muscles are already tired and shaking. It makes him laugh to see it.

He palms my pussy and makes a noncommittal noise. My face goes hot. Even if there were a mirror here, I wouldn't see myself blush. The blindfold took care of that.

"Your body is made for punishment," he muses. "And so are you. Do you know why?"

I shiver under his touch, wanting to rock back into his

hand but stopped by the bindings. "Because I went outside without you?"

"Because you belong to me, and you put yourself in danger."

"I won't do it again."

"No, you won't." His hand leaves the space between my legs, and I'm in the middle of whimpering for it to come back when he spanks me there. Hard. And then again. If I worried he changed, that he'd become someone else, then I was wrong. Hades is as cruel as he's always been.

I relish it.

His hand snaps between my legs again and again, and now I know why he touched me so much before he began. He wanted me to be ready for him. To be wanting. He is showing me now what happens when the wanting comes face-to-face with consequences. These are the consequences, and it makes me unbearably wet, even when it hurts. Especially when it hurts. I keep thinking he'll stop, but he doesn't—not until there are tears running down my cheeks and splashing against the backs of my hands.

"Yes," he hisses. "Now you understand. But I think you could understand more."

There's a release near my ankles, and then Hades turns me over, still blindfolded. Now my wrists are stretched above my head. It was one thing being bent over for him. It's another to have my whole body exposed like this. He spreads my legs wider, and I let myself sink into the lingering ache between my legs and the slow panic coming in like the tide. My body knows better than to think this won't hurt, and it wants to get away.

I want to stay.

Hades brushes his hands over my nipples and my ribs then rakes his nails down my belly. Spreads my folds open with his fingers and sweeps one inside, testing. He's working me, arranging my legs so my pussy can take more punishment.

But it's the soft insides of my thighs that get the kiss of a belt.

It snaps my mind in two. One is the woman, the queen, who is stoic in the face of danger. And the other is the girl who met him in the field that night. One of them is gritting her teeth. Both of them are crying, begging, but he doesn't stop until my thighs are burning too.

A sudden slack in the tension at my wrists startles me. Hades rips off the blindfold and takes me up into his arms, kissing me with an angry, desperate bite. I don't know what's happening or why I'm free, and I'm so off-balance. The only thing that's steady is him. Steady arms, steady legs, a vicious mouth on mine. He kisses me hard, then again, staring into my eyes like he's searching for a secret there.

Then he pushes me out of the bed.

I land on the floor, on my knees, and catch myself on the bedspread.

His eyes meet mine, and I get my first real look at him of the morning. He's wearing a dark T-shirt and underwear, and if he were anyone else, I'd think it made him look vulnerable. Human. But he is a king no matter what he wears.

"Run," he says.

My body obeys. I sprint for the door, getting through just ahead of him. I cross the sitting room and escape into the hallway. His fingertips brush my skin, but I put on a burst of speed. At his office, I hook a hand on the doorframe and fling myself inside the room. I have some vague idea that I'll circle his desk and skirt around him on the way back out, but being chased…

It turns me into prey.

I'm afraid of him in an animal sense, my eyes and ears

working in overdrive to hear him on the hunt. He is not subtle. He doesn't have to be. He doesn't have to rely on the element of surprise to get what he wants. I'm two steps into my plan when his arm comes out and catches me around the waist, knocking the wind out of me.

I end up on the floor.

It's different here than it was on the bed. I'm still scrambling to get away from him, because he hasn't told me to stop. My hand hits the side of an end table, knocking it over. A lamp crashes to the floor. I gain six inches on him, and he drags me back, my peaked nipples electric on the rough rug, and he jerks my legs apart. Wider.

"I caught you," he says, sounding almost breathless. "I'll always catch you."

And then he drives himself into me in a single impatient stroke, pinning my hands behind my back while he does it.

I'm a mess.

Cheek pressed to the carpet, hair in my eyes, tears making everything slick. I keep struggling. That's what he told me to do, and I don't disobey. Something else falls off his desk. He opens the drawer without slowing his pace. He fucks me so hard I can't get a breath, and then he lets go of my hands to spread my ass. The cool, slick wash of lube comes down onto my heated core and then something thick. Not a finger. Bigger. Harder. Cold.

I fight it, because I know he wants me to, and because I can't help it. He tenses inside me, pulsing, and forces it in another fraction of an inch. I can't let it inside, so he delivers a slap to the outside of my thigh.

"Open," he orders. "Now."

No other choices, then. A sob breaks loose from me. I'd confront an army for him in a heartbeat. It's big, what he's putting inside my hole, almost too big, and I'm sweating by the time he's finished, splayed over his lap, my face in the carpet. I'm destroyed.

But when he starts to move inside me again, taking his time, I'm remade.

Hades fucks me until he gets a hitch in his breath, and then he fucks harder, each stroke bringing the full force of him to bear on my body. In the end, he growls at me to hold still and empties himself into me, the heat of his release making me even hotter.

And then he pulls out, putting a hand beneath my chin and turning me around so we're eye-to-eye. "Who do you belong to, Persephone?"

"You," I pant. He hasn't let me come yet, and it isn't fair.

"I couldn't hear you."

"I belong to you." It breaks me open a little. I won in the end, but death was at my doorstep. I still feel its kiss everywhere I go. Or maybe that's just Hades. He's more powerful than death.

He pinches one of my nipples and twists, pain making me arch back against him. "Do better."

"I belong to you," I cry. "I'll be good. I'll be so good. I won't leave you again."

"I want all your seasons, summer queen. Every fall and winter and spring and summer until you don't have any more left to give."

"They're yours." My sobs are a promise. A vow. "All of them. All of them, I promise. I love you."

Hades releases me then, but I'm only free for a moment before he pulls me up into his arms.

"They're mine," he murmurs. "You're mine." And then he kisses me, deep and hard, for proof.

TWENTY-NINE

Hades

THE TRAINS HAVE STARTED RUNNING AGAIN, BUT THE schedule has shifted.

I spend an hour in my office shifting it back.

There are new orders to fill. After Demeter's tantrum, she went into hiding, either on her property or elsewhere. No more army. So far, she hasn't risked her visits with Persephone.

She'll have to find some other way to entertain herself.

I'm desperate for Persephone by the time evening comes. Finally I tell Oliver he needs to manage things and leave the office.

There's no evidence of the panic in the rotunda. Not so much as a chip in the tile.

There are no reminders my brothers were here. There won't be, unless they visit again.

I'm not opposed to that idea.

Zeus is back in the city and quiet. Too quiet. It puts me

in the awkward position of having to check in. Poseidon is at sea, God knows where.

It took the three of us to settle the mountain after Persephone came home. Poseidon left soon after. Zeus came upstairs with me one more time.

We found Persephone asleep on one of the sofas in the living room, exhausted from the events of the night. And the morning. Exhausted from everything.

I tugged a blanket over her shoulders and sat on the floor, leaning against the front of the sofa. Conor pressed himself close. Zeus dropped down on my other side.

"What now?" he asked, drawing a knee up and slinging his arm across it.

"Hell if I know."

"Are you…" He paused. "Fine? With the painkillers."

"For the moment." There was a long silence, and I was too raw to keep my mouth shut. "I hated you for keeping me alive. The whole enterprise seemed worthless."

"That's very past-tense of you, Hades."

"It doesn't seem that way anymore."

Zeus stared up at the ceiling. "I hated you for wanting to die, you stubborn bastard."

"Did you?"

"Yes. In the past. Now I just hate you for being so obstinate."

He didn't leave until the next morning.

I return to our sanctuary. The lights get dimmer the farther I go into my space. My cock stirs at the thought of using Persephone. The painkillers might not be addictive, but she is.

Conor sniffs around in the hall, looking for anything out of place. He finds nothing. I have a new habit of watching him closely as we approach my rooms. He's on edge if Persephone is not inside. The farthest she'll be is elsewhere on the mountain, if she's learned her lesson.

My dog follows me into the sitting room and curls up on his bed by the fire. It's been an exhausting day of defending me from all the factory lights. He's earned his rest.

I go through to the bedroom to find one final pool of light in front of the window.

Moonlight.

Persephone is kneeling in it, naked. Her hair falls down over her shoulders in waves that catch the light too, and something dark rests in the palms of her hands.

Fuck.

How am I supposed to keep breathing when she's this gorgeous?

I'm already hard, tensed and ready and throbbing. It hurts—that's how much I need to be inside her pliant body. Her face is in shadow, but I can tell from the angle of her chin that she's looking at the floor. Her shoulders rise and fall with each breath. The dusky shadows of her nipples tell the story of her waiting here.

For me.

I go to her and put a hand under her chin, tipping her face slowly back so her neck is exposed, and her eyes meet mine. She rises with my hand until she's up on her knees, legs spread for easy access. It's breathtaking. Her lips part under the pad of my thumb, and I test her teeth, her tongue.

"You're waiting so patiently," I tell her. "Is there a reason?"

"Because I belong to you." She knows I like this. Knows what it does to me to hear it. "And I brought something else."

"What?"

She lifts her hands and shows me the shadowy thing I saw there before—a jewelry box. I angle it into the light and open it. Two diamonds glitter at the center of the velvet. Neat, matching clamps. Perfect for her nipples.

"For you," she says, voice soft and needy.

"Up on the bed."

Persephone hurries to obey me. She was so mortified the first time I made her do this. She's still mortified, but she lets it burn over her skin. Withstands it. My summer queen kneels at the edge of the bed.

"You deserve for me to use these now." I pull one clamp out and drop the box next to her knee. She's been thinking about this. Her nipples are ready and waiting. Persephone keeps her hands at her sides and lets me put the first clamp on.

It hurts.

She makes a delicious hiss, her hips working. I add my mouth and lap my tongue against diamond and flesh. This earns me a desperate whimper.

The second clamp makes her knees give out, her bottom meeting her heels. I pull her upright again so I can lash her other nipple with my tongue.

"It's so bad," she gasps. "It's so good."

"Pain and pleasure are always better when they're mixed, don't you think?" Her hands reach up to try to take the clamps off, and I pin them behind her back a second time. "Touch them and I'll tie you down. Stay here. Don't move."

I go into the walk-in closet and strip off my clothes, the day falling away along with them. Persephone's tiara is on a shelf at eye level. Back in the bedroom, I stand in front of her. She pants with the intensity of the clamps and my order, and I crown her again, the diamonds winking in her hair.

"Are you ready to be a good little queen?"

Her lips part. If it were brighter in here, I would be able to see the pink in her cheeks and the flush of her breasts, the way that red goes all the way down to her belly and between her legs. But I don't need the light. She's enough light all by herself.

"Yes. I've been ready all day."

"Does it hurt?"

"Yes." Her head falls back and her eyes flutter closed, but I twist my fingers through her hair and make her open them again. It's hard for Persephone to hold her hands behind her back.

She manages.

"Do you like it?"

Her tongue peeks out to wet her lips. "I need it," she whispers.

"That's right."

And then, because she is mine, I take the liberty of fisting her hair until she whimpers. I shove her face into the blankets. I knock her legs apart and spread her open, and then I lick her cunt while she begs for me to take the clamps off.

It's all a ruse. She doesn't want them off. She wants more.

I can tell, because when I lick her again, she rolls her hips, trembling, on the edge. I turn her over and nudge myself to her opening. Every touch is a lesson, a reminder that she belongs to me in every possible way. Now and always. She's mine.

Mine to use.

Mine to keep.

Mine.

"Hades," she murmurs. "Hades, wait."

I pause, gritting my teeth against the need to thrust. "What's wrong?"

"I'm your queen." She's breathless. Fuck. Did I hurt her? A tear runs down her cheek, but she isn't really crying. Not with her trembling smile. "And I'm pregnant."

A fist around my throat. It's love, that fist. I'm not an urn after all. Not burned to ashes in the sun. I'm alive. Blissfully, achingly alive.

"Are you sure?"

"Yes." So solemn. So brave, linking herself to a man like me.

"I'll never let you go. You know that, right? Persephone. God." I pull out, even though the cool air feels like nails on my hungry cock. It doesn't matter. I palm her stomach, which is still flat. No sign of the child inside. "Are you all right? Have you seen the doctor?"

She laughs softly. The sound washes over me, rain on a desert. "I'm fine."

"Are you sure? Do you feel sick? Do you need…" I know nothing about babies. Or pregnant women. I'm the one who feels faintly sick. "Pickles? Or ice cream?"

Her smile looks fully serene. A queen on her throne. Her arms pull me down. Her body cradles me—her breasts, her stomach, her wet cunt.

"Only you." She licks my bottom lip. "You're all I need."

When I bury myself inside her, I know I've finally come home.

And home doesn't hurt at all.

EPILOGUE

'VE FINALLY FOUND A PROBLEM I CAN'T FUCK MY WAY OUT of.

 It's a mindset issue, really. Being this despondent makes it difficult to be interested in sex. It's not that I can't fuck—that would be a cold day in hell—but that I have no interest. I might as well be dead. As dead as all the people I've killed. My hands flex, thinking about slim throats in my palms. It's not the killing that gives me a rush, I've decided. It's being the one to go on living.

 Right now, it doesn't feel like a rush. It feels like cement boots. It feels like being caged.

 At any rate, it's very charming, this desolate look I have going on. Staring out the window is a regular habit in a whorehouse, where one needs to rest his eyes every so often to avoid too much tampering with the merchandise. A certain amount is allowed if you're the owner, which I am, but even now, I've cleared out the prizes I usually use to decorate my office.

 I've never felt this unsettled. This…

 Jealous.

On the whole, it should be progress. Once my brother found Persephone, things changed.

My sister went mad when her daughter ran away. Not quite accurate, is it? She was already out of her mind, but when Persephone left, Demeter begged for my intercession.

I'll admit—I saw an opportunity there. Placate Demeter. Keep her supplies coming. I knew she'd stopped sending essential shipments to the mountain, where Hades lives, and I thought I could set things back in order. Keep us from each other's throats for another day.

Of course not. I underestimated the depth of his possession of Persephone. Having her brought from the mountain led him to do the unthinkable—come here, along with a gang of federal agents.

The situation escalated quickly, as it does. I went to the mountain. Threatened to attack. My frustration got the better of me, and we fought. Fists. Fury. All of that.

My father would have been proud.

A ghost drags her fingers along the shoulder of my jacket. Whispers in my ear. He wouldn't be proud.

He would.

Proud to know I'm as much of a bastard as he was.

I tug my collar away from my neck.

"Not now," I say to the ghost. She disappears.

After we fought, I saw what Hades had been hiding.

I saw how close he was to death.

What was I supposed to do? Let him die? Of course I didn't.

It's peaceful between us, for the moment. I could almost call it reconciliation.

I don't trust it. I don't know where to go from here. Relationships are a fucking nightmare. Too much to lose.

Seeing what Demeter had done to Hades chilled me to the core. And more than that, seeing him with Persephone made me aware of an uncomfortable absence in my life.

When our foster father Cronos died, I took over his business and his cold, dead heart. It all belongs to me now. The custom suits. The city's most expensive, most sought-after whorehouse. The emptiness inside my chest.

This place looks like paradise. Today it feels like prison.

I drum my fingers over the note on my desk. Thick paper, folded once.

If you don't answer my messages, I'll assume you're dead and come to close down the whorehouse.

—*H*

As if Hades knows I'm thinking of him, my phone rings.

"I got your note," I say when it connects. "So lovely of you. Does it mean you'll be paying me a visit?"

"No. Was it you?"

"Was what me? You'll have to be more specific."

Hades sighs, the sound sharp. "A shipment arrived on the mountain today."

"Then it must have been someone else."

Technically, I did send several men to Demeter's property to search it and find any remaining stock of a very specific pain-killer. Technically, I did put them on the train.

A silence.

"Are you all right?"

"I'm the same as ever." I laugh, as if our lives have been one great joke instead of an endless wasteland dominated by a psychopath. "Come visit me, Hades. We could talk. You might learn something."

"I would, but the company is fucking terrible."

He hangs up.

Good. The things I sent to the mountain did arrive. I'm still going to keep him at arm's length while I figure out…

Whatever the fuck is happening with me.

Back to the task at hand.

The women who want to work at the whorehouse like to show up late and in the middle of the week, when things are quieter. Perhaps they think it'll be simpler to deal with the men who are the most desperate for a fuck. I don't know.

What I do know is that there was a bit of a crowd not long ago at the backdoor. I've never posted an ad online looking for new whores, and yet they all find their way to the correct entrance. I long for the day one of them shows up at the front and makes a fool of herself. It would be fun for me.

As it stands, the street in front of my establishment is quiet. The occasional car edges up to the curb, deposits a client, and disappears into the clear night. No clouds. My brother's mountain will be visible from here.

Safe.

Secure.

I envy it, on occasion. How remote it is from the world. Hades disappeared into that fortress the very moment it was completed.

I wouldn't mind an escape.

Being there in an emergency situation made me wonder if that's all there ever is for my fucked-up family.

Not that I care.

A knock at the door.

"Come."

Savannah is pretty, like all the others, but less timid. Spent hours on her makeup, obviously, and probably more on her hair. She chose a nice dress. And now she is here in my office with red lips and a coy smile.

"They're waiting for you downstairs. Six new girls." An edge in her voice. Savannah is always nervous that someone might usurp her as the one most obnoxiously obsessed with me. She brushes her fingertips lightly over my things, which is asking for me to pin that hand behind her back and march her out of here. "Reya sent me to tell you."

"You volunteered and you know it." I've fucked her before. It was fine. A nice distraction. I would consider it a mistake, but I find it unproductive to dwell on those kinds of things.

"You're right." A pout. She tosses her hair over one shoulder. "I thought you might want to relax a little before you go downstairs."

"No need."

"Are you sure?" I stand up and straighten my jacket.

Savannah makes a sad face, the corners of her mouth turning down. "You look sad. I could make you feel better."

When she reaches for the fading bruise on my cheek, I catch her wrist in my hand and squeeze. Tight. Tighter. Then I settle a calm, pleasant mood over the whorehouse and brush past her.

Savannah hurries to keep up with me, rubbing at her wrist with a pasted-on smile that becomes a real one before we're down the hall. She's good, but not the best. I expect more of the same from the new girls I'll be inspecting in thirty seconds. What's important is the ability to craft them into human illusions. The sexiest. The most expensive. It's just good branding.

She acts as my own personal shadow all the way down to a room on the first floor, which is conveniently close to the loading dock and the back entrance. I can feel myself becoming the man who owns this place and everyone in it. A benevolent dictator, emphasis on benevolent. Buttoned suit. Perfect posture. Smile. Best not to scare them off before the real work begins.

Reya, my personal secretary disguised as a whore, is waiting with the new hires. All six of them are stripped down to panties and bras. If they can't handle this, then I won't put them out on the floor. Each one has her own attitude. The blonde on the far left is the first to meet my eyes and stick her chin in the air. She lets me turn her face from side to side and winks at me when I let her go. Saucy.

"Promising," I tell Reya, who makes a note in my ledger. She's good for many things, one of which is record keeping, another of which is hiding in plain sight. It would startle most people to find out what she really does for my business, but that's neither here nor there.

The redhead next in line is promising too, but the third girl is trembling. Her arms are locked over her chest, and when I touch her face, she clenches her teeth. I'm not in the business of making pity hires, but what the fuck else am I going to do? Reya was one of those women, shaking and white-faced, blinking back tears. She's become quite useful over the years. The girl in front of me now is hungry, judging by the peaked lines in her face.

"I think you'd be better off in the kitchens. Can you cook?"

"What?" She licks her lips. "Yes. I cook all the time."

Lie. Maybe she used to cook, but not now. "Reya, she'll start on dishes and work her way up. She can eat whenever she wants."

When I step away from her, she sags, letting out a relieved breath. Reya goes so far as to take her out of the room ahead of the others. She hands the girl off to a waiting staff member, who will give her clothes and a bed.

Four and five, beautiful but unmemorable. They're doing their best, putting on a pretty show, and it's fine, fine, fine. Excited to be here. They should be, because they know I treat my staff well. They bounce up and down on the balls of their feet when I move on, eager to get to what's next.

And then there's the last woman.

The sixth.

One glance, and I am far less interested in rushing through this and far more interested in looking at her.

She's gorgeous. A doll come to life. Hair in luscious waves the color of sand kissed by the sun. Huge green eyes flecked with little chips of sparkle, like diamonds. But her eyes are not the most arresting thing about her. Not by far.

It's that she's giving me absolutely nothing.

Not excitement. Not fear. What the fuck is she feeling? A long look into her eyes reveals no insight. She stares straight ahead, as if I'm not even here. I spend most of my waking hours reading women, getting their worth out of them, and this one?

A closed book.

A book with uncut pages, wrapped in locks and chains.

I want those chains off.

I have the immediate sense that if I were to free her, take this stoic weight, she'd soar off into the sky.

She's not even responding to me, damn it. To the energy in the room. I do it so the women are not so afraid that it becomes tedious, but the closed-off expression on her face…

Her lips part. "If you're going to look any longer, you could at least pay me for my time."

The rest of the room goes silent. Out of the corner of my eye, I can see Reya's hand frozen above the ledger, her mouth open in shock. The ripple moves through her and into the other women, who shift and titter and wait for me to react.

To retaliate.

"Take them out, Reya. Show them their new rooms. We're done here."

All of them start to file toward the door, but I hook a hand around her elbow and stop her. *This* woman. This alluring, irritating woman. Reya hustles the rest of the girls out into the hall. She leaves the door open—a silent sign of trust. Reya, the poor thing, has come to the mistaken belief that I'm not as dangerous as I used to be. I'll let her keep believing it for the moment.

"Is this part of the interview, then?" She crosses her arms, and I slip my fingers between them to pull them down. Her eyes flare. There. I've gotten something out of her. Now I know it's possible.

"It's an inspection, sweetheart. And I don't think you've passed."

I circle her closely and breathe her in. She smells like cheap shampoo and something sweet, which is at odds with the fire in her eyes and the games she's playing. The blank expression was bravado, meant to hide something else. Cheap shampoo, but her skin is flawless, and her little bra and panty set looks new. She hasn't been on the streets.

A mystery.

A thousand questions, all wrapped up in one person.

I should show this woman the door. For her attitude. For her games.

And yet...

"Why not?" She's trying to keep me in her line of sight, but I stand behind her and make it impossible. I might act like a benevolent dictator, but inside I am a consummate asshole. A monster. "Am I not pretty enough for you?"

"Men will want you sweet and compliant. Stand still."

She does, but I can tell it's difficult from the way she tenses. Like a little bird forcing herself to stay on the ground. I stroke a hand over the naked skin of her belly. I feel those muscles tremble. I am so fucking tempted to force emotion out of her that it feels like my blood has gone up in flames. I could do it. I have the skills, and the inclination.

"I'll spread my legs," she says, and the tiniest wobble in her voice makes my cock hard. "What more do you want?"

I brush my fingers up to the tiny bow in the center of her bra and higher, seeking out the delicate flesh underneath her chin. She lifts it for me, and fuck, I'm pulled into her, stepping far inside her personal bubble until the front of my suit makes contact with the skin of her back. I only mean to kiss the side of her jaw, touch it with my lips, really, but at the last moment, she turns her head and kisses me first.

It's brief, glancing, her eyes fluttering shut for the shortest surrender I have ever seen.

A spark.

A single match in the night.

A thrill.

I let go on instinct—*hot*—and marvel at this development. My heart has gone out of rhythm, racing, getting ahead of me. That's what they mean when they say *thrill*. A lifting sensation, like hurling oneself off a cliff and into miles of open air.

I've felt this before.

Once before.

It was never supposed to happen again.

She turns her head away, putting an inch between us, and looks toward the door, a slight color to her cheeks and a hitch in her breath the only evidence of the jolt that's left my skin sizzling. I move back in front of her so I can see her face. It's all I want to see.

I'm going to keep her.

It's a rash decision, but sometimes there are only rash

decisions. This one seems monumental, earth-shaking, even though the building stands and I do not fall.

No one will touch her until I've had my fill of her. None of the men prowling downstairs will get to do anything beyond look at her. Even the thought of their eyes on her makes my stomach curdle. Fuck those men. They can stay far away, floors away, and keep their hands to themselves.

Until I'm ready to sell her off. To rid myself of her. To put her on the windowsill and nudge her into flight.

Until that moment, she's mine.

Thank you so much for reading HADES & Persephone! If you loved Hades and Persephone, you will fall hard for Zeus. Find out what happens when a desperate virgin throws herself on the mercy of the city's cruelest billionaire in OWNED BY THE BILLIONAIRE, Zeus's completed trilogy in one volume!

I'm the city's cruelest billionaire. And I'm the only one who can save her.

In a life like mine, there is only danger dressed up in money and power. I'm a monster in expensive suits and an opulent home. Brigit is an innocent angel with only the clothes on her back.

She's on the run from a nightmarish arranged marriage, and I'm her only hope in the city. If she works my business she'll be able to buy herself a new life.

But the moment she steps into my life is the moment she's trapped forever.

She thinks she can tempt me and slip away like a thief in the night. She thinks I can make her mine and then let her go.

She's never been so wrong.

READER'S NOTE

The Price of Diamonds exclusive short story contains spoilers for the Richer Than God trilogy. If you haven't met Zeus yet, read at your own risk.

The Price of Diamonds

ONE

Hades

MY DAUGHTER IS TEN HOURS OLD.

I've been intimately acquainted with the passage of time since I was a child. A necessity, really, when you've only got so long before your brain scrambles itself into a total shutdown. But now time has burrowed beneath my skin. Every heartbeat marks another passing moment.

Each moment is an enormous bell, tolling outside my heart. The vibrations come down over me again and again and again. I'm alive. Persephone's alive. The baby is alive.

The baby is more than alive, though she remains nameless. Persephone didn't want to choose a name before the birth. Afterward, she was so love-drunk that she did nothing but murmur to the infant until her exhaustion caught up with her.

Now she sleeps in a hospital bed I had custom-built and shipped to the mountain. I don't use any of the hospital beds here, as a rule. But they are sometimes occupied. It's good

hospitality that they aren't made from sheetrock like the usual kind.

Persephone sleeps, her curls a mess on the pillow. Conor sleeps in the hall outside the door. Oliver kept him away until after the baby was born, and now he's guarding, the way he always does.

I hover over my daughter's bassinet like the superstitious bastard I've discovered myself to be.

She's just so small. So fragile. I cup a palm over the downy top of her head and feel her heartbeat there. She doesn't stir, wrapped up in her swaddle, only breathes soft breaths. A little bird, hatched in her nest made of twigs and leaves.

I don't let myself think about the inevitable flight away from me.

Stepping away feels like a bad idea.

We should be safe here. Triply so, though I didn't tell Persephone how many people I've vetted and hired and over-paid to surround the mountain. My brother Zeus and his fi-ancée Brigit remain unaware of the twelve-person team that accompanied them on the train ride here. No one is coming in that I don't expressly invite.

That, and I gave Oliver, my head of security, permission to wake Zeus up if anything goes wrong. Both of them like a good fight.

None of this eases the worry that's taken up residence near my heart.

My daughter cried when the light hit her eyes for the first time. Of course, the baby has been in the comfortable dark for long months now. It would be excruciating for anyone to be confronted with light.

It could be normal.

But.

There is a possibility that follows me around, close as a shadow.

Close as a diamond.

"Is she all right?" Persephone's whisper falls through the darkness like a jewel, and I go to her, though it means leaving my own beating heart sleeping in the bassinet.

"Yes." I sit on the side of Persephone's bed and brush her hair back from her face. "She's still asleep. No signs of trouble."

She rolls over onto her back and presses my hand against her cheek. "And what about you?"

It's dark enough, and late enough, for raw truth. "It's painful."

"Your head?"

"No. Loving her so much."

Persephone sighs, but it's a happy thing. "I know."

"Did you think of a name?"

A low laugh that makes me wish I could take her to another bed. "No. I was dreaming about a pearl on a ship. Isn't that so strange? A box of pearls."

"Maybe that's her name."

She turns her head to kiss my palm. "No, no, not yet. The sooner we decide…"

"The sooner we'll have something to call her, other than *sweet baby*?"

Persephone meets my eyes in the faint light of the hospital machines, which stand by in case of emergency. "She'll be so grown up if we name her. A small person, all on her own. It'll be the name we say when she leaves home."

I lean down to kiss my wife then. She tastes like the Tootsie Pop she demanded thirty-five minutes into our daughter's new life. Persephone's been eating them for weeks. It's not for me to question it. "We have time. But you know Brigit is going to ask you in the morning."

"The morning, then." She tugs me down onto the bed with her. This only works because Persephone is so petite. "We'll decide in the morning. Come to sleep with me. You've been awake all night. You must be exhausted."

She's quiet for a long time. So long that I chance putting voice to the worry. I know before I speak that I'll have to under-sell it significantly. *Worry* is an inaccurate term. What I feel is a clawing fear. It began as a thought five minutes after I learned Persephone was pregnant. It grew and grew until it reached its current size. Large enough to eat me alive.

We agreed a long time ago not to keep secrets, Persephone and I, so I don't keep things from her, as a rule.

Except this.

I could never bring myself to say it out loud.

"She could be like me."

Persephone curls her body close. "Good. I hope she is. Only not as tall. That would be a little much."

My eyes. "I meant—"

"I know what you meant." She turns, putting a hand over my eyes. "I'm not afraid." Persephone takes her hand away and brushes a kiss across my cheek. "Come to sleep. I love you."

"I know."

"Such terrible manners."

"I love you too."

I mean to stay awake, listening for any sound from the bas-sinet. I'm determined to do it. I can hear my daughter breath-ing from here. Tomorrow she'll have a name. But tonight the easy flutter of her breath sends me drifting into a dream. In the dream, a little bird lands on the window by my room.

She's come home.

TWO

Persephone

WE NAME HER DAISY.

Or *I* name her Daisy, and Hades agrees. My dreams are so vivid during Daisy's first day of life. I keep thinking I can't fall asleep, and then I can't stay awake, and the dreams. The *dreams*. One of them is filled with daisies. Innocent flowers. Full of possibilities. When I wake up from that dream, I call the baby by that name for the first time and it becomes hers.

Like it always belonged to her, even before I gave it.

The first two weeks of her life are a complicated bliss. I'm sore in places no one warned me about. My body has taken a strange shape and a strange sensitivity. I can only stand to wear the same four dresses. They double as nightgowns. It doesn't matter. We don't go anywhere, and Zeus and Brigit don't leave.

I never thought I would say that it's good to have them here, but it feels almost necessary. A very pregnant Brigit sits with me during the long afternoons when Daisy wants to do

nothing but nurse and I can't summon the energy to get up. We watch movies I've never seen. Zeus annoys the kitchens with his requests for food and snacks. He can't stop playing host.

Hades is always close by. The moment Daisy cries, he lifts her out of my arms. Changes her. Rocks her. Walks her around the halls of the mountain. While he's walking, Brigit and I take naps on the big couch in Hades's sunken living room.

It's weird. I don't mind the weirdness. What I mind is Hades is keeping a secret from me.

I can see it in his eyes.

He knows that I know, but we have a silent agreement not to talk about it yet. I don't push him. He doesn't say it out loud. There's technically no time limit in our agreement.

When Daisy is exactly two weeks old, a new team of people arrive on the mountain for a checkup.

A pediatrician, vetted by Hades and Zeus. He arrives with Carina Jain, who is Zeus's personal physician, I guess. They come to our home, to where I'm still ensconced on the couch. Brigit and Zeus have stepped out. Hades sits next to me, Daisy in the crook of one arm. I'm so tired.

"Who are these people again?" I ask him through a yawn. "We had a different doctor when she was born."

"It wasn't a long-term contract," Hades says, not looking at me.

I haven't attended a lot of doctor's appointments in my life, so I'm not sure what's normal. This seems fine. Other people in scrubs, surrounded by security from the mountain's staff, bring in equipment. A scale, I think. Other things.

"We'll check her vision and hearing," Carina Jain tells me. She's a kind woman, with kind eyes, and I'm just so tired. I trust her. Nothing's going to happen with me in the room. Daisy seems healthy.

I'm not worried.

And anyway, there's only space here for one person as intense as Hades. He's the one who stands over all of them.

While I...

Drift.

I know it's not right. I should be paying attention, but I'm so tired... and he's standing right there.

At some point Hades brings Daisy back to me and she nurses. No one ever told me about the rush of chemicals. They make me feel warm and sleepy, sleepier than before, if possible. Hades sits close by. Nothing has ever smelled as good as a newborn baby. Nothing in the world, except maybe him. *He* always smells clean and slightly cold. Sharp like diamonds. He tells me Daisy has regained the weight she lost after the birth. And they did some tests.

"And she's perfect," I say through a yawn.

I don't hear if he answers. I'm falling asleep.

Hades puts Daisy in my arms a while later, and I only stir when I register the soft weight of her. Oh, I'm not awake enough for this. Not awake enough to hold her. But it's all right, because Hades crouches at my side, holding her there for me while she nurses.

"Go back to sleep," he says.

I do what he says. I always do what he says.

The next time I come out of sleep, it's dark. Late. I had vague dreams of nursing Daisy, which were probably not dreams at all. But now the living room is empty. Getting off the couch is a process. The silver lining is that I feel slightly less like I was hit by a train. All that sleeping. No one ever said I would be this tired. No one ever said, *Persephone, you will be crazed by how tired you are. You'll fantasize about sleep while you're already dreaming.*

I rub my eyes and pad down the hall toward the bedroom. A shower. A fresh nightgown. I think I could bring myself to climb into Hades's big bed for a sleep. I haven't been up for climbing lately, which is why I've been living on the couch. He doesn't mind.

As I move down the hall, it's illuminated by the softest possible glow, one section at a time. There's barely any light in the sitting room. All of them turn off when I reach the doorway to our bedroom. They're programmed so there's no rush of brightness when I open the door.

Hopefully he's sleeping. Hades is awake all the time lately. He has to be tired.

I open the door as quietly as possible, holding my breath.

He's not sleeping.

Hades sits in a chair by the window. He is bathed in starlight and cast in the moon's reflection. Dressed in black, always black. He looks made from the stars.

And he looks wrong.

My heart makes a wild leap and slams against my ribs. Wrong, wrong, wrong. Something's wrong. The silence in the room is so thick it's hard to breathe, and it's a bad silence, filled with fear and dread.

He's leaned forward in the chair, strong arms making a cradle for Daisy, but such agonized tension runs through his shoulders that it hurts to see it. A tense, worried Conor presses in close. Hades wears a purposefully blank expression. It usually means the pain from his eyes is heightened and reaching a peak, but there's something different about it. I don't know what. I only know it's not right.

I'm three steps into the room when I understand the gutted curve to his shoulders and the silver sheen on his cheeks.

He's crying.

THREE

Persephone

MY HEART FALLS, DROPPING TO MEET MY FEET AT THE floor and sinking under. Still my pulse throbs. Still my blood pushes at the boundaries of my veins. I don't know what I'm walking into right now, but I'm going to keep my head up.

No matter what.

I go to him. Around the bed. Across the floor. It must be bad. It must be awful, because Hades doesn't cry.

I didn't think he *could* cry. I thought it was another side effect of his eyes and his pain. But now tears fall freely down his cheeks. He doesn't seem to notice them. He doesn't seem to notice anything, except for Daisy. Her tiny head rests in his huge palms.

And she is…

Alive. She's all right. I lean over her and breathe her in. She stirs, her tiny mouth forming an O as if she's dreaming of milk in her sleep. A bright flash of relief. And then it dissolves.

He's crying. He's *crying*.

I put my hands on his face, the way I do when his head hurts. Conor cedes a few inches of space to me. Hades doesn't take his eyes off Daisy. My heart could burst from panic. What is this? What's happening?

"Are you hurt?"

"No," he answers, voice matter-of-fact. The level tone scares me more. This is how Hades hides from other people. It's how he keeps them from seeing him as fallible and human. As weak.

He's the strongest person I've ever known, but he obviously doesn't feel like that now. He looks like he's been beaten.

I wait.

Wait, and force air in and out of my lungs. It's not easier to breathe yet. Until he tells me what's wrong, it won't get easier. The only thing to do is survive these seconds.

Hades takes a breath, then another. They sound tight and pained and unfamiliar. "The doctors ran some tests on Daisy today."

"I know." I run my thumbs over his cheekbones, again and again. His tears are hot and fresh, and each one breaks my heart. Hades doesn't have any of the habits of a person who knows how to cry. He doesn't wipe at his face with his sleeve. He doesn't try to blink them back. If I couldn't feel the tears on my hands, I wouldn't know he was crying at all. This is happening *to* him, I think. Something terrible must have happened, something devastating, to override his iron control. "You said her weight was fine. They said she's perfect."

But they didn't. I know it as soon as the words are out of my mouth. They didn't say that. I said that. Because that's what I wanted to believe.

That's what I did believe.

My hands freeze. My face freezes, but I won't stop touching

him. I'll stay on my feet through whatever this is, because he had to face it alone. I should have forced myself awake. Hades wouldn't have tolerated that. He would have insisted I rest. He's been doing it since our daughter was born. Since before.

His hands stay steady for Daisy, but the rest of him is trembling.

"One of the tests was to determine if—" Hades swallows, and the ache in my heart flies out to my fingertips and down to my toes. "To find out—fuck."

I can't speak. I want to say, *Tell me. Tell me anything, because it will be okay.*

But I can't.

Hades lets out an unsteady breath and steels himself.

"The test confirmed that she has the same sensitivity as me, in a similar—a similar severity to what I probably started with as a child. Her eyes—" He meets my eyes for the first time. His are as black and blown out as I've ever seen them. No ring of lighter color, here in the starlight. They're the bleak shade of stress and grief and pain. "She's like me, Persephone. I'm so—" Hades takes a huge gasp of a breath. "I'm so sorry."

FOUR

Hades

A NYTHING. I WOULD DO ANYTHING TO RELEASE SOME of the tearing, cracking pressure in my chest. Anything, but I don't know what to do.

This is my nightmare.

There was always a hope—I always had a foolish hope—that there wasn't a genetic component to my suffering. I'd hoped it was a freak evolutionary accident made worse by my foster father. A dead end just for me. That Persephone's brightness would win out in the DNA lottery.

And now—

Now—

Zeus brought Carina Jain here, and Carina Jain brought the best pediatric specialist in the country with her, personally recommended and vetted by her team. Those were the people who had to look me in the face, in my own fucked-up eyes, and tell me that I've promised my own daughter a lifetime of pain.

And I've had to tell Persephone.

She hears this news with a calm, thoughtful expression. She looks into my eyes as if she finds nothing wrong there. Nothing at all. Like this is the way I was meant to be.

And then she bends and lifts Daisy from my arms, holding her so easily, so naturally, like she's done it all her life. My summer queen lays our baby in the bassinet behind her and turns back to face the apocalypse.

She's dressed in all black. For me. Me, the man who has ruined our daughter's life before she had a chance to live it. My heart tears itself to pieces again and again. My lungs choke off access to air.

I'm the one Persephone is saving now.

She shouldn't bother.

Persephone steps between my knees, sits down in my lap, and gathers me into her arms.

"There's nothing to be sorry for," she says. "You did nothing wrong."

I'm too big for it. Too tall. Too strong. But the moment her arms fold around me, the moment my arms go around her waist, the dam breaks.

It feels terrible. Overwhelming and overpowering and wrenching in a way I can't remember experiencing before. Persephone runs her fingers through my hair and down the back of my neck. Again and again.

She's shaking.

No. It's *me*. It's *me*. Conor curls himself on the floor at my feet and trembles. He must be terrified. All the fear and dread I've swallowed for the past nine months fights my rib cage and squeezes my heart and forces its way out of me in what I think must be sobs. I don't recognize them. Don't remember the last time this happened, if it ever did. So painful. I shed tears for Rosie, but this is so much more, so much worse. I've lost something I never had in the first place. Daisy has lost something. She'll never know what it's like to be—

To be—

"I did this to her." I feel all the doors of her future slamming shut. There are so many things that will be harder. That could be impossible. Because of me. "I hurt her."

"You didn't," murmurs Persephone.

"I did. If I had tried to fix it, if I had tried to find some kind of cure, if I had pushed harder—"

"There isn't a cure." Her voice is far gentler than I deserve. "You've known that for a long time."

"It's like he followed me here," I admit through clenched teeth. "Like it's still happening."

The thing I would never say, never in a thousand years, not to my brothers, not to anyone. That this moment, this anguish, feels like being dragged out into the sun. It feels like being trapped in a small body without any way to fight back. It's like knowing, *knowing*, that the pitch-dark pain of an attack is coming and being powerless to stop it. It's like living the excruciating ramp-up to a terrifying unconsciousness again and again and again.

It's like Cronos himself has reached out of the grave, grabbed the back of my collar, and pulled me into hell.

This is the risk of crying. Of losing control. I hate it. I fucking hate it. Persephone runs a palm over my shoulder, as far down my back as she can reach.

She takes a long, slow breath. I can feel my lungs trying to do the same. They fail. But Persephone continues to breathe. I wonder where she learned this. Not her own mother. Not her own house. By some miracle, she knows how to comfort. She knows how to love.

We sit in the dark like that, Persephone rubbing my

back, for a long time. Until I can breathe. She waits until I can breathe again to speak. I don't know if I feel better. Mainly, I feel wrecked.

"Daisy is safe here. You've made her safe. He's long gone, your foster father. He can't hurt her. No one will ever be able to hurt her." She runs a fingertip over the shell of my ear. "Nothing that happened back then was your fault. This isn't happening because you fought him, or didn't fight him, or because you were too small to get away."

"It's impossible to know that."

"I do know it." Persephone's voice rings with certainty. "It wasn't a failing, what happened to you. You didn't fail Daisy by having to survive. You *made* her by your own survival."

It sounds true. Like something I could believe. I didn't know I needed her to say it until she did. Some of the biting tension in my shoulders releases. A spike drilling into my spine lets up. I don't know how she does it. I don't know how she sees through everything I say to the naked heart below.

"You're safe here too, you know." Persephone puts her hand flat on the back of my neck, just above the collar of my shirt.

"It could be the same for her. Diamonds and agony." I gather Persephone's nightgown in my fist and hold her closer. "How will you ever forgive me?"

My summer queen, my sweet thing, puts her hand under my chin and raises my face to hers.

"I won't," she says solemnly. "I will never forgive you for giving me a perfect daughter."

"She might suffer." I tighten my grip on her. Terrible possibilities crowd into my mind, one by one. Many of them have happened to me. "She could feel—"

"Some pain is inevitable, I think." Persephone traces a

finger under my collar. "But the suffering?" She looks out at the stars, at the moon. "Her dad won't let that happen." I open my mouth to name the terrors. There are hundreds. Thousands. But Persephone puts a finger over my lips. "Don't let your fears run away with you."

"This is fucking mortifying."

She kisses me then, sweet and soft, and the wrung-out parts of me bend to her. Pull her in. I want to feel more of her waist, her hips, her body on mine. Persephone laughs into the kiss.

"It's too early," she says. "You can't."

"Because it's too early or because I'm an embarrassment?"

Persephone makes a low noise. "I'm not embarrassed."

And if she is not, if she's calm in the face of this storm, then there's hope. If I can show her this base part of me and she does not flinch, then I can survive the rest. Then I can wake up tomorrow and be the shield between Daisy and the world. It will require carrying these fears in a way that's manageable.

To do that, I had to feel them first. They're larger and more dangerous than I thought. It was worse than I imagined to be at the mercy of emotions like this. But it was survivable.

She's strong, my summer queen. To feel so much. To let herself feel it so publicly, where other people can see.

Conor pushes his head onto my leg. I run a hand over his head—*I'm fine*—and it's only then that his body relaxes. When he's satisfied I'll live, he returns to his bed.

I press another kiss to the hollow of Persephone's throat. "It hurts."

"Waiting?"

"How much I love you."

My summer queen sighs. "Prove it."

I laugh in spite of myself. "What would you accept as proof? Diamonds? Ice cream?"

"Lay with me in bed."

I take her in my arms and stand up. "You should raise your standards," I tell her. "Negotiate for more."

Her smile is a kiss of heat against my neck. "I have more than enough."

FIVE

Persephone

THREE NIGHTS LATER, I'M WALKING FROM THE NURSERY back to the living room when I hear voices.

Low. Steady. Even.

Brigit's waiting for me with Daisy on the couch. We've been watching a new show during the odd hours when I'm awake during the night. I creep toward the rectangle of light—dim and soft—coming from Hades' office.

From here, out in the shadows, I can see them.

Hades sits at his desk, hands clasped, leaning forward. He wears the soft clothes he's been wearing since Daisy was born. A collection of black, long-sleeved shirts and black pants. He will never admit his custom suits bother him when he is stressed.

He won't admit he's stressed, either, but I know him.

Zeus leans against the opposite bookshelf, near where Conor sleeps by the fire. It's a large office. Too large for me to hear what they're saying over the echoes from the movie and my own beating heart. I don't have to hear to know it's about

Daisy. Hades motions to his own eyes, a quick gesture he only makes in private company, with people who already know.

Zeus's eyebrows go up. He asks a question. Hades answers. And then Zeus nods, slow and deliberate.

Oh—I shouldn't be watching this. I don't want to disturb the moment, so I tiptoe past.

As I go, Zeus steps forward and puts a hand on Hades's shoulder. He doesn't hesitate in this movement, not exactly. What he does is hold his hand up and out for a heartbeat before he does it, this part so fast I could blink and miss it. I think he does it so Hades sees. So the touch doesn't come as a surprise. So Hades knows his palm is empty and not a fist.

It's the closest I've ever seen them.

And it's good. Hades is telling people about Daisy. Zeus, at least. And if he's telling people, he's not letting his misplaced guilt eat him alive. It means he's searching for answers. Looking for hope.

My heart aches, a flash of pain that pulls on my love for him and for our daughter. He loves her more than the world.

Brigit looks over at me as I settle onto the couch next to her. "Should we keep watching, or are you going to bed?"

I shoot her an incredulous look. "I brought clean swaddle blankets. We're finishing this movie."

She laughs and rewinds the movie a few minutes. It's not long after when Hades and Zeus come down the hall, their voices preceding them.

"You've lost your touch," Zeus says as they enter the space by the living room. "Gone soft."

"Fuck off." Hades's glare is familiar and cutting. It's a relief to see it. I've been worried about him, which isn't the usual order of things.

"Manners," Zeus scolds.

Hades shoves him. Hard. Hard enough to send him into the opposite wall, but Zeus catches himself. Shoots out a hand and shoves back.

"Not in my house, asshole," Hades hisses.

"Fine." Zeus grabs the front of Hades's shirt, and Hades bats him away. "I can beat you up outside."

Hades stalks toward him.

Zeus runs.

They're surprisingly fast. Zeus's laugh floats back from the hall as the two of them sprint away. I hear the door out to the valley slam open and bang shut.

On the couch next to me, Brigit sighs and stretches. "Should I make popcorn?"

"For the fight or the movie?"

She laughs, rolling her eyes. "I'm not getting up to watch those two act out their feelings, but I *will* get up for popcorn. With extra butter."

"Agreed," I tell her. "We'll have it waiting when they come inside."

Daisy stirs in Brigit's arms, mewling for me. I take my daughter from her and pull her in close. Breathe in that new-baby scent. That perfect scent. I nuzzle her nose with mine and she opens her eyes. They're a dark, dark newborn blue, with big black pupils.

Perfect. She's perfect. They're her father's eyes. "You don't have to worry, sweet pea. He'll be back soon."

Thank you so much for reading THE PRICE OF DIAMONDS! If you loved Hades & Persephone, you'll love the second generation…

Rough. Tattooed. Dangerous. Hercules learned to be tough on the streets of Bedford Park. Money can't change what he is inside. He's still too broken for Daisy, the delicate beauty from his adopted family. No matter how much she tempts him.

He can't have her, but he can protect her. Except his dark past catches up to him. It threatens her, which breaks down every wall he put between them. He'll make her safe or die trying.

Read HERO WORSHIP on Amazon, Apple Books, Nook, Kobo, and Google Play.

Hide & Seek

ONE

Persephone

HIS HAND IS OVER MY MOUTH BEFORE I HAVE A CHANCE to scream.

And I would scream, because it's pitch-dark in what I thought was an empty room.

I bite back my shrieks against his palm as my heart pounds, his body a tall, unyielding cage behind mine. He has me pinned. Trapped. My arms useless at my sides, held in place by one of his. Who could blame me for fighting? For testing his grip?

My husband laughs.

The sound is low and dark and dangerous in my ear. "I love when you put up a fight, summer queen."

He can't do this. Not because I don't want him to, but because there are multiple people engaged in a game of Hide & Seek throughout our mountain home. Eleanor. Daisy's nanny. Oliver. Whatever other staff members Daisy saw before the game started. It's only a matter of time before they come looking. The game will have started with Eleanor finding Daisy in

the hiding spot she always chooses—behind the big couch in the round cove of our living room.

Then the two of them will search for the rest of us. They won't stop until we're found.

But I've been found first, by Hades.

He answers my muffled protest by shaking my head in his hands.

"If you're going to beg, do me one better and cry." The sound I make against his hand is more moan than protest. Hades is already hard as steel through his clothes and mine. "That's moaning, Persephone. Not crying."

It would be easy to let the tears fall now. What can I say? My body responds to him just the way it always has—with an almost fanatical obedience. Tears prick the corners of my eyes. He's not even doing anything. He's just suggesting it, and I'm willing. I press my thighs together under my dress and push back into him.

His hand tightens over my mouth.

"I'll fuck you for that," he says into my ear, and then he lifts me off my feet and drops me.

My knees hit carpet first, my hands following a second later, then my face. Hades fists my hair with one big hand, driving me into the carpet behind the antique wardrobe that was my hiding place. This particular room houses part of his collection. Pieces come in and out as he acquires and sells them. He was probably waiting in here when I came in. He would be. He's like that.

Daisy turns four this spring and Hades is as insatiable as he always has been. He pushes my dress up above my waist and tests my hips with bruising pinches until I cry out.

"No more noise." The order drops from his lips as naturally as anything he does. He's used to being in charge, and right now, being in charge means pinning me to the floor and fucking me.

It never gets less hot, feeling the way he rips through the cloth of my panties like it's nothing. He's a destructive force, and it feels so good to be destroyed by him. I inch my knees apart and brace myself to be fucked.

Hades rewards that with a sharp slap against my pussy. "You are such a sweet thing, spreading those legs for me. Now show me how you take a cock." I start to answer him but his hand comes down on the back of my neck, pushing my face farther into the carpet. "Show me *silently*."

I have to hold my breath, because with his other hand he strokes between my legs and pushes three fingers roughly inside me. No warning. It doesn't matter. I'm already wet. I can't help it. It's shameful, how much I want him, and I lean into that old shame and let it make my thighs tremble. Hades twists his fingers and my inner muscles flutter around him. He knows me so well. He knows me better than I've ever known myself. I'm the woman who pants on the floor under this god of a man. I'm the woman who loves to be filled with his fingers and humiliated.

It's the sweetest possible embarrassment.

The sound of his zipper warns me about his cock with a second to spare. The new absence of his fingers is replaced by his thickness and a hard, possessive thrust. It knocks the breath out of me. It tells me so much about him. That he's having trouble staying at the office because he wants to fuck me. That all his tension would go away if he could just spill it inside my body.

Hades doesn't waste time. He reaches a hand around and works my clit while he strokes into me, efficient verging on disengaged, and it's so cold, it's so mean, it's so hot. He fucks me like I'm just a body, just flesh he can use in service of his own orgasm.

Fine. It's a little fucked up that I love this so much. It's a little fucked up that he shows me his love by fucking me like I'm property.

I am, in a way. I've belonged to him since the first night I saw him. Thinking of him there in the moonlight makes me hotter, makes me tighter, and it's Hades's turn to stifle a groan. This, this, this. I love this. I love bringing him right to the edge of his own control. I love doing it by doing nothing. By being obedient. By letting him take as much as he wants of me. He gives me more in return than I ever could have dreamed.

Hades tilts his hips and I have the electric, bruising sensation of him bottoming out. He adds a bit more pressure, stretching me around him, his fingers expert on my clit, and—

Oh. *Oh*. He's going to make me come this way. This way, with the length of him as far inside me as he can go.

"Come," he says, and I do. Instantly. Hard. Impaled on him. My hips buck and try to get away from the intensity but he pins me in place and waits for my release to peak before he fucks me again in earnest.

"You're filthy," he comments. "You're dripping on the carpet, you're so wet."

He pulls out with a bitten-off groan and hauls me up to my feet. One push sends my back into the wardrobe. Hades forces my thighs apart and kneels between my legs. When he eats me, he does it with the air of a man who only has moments to live. Licking like I'm the last thing he'll ever taste. Memorizing me with tongue and teeth. He laps at my clit, forcing the nerves to respond to him. To crest and peak and make me shudder and come into his mouth. While I'm still coming, he bites my clit.

The pain takes the pleasure in its teeth and wrings another orgasm out of me on a gasp I don't manage to hide.

And then he's up, lifting me, pushing me back against the wardrobe and bringing me down onto his cock. My head knocks against the wardrobe with every stroke but I don't care I don't care. This angle is heaven. Being taken by him is heaven.

His need is written all over him. In every movement. He hunted me because he craved me, and he shows me that in every nip and bite and lick of my skin. He fucks me like a man possessed, standing up, his muscles tensed. I drive myself down on him. Make circles and figure-eights of my hips.

And then—

I feel it. The moment he loses control.

It's my favorite thing. The hitch in his breath. The change in his strokes. They get deeper and more frantic, and he grips me harder, like he doesn't care if he leaves bruises. He doesn't care. It's unbearably hot. I like to see them on my skin. I like when he kisses them in the shower the next morning. Hades pulls down the collar of my dress and bites one collarbone. He makes his own sound when he comes, a low hum across my skin. It's a sound that means *there's more*. It's a sound that means get ready, *sweet thing*.

Running footsteps in the hall. Hades is still fucking me through his release in long strokes, and he presses a frustrated kiss to my collarbone.

"Hide and seek!" Daisy shouts.

"Watch the table," Eleanor calls after her.

Hades kisses me with a growl, lifting a hand to grip my face. "I was going to fuck your ass, summer queen."

I can't catch my breath. "Not enough time," I pant. "You know there's not enough time."

He lowers me to the ground and rearranges his clothes.

Daisy runs up and down the hall outside, laughing. I push at my dress until it falls into place, my hands trembling from the rush of being fucked by him. Still a rush. Always a rush. He leans down and kisses me again, his teeth digging into my bottom lip.

"You'll make time later."

Oh, I will.

Hades leaves me standing there and strides to the door. He opens it. Steps into the hall.

"I found you," he calls. Daisy shrieks and dissolves into laughter, the sound of her voice getting louder and louder until finally she sprints into view. She's almost four, all blonde hair and big dark pupils.

Like her father's eyes, Daisy's have a thin ring of blue.

At the last moment, she leaps. Our daughter jumps with absolute faith that her father will catch her.

He does.

Every time.

This time, too.

He spins her around in his arms and swings her up and over his shoulder. I cover my mouth with both hands to keep from laughing with her. Hades puts a hand around her waist.

"Let's get out of here," he says, pretending to walk away.

"No!" shouts Daisy. She flings her arms around his neck and pulls. "We have to find Mama. She's lost. We have to find her."

Hades's eyes widen. "Lost! My God, sweet pea, you're right. She could be anywhere. And she can't see in the dark."

"What is she gonna do?" Daisy howls with laughter. *Howls.* Her little body shakes over Hades's shoulder. "She can't see anything!"

"We'll find her." Hades meets my eyes as he says it. There are so many promises in that look. I want them all. He sets

Daisy on her feet and she sprints into the room just as I hide myself behind the wardrobe.

Daisy finds me immediately and throws her arms around my waist. She tugs me out into the open.

"I found her, Daddy. Look! I found her." She brings me to Hades, who pulls me into a tight hug and kisses the side of my neck.

"Found you," he murmurs against my skin. "You won't get lost again.""

CONNECT WITH AMELIA

Amelia Wilde is a *USA TODAY* bestselling author of steamy contemporary romance and loves it a little *too* much. She lives in Michigan with her husband and daughters. She spends most of her time typing furiously on an iPad and appreciating the natural splendor of her home state from where she likes it best: inside.

For more books by Amelia Wilde, visit her online at

WWW.AWILDEROMANCE.COM

Made in United States
North Haven, CT
05 April 2023